Currituck comes from an Algonquin word
meaning "Land of the Wild Goose."

The large, brick Currituck Beach Light stands
guard over Currituck Sound, a mostly freshwater body that opens to Albemarle Sound (and
eventually the Atlantic) through a narrow gap at
its southern border.

Currituck Sound has no tides and averages five
feet in depth, with most areas no more than
knee-to-waist deep. You can conceivably walk
it from side to side but beware of the mud flats
and snakes that lie in wait for the unwary.

BLOOD COUSINS ON CURRITUCK SOUND

BLOOD
COUSINS
— ON —
CURRITUCK
SOUND

AN OUTER BANKS MYSTERY

FARLEY DUNN

BLOOD COUSINS ON CURRITUCK SOUND, Dunn, Farley

1st ed.

Subtitle: An Outer Banks Mystery

Dedication

To all the Diane Turnipseeds, Sean Taylors, Jason Romneys, and Emily Bryants who keep the world safe for the rest of us.

I'd also like to give a shoutout to the Cynthia Ellisons, the Mary Wilsons, and the Steven Hills.

My characters faced fictional dangers in each of my Outer Banks books, but I controlled the damages that impacted them while in pursuit of their jobs.

In the real world, the dangers are frighteningly real. The true heroes are not those within the covers of this book but the ones who patrol our streets and keep us safe from those who wish us harm.

Thank you.

Introduction

Book 1 in this series, *Dead Body on Bodie Island,* was born from a wedding, a drive halfway across the country, and a weekend on the Outer Banks for a sister who wanted to see one thing: Ocracoke Island.

Book 2 came about because I liked my characters so much that I couldn't not give them another adventure.

In Book 3, the core team from C-District in Dare County, North Carolina, is back as dead bodies pile up like driftwood on the beach.

Book 4 gives my main character, Diane Turnipseed, a promotion and a new team to enable her to facilitate order out of chaos on the far-flung Outer Banks of North Carolina!

Welcome to *Blood Cousins on Currituck Sound.*

TABLE OF CONTENTS

Prologue

THE LATE-DAY sun glistened off the Currituck Sound beyond the Whalehead Club, and across the small harbor with its restored boat house, the thick brick column of the Currituck Beach Lighthouse thrust confidently through the trees.

Five months in and she still felt a fish out of the water.

Of course, at the Whalehead, she was, as she was no longer in Dare County. She'd crossed that line half an hour before when she'd driven north from Duck into Currituck County. No one had noticed, though, as she was in her county-issue Ford Explorer, a high-powered beast in unmarked black with its emergency lights safely tucked into nondescript locations.

The sound of revving motorbikes pulled her eyes to the parking lot near the boathouse. The park was generous, but the substantial truck and trailer sucked up multiple parking spaces. A lightbar atop the cab suggested off-road capabilities. On the trailer, two slim youths in colorful offroad gear hovered over the bikes. Matching black hair likely meant they were brothers, although Diane could hardly make out more than that, except that from a distance, she could hardly tell one from the other.

One of the youths twisted a grip, and the bike's engine screamed then chirped and chattered as it settled down. He climbed on, his companion turned to the second bike, and as he began to work the bike off the trailer, the second bike roared to life.

"Grown up is as grown up does," a voice shouted from outside Diane's Explorer.

She looked over to see a tall, thin, weathered man with thick jet hair shot with gray shaking a fist towards the two motorcyclists. She scanned for the man's vehicle and found a green Dodge truck that had seen better days. It was the only one nearby, and in her mind, it became his. She exited her SUV and took two steps in his direction.

"Evening," she said with a nod. "Diane Turnipseed from down Dare direction."

"Oh?" His eyes assessed her. "This isn't Dare County."

"And I'm off duty." She smiled. Her uniform would have given her away even if she hadn't said anything. "Thought those required beach permits."

"Not that those Currituck interlopers know. This is Brayboy land, like Papa always said, and I don't take nothing from lowlifes like them."

As if Diane wasn't there, the man turned and walked angrily to the green Dodge, drew himself inside, and with the squeal of a slipping clutch, disappeared into the September evening.

Brayboy, Diane mused. Now, that's not a name that gets dumped on you every day.

—— Chapter 1 ——

Churning the Waters

CAPTAIN DIANE TURNIPSEED let the oddly shaped name drop hard.

"Brayboy."

She soaked in the A-District team gathered in the Dare County Sheriff's Office's sub-station situation room in Kill Devil Hills. In the previous five months, she had begun to learn them for who they were.

The newest person on the job was K9 Handler Sergeant Edward "Ed" Walters, although at the present, he had no K9 officer to handle. Ed's hiring had been one of Diane's first assignments, but to hoggletie a trained dog was another matter.

Sergeant Wallace "Wally" Styles was the lone carryover from the previous A-District team. Diane had teamed Wally with deputy Nathan Preston who had just completed the North Carolina BLET program and was a new hire doing field training. Wally enjoyed teasing the former Texan that as his Field Training Officer, the young man's first job each morning was to make sure a fresh cup of coffee appeared on his desk.

Deputy Nathan Preston had become familiar with Dare County when visiting the area for his cousin's wedding some time earlier. He and his wife, Paytyne, had become involved with a case involving a dead man on Bodie Island, and his desire to enter law enforcement had been piqued. His wife and small daughter were at home with her parents while Nathan was getting established.

The final permanent member of the team was also a new-hire, Deputy Clara Del Ray, who had previously worked in Brunswick County but wanted to get her feet wet in Dare County—literally, as she was living in her parent's vacation home on the beach and spending her off-duty time windsurfing.

The A-District building was a vast step-down from Diane's previous assignment in C-District, but she would be above her knees if she let anyone in this room hear her complain. The temporary-looking structure nestled among the trees under "The Bong," actually the Colington Water Tower, so called by the locals for its unusual method of construction. The water-containment portion was constructed on the ground before being elevated to the top, and while under construction, it had resembled a pipe—or a "bong," something associated with the illegal drug trade. For so many people to label it as such suggested no end of possibilities for keeping Diane busy seining the waters for offenders.

From beyond the room's closed door, the receptionist's landline began to ring. Diane frowned but was satisfied to hear Paloma Ronson's old-soul voice begin, "A-District, Paloma here. How can I sweeten your day …" before fading into a question from closer to hand. Rain had begun to thump the sides of the wood structure, and the loudly voiced comment drowned out Paloma.

"So, Brayboy." The response was Clara's, and her hand was partway into the air. "I've never seen or heard that word, and my parents have had a house here for ages."

"Wally." Diane nodded his direction. "You know the northern parts of the Banks best. You might could tell this better'n me."

"You people will learn," he began. He held his cap in one hand, leaving his thinning hair exposed, and to ease his thickening waistline, he leaned back in his chair with one foot cocked over his knee. "Some people say there's not no Brayboys any longer—"

"But what is a Brayboy," Clara persisted. "It's gotta mean something if we're holding a meeting about it."

"Oh, it means something, or it used to." Wally chuckled. "Just let me show you this."

His chair creaked as he stood, and he stepped to the desk beside Diane. He lifted a folder and removed a printed flyer. It revealed a substantial home on the water with a large, shingled roof, a covered porch running its full length, and multiple dormers filling the expanse of shingles.

"I've been there," Clara began.

"I expect so. The Whalehead Club. It's now a state park, but it used to be the home of Edward and Marie Knight. A woman named Juno Brayboy worked there back in the twenties and thirties of the last century, and she claimed that Edward fathered her son, Creighton Knight. Truth is, the boy was illegitimate, but she put her employer's name on the birth certificate, and there we are."

"I'm following you," Nathan Preston said, but he looked puzzled. "But seeing it my way, the mother's name hardly matters anymore."

"Except for Edward's granddaughters in France," Wally countered.

Nathan laughed. "They're in France. Why would they even care?"

"One of them came back to New York and became an influential designer. You might recognize her last name: Rothschild."

"Like the French winery." Clara's eyes widened, revealing her affluent upbringing in a tony household.

"Rothschild's stepdaughter became an actress, had children, and a whole slew of them live up in Currituck on the mainland. Not our county except for when they bring their shenanigans south. We team up with Currituck County to double down on them when necessary." Wally grinned in pleasure at the opportunity to pass his wealth of shared knowledge to the untaught.

The door opened, and Diane realized the rain had slacked off, even though the wind was still whistling. She had heard the phone multiple times, but Wally's storytelling tended to reel in her interest in all things Outer Banks.

She also enjoyed the idea of collaborating with Currituck County, as she had an interest in teaming up with Sheriff William Barnett, who she heard had an equal dislike for the previous Dare County sheriff, Morton Kringlebach.

"Paloma," Diane started, "you might as well dump it on us, whatever it is."

"Yes, Miz Turnipseed." Paloma was a solid, round woman with artificially red hair and a dusky complexion that she swore allowed her to pass for white. She also moved with the quickness of a teenager, although she had long since relinquished her teen years to her grandchildren. "We got a pounding of homeowners out there can't get in out of the rain. Instead, all they got to do is look out their windows and see what-all everybody else is up to. Well, those Ballinger twins are rained off that beach up in Corolla, so them done come down here to make trouble. You want to go see about it, or should I just tell them back on the phone that the rain'll send them boys back home soon's they feel wet behind the ears?"

"Wet behind the ears. That's how it goes?" Diane almost smiled.

"Well, Miz Turnipseed, I may look white, and I don't like to criticize them much who claim to *be* white, but my grand-pappy always said that if you don't got the sense to get out of the rain, well, the rain gonna find you one way or the other." Paloma nodded her head decisively as she peered at Diane over oversized black hornrims. "Now, we gonna do anything about them boys or just let 'em soak?"

"Hold your taters, Paloma. I'm on it." She turned to Sergeant Styles. "Wally, this is your pot I'm about to put my spoon in. You know these sandfleas better'n anyone else on this team, so how do you tell the story? Is this a reason to head out into a storm, or is this a big no?"

The man was truly the expert on all things A-District. The previous head of A-District, Captain Foster Le Grange, only thirty-four but domineering in his reddish-blond hair and beard, had taken two of his officers with him, leaving Diane with a vacant K9 handler position—now filled—and two newbies that were little more than minnows working hard to swim upstream. From Wally, she understood that Le Grange had been a team player if you wanted to be on his team, but anyone with an opinion? He was quick to make judgements and refused to back down. She considered the two he'd taken as good-riddance, as they were likely bottom-feeding lackeys, and she had no use for anyone of that caliber on her team.

"Yes'm, Captain. You might know these are Brayboy players."

"Brayboy players?" Clara giggled and covered her mouth. "Paloma called them Ballingers."

Wally paused, realized he'd forgotten his cap, and frowned when he located it still on his chair. He ran a hand over his thinning hair. "Well, let me tell it right, and you're correct, Clara. There's not no more Brayboys, that's sure, but their descendants are thick as molasses on toast. The Brayboy Knights stick to the island, and the Brayboy players come down from Currituck to stick it to the ones on the island."

"High five, Wally!" Deputy Preston held a palm in the air and leaned forward for Wally's slap. "We're gonna stick it to them, right? Do I even need to ask?"

"So that's a big yes, Paloma," Diane said with a nod in the receptionist's direction. To Wally and his freshly minted charge, she said, "You boys heading out to see what the tide's turned up? Or is it too close to sunset, and you're hoping I'll pull my feelers back in and snap my shell shut? Deputy Preston, you're with Wally. Now make a change and be the boy your parents want you to be."

"Yes, ma'am!" The young deputy stood abruptly, startling his chair, and its legs squawked on the hard floor. He grinned sheepishly. "My bad."

"Wally?" Diane gave him her full attention. "Before the sun goes down, a report on my desk. That deputy's got a few holes in his drain bucket, and I want you to start filling them in."

"Nah, just a glitch of enthusiasm. Done this before, so leave it to me." He nodded his assurance at Diane and turned to Deputy Preston. "C'mon, wet pup. Let's get outside and let this weather wash some of the new off you."

"Sure. It's why I got this job—"

They were already headed out the door, and Diane missed the last part of the green deputy's remark, but with the young man's enthusiasm, she could hardly blame herself for thinking of Deputy Sean Taylor from her previous post in C-District. The man's aberrant enthusiasm, his constant affirmations, and his repeated efforts to annoy her reminded her that while A-District might stir up a whole new bucket of rowdy minnows—like the Brayboy feud—one of them was no longer Sean Taylor.

She noted Sergeant Walters on the edge of his chair. His hand wasn't raised, but his expression said he had something to say. Only three people remained in the room: her, Ed, and Clara. She wondered what was so important to say just between the three of them.

"Ed, so what's the tide turned up?"

"The tide?" He frowned, puzzled. "I don't get it, Captain."

"I do," Clara inserted with a bright smile. "What's on Ed's mind, right, Captain?"

"Um …" Diane hesitated. She'd never been asked that, as she thought it obvious what it meant, but she nodded. "Yes, on your mind, Sergeant. You look like you have something to say."

"Are you sure, um, that Preston got the memo?"

"Memo?" Diane looked at Clara. "Clara, can you explain that one?"

"Oh, sure, Captain. I heard that expression all over back in Brunswick County. It means does he understand what he's supposed to do."

"Shush that!" Diane couldn't stop the smile from growing on her face. The image of Sean Taylor leaped before her eyes and faded just as quickly. It seemed someone had their hand in the same minnow bucket. She shifted her response to Ed. "I assume you mean his enthusiasm—" at which Ed nodded "—but that's why he's teamed up with Wally."

"But caution—"

"For all sakes, Ed," she said, then immediately stopped herself. "My apologies. I didn't mean it that away. We had a man just like that in C-District, and he proved himself a good officer. He got above his knees a few times, but he always waded back out better than he went in."

Diane saw Clara lean towards Ed and heard her whisper, "Above his knees means out of his depth."

"Thanks," Ed replied just loudly enough for Diane to hear.

A ruckus from outside the situation room diverted their attention, and Paloma's substantial voice called, "What's this on my floor? Water?" Then, the situation room door opened and slammed wide.

"That didn't take long." Deputy Preston fell into the room, still dripping water from his cap and shoulders.

Just beyond him, two carbon copies stood side by side, slim, well-proportioned youths touting thick black hair. Wet black hair. Their differences were in their clothing. Both wore full leather dirt biking regalia, although in different and distinctive colors.

Oh, and one had a black eye. And blood running from one ear and from a gash beside his left eye.

"Move ahead, boys." Wally Styles' voice was a wave of authority forcing them forward. "You can take your time if you want, but we've got a slew of time, too, so's we can wait as long as need be."

"Give me a second, Wally," Deputy Preston called. He moved two chairs out of the way and said, "No reason to hang back now. Move, boys. Time to meet the new boss."

Boss. Diane remembered Taylor using that word, and she hated it as much now as she had back in C-District. She also noted that the "boys" were hardly younger than Preston. Boys, indeed. *Watch yourself, Deputy Preston.*

Wally appeared as the two detainees shuffled into the room, and he motioned them forward and called to his companion, "Good job, Deputy Preston. Boys, follow his instructions."

Diane felt reprimanded, even if only in her head. Preston wasn't Taylor, and she would need to remember that. The first of the two youths—the one not bleeding—mumbled, "We're m-m-moving, m-m-m—" before shaking his head in frustration.

His twin filled in with a growl, "We're moving, man." He glowered at the officers as his mirror image glanced at him in appreciation.

"Hold your taters, Team," Diane barked. Wally and Deputy Preston froze. A frown passed across Clara's face, and Ed, still seated, started to grin. "You two," pointing to the two dirt bikers, "mouths closed unless you're spoken to—"

"We were—" the one with the blood began, when Diane whipped her handcuffs off her belt and slammed them down on the desk.

"You are above your knees," she spat. "I might could guess why you're the minnow that got banged up going back in the bait bucket. This is the county sheriff's office—" even if it looked like a portable storage building "—and these are my officers. You will respect them."

"Yes, m-m-m—" the uninjured one began.

"He said yes, ma'am," the second finished.

"By all sakes, I heard him. You finishing his words for him, can't he speak? Dump it on me. I'm listening." The boy didn't look slow … at least he'd not gotten himself smashed in the head. He might could be the smartest of the two.

"He doesn't like me to use the word." The blood had started to irritate him, and he rubbed some from underneath his ear. Clara pulled a tissue from a box, and he accepted it from her.

Diane caught Wally's lip movements. *Stutters.*

"Okay." She backtracked. "Clara, you got your notepad?"

"Right here." She pulled it from her shirt pocket and held it up.

"You write for me. Names, first." She drilled her eyes into theirs, even though only the vocal one seemed ready to confront her. The other watched the patterns on the vinyl floor.

"Sergeant Styles knows—"

"Not what I asked." Diane pressed her mouth tightly and crossed her arms.

The young man's posture sagged, and he said, "Philippe Ballinger. My brother is Creighton. He doesn't like to answer strangers. They make him nervous."

"Creighton?" Diane was satisfied when the youth looked up at her. "Is that so?"

He nodded, glanced at his brother, then back to the floor.

"You two twins?" The family resemblance was so strong, she figured they must be. She also was aware that at first glance, she'd assumed they were taller, but now, standing between Wally and Nathan, they were average height. Being well-proportioned had tricked her eye.

"Duh—" Philippe began to roll his eyes.

"Might oughta learn this now. Not going there." Diane pointed in Wally's direction. "Wally, cuffs, please?"

"Bro, sh-sh-shut up," Creighton hissed at his brother. "D-d-don't want any trouble."

"Trouble, huh, that's what this is." Philippe forced the bloodied tissue near his brother's face. "Already got trouble, so let it go."

"Boys!" Diane barked the word. "Make a change and be the boys your father wants you to be. While we're at it, clamp your mouths closed and let me talk to my officers."

"Yes'm." That was Creighton, and he elbowed his brother who let out a grudging, "Yes, ma'am."

Diane turned to Wally. "By their outfits, might there be motorbikes floating on the tide? And other people? Someone's bound to have caused the blood." She indicated her left ear and temple.

"Reckless driving, I believe. Running their bikes on public roads without certification. Endangering the public and, I believe, that head damage is from impacting a light pole beside the donut place in Duck."

"Which one?" It likely didn't matter, but Diane would like to know.

"The, um," and Wally pulled a spiral from his shirt pocket and flipped it open, "Duck Donuts by the Big Red Chair."

"At Superwings?" Diane asked.

"Yes," Wally confirmed, and he laughed. "Tourists holding umbrellas were running down the Duck Town Boardwalk toward the Sound for safety. Not safer, I thought, as the water is the only exit!"

"And the bikes?" Wally hadn't answered that.

"Back on their trailer. They have a truck they bring over. Isn't that right, boys?" Wally cleared his throat as he waited on a response.

"Are we impounding it?"

"Seems we have to, public nuisance and all. The law's the law." Wally was grinning.

"You can't—" Philippe still had his tissue at his ear, and he looked ready to punch someone as he surged forward. Both his brother and Wally broke his stride with a firm grim on his arms. Philippe turned to his brother, "Creighton, they can't do this. Our stuff—"

"Bro," Creighton cautioned him, as he gave a jerk of his

head.

"Our stuff! And how will we get home—"

"Shush it, boys. One of my officers will see you home. Wally, any forms I need to sign or anything else I need to take care of for this impounding?"

"Truck's in the lot outside, bikes attached. Just lock the gates when we leave, and it's good. I can take care of the paperwork when I write up the report."

"Can I see you out yonder for a minute, if you think the good Deputy Preston can manage your charges?" Diane nodded towards the door leading into the lobby.

"Yes, ma'am." He turned to the deputy. "If these Brayboy players so much as twitch, use these." He unclipped his handcuffs and held them out to Nathan with a wink.

Philippe's eyes narrowed at the perceived Brayboy slur, and Creighton's eyes were red—whether with tears or anger was unclear.

Outside, Diane quizzed her sergeant. "I seen these two up towards the lighthouse a while back, or two boys very nearly the same." She paused, thinking. "By your story of what they were doing, yeah, the same. That weren't my county, so I didn't get involved, but you said earlier they like to bring their shenanigans down the island, correct?"

"Tide rolls out, and the Brayboy players roll in." Wally held his cap in one hand, and he pushed his spare fingers through thinning hair. He grinned. "A whole covey of cousins lives in a converted warehouse in Currituck, one originally belonging to the Knight family. They appeared out of thin air a few years or so back."

"No Brayboys in the fish pen, though?"

Wally laughed. "You've got some descriptive language, Captain, not that I'm complaining. But no, not on that side of the Sound. These two are Ballingers, but you know that. The rest are Sereys and Beaumarchaises."

"From France, then." Language, customs … the very way they thought could be out of kilter with the Outer Banks lifestyle. A deeper look-see into their background might be wise.

"Likely but I can't say for sure."

"I appreciate the honesty. Now about that blood—"

"Already thinking that through. There's an Urgent Care just south of the Wright Brothers Memorial, and I can head further south to Nags Head if that one's closed."

"Outer Banks Urgent Care."

"In Nags head, yes. Surprised you know that one."

"I grew up on the Banks, Sergeant. I might'a come up from C-District, but this is my home. You get that boy checked out— take one or both, you choose—but I want those bikes impounded long term. They must need permits to run on the beach. How about we rattle the minnow bucket up north about whether they had them? Or are you thinking they might have been on the Dare side of the county line?"

"Either way." Wally glanced at the ceiling as he pulled his answer together. "These boys know Southern Shores is off limits, though that might not stop them, and as far as Corolla, I'd need to put in a call to check." Southern Shores was at the very northern extremes of Dare County, with Corolla and Currituck County just beyond.

"You thinking that'll be a problem?"

"Not with Currituck. They are good at working with us on the Brayboy problem, as they know it affects us both. Which do you want me to do, the clinic or the beach permits?"

"You take the clinic and reel in Preston to go with you. We need to keep him on his toes. We'll sort the rest here." She studied his face for a moment. "We're good?"

"Just another rock to turn over, Captain. Yeah, I'm good."

"I'm pouring myself a cuppa blackie while you and the deputy help those two sandfleas to your patrol car. Maybe your report can wait until morning."

"You'll have it tonight." Wally felt his pockets and pulled out his car keys. He held the keys and his cap in one hand and grasped the doorknob into the situation room with the other. "As I said, just another rock to turn over. See no reason it'll slow me down."

As the door opened, and Wally moved inside, apparently the young men's patience was ready to snap, and one of them—the one that didn't stutter, obviously—tried to give Wally a dressing down.

"Blood? You see this? I don't even live in Dare County. I'll get my papa to call the sheriff back home. He knows Sheriff Barnett—"

"We can call him now, young pup. He's right here on my speed dial—"

The door closed and cut off the conversation, but Diane had seen Deputy Preston's eyes sparkle at Wally's snapback rebuttal. As long as the fledgling deputy continued to pick up on and emulate the sergeant's obvious skill, maybe Wally could keep him out of the collards.

She pulled down a cup from an overhead shelf and reached for the coffee maker. The one in the A-District sub-station was just a coffee maker. The high-end Wolf unit in her aunt's old beach house didn't belong to her, so she had left it for when Jason Romney decided he wanted it back. The coffee that poured from this pot paled in comparison, but black was black, and she wanted a cuppa sooner rather than later.

Her cup was a quarter empty—although steam still washed her face—when the four men exited the situation room and paused at the main door. She studied the off-road-liveried youths, clean-shaven—although the dusting of light hair on their jaws suggested it wasn't by choice—and yes, next to Wally, no taller than she was. Their leathers boasted scuff marks that said they were well used. Was that out of pride or necessity? One was bragging at what they'd accomplished, and the other said that they were likely up to something. There was a big difference between the two.

She called, "Boys, I'll be checking on your beach permits. I'll know if you requested them before you headed out on your bikes today."

Deputy Preston's hand was on Philippe's shoulder, and the youth jerked free, glared at Diane, and threw the door wide and disappeared outside. His brother followed him, less aggressively but with a shared glare. Wally gave her a shrug, and Deputy Preston was a lightbulb, like this was the best part of his day.

Likely it was, until the guns came out, blood spurted, and dead men were left on the side of the road.

Or floating in the Sound.

Or on the beach alongside a creek or behind a filing cabinet in a basement bunker.

That last one still made Diane cringe.

"PALOMA, I might could use the number for Corolla." Diane rinsed her coffee cup before setting it beside a small sink, and the receptionist's response caught her by surprise.

"Take this like I say it, Miz Turnipseed, but there's more numbers in Corolla than white people on the beach. You care to give me a clue for which'n you want?"

Diane turned to find Paloma with her old-fashioned Rolodex at her fingertips and ready to spin. She moved her hand on one of the knobs, and several of the contact cards flipped over as the device rotated.

"For all sakes, whoever issues beach driving permits. You needing me to come over and find that for you?"

"No, ma'am, Miz Turnipseed. You made me plenty happy by doing something about those boys, so I guess I can do what you need all on my own. You want me to call 'em, too?"

Diane held up one finger and glanced in the situation room, which also served as the break room, an occasional kitchen, and A-District's overflow storage space. Deputy Del Ray and the A-District K9 Handler-without-a-K9 were in conversation, with Clara sharing an animated story that involved claw-like hand motions in a parody of what could only be a bear attack. Ed laughed and replied, while tapping his pointer finger on a table for emphasis.

"Don't you worry yourself about it. Just the number. And I appreciate it."

When Paloma handed her the number on a sticky note, it also said Corolla Visitor Center. Diane folded it over to trap the adhesive and slipped it in her shirt pocket. She stepped to the situation door and waited for Ed's and Clara's attention. Eventually Ed saw her, and he motioned to Clara who slowed her story and rested her hands on the tabletop.

"Yes, Captain?" Clara smiled, part of her friendly eagerness to be involved and helpful.

"You done with your story?"

"No story, Captain, just filling in a blank space." Her face settled but laughter fought with her attempts to seem serious. Next to her, Ed cleared his throat as he also worked to bring himself in line.

"For all sakes, Clara, I don't mind you telling a story. To tell the story honest, I might could listen once in a while, if you don't think I'm above my knees. But now, I got a job for you."

"A job, Ed." Clara's eyes sparkled. "With Wally gone, maybe I'll get an important one. Some real experience."

"It's not like I've not been listening, Clara." Diane pulled the paper with the number from her pocket. "This place seems slow next to Brunswick, but that's why people come to live here. Not much that does happen. But now that it is—" She held out the folded sticky note.

"This is?" Clara took the paper.

"A number to call to verify beach permits for those two sandfleas Wally has in his fish basket."

"Might not reach them on the phone," Paloma called from her desk.

"I might could guess that our receptionist is listening in to our conversation." Diane shook her head.

"I don't mean to step on your toes," Paloma said, as she frowned at Diane, "but nothing much to do makes me curious about what you people do. Might need to become a deputy just to fill my time."

"So that's a big no on calling. Is that right, Paloma?"

"Yes, ma'am, unless you like leaving voicemails. Me, I liked it better when we dropped a letter in the mail and had three days to recover before getting busy again."

"And you have nothing to do?"

"Not now, I don't. I'm talking to you, trying to get you to see the error of your ways. I'll go back to nothing to do when I get you people straightened out."

"Keeping me on my toes—"

"Yes, ma'am, I'm trying."

Diane laughed. "Clara, before Paloma gets above her knees, you and Ed head up to the Corolla Visitor Center and ask them about those two bikes outside. If they don't have permits filed, let me know so I can start impound proceedings."

"If they do?" Ed had already gathered his things and was standing.

"Them boys rode in on the tide, but the net's all ours." Diane heard her words, saw the man's puzzled look, and revised her response. "To clarify, there's more'n one way to collar a ship's cat, so leave that to me."

The frown on Ed's face deepened, but the copier behind Paloma's desk drew her attention. Clara tapped Ed's arm and said, "I'll explain in the car," at which Diane took her exit towards her small office.

Paloma stopped her with, "Miz Turnipseed, I heard you people talking about the Brayboys. I expect you might find this good reading." The stack of printouts was an inch thick.

"For all sakes, I might need another cuppa blackie for all that." She took the stack, and the aroma of printer ink surrounded her. "To tell the story honest, for there not being any Brayboys, this is a lot of Brayboys."

"That's how my grandpappy always said it. Too many Brayboys, he used to tell everyone in earshot." Paloma seated herself and lifted her glasses from where they hung from a decorative leather strap running around her neck, and she placed them on her nose. "You read that, and you'll learn a lot."

Diane expected family history, residential disturbances, even the possibility of intermarriages between cousins. Yes, there was some of that, but police reports and local news articles revealed an excessive number of recent incursions into Dare County, which explained the cooperation between the two sheriff departments, but much of what she was reading suggested this was more than just two rowdy youths behaving badly with their two-wheeled toys.

"Some things aren't ours to wish away," she muttered to

herself.

"Yes, ma'am, I hear that," Paloma called.

"My aunt Lucille used to say doors are for privacy." Diane pulled her office door wide, surprised to see Paloma still at her desk and touching up a document at an old-fashioned type-writer. "That White-Out?"

"Works now as good as it did then. And my grandpappy used to say that sardines in a can know everybody's business. How'd you like those papers?"

"I bet tomorrow's breakfast we got a family feud simmering up in Currituck. Might be boiling over into A-District—"

"It has in the past." Paloma nodded firmly, taking no account that she had interrupted her boss.

"I'd be above my knees to not think I could use some backup when it does. Please set up an appointment with Sheriff Glynne this afternoon, if possible."

"Yes, ma'am. I'm plenty happy to do that for you." She already had her Rolodex spinning.

Diane stepped back into her office and closed the door, as if that gave her any privacy at all.

DIANE GOT HER meeting quicker than she expected. Paloma knocked on her door barely minutes later to relay that the sheriff was happy to see her, but it was within the hour or next week, as he and his family were heading out to his wife's family reunion in West Virgina. They needed an early start as it was a two-day drive with two preteens and a rescue dog that took up half their luggage space.

Diane had her keys in hand and was headed towards the door before Paloma was back in her chair. She paused before exiting the building and raised an eyebrow in Paloma's direction. "To tell my story honest, I expected tomorrow or the next day. I wisht …" She shook her head and said, "I appreciate you catching the man before he left, but you are keeping me on my toes."

"Yes, ma'am. That's what I do." Paloma never looked up from her typewriter.

In her truck, her very familiar Ford Explorer with its black paint and tinted windows, she noted the coffee cups lining the footwells. Many were crushed, but a number of clean ones were nestled among the chaos. They had been there so long that she could almost locate them in the dark. She had to do better. But better was for tomorrow. Now was for Sheriff Glynne.

She started the engine, and her rear wheels hopped in the gravel before she backed off the accelerator. She pulled around the white truck and trailer with its load of bikes and frowned at the BALLIN II on the license plates. Once she set her tires on tarmac, she let the engine strain as she headed east on Covington towards Hwy 158 and Kitty Hawk proper. The other direction on Covington, and she could see across the Sound to Manteo proper, but that required a boat, which she didn't have. To drive it occupied a full half hour in light traffic, and longer during the height of the tourist season.

Part of the journey took her across a small bridge fronting Blount Bay on the left. Fingers of residential docks extended from the shoreline, and farther out, Baum Point Island was a fishhook of a peninsula, like a giant finger crooked to say, "This way. I gotcha." Gotcha for what, Diane couldn't say, but since no one lived there, she supposed it didn't matter much.

Past Colington Creek Inn, a longer bridge took her across Colington Creek, which was more channel than creek, with Gorilla Island to her left—also uninhabited—before leaving the Colington Islands and approaching the Wright Brothers Memorial, where Colington cut across part of the Memorial's runway and twisted left to take Diane towards 158.

She couldn't see the beach as she headed south, unlike much of Pea Island and Hatteras down in C-District. Instead, stores and shops, including Dirty Dicks Crab House and Nags Head Elementary School, filled up her eyes along the drive. Once she left the sand dunes of Jockey Ridge behind, she relaxed. A bit more of city, then right on 64 to Roanoke Island, and right again to the Dare County Courthouse.

She was surprised to discover the tall, athletic sheriff in the parking lot outside the courthouse and standing beside a white Range Rover. The back passenger door was open, revealing a sumptuous tan leather interior. Beside him, a Belgian Malinois, an animal Diane recognized as fast, powerful, and built differently than most American couch potatoes, sat on its haunches and watched the sheriff, its large ears erect, and its head tipping from side to side as it watched Glynne try to work a padded and rubberized blanket over the seat.

Diane evaluated her parking options and chose a space to give them some room, parked, and exited her vehicle. The dog, with its chocolate fur and black muzzle and ears, turned her direction, studied her until it was satisfied, and then gave its full attention back to the sheriff. She cleared her throat and was satisfied to see Glynne look in her direction and turn his back to his SUV.

"Captain Turnipseed, I'm glad to see you made it. As you can see, we're fixin' to head back to West Virginia for my wife's family event. I wanna take the dog, but there's the luggage. I suggested a roof rack, but the wife has an opinion, and mine hardly counts, it seems."

"That's a pretty interior to carry a big dog like that. You had him long?"

"She, and no. She's a shelter rescue from West Virginia. My

wife brought her home, and it seems we're stuck with her. The dog, not my wife—" He shrugged and smiled.

"But your wife has an opinion." Diane smiled. The sheriff had taken over the county fishing hole about the time she accepted her transfer to A-District. She had been surprised—and pleased—to discover his opinion of Morton Kringlebach was about the same as hers … but less pleased when he brought up Jason Romney's name in a recent meeting. It seemed Jason had spent the five months since she left C-District in training and was now assigned to the Manteo facility as the county's Detention Officer. That hadn't disturbed the tidepool of good rapport she felt with the new sheriff, just reminded her that she hadn't left all of C-District behind. "She rides in here?" She stepped closer to inspect the interior.

"In the back, yes. This—" He held up the rubberized blanket. "—goes in back so she doesn't damage anything. We have one ordered for the back seat, but—" He shrugged again.

"You'd be above your knees if you said it was here." She took another long look at the dog. "She seems mannerly enough."

"Yes." He smiled at the dog, and she seemed to smile at him, either that or she was thirsty, who knew? Anyway, she panted a few times before growing still once more. "For a rescue, she is very well-mannered. She does like to be busy, maybe requiring more time than I have. Well, enough of that, and I'll get back to her later. You requested a meeting. Here, or would you rather be inside?"

"Here is good. No need to slow you down more than need be." Besides, the memory of her hours with Morton Kringelbach inside that building did nothing for her sense of calm once she stepped through those doors.

"Then I'm listening." He sat back onto the Range Rover's

rear seat, ducking his head so that it just cleared the top of the opening. He snapped his fingers at the dog, and she stood, moved just in front of him, and immediately sat, giving the sheriff her full attention.

"Had a dog in C-District much like that one." Diane nodded approvingly, and then she shifted to her real purpose. "Does Brayboy mean anything to you?'

"Gotta check the book on that one. Brayboy, let me think." He looked skyward, rubbed his chin, and sighed. "For what it's worth, not that I can say. I'm gettin' something that says it might be important to you. So, tell me, Captain. What should it mean?"

"I might could expect nothing." Diane adjusted her belt, unsure if her request would be met with scorn or support. "It's a family name from a school of tadpoles that should'a developed legs and grew forked tongues instead."

The sheriff laughed. "I'm fixin' to bust a gut. You might wanna explain that one to me."

"My new K9 officer says the same." Diane felt her face warm. Then she explained the story of Juno Brayboy and her connection to the Whalehead Club north of the county line, from the early claims of the Knight bloodline still in Corolla to their conflict with the French branch of the family now invading Currituck.

"Sure. All their hoopties livin' too close to be sociable. That's West Virginia everywhere. How's it affect us?"

"I'd be above my knees if I made it out to be bigger than it is. In my five months up here, they've kept a low profile. That changed today—" and she recounted the morning's events and the truck and trailer in the A-District compound, and the two lookalike youths at the Urgent Care in Nags Head. "One of them was busted up like a leaf peeper that forgot to look out for the trees."

"You can handle that. Your track record in C-District says so. Why bring this to me?" He had his hand on the dog's head, working the fur around her ears, and she remained focused on his face, only occasionally glancing at Diane.

"My receptionist makes sure I stumble over everything she thinks I should know. Today she dumped on me a stack of police reports and news articles about those boys and their families. They cross the county line like a heat-crazed crab crossing the sand. I might need to coordinate with Currituck County to reel them in. I don't want to step beyond my rank when deciding how much to share with them."

"I see." Sheriff Glynne pursed his lips. "You've had your wings clipped before. Well, that was Kringlebach. New sheriff, new plans, Captain. I would say I need to check the rulebook, but this'n's one in my own head. I make it up as I go, and I like your track record. Besides, I know Sheriff Barnett. He knows of you, and he'll be glad for your help, I assure you."

"Thank you." The buzzing in Diane's head began to fade, and she was able to think again.

"Oh, Captain." The sheriff had knelt to give the dog more attention. "I told you we were leavin' to see my wife's family. Tell me, how are you with dogs?"

"Not sure what you're asking." She was guessing, though, and she hoped she was wrong.

"For the next week, how about it? Roxie here is a fine example of a Belgian Malinois. She's housebroken and a fine guard to sleep beside your bed. I'll loan you my blanket for the back of your vehicle." He stood, smiled at Diane, and the dog shifted her focus from the sheriff to Diane without hesitation.

"The next week, you say." He had given her unqualified support, more than she had expected to wrangle from him. But, a dog. And a Malinois. She knelt and called, "Roxie?"

The dog snapped to position just in front of Diane, from seated in one location to seated in the next with no spare movements or hesitation. Her big eyes studied Diane's face as if willing her to please say yes.

"We gonna do this? My wife will be your fan if you do."

"Your kids won't be."

"You might be surprised. They'd have the entire back seat."

"The back seat ruse, I see." Diane stood. "It's not like I weren't listening, so I guess it's yes. She must take a lot of food."

"She does. I have a fresh bag in the back. You want me to help you ..." He motioned from the back of his SUV to the back of hers.

"And a leash?" She stroked the dog's collar, questioning whether a harness might serve better. She was a very sturdy dog.

"Likely you won't need it, but yes. She does like an egg on her dried food first thing in the morning." He had opened the liftgate, and he paused before lifting the bag of food. "Seriously, scrambled but not too dry."

Diane shook her head and hit the button to open her own liftgate. While the new sheriff shifted the dog things from one vehicle to the other, she realized she wasn't all that displeased. Whoever had owned the animal before it had made its way to the shelter had known what they were doing. Once the padded blanket was in the back of Diane's Explorer, the sheriff patted the floor of the cargo area, called, "Inside, Roxie," and the animal leaped inside and laid her head down. Her eyes studied the sheriff's until he turned away, then all her focus was on Diane.

"New sheriff, new plans," Sheriff Glynne repeated as he closed the back of his Range Rover. "For what its worth, I'm the leader in Dare County, and if you're on board with me, that's all that counts. Thank you, Captain. She really is a good dog."

He smiled and disappeared behind his tinted glass, and Diane opened her own door. After seeing the pristine condition of his tan leather, her floorboards disgusted her. Funny how she'd never been bothered before. Now, she wanted to visit the first carwash she found, as she was certain the cups weren't the only things residing in her floorboards.

"Roxie, you and me," she called to the back of the vehicle. The dog's ears perked up, but her attention was on the Range Rover as it pulled away from the curb. "A cuppa blackie, how does that sound? Then maybe somewhere to clean out the car." The last part she breathed to herself, less intended than hoped for. The Caliber Car Wash was south of Colington and so, convenient, and she notched that as her plan.

Back on South Croatan—the local name for 158—and headed north, just past Food Lion, the Urgent Care parking lot caught her attention, especially as a Dare County Sheriff's Office vehicle stood with a back door open and no one around. The Urgent Care building sat apart from the larger strip shopping center it fronted, and while the larger parking area held a smattering of cars, the police car hunkered alone in front of the Urgent Care.

"For all sakes," Diane muttered, as she hit her blinker and slowed to take a left into the lot. "Some things aren't ours to wish away, but to tell the story honest—"

She was there by then and didn't finish her sentence. Instead, she slammed her SUV into park, threw open her door, and had her feet on the pavement in one quick motion. She held one hand just on her holster where she could access her firearm if necessary.

"Sergeant Styles, you there? Deputy Preston?"

With no reply, she worked her gun free but left it partially holstered. She moved around her SUV door, keeping an eye on the dark void left by the opened car door, as she swept the parking lot with a practiced glance. With no apparent movement, she stepped toward the car and leaned inside. Blood on the plastic that served as a back seat, and a bloody handprint on the clear polycarbonate divider between the front and back seats assured her that this was indeed Wally's car. Then, where was everyone?

She stood and looked towards the building. "Styles, Preston? You might could answer about now."

Something about the handprint, although fully explainable with the damage the youths had boasted, now had her fully holding her weapon. She clicked the safety off, glanced at her SUV to ensure that Roxie was fine, and moved toward the building. A side entry with a wide porch faced half the building, with glass sliders giving more direct access from the broad sidewalk leading directly from the parking lot. The heavily tinted glass gave no clue to events inside, or if there was anyone present. Then the glass doors slipped soundlessly aside and out walked Deputy Preston with one of the detainees handcuffed to his wrist. The detainee wore patches, so she assumed it was Philippe.

"Deputy, is everything ok?" She wanted to say, *Dump it on me*, but she'd had enough confusion over her terms of speech that she opted for something more generic. "And where's Wally and the brother?"

"Sorry, ma'am," Deputy Preston said, as he lifted his hand to reveal the handcuffs. "The boys got rowdy. This one's brother did a runner. I was inside, so Wally's after him."

Diane touched her radio mic on her collar. "Diane Turnipseed to Wally Styles. You there, Sergeant? Over."

"Coming around the building, Captain." Creighton appeared

first, hunkered over, with his arms twisted behind his back, clearly cuffed. Wally held the cuffs in one hand, and his other hand pressed against the back of the detainee's head. "Guess he thought he needed something from the market over there."

Sure enough, one of the stores in the strip mall wore signage that proclaimed The Fresh Market in giant green letters. Diane quizzed the youth, "You hungry, Creighton?"

"I-I … w-w-why are you asking?" He jerked his head as if trying to free it from Wally's hand before glaring at Diane.

"He says—" his brother began when Deputy Preston jerked the arm attached to the cuffs and hissed, "She understood him just fine.'

Diane felt a twinge of nostalgia for C-District as she spat, "Yonder is The Fresh Market. You visiting maybe for board shorts, maybe a new surfboard? No, a new plant for your bedroom, that's it? Home Goods is the other way. So tell me, where were you headed?"

"H-h-home."

"He says—"

"Enough," Nathan commanded. "We've just had enough of you two."

Diane took control. "Here's how it's going to go, boys. If the deputy here says those injuries are good, I'm keeping your truck and bikes, but you two I'm taking home to Currituck. In my car. I've got my police dog in the back. Roxie is well behaved when I want her to be, but she likes the taste of a hand or two just fine. Don't make me give in to her."

"We've got a—" Deputy Preston began when Diane cut him off. No, they didn't, but these two tadpoles didn't need to hear that.

"Wally, I'm ending my day here, if you'll let them back at the sub-station know. Currituck is mostly on the way, so's I can empty this bucket on their doorstep and find my own way home. You good with that?"

"That's for sure, ma'am." He grinned. "You be sure to tell Roxie hello for me, and I want to hear all about her day the next time I see her."

"She'll love to share. Let's hoggletie these two into the back seat." Diane opened the doors as she heard Wally mutter to his charge, "Move ahead, young pup."

With her car closed up, Diane was aware of the young men's long day, as the aroma assaulted her. She flipped the air on high to give herself breathing space and called into the back, "Currituck. You got any place in town specific? My GPS is right here."

"You can't keep my truck," Philippe said, swelling up in anger as he spoke.

"Yeah," his brother added, surprisingly without stuttering, giving Diane the heads-up that his speech difficulty likely was exacerbated by stress. Or maybe anger eliminated it.

"Let's do it this way, boys." She turned partially in her seat to look them in the face. "I just came from the county sheriff, and he said two things. One, he's in charge. Not me, him. Two, I have authority to handle this. So, yes, I already did. It's impounded. You got a problem with that, you take it up with the sheriff down in Manteo."

Diane put her truck into gear and headed north on Croatan. Well, 158, but a fish on one side was a fish on the other side as well. Just before Croatan angled left to cross the Currituck Sound and wind its way to Elizabeth City, the tall porte-cochere of Beach Medical with a prominent sign shouting URGENT CARE claimed her attention. So, why did Wally go so far south to Outer Banks Urgent Care? Then, there were no cars in the lot, so maybe he'd stopped and was encouraged to head on. Or, maybe he'd decided that once he'd selected a destination, Diane would know where to find him if he didn't alter it. Good for you, Wally, she thought. Except for the two bottom feeders in the back seat, it had worked out perfectly.

"So, an address, or you two expecting me to wander around and just pick a spot?" Like in the Sound, but she didn't say that.

"How about cleaning your car sometime?"

Diane riveted the faces in her rearview mirror, certain the damaged one was the instigator. "That's how it goes, Philippe? You're not above your knees for all that, so I might stop up here at the car wash and let you earn off some of the cost for my delivery services. We're good about that?"

The other one sank lower into his seat, nearly disappearing from the mirror, but Diane had no trouble seeing the effects of what must have been a jab to Philippe's ribs. She heard, "Just s-s-shut up, s-s-sometime, won't you?"

"Address?" Diane didn't see a car wash, but there were usually trash receptacles at the Outer Banks Monument to a Century of Flight just past Beach Medical. She hit her blinker and pulled in at the crossing to wait on the light. At the change, she surged forward into the entrance and circled around to a parking area on the backside of the trees. An empty space near a receptacle invited her to stop, and she nosed her big SUV in.

"You serious?" came from the back seat.

"Some things aren't ours to wish away," Diane muttered, as she opened her door. The rear ones were disengaged from the inside, so she didn't worry about them making a dash, but once the door was open … well, she hadn't forgotten the scene at the Urgent Care. She opened the liftgate and was caught off guard at the sight of the Belgian Malinois looking back at her. "Almost forgot about you, Roxie. Sheriff Glynne wasn't above his knees when he said you were a good girl." She gave the dog a quick rub behind the ears and pulled two trashcan liners from a box.

Evidence collection, normally. Today, busywork for the two detainees. She opened a back door and offered them the bags. "You might get to it."

"You're not letting us out?"

"For all sakes. You done tried to run once. To tell the story honest, I don't trust you further than I can cast a line. Since those cups are bothering you, pile 'em in these bags and you'll have all the room you need." She offered the bags a second time.

"J-j-just do it, Philippe." Creighton grabbed the bags roughly, shoved one at his brother, and opened his. He began stuffing used cups inside.

"Why do you people harass us and leave those Banker cousins unmolested?" Philippe was slower at opening his bag, but he finally stowed his first cup inside. He muttered, "They're the ones with the money."

Diane would bet tomorrow's breakfast she was seeing part of the conflict. She countered with, "I'm still waiting on news of your permits to be on the beach with those bikes—"

"Don't bother yourself about it. It's not your county."

"That's a big no," Diane retorted. "You brought it into my county. You want me to leave you alone, you might try the beaches in Hatteras. They'll give you all the beach access you want down there, and it might even save you some time in that truck of yours."

"M-m-m—" Creighton began, before he crushed the cup in his hand in frustration and gave up.

"Yes, Creighton? You were saying?"

"He says you're missing the point." Philippe held out his sack. His side of the floorboard was clear.

"Hold your taters." She took the sack but didn't move towards the trash receptacle. "You got those nice bikes. How's a better beach beside the point?"

Creighton snorted in contempt, and Philippe said, "Maybe that's not all we go to the beach for."

"S-s-shut it, Bro." Creighton grabbed his brother in a head-lock and attempted to wrestle him into a position of surrender.

"Hey, my head!"

"Enough, boys!" Diane grabbed the shoulder of the one closest and pulled them apart. "Creighton, settle! I can see seep-age, so Philippe, you sit still until I get you home. Creighton, you done with that bag?" She no longer cared if the floor was cleared. She wanted these two out of her truck.

With both bags in hand, she closed the door to contain her guests and disposed of the refuse. Back inside, she pressed them once again. "Address?"

"The Wharf," Philippe sighed. "You know where that is?"

"It's not got an address?"

"If it does, I don't know it. I just live there. I don't write myself letters."

"T-t-turn right at the F-f-feed and Seed." Creighton.

"Good job, Bro," from Philippe. "He's right. It's down that road. Everyone knows it."

Diane didn't, and to tell the story honest, she didn't care if she ever did, but she did want free of these two sandfleas. The Feed and Seed turned out to be an easy landmark to locate, down what the sign touted as Bells Road, and she easily pinpointed the big building directly on the Sound. The name was high on the street side of the structure, The Wharf, but the letters were faded to the same weathered brown as the rest of the siding. She recalled the story behind the building, an old Knight-era warehouse that had been used for construction material storage from when the Whalehead was built. It was bought by a devel-oper and converted into lofts back in the 70s.

Due to a history of catastrophic flooding during heavy

weather, especially during strong southerly events, it was abandoned a decade later. It was in and out of the news as a location for transients and an occasional drug den for years. The structure's age and condition didn't suggest robust finances, but Diane allowed that as the place was quite large, perhaps this branch of the Knight clan had invested as a group and divided up the apartments among themselves. Or maybe the abandoned property had reverted to the original owners, which could mean Knight descendants. Clearly there had been no money to remodel or upgrade. With its capacious size—and the waterfront location—maintenance costs would be like holes in a fish strainer, eating up everything they dumped inside.

Diane shivered at the thought of the building and its probable condition inside.

Her drive back down to 158, which became Shortcut Road at Barco, truly provided her a shortcut, and she hooked a right on Barco Road and saved a mile or so before taking a second right back onto 158. She passed the College of the Albemarle to the north, where she would find Sheriff Barnett's office, but it was nestled behind several campus buildings and three softball fields. It was as good as invisible to her.

Elizabeth City—and home—appeared less than half an hour on. She missed her aunt's place on the beach, but this was better for her for now. She pulled into the drive, noted that Professor Shelton's car was outside the garage apartment he rented from her, and she pushed the remote to open the garage door. It was noisy, so he would know she was home, although she doubted he would make an appearance.

Good. A quiet evening and a night without footwork would do her good … as would a clean car and two sandfleas on deposit back in Currituck.

Good riddance to bad rubbish.

She shook her head as she closed the garage door and walked towards the house. That was unkind of her, even if it was sure as taters in a bag. Although they might be rubbish, they still needed protecting.

"With me, Roxie." She snapped her fingers for the dog to fall in line and smiled at the thought that it was Sheriff Barnett's protection they needed, as she would just as soon never see them again.

"MAN, I THOUGHT I would be busy in Manteo, and you send my first two prizes back to Currituck County. Let me think, yes, Rodney Dangerfield."

Diane looked up from her computer, and seeing Jason Romney at her door had her tongue-tied. Not only had she left him in C-District, the twinge of butterflies in her stomach suggested she had only left part of him behind.

"Might could invite me inside, if you want to." Jason crossed his arms and leaned one shoulder against the doorframe.

"What about Rodney Dangerfield?" That was a safe question. She lifted her coffee cup to take a sip, only to find the temperature off, and she returned it to her desktop.

He laughed. "I should have expected that. 'I don't get no respect.' Classic Dangerfield."

"I got no idea where that's coming from, Jason. I bet tomorrow's breakfast you got an explanation in that head just waiting to come out, so dump it on me." She clicked her monitor off, leaned back in her chair, and crossed her arms, tit for tat.

"You do know I'm no longer in C-District." His eyes twinkled, and he seemed to fight a smile.

"So the leaf peepers say." She could wait him out, and she would, even if it was good to see his face. She just didn't have space for him in her life. He distracted her from the important things, like protecting the life, liberty, and happiness of her constituents. The sound of the front door let in the voices of two of her A-District team arriving for her morning briefing, Sergeant Styles and Deputy Preston. The two men were sharing a joke, which they broke off to greet Paloma Ronson. After Paloma shooed them into the incident room and things quieted down, Diane said, "I got two more people to show, then this conference is over. To tell the story honest, I need to get in there now."

"Aw, Diane. Don't be like that. You know why I'm in Manteo. When that La'Von character got loose and Jimney wound up dead, I knew I could be more use up here as a detention officer than mucking around in Hatteras—"

"Not to mention Manteo is a look-see away from Kitty Hawk. I know the map as well as you, Jason. Don't be rattling around in my minnow bucket."

"Seriously? That's that you think? I'm hurt, Diane. Really hurt." His face twisted into a grimace.

Diane laughed. "You are getting more above your knees with every word you say. Tell it honest, Jason. Why are you here?"

"You likely should have held those two from last night."

"Oh?" The suggestion hit hard, and she berated herself. She'd felt it in her gut, but with nothing to hold over them and Sheriff Glynne dumping his dog on her, she'd had no choice.

"Deputy Del Ray phoned Manteo with her report on the beach permits from Corolla—"

"And there were none." Bushwacker country! "I wisht … no, shush that. Did Clara say if she and Ed found anything else I can use?"

"You mean Sergeant Walters?"

"For all sakes, Jason! Who else would I mean?"

"Sorry, Diane. I'm new up here. I got Deputy Yates on my radar, and I'm still learning everybody else. For a change of topic, what's with the big pup on that dog bed in the lobby?"

"For all sakes!" Diane stood, and her chair rolled back, bumping the metal cabinet behind her desk. "Roxie's food is still in the truck. Jason, take my keys. The dog hasn't had breakfast, and she needs fed twice a day. You do that and I'll let you know if you can slip your hand into our minnow bucket for the morning."

Diane exited the room, leaving Jason behind, only briefly acknowledging Paloma, before pausing to assure herself that Roxie was fine. The previous evening and night, the dog had amazed her with its self-control and obedience to commands. It was like someone had trained it, but who would abandon such a highly skilled and obviously intelligent animal? Roxie didn't move, but the eyes in her black face locked on Diane and tracked her every expression.

"Good girl, Roxie. Stay. Food is coming."

"About time," Paloma snorted. "Seems I can hear her stomach rumbling. My grandpappy always said a full dog is a well-behaved dog."

"I'm glad you're so worried about her, Paloma."

"I have been. I nearly offered her half a can of sardines, but I decided you needed to be the one doing the offering." Paloma had hardly glanced up from her keyboard.

Diane heard Jason returning with the food. She held up one finger to Roxie, said to Jason, "No more than a cup and a half," and headed for the situation room.

"You're welcome, Diane," he called.

She ignored him, choosing to wish his presence away for the moment, as she structured her thoughts on her team meeting. She was surprised to see all four team members present and wondered briefly how they had all managed to arrive without her knowledge. Clara's face was bathed in steam from a cup of coffee, while Nathan and Wally were haggling over whether to choose a cinnamon roll or a croissant. Ed, the K9 Handler-without-a-K9, had out his phone, filling in the time until the meeting started with whatever he had on his screen.

"Ed, Clara, good job at Corolla." Diane gathered their attention as she moved toward the front. "No beach permits is good news, for us, of course. That leaves our bikers open to a possible warrant. I'm interested in learning what else you uncovered from up that direction." She noted Jason watching as he opened the container to share with Roxie. "Wally, Nathan, I haven't had time to review your reports from Urgent Care. Can I get you to fill me in now?"

Diane smiled as she gave her team the floor. She wanted Jason to see that she knew each one of them, and on a first-name basis. He might not have the sense that God gave a minnow, but she bet tomorrow's breakfast that she could make her new team into the best on the Outer Banks.

Just watch, Jason. See how it's done.

Chapter 2

Blood on the Sand

K9 HANDLER ED WALTERS looked up from his phone as his new boss called the meeting to order. The aroma of the pastries was a fondly remembered passion but one he'd given up years before. Even a taste was walking the rim of a deep pit he could easily tumble into. So, it was easier to just not.

The coffee? Nah, but for a different reason. The aroma nauseated him. He was grateful the machine was in a different room, and he tried to keep his chair positioned away from any steaming cups. Clara clearly had no such predilections against the stuff, as her head had been wrapped in a coffee haze since arriving. Yesterday's trip up the islands had been several hours of coffee nausea, though he would never criticize another team member for their preferences.

His interview with Captain Turnipseed had been especially difficult.

"Coffee's on me, Sergeant Walters."

The businesslike woman with the carefully casual hair, tired eyes, and full law enforcement regalia—down to her badge and holstered weapon—placed a brimming cup of blackened tar on her side of the booth and slipped into the seat. He and his wife, Hazel, lived some distance from the coast, so she had agreed to meet him in Edenton at a McDonald's just off the highway. On his arrival, he noted Taco Bell and Burger King aligned on the same side of the street, we-three-kings-of-Orient-are, but accepted the captain's preselected choice of locations. He might prefer those, but this was Captain Turnipseed's dime and interview, and he had been waiting for a K9 opening for some time. McDonald's was all right with him.

"Before we go further, let me introduce myself. Captain Diane Turnipseed with Dare County. I'm glad to finally meet you, Sergeant." She pulled a small spiral and pen from her shirt pocket and flipped it open before laying it on the table. "I've reviewed your qualifications. To tell the story honest, your record is impeccable. The one thing, I see a health scare several years back. Talk to me about that."

Always that. Ed sat up, cautious of appearing to take up too much space. He knew it was a holdover from the weight, but that was gone. He had worked on relearning his spatial awareness, but sometimes he slipped backwards. The aroma from the cup, like a deadly fog, squeezed his throat. He smiled and said, "Too little exercise and too much caffeine. I still need more exercise, but I've given up the caffeine. You'll have seen my medical report. I'd have to be twenty years younger to be any fitter." He didn't mention the weight. He wasn't proud of it and used the caffeine as a distraction, though it wasn't the real reason for dodging the curse of a daily coffee. Any excuse was as good as another if it kept tongues from wagging and the coffee-lovers from offering.

"Then my apologies for offering. Never again. A-District doesn't currently have a K9, but I noted that you've completed your training. I'd be above my knees if I didn't ask if you are prepared to participate in selecting a new pup. I've never done that, and I understand it can be exhausting."

"Yes," he said, blinking his way through the coffee fumes. "Here's the picture I see. Many of the best come from Europe, either Germany, Belgium, or the Netherlands. There are some organizations in the States we can look at. One is the Police Canine Association, though I would need to pursue specific trainers and their locations through them."

"I might oughta know you would be on top of this. You wouldn't be above your knees to check out Tarheel Canine Academy down in Sanford. They're a good group. My previous district here on the islands just replaced their retiring dog using one from Tarheel. The K9 handler down that direction sings their praises."

So, Ed mused, no easy access to a dog, as it was months to train a good K9 through a law enforcement program. Most pups were weeded out, and those that passed were in high demand. That sapped his enthusiasm. Through research, he knew as much as there was to find out about the Dare County Sheriff's Office and its three patrol districts. There had been almost nothing on the A-District, meaning it was quieter'n the backside of the moon. A small office like A-District wouldn't land high on the priority list for a new K9 officer, suggesting that Ed would likely be patrolling more than he was policing.

"So, we're good." Captain Turnipseed took a last slug from her cup of tar and stood. She looked around for the trash container, located it and said, "I'll be right back."

Ed wasn't certain, but he thought he'd just been hired. He

worked his way out of the booth, moving like there was too much of him to shift all at once, even though he had plenty of space. Nerves, he considered. Spatial awareness. Get a grip, man.

"Ed, if you'll join me. It's our turn."

Ed blinked, and he was back in the situation room. Clara touched his shoulder, and he smiled and stood.

"Of course. The permits. I have it all in my notes." He patted his chest pocket. That was something the new captain had impressed upon them, giving them each a small stack of spirals and short pens that just slipped into the wire rings.

As he and Clara approached the lectern, the corner of his eye revealed Wally and Nathan approaching their seats, with Nathan reenacting the scene with the runner from Urgent Care. Despite Ed's mind being on his interview, in that singular glance, he recalled everything in the two men's report about the twin brothers and their arrogant attitude.

Two things at once. It was something Ed was good at and what he figured made him successful at his job. It would be helpful if he had a dog so that he could do his job, but that was coming. Perhaps five months away, but it was at least something to look forward to.

"Ed?" Clara finished up and gave him the floor.

"Thank you, Clara." Ed stepped to the lectern, pulled the spiral from his pocket, and flipped it open in one motion. "When Clara and I talked to the docents at the Visitor Center in Corolla, they knew our boys. One lady, um," and he glanced at his spiral, although he had it in his head, "Mrs. Sally de la Palma, knew immediately who we were asking about." He looked at the faces giving him their attention and thought how much easier this would be if he had a dog. He steadied himself and continued, "I'm under the impression from talking with her that it's not what's in the picture but what's behind it that matters. Something behind the scene that she either didn't say or doesn't know."

Clara Del Ray had her hand about shoulder height, and she wriggled her fingers for his attention.

"Clara?"

"I've been doing some thinking about something else Mrs. de la Palma said, and since we're holding a meeting this morning, maybe everyone should know." She faced the room and smiled brightly before letting it go. "The beach is open during the day, and that's when most people go. But these two break the rules at odd times. Like yesterday, a storm coming in, and driving over an hour to get up there. Don't know that I would do that is all that I'm saying."

"Clara's right. I agree completely. Here's the picture I got from our visit. The main thing, besides the lack of permits, is when it happens. I didn't ask to see their records, as it's not our jurisdiction, or likely not. I'm uncertain exactly where the border between counties lies, and I'm unsure of how much cooperation there is between us and Currituck. Anyone have any questions?"

Diane took over again, leading a discussion of whether the truck and trailer in the yard needed to be sent to Manteo or released to the owner, which Diane eventually tabled as the sheriff was out of town. She questioned Wally about his plans with Deputy Preston for his required field training. He had a slot reserved at the Outer Banks Gun Club just south of Manns Harbor, and she nodded her approval.

"Wally and Clara," Diane pulled them aside once she wrapped up the meeting. "My aunt Lucille used to say that you can't fix stuff until it's broke, but by then it's sometimes too late. To tell the story honest, these brothers aren't going away no matter how much we wish it. They may live up in Currituck County, but I don't expect them to stay there. We saw that yesterday. How about you two head back up the island to see what the slack tide's turned up?"

"Anything in particular?" The question was Jason Romney's. He had joined the impromptu gathering.

"Hold your taters, Jason. This is A-District matters—"

"You might see it that way." Jason gave half a grin. "Here's the thing. As the County Detention Officer, I get to be here, there, and everywhere. Those two are mine if they wander back this direction. I'm not trying to intrude, just to do my job, so let's leave it at that."

"I wisht—" She tightened her jaw but turned away and continued her instructions. "If those two intend to put their spoon into our pot, I want to be the one doing the stirring. You two are new here, so head up and have a look-see at the border. Sand don't say nothing, but jurisdiction does. I want to keep them on their toes. We're good?"

Ed and Clara headed out, but not before Ed overheard the captain berating Jason Romney with, "You don't got the sense God gave a minnow ..."

Once inside the vehicle, Ed said, "I do believe I'm starting to understand what she says." He slipped a glance at Clara, with her blonde hair snugly wrapped into a bun, and her red lips in a grin.

"It's just a little practice. You'll pick it up. Can we stop by the Circle K? I'd like a cup of coffee."

"You'll keep the lid on?" What he didn't want to say was that he cringed at saying yes.

"Please and thank you goes a long way." She smiled when she said it. "I'm perceptive, and I'll try not to offend you with my coffee."

"But you have to have it, right?"

"I knew you'd make a good partner. Thank you, Ed." She laughed and settled into looking out the window at the passing scenery.

ONCE THE COFFEE was at Clara's fingertips, Ed headed up 12 the same direction as yesterday. The rain the day before had closed in the view, but today, the haze was of the wind-blown variety. Drying sand gathered on the roadways, only to be swept aside by humming rubber and burbling exhausts of luxury cars. Where the highway cut left towards the mainland and Elizabeth City, 12 took them right, and the city turned into trees, large beachfront houses, and more trees. The roadway wandered west to the Sound side and alongside the Duck Town Boardwalk. Eventually, the residences cleared, the U.S. Army Corps Field Research Facility on the right pointed a long finger into the ocean, and the Duck Fire Department made itself known.

Then, the trappings of civilization returned, with flowering, shrub-lined roadways, the roofs of private homes, and occasional shops for the convenience of the well-heeled. The Sanderling Resort touted itself as a location for charging electric vehicles, the beachfront homes grew to resort-like dimensions, and the road took a sudden curve toward the ocean.

A landscaped, wooden sign on the left side of the road boasted DUCK. Several hundred feet down, on the same side, a similar sign yelled, COROLLA, and under it, Currituck, North Carolina.

Ed pulled to the side of the road and glanced in his rearview mirror. "Somewhere in between those two signs in my guess."

"How do we get on the beach? That's why we're here."

"Dunno. I didn't see any beach access points driving through Duck. But remember, it's not the sand, it's the jurisdiction." Ed laughed.

"But the sand is where our boys ride their bikes. Head north and see what we find, hopefully before the Visitor Center four miles ahead. That's a long way to walk back on the sand."

"What? We can't use the car?"

"Are we in a four-wheel-drive?"

"Okay. Searching for an exit. Let's see where it takes us."

A couple of miles on they passed a divided, tarmacked entrance on the right, with unobstructed dunes towards the sea, and Ed slowed. Clara shook her head no, as it was clearly a new community opening up, and Ed pressed the accelerator and continued forward. He slowed again at Hampton Inn and Suites, and this time, Clara noted the beach access likely for hotel guests only but surely available to county law enforcement. She motioned for him to continue towards Corolla. Just further on, the Corolla Fire Station appeared on the left, and on the right, a sign read Currituck County Southern Public Beach Access.

Ed pulled in. "I didn't notice this yesterday. The Visitor Center is just there." They couldn't see it, but ahead past a tree-shrouded curve in the road was the location they had visited the previous day.

"Blame it on the rain," Clara chirped. "That's a very long hike back to the county line."

"Only if we could rent a four-wheeler ..." Ed let his complaint fade away. He didn't know if that was even possible.

However, Clara already had her phone out and clicked on the voice feature. "Please locate four-wheel-drive rentals in Corolla, North Carolina."

The phone replied, "Corolla Jeep Adventures just south of Currituck Light in Corolla provides rentals for ATVs. Would you like directions?"

"Absolutely! Yes!" As the information popped up on her

phone, she said, with a pleased expression, "I didn't expect this. I don't mind being on the beach. It says to continue north another … five miles?" She looked up in dismay.

"Five more miles? That's a lot of ATV back down the beach. There's got to be an easier way." Ed had begun to pull forward, but he moved his foot to the brake.

"The captain did say to have a look at the border. We're not getting there by foot."

"And they were on dirt bikes. They wouldn't notice five miles, would they?" He pictured himself on a tiny ATV. When he was heavier, he wouldn't have dared. He glanced at Clara's coffee cup, thankful that the aroma had remained mostly contained. He rubbed his eyes, trying to see this logically. "Don't know if the district will cover this. The rental, I mean."

"I have a credit card from my parents. I can cover it with that." When Ed looked astonished, she said, "Just for expenses, Ed. You know, emergencies."

"This is an emergency?" It was her money, but still.

"If I say it is. Anyway, I'm sure the captain will reimburse us, and if she doesn't, my dad can count it as a business expense."

"Your money." He checked for cars, waited on a large Lexus SUV, and pulled out headed north.

The Visitor Center appeared on the left and was quickly behind them as their vehicle clicked through the miles. The houses remained large and well-maintained, the shrubbery flowered as if on command, and the businesses fell in line with welcoming porches, discreet signage, and parking areas neatly partitioned with screening shrubs or flowers.

Neither the ocean nor the Sound was anywhere to be seen, although according to Clara's phone, they could hardly be a five-minute walk from either. They noted a turn that would take them to the Herring Street Beach Access point but continued past it another mile and discovered more beach access points at Shad Street and a more substantial access point at Corolla Village Road, with a wide avenue bordered by parking for nearly a quarter mile towards the beach.

Their plans for an ATV rental began to fall apart soon after they reached their destination. The building boasted a bait-and-tackle shop that included an ice cream parlor under the same wood-shingled porch. A small sign hanging from the porch said, WILD HORSE TOURS all in capitals, and beside it, ATV TOURS. When they stepped in, Marjorie Winters, a no-nonsense type in cargo shorts with her sleeves rolled up and buttoned with a strap, noted their police-type clothing with a glance.

"Dare County. A bit out of your territory. What can I do for you?"

"A couple'a yours found us down in Kitty Hawk. We have their truck and bikes in impound—" Ed was surprised to be cut off.

"What?" Marjorie clapped the counter. "Jeromy, get in here!" She nodded towards Ed and Clara. "My apologies, officers." She leaned through a door. "Jeromy, now!"

A young man, likely still a teen, with rough hair, also in cargo shorts and a shirt that said Corolla Adventure Tours, appeared. His shoes said he'd recently been on the sand. He said, "Yes, Marjorie?"

"Is any of our equipment unaccounted for?"

"Um," and Jeromy pressed the heel of one hand to his hairline just at his temple, searched the floor as if the answer was there, and looked back to Marjorie. "No."

"Okay, then." She turned her attention back to Ed and Clara, letting Jeromy slink back into obscurity. "That's Jeromy

Travers. He's working for college money. Hopes to attend next year. Anyway, I'm guessing that whatever you've got isn't mine."

Clara stepped up. "We had trouble yesterday with two people from up here. It's their vehicles. We're learning they tend to cross the county line, and we're needing to discern exactly where that is."

"Sure. I get that. They cross over, they become your responsibility." Marjorie frowned as if unsure she understood but didn't want to be disagreeable. "There are signs on the road."

"On the beach." Clara smiled brightly. "They were creating a hazard with their bikes on public roads, likely because they were rained out on the beach. We understand this isn't the first time—"

By then, Marjorie seemed to be catching on. "Can I get their names?"

Ed pulled out his spiral, flipped it open and read, "Ballinger, Philippe and Creighton."

"Oh, my word! Jeromy, you hear that? Those brothers are stirring the pot again!" She closed her eyes and shook her head. "Any blowback from the Knight clan?"

"Um, not yet." Clara seemed unsure. "We're just getting our feet wet. The Knight clan?"

"They're all cousins, the Corolla Knights and the Currituck bunch. The Knights have been here the better part of a century, but the Currituck cousins, well, they should'a stayed in France, if you want my opinion. They're like two pieces of sandpaper, that's what they are. But enough of that. What else can I do for you? The beach, you said. Unless it's up towards Virginia, I don't see how I can help. We operate on private land north of here near the border on the old Guggenheim hunt club. We offer views from the highest point in Currituck County. Alas, not any beachfront down your way. If you need on the beach down there, here's what you do."

She shared that law enforcement often accessed the beaches, even in private areas, through private access points. Homeowners were generally very accommodating, as protection of their property was paramount. As long as it was in an official capacity ... and their clothing and badges would attest to that.

Headed south once more, after crossing the Dare County line, they took the first left, labeled as Baum Trail, into a subdivision marked as Palmer's Island and clearly posted as private. They headed left to locate the property adjacent to the county line. Leaving the car on the road, they entered the driveway. The house and extensive grounds appeared to be closed for the season. They circled past the front of the house, by what must be a pool, to an extensive parking area with its own expansive structure. Behind that, a landscaped walkway revealed sand and the unbroken expanse of the Atlantic. The wind forced dry sand to skip along the beach and across the rough dunes, and steady waves rolled in, hitting the hard-packed sand with loud thumps that seemed to vibrate under their feet.

The rain the day before had been atrocious, but beginning just beyond the beach access point, just at the high-water line from the most recent tide, scattered debris suggested dark deeds had indeed taken place on the Currituck County line and had splashed across onto the Dare County side.

Dark, bloody deeds, even if a body was nowhere to be seen.

DEPUTY CLARA DEL RAY dropped her phone from her ear. Her radio was virtually ineffective so far out, except to contact Ed, and her phone barely had enough signal to make a call. She glanced at the detritus strewn along the beach and shook her head.

"I know I say it's not what's in the picture, but maybe this time it is." Ed had walked a short way along the sand, keeping to the area that had been washed clean by the tide. He called to Clara, "Were you able to get through?"

"Yes."

The wind whipped her voice away, and Ed motioned for her to join him via the undisturbed sand. When she was closer, he asked, "This is people's lives. What did they suggest?"

"I told them things were likely washed up in both counties, but access was difficult. They said that Dare County doesn't have a dedicated marine division, and the state-level marine officers assigned to us concentrate on fisheries management."

"So, it's up to us." Two counties. Ed considered what that meant.

"Maybe not. The captain is contacting Currituck County."

"Does that mean Currituck has a dedicated marine division? If not, did she mention the Coast Guard? This seems like Coast Guard level nastiness to me."

"I didn't ask. I just said that boat access was the only viable option if we wanted real feet on the scene. I stuck to please and thank you, as they go a long way."

Ed blew his cheeks out in a heavy sigh. "You know this would be easy with a dog. But I don't have one assigned yet. Still, I got my own senses." He paused when Clara laughed. "What, young lady? That's funny?"

"No, go on." She held up a hand and waggled her fingers at him.

"Here's the picture I see. A fight, maybe. Two people having a go at one another, things get out of hand, and one punch becomes two. A nosebleed at first, then more damage. Blood everywhere, maybe even everyone heading home to get cleaned up." He paused to study the beachside views of the large and imposing homes fronting the ocean.

"This hardly seems to be a fistfight sort of neighborhood."

"Right. So, let's turn the picture around and see it from another direction. Remote area, limited access. Private road and likely lots of security cameras. Why here?"

"An animal attack?"

Ed frowned. "What sort of animal? This is a beach."

"I grew up summering just south of here. I'm a water girl, remember. North Carolina does have sharks."

"Corrected. This is new to me, so I didn't think." He frowned, considered Clara's input, studied the clothing caught in the sand and on the tough, wiry plants that forced their sturdy shoulders from the windblown dunes, and continued. "This isn't beach attire, not that I can see. I would expect towels and swimwear if this is the remains of a shark attack."

"My turn to be corrected." Clara smiled. "Shark attacks often leave no evidence if the shark is really hungry. If there's no body washed up, I mean."

"Understood." Ed faced the ocean. "You can't get here by road, but there—" He pointed into the incoming waves. "—is easy access. Perhaps not today, but someone comes in, not wearing beach wear because they aren't here to swim, and there's a disagreement ..." He let his words trail off.

"Over what?"

"Those bikes back in the sub-station lot. They're perfect for this sand, wouldn't you say?" He looked up the long, unbroken Currituck section of the beach towards Corolla.

"I like a man who thinks. What are you thinking, Ed? Smuggling? They didn't look like smugglers, but then what do smugglers look like? We didn't see many of those back in Brunswick County."

Both their radios blipped at the same time. As if in stereo, a voice said, "Sergeant Brannigan Calmont with the Currituck County Sheriff's Office. Is there anyone nearby by the name of Ed Walters? Over."

Ed hit his mic at his collar and said, "Walters, here, with Deputy Del Ray. Where are you? Over."

"On 12. I don't see your vehicle."

"We're parked in—" He looked towards Clara for the name of the community.

"Palmer's Island."

"—Palmer's Island, Sergeant. That's on the Dare County side."

"I'm familiar with it. I can see it from here. How do I get to where you are?"

"We're parked at the big house closest to the county line, the one on the far left. There's a private beach access point behind the garage."

"Be there shortly."

Ed released his collar and said to Clara, "Backup. No boat, though. I don't guess Currituck thinks this is serious."

"Maybe they don't have a dedicated marine division." Clara laughed.

After some minutes, Calmont appeared, a tall, muscular man, with his face shaded by a lightweight cowboy hat over freckles and red hair. His eyes were covered with black sunglasses with equally black wire rims. He had one hand at the brim of his hat to fight the wind attempting to wrest it from him.

"Walters, Del Ray," he called, lifting a hand. A sideways grin gave him an approachable vibe.

"Took you long enough," Ed said. "Did you walk here?"

"Actually, yes." The sideways grin was back. He pointed to the houses on the Dare County side. "High-dollar places. No sense in placing my out-of-county car in view of their security cameras. Private security is no joke."

"Then they have us." Ed shrugged. "So be it. What about this, though? Are you with a marine division by any chance?"

"I am in a car." Calmont seemed amused. "My official title is Beach Duty Detail Officer. I do ATVs, not boats. Do we need a boat?"

Clara stepped in and held out her hand. "Deputy Clara Del Ray. Glad to meet you, Sergeant Calmont—"

"Brannigan, please." The redheaded man took her hand and shook.

"Thank you, Brannigan. I like Clara, if you don't mind. Ed and I were hoping you could tell us how to move forward with this. We're new to Dare County, or at least to the Sheriff's Office, and we're told the state marine division officers working with Dare County prefer to tackle fisheries management."

"Right. I've been told that. Currituck has its own marine division, so lucky for us. We can do what we want. Show me what you have, and we can go from there."

"Follow me." Ed indicated the dunes just to the north. "Brannigan, right?"

"Yessir, if you insist. Follow you, that is. My name, well, it just is." The Currituck County officer gave his half grin.

"Right. Ed. I didn't introduce myself earlier." He offered his hand.

"Yessir, got it, Ed. Glad to meet y'all." His eyes skipped along the detritus along the high tide line. "This is what you've got?"

They were moving along the dunes while staying just below the high tide line to avoid impacting the site. The offshore breeze was hitting at a clip, and various items of clothing whipped in the wind. Portions were partially buried, with others suspended on prickly beach growth. Ed knelt at one point to show Calmont a sleeve cuff. Only part of the sleeve was visible, meaning the rest of the shirt could be buried, but several tears in the fabric suggested it had been ripped from the main article of clothing. Darkened blotches could be blood, if Calmont saw it that way.

An athletic shoe, on its side and half buried, wore similar blotches, yet the worn white leather revealed them as deep red in color.

Ed was unsure about several places in the sand that didn't seem like natural windblown textures. Dips, divots, troughs that were out of character with the rest of the undulating dune surface. Calmont knelt at the suspicious surface to calculate his opinion. Even as they watched, sand began to fill more of the shoe, and the sleeve attached to the shirt cuff had begun to disappear.

"Do you have stakes and tape?" Calmont stood and looked out to sea. The whitecaps on the water suggested weather on the way.

"I can check." Ed called to Clara, "Do we have stakes and tape for all this?"

"Maybe. I haven't seen them, but I can check. I'll need the keys."

Ed pulled them from a pocket and hefted them to her through the air. She caught them handily. Calmont called to her, "I'll join you." To Ed he said, "I need to call in. If this is a crime scene, we need to stop the sand before it obscures everything."

"You've got a plan, then. Good. I'll wait here." Ed pulled out his phone and began to snap pictures of the items on the beach and their relationship to the residences on either side as Calmont headed back to the road and his county vehicle.

Clara returned carrying a bag. Inside, Ed located wooden

stakes, a mallet, crime-scene tape, and a power stapler. Together, they began driving the stakes in the sand in a long, snake-like oval, ensuring that they were far enough back in the dunes to avoid contamination of the scene. On the beach side, they aimed for the high-tide line, as any lower would likely be washed away within a few hours. Clara carried the stapler and followed Ed as he unrolled the tape and held it for her to attach to each stake. They were almost finished when they noticed a red-and-black ATV speeding down the beach from the north. A hand on a cowboy hat told them who it was. When it pulled up, Calmont killed the engine and stepped off.

"They couldn't give you a windscreen?" Ed teased him.

"We have them, fully enclosed for inclement weather, if we need them. I didn't take the time to attach one. If you think it best, I can go back and do that." The man grinned. "Otherwise, I brought something to help with the sand."

The back of the ATV boasted a sizable roll of landscaping fabric with substantial metal stakes. As they unloaded it and searched for where to unroll it, the Currituck officer noted the Dare County team's work in marking the site and that it gave him a good indication of where the fabric needed to be. They dropped it along the section of dune that held the suspicious items and kicked sand on it to hold it in place. The stakes were much more substantial than the wooden ones and had attachment points for the fabric. Calmont laughed when Clara offered him the mallet.

"No ma'am," he said. "That won't make any headway at all. I've got the real deal back on the ATV."

The real deal was an actual sledgehammer. The three of them made good progress on the stakes. Halfway through, Calmont pulled a package of fasteners from his pocket and offered them to anyone who wanted to begin attaching the fabric to the poles. Clara volunteered, and after a brief tutorial, she headed back to the beginning, while he and Ed continued with spearing the stakes into the sand.

In the haze being kicked up by wind, Ed noticed a boat on its way down the coast. It was a good ways out but easily identifiable as a Boston Whaler design, and as it closed the distance, he could read the word SHERIFF on the side.

"Your people?" He pointed it out to the Currituck County officer.

"Likely." Calmont held the sledgehammer, and he only gave the seacraft a cursory glance. "They said they would try to send someone in, and our two someones relish this type of weather."

"I don't get the picture. Sorry."

Calmont dropped the head of the hammer to the sand and leaned on the handle. "Surf is hard to land in. Barker and Krazinski, our Marine Patrol team, beg to go out in this."

"How do they keep the boat from washing back out?"

Calmont laughed. "The boat doesn't come ashore. Can you see what they're towing?"

Ed could just make out two smaller vessels in the Boston Whaler's wake. Personal watercraft. Three people occupied the larger boat, and two were in the process of donning protective, waterproof gear and flotation devices.

"That looks like fun!" Clara had joined Ed and the Currituck County officer in observing the actions out to sea as the men slipped on backpacks, reeled in the smaller vessels, and mounted them.

Calmont chuckled. "Barker and Krazinski think so."

The third person waved to shore, Calmont waved back, and as the boatman released each individual jet ski, a rooster tail shot skyward, and the smaller craft separated from the larger one.

Once the two smaller boats were headed in, the Boston

Whaler looped around and lifted its bow into the waves and began clawing its way north, sending spray flying as it lifted on the wind-tossed waves and repeatedly slammed back down again.

ED HAD EXPECTED the two men to slow down, come in gradually, and dismount while still in the surf. They would run a line up on the beach and secure it, although in retrospect, that didn't make any sense. There was nothing to secure it to, so that wasn't the picture that played itself out. Then, Ed wasn't a beach person, and his familiarity with the small water scooters came from movies where the shore consisted of wharves, docks, or lakeside picnic areas.

Instead, Ed felt his heart tighten as the men didn't slow but came at the shore at what must have been top speed, tearing through the swells. Just where the water turned to sand, they soared into the air in an impossible leap across a bridge of spray-infused sky. Actually, it was likely a leap of inches, but in that moment of unexpected and heart-throbbing surprise, Ed expected them to take flight and wind up on the highway.

Marine Patrol Officer Scotty Barker, a man with a ruddy complexion and a bit of a gut, sorted the best landing. He pulled the nose up just as it left the final whitewater barrier, braced for a small skip on the sand, and came to a complete if abrupt stop. He killed the engine, stood, slapped the machine on the side, and called, "Yeah, Sissy. Good job, girl!"

His companion, Marine Patrol Officer Dillon Krazinski, a fresh-faced youth with strawberry hair and a rash of freckles across his nose and cheeks, did his best, but the nose of his watercraft impacted the sand, leaving the back of the craft in ankle-deep water.

Barker took in his landing and yelled, "Gotta keep the nose

up, Dillon!"

Krazinski didn't reply as his craft had his full attention. He watched until a wave built and crashed just behind him, and as it lifted the tail, he hit the power and let it carry him forward another two feet. Before the water had a chance to slink back into the ocean, he was off, with water swirling up to his knees, and pushing on the water scooter to move it onto the beach.

"I gotcha." Barker moved forward, grabbed the mooring line, and wrapped it around his forearm. Together they got the small craft from the waves to safety and turned to greet the personnel already on the shore.

"Showing off again, I see." Sergeant Calmont had his arms crossed. Despite the wind-driven moisture in the air, the glare from the sun was brutal, and his black wire rims disguised the expression in his eyes. His voice, however, said he was laughing.

"It's the best job ever!" Krazinski had sloughed his pack to the sand, and after he removed his flotation device, he unzipped his jacket to expose County attire underneath, consisting of a light-colored shirt with insignia and the waistband of khaki pants. A rolled cap with Sheriff on the front appeared from an interior pocket and found its way to his head.

Barker wore the same under his waterproof wear, with the exception of not boasting soaked trouser legs. He had moved his pack farther up the beach and allowed only a moment's frown at Krazinski's closer to the water. He did point to the pack and nodded when his companion shifted its position away from the surf.

"What I expect, Calmont," Barker had knelt and was open-ing his pack, "is for you landlubbers to hustle and make more of these opportunities possible. Quite trying to handle everything yourself and just give us a call. We want to step in and get involved."

"I thought y'all were all about tooling up into Sound estuaries, either that or kicking overzealous college girls back onto the shore."

"Only when they're drunk and a danger to themselves or others." Barker stood with a smaller pack of supplies. He looked up and down the landscaping fabric and moved closer to peer on the other side. He glanced from one end to the other and let his eyes rest on the section to the south. "This is Currituck, but I'm guessing that's not."

"There is a reason I have two Dare County people with me. Scotty, this is K9 Handler Ed Walters and Deputy Clara Del Ray. Ed and Clara, this is our very own, rough and ready Sergeant Scotty Barker."

"Folks." Barker nodded.

"And that's Deputy Dillon Krazinski. I don't vouch for him. If Scotty wants to, that's his call."

"Hey, y'all," Krazinski called with a wave, as he stood from his pack. The sand around him had become littered with similar supplies to Barker's.

The mood among the men shifted from teasing banter to focused police work with as little notice as stepping from one room to another. The supply packs supplied evidence bags, markers, numbered plastic tabs, and surprisingly, a camera, more than seemed possible in the compact backpacks.

Clara laughed as the camera appeared out of yet another, smaller bag. "Don't know that I would do that."

"Do what?" Krazinski held the camera as he prepared it for use. It was enclosed in a sturdy, inner clear bag.

"A camera with all this water."

"Oh, why?" The strawberry-haired officer held it to his eye as he ensured it showed what he wanted.

"Salt water. That was you out there, wasn't it?" She caught Ed watching the banter, and she winked at him.

"Oh, the inner bag is waterproof." He looked away from the viewfinder and grinned. "All of the bags are."

"Just not your clothes."

He glanced down. His waterproofs were off to the side, and indeed, his khakis were dark up to his calves. He shrugged. "I'll dry. The camera won't."

"Dillon, quit jawing and catch." Barker tossed him a set of the numbered tabs. "Everything in this taped off area I want numbered and photographed. Then we'll start collecting and bagging. Maybe the Dare County people will stoop to help."

"I'm all in," Clara chirped. "I've been waiting on this for ages."

"It'd help if you had a K9 here, K9 Handler." Barker paused to give Ed a long look.

"I've got an idea," Ed retorted. "If I had a dog, I'd offer his services. That's not in the picture until we get one trained."

"I see. Didn't mean offense." Barker nodded. "No dog means you get beach duty. Lucky you." He laughed. "Least-wise, that's what young Krazinski over there thinks."

"No offense taken." Ed shifted his position to block the stinging sand. It had already begun to pile up in a loose accumulation at the base of the jet ski hulls. The landscape fabric fluttered in the stiff breeze and made a popping sound as it strained at the metal posts and vented its frustration. Clara followed Krazinski, taking pics with her phone, even as he knelt with his camera at each location.

Good for you, Clara, Ed thought. *We might need a record, too.*

Sergeant Calmont joined Scotty Barker, smoothly accepting a roll of evidence bags, thin nitrile gloves, and a permanent marker, the action suggesting that they had a comfortable and familiar working relationship. The Beach Patrol officer eyed the pair photographing the items in the sand, spoke to Barker—which Ed couldn't hear over the sound of the surf—and Barker pointed. Calmont nodded, circled the end of the landscape fabric wall, placed one foot on the police tape to make a temporary entrance, and stepped into the potential crime scene.

At a tap on his shoulder, Ed was surprised to find Barker at his side. "Yessir, how can I help?"

"Look there." He nodded towards Krazinski's watercraft. "Notice anything?"

"Surf."

"Just watch."

Occasional seafoam peeled off the whitecaps and went for a run across the sand. The waves rolled in, collapsed, then sank back down the beach in retreat before trying again. One shell caught Ed's attention. It had been dry, but now it glistened. After a moment, a larger wave rolled over it before slicing back out to sea. When the water was gone, the shell was, too.

"Tide?"

"And the wind. Dillon and I need to hustle if we want to get back out."

"I was thinking about that. What can I do to speed things up?"

Barker seemed to relax as he handed Ed a stack of evidence bags similar in volume to Calmont's. "You're familiar with the procedure?"

"Don't expect it would be much different than anywhere else. Anything specific?"

"We don't have a case number, so that's not a thing. The item number is from Dillon's tabs, plus the date and time of collection, and a brief description of each item." Barker added a permanent marker to Ed's stash.

"And my name and position with the county. For the location, do I need to identify the specific county each item is in? Or is the name of the beach enough, if it has one?" That was part of the issue and the reason both counties had officers present. Depending on each item's exact location, it could be in either.

"OBX for those at that end." Barker indicated south. "Currituck for this end, I suppose. There's a line somewhere, but if you're not sure, you can add both. Now, let's step up and get involved so Dillon and I don't get stranded."

Krazinski had several items bagged and placed on the sand just outside the "crime scene." Of course, Ed reminded himself, they had yet to determine if that's what it was, but good police work was a practical matter. Matter of fact. Logical. Caution was tantamount to effective crime scene investigation, so it made sense to collect the information while it was available rather than wish they had done so, and a criminal remained free to strike again.

The beach was steep—as Ed was learning about much of the Atlantic side of the Outer Banks—and his feet dug in as he pushed through the sand. He noted the numbered tabs in the bags along with the retrieved evidence and picked up one to read Krazinski's description.

"Shirt sleeve, plaid, dark stains." Then he had added the other required information, with the location identified as "beach—OBX/Currituck, Atlantic side."

Then that's how his labels would look, Ed decided. He replaced the bag, worked out one of his own, slipped on a pair of the protective nitrile gloves, and headed towards the closest available tag to begin his participation in collecting evidence from the scene of this potential crime.

BY THE TIME the bits and pieces were cleared from the taped-off area, the attending officers had a better understanding of what Ed and Clara had inadvertently stumbled on. In their attempt to satisfy Captain Turnipseed's request to draw a line in the sand between Dare County and Currituck County, they had separated nothing but had created a link that would—of necessity—require the cooperation of both counties to cast a wide enough net to pull in whoever had done whatever had been done.

The occasional sleeve stained with dark fluids could be anything. A crime lab would determine what, but in their minds, it was likely blood. As they pulled partially buried clothing items from the sand, several ragged areas suggested bullet holes. Barker remarked that black marks around one seemed to be powder burns, indicative of a shot taken at point-blank range.

At that assessment, Clara had blinked hard and taken a deep breath before continuing.

Krazinski found the first evidence of drugs, and not the used sort that sometimes turned up on the beach. Used paraphernalia could wash up after any storm, sometimes cast off from fishing boats and floating in on the tide. A canvas strap protruded from the sand, with the surface worn to near breaking. As he worked it out, a satchel—also boasting dark stains—grew out of the sand. The side was torn—gunshot damage?—and out tumbled several small bags of powder.

Krazinski stood, taking photos of the tear and the scattered bags, and he called to Barker, "Hey, Scotty. Come see this."

That wasn't the most interesting thing they uncovered, however. Yes, there was damage to many of the items, and a number appeared to be gun inflicted. That wasn't surprising, what with the stains that had originally attracted Ed's attention. With Krazinski's skill at placing numbered tabs where there seemed to be nothing, even the shell casings that had appeared like sand crabs from the soil seemed almost normal.

The pistol got everyone's attention.

Sort of that "smoking gun" thing, where the proof is in the pudding ... or as an English scholar might say, the *proof* of how *good* your *evidence is* can be found in the *tasting* of the pudding.

"Well," Ed said, as the weapon entered one of the evidence bags. "That looks pretty much like pudding to me."

An English scholar might disagree with Ed butchering the old idiom, but no one could disagree with Ed's conclusion. After all, a gun in the evidence bag is worth two in the sand.

Or something like that.

MARINE PATROL OFFICERS Barker and Krazinski conferred with their county teammate and suggested that carrying the evidence bags out via the ocean was unwise.

Barker looked over the water, his eyes taking in the wind stripping the foam from the whitecaps, and he nodded. "Transporting the evidence bags by ATV certainly makes more sense. Sissy'll take that surf, no issue, but there might be a little water involved."

"A little?" Calmont laughed. "The bigger question is, can it be done? You guys were nuts to bring those out."

"At your request." Barker was moving the collected items to the ATV to load them.

"I called for backup, not for crazy. I can head up for a trailer."

"Hey, no!" Krazinski's face fell. "These are the best waves ever. Scotty, no."

"My partner has spoken." Barker clipped the cargo box closed. "That means we need to quit jawing and hustle on outta here."

"Still the best day ever!" Krazinski's face brightened, and his grin revealed his excitement.

"If you think it best. I want to see some headway out there before I drive off, though." Calmont tipped up the brim of his cowboy hat and adjusted his sunglasses before taking them off and polishing them on his shirt. His eyes revealed the need for the sunglasses with their clear blue irises. "I've got room for the packs, too, if you want."

The packs didn't fit in the cargo box, but Calmont had plenty of straps. Barker and Krazinsky suited up in their waterproofs and repositioned their watercraft units to face into the surf and fired them up. They waited for a large swell to bring in enough water to just begin to float the hulls, and their engines roared. Smoke, spray, and rooster tails followed them as they skipped and danced through the breaking waves into easier water off-shore.

"Those guys are the real deal." Calmont looked from his ATV to the house on the Dare County side. "You people need to call in before I take off? Or you think it best to just head on out and let your people sort this out with mine?"

"All this." Ed indicated the police tape and the landscape fabric. "We're just leaving it?"

"Right. You're a mainlander. Well, were a mainlander, I suppose, but yes. One of our departments may well decide to comb this area again."

Clara said, "Ed, we can come back if the captain suggests it. These people have closed their houses for the season, so this can stay here for ages, and no one will complain."

Ed nodded his agreement, shook hands with Calmont, and watched him for a moment as he mounted the ATV, secured his cowboy hat with one hand, and did a U-ie before spinning his tires and heading back up the beach toward Corolla.

"Ready, Ed?" Clara had their supplies bagged and at her feet.

"Just thinking." He felt he was good at picking up details, or perhaps it was just being able to focus on one thing and still be aware of what was around him. He just *knew*, sometimes without being aware of it. But then, police work was practical, and he saw things in a logical manner, so he was convinced that was part of it. "A dog would make this easier."

"Please and thank you. I think we did a good job." A strip of hair had worked its way out of Clara's tight bun, and she had her arms at her neck working it back in.

"Dogs can connect things we can't. Aromas are invisible, and we don't have the nasal cavities that canines do."

"On a beach? Thank goodness for that." Clara returned a bobby pin to its rightful location in her bun and shook her head, ensuring she had done a good job on the repair. "Otherwise, no one would want to be here."

"I dunno. I suppose. Okay, let's head up."

As Ed slowed to pull out onto 12, a tired yellow Toyota opened its door on the opposite side of the highway. A man with thinning hair in a reddish tinge and a thick moustache in white grasped the roof drip rail and pulled himself up. Standing, he was of medium height, with off-island clothes that had survived a washing machine too many times.

He waved at the officers, looked both ways, then strode across the highway with a surprisingly brisk step for a graybeard, er, a man with a gray moustache.

"Yessir," Ed called from his window. "What can we do for you?"

"Waited long enough for ya'." The man's face broke into a laugh. "Thought you was lost, maybe the tide gotcha and ate you up." This time the laugh took over his whole body.

"So, what can we do for you?"

"That's my car there." He pointed with his head. "I guess you saw it well enough. It's a Corolla."

"Sure," Ed said, puzzled. "Your point?"

"You must not be from around here." The man laughed again and this time offered a hand. "Gippy Knight, from Corolla." This time he pronounced the word differently, Co-*rahl*-la rather than Co-*roll*-la. "Get it? I drive a Co-*roll*-la and live in Co-*rahl*-la."

"That's good." Ed glanced at Clara and found her fighting a smile. "Gippy, is there something specific you stopped us for?"

"Specific?" Gippy chuckled. "I may be a Banker, but I'm a Corolla Banker. I'm no coward just because my Corolla has a yellow tail. You follow me?"

"Sort of."

"I'm guessing you ain't been here long enough to be *aware* of the feud here on the Banks."

"You said Gippy *Knight*." The light was coming on for Ed. "The Currituck—"

That's as far as Ed got when Gippy lifted a hand into the air with his finger pointed for emphasis. "Not as slow as I thought. I learned the Sound from my daddy, who said you can walk across given any sense, though I never tried it. Anyways, Bette—that's my wife—was by this morning and talked to Brannigan. You know Brannigan?"

"Officer Calmont," Clara called her answer from across the car. "Dare County has been working with him, so yes."

"Oh, howdy, little lady." Gippy leaned down to peer in. "Wasn't sure you was a real policeman. I see your uniform now. Hello." He stood and seemed to relax into his story. "Brannigan didn't say much to Bette. He's a good man and does his job right, and you can tell him that." He paused and seemed thoughtful.

"We sure will," Clara called.

"And?" Ed prompted the man, hoping he would get to the point. This had to be more than singing Calmont's praises.

"Just thinking how much to say, but I will say this. We Corolla Knights don't care much for those Currituck folk. They claim to be Knights, but not a Knight among 'em. They use some name they got from over there—" He motioned vaguely with his hard toward the ocean. "—and say they're our cousins, but real blood cousins feel it. There's a link. They're not no cousins of mind, I'll say that."

"We do have business elsewhere, Mr. Knight." Ed shifted to the man's last name. Crisp. Concise. Let's get this over.

"I hear you got hold of two of 'em yesterday down in your part of the Banks."

"And released them." Ed looked at Clara and nodded. This might be something.

"Maybe shouldn't have. Before that squall, them boys was out here on this beach. Whatever you found out here, the acorn don't fall too far from the tree. If you've got the notion, don't think any of my family would mind helping you out if you asked."

"Thank you, Gippy." Ed relaxed. This was the real reason for the impromptu meeting. "We'll keep in touch."

"It's the reason I came down to wait on ya'. I knew if I parked right there, I'd see you." He chuckled. "I said I never walked the Sound, but that's because my daddy allowed it was filled with snakes and gators and said to never do it. Still, no more than knee-deep in most places. Done it myself many times … walked across, I mean, though I never told Daddy."

Gippy somehow decided he was through, and without a goodbye, he looked up and down the highway and almost skipped across. He did the second U-ie of the day, sending his car northward with whining gears that revealed the car's meager horsepower.

"That gun." Ed gave Clara a moment to process. "Are you thinking Gippy said what I think he said?"

"I'll contact the sheriff's office in Barco. When Brannigan gets there, they can run the serial numbers."

"You ... Barco?" Ed was surprised for the petite blonde to throw out that extra bit of information.

"I summered here all my life." Clara grinned.

"Right." Ed pulled out and headed south. *And I still don't have a dog.* He was certain he'd feel better when he did.

PULLING IN AT the sub-station and seeing the impounded truck and the bikes caused Ed to picture the three vehicles in a new light.

A sand-covered pistol light.

There had been blood when they were brought in. Was it pistol-type blood? Hitting someone in the face with the butt of a gun could do immense damage.

Had Styles and Preston transported victims or perpetrators to the Urgent Care ... or were the two young men misconstrued innocents?

Whichever, they were now persons of interest. It's a shame he didn't yet have a dog. A dog's nose out there on the sand ... the rain and surf at high tide would have weakened the scents, but a good dog could pick up information from near nothing, even after extended periods of time.

Paloma was at her desk when Ed and Clara entered the building, and she paused at her typing and looked at them pointedly.

"A bit of wind out there?" She smiled.

"You can tell?" Clara brightened to the question. "Is my hair still in place? She pointed to her bun where she'd made repairs.

"Take this like I say it and don't get offended, but as good as can be for a day like this."

"I'll take that as a yes. It's just a little wind out there, and if I didn't enjoy the beach, I'd be working back in the city."

Ed moved on past, greeting the red-haired woman with a nod and, "Paloma," before heading back to his assigned desk.

Behind him, Paloma called, "Honey, I didn't mean to step on your toes."

"Report to write up," he called back.

"Not yet. Get back in here."

"Yes, ma'am."

Ed and Clara learned that Barco had taken Gippy's information seriously. Paloma, with connections to everything and everyone north of Manteo, didn't seem surprised.

"The Knights up there in their Corolla hidey-hole are urchins on a rock, prickly on the outside but good enough on the inside, I suppose. They keep to their business and mostly it doesn't spill into our business. Barco might say differently, but I don't mind them … when they stay up in Corolla." She peered hard at them as she paused. "It's when they get riled that their spines start poking into everyone's business, and those people in Currituck, well, they rile the Knights every chance they get."

"Wait, wait," Ed said. "There's something I need clarified. Currituck. It's a county, right?"

"You, an officer of the law asking that?" Paloma said it dramatically but with a smile.

"It's a town, also, Ed. Well, maybe a village, and a small one at that." Clara seemed to find it amusing. "When you recognized Barco, I assumed you knew about Currituck."

"Barco's one of the places I sent my resume, but they

already had a K9 handler. That's the only reason I know the Sheriff's Office in Currituck is there."

"Fair enough," Clara conceded.

"So this," and Paloma pulled a thin file from a rack on her desk, "is a file the captain asked me to start on those boys. It includes those vehicles out front. Note, nothing to show." She opened the file to reveal it was empty.

Ed was seeing it, what was being asked of them. He looked towards the door, could just see the rig outside, and worked his mouth before saying, "What's expected of us?"

"License plate check, inspection verification, records check for possible violations." Paloma pulled out and placed a separate form for each item into the folder.

"What sort of violations?" Ed reached toward the folder but hesitated when Paloma didn't immediately offer it.

Clara answered, "Parking tickets and fines, and whether it can be deemed unsafe. That can keep vehicles impounded for weeks if we request and delay an independent inspection."

"If the current inspection's good, though—"

"Sometimes what's good is to keep the vehicle out of someone's hands for a while. There's a way, Ed. This isn't new to me." Clara asked Paloma, "Anything else?"

"The captain specifically asked for gun residue tests. Are you familiar?" Paloma peered over her glasses as if in doubt.

"If there's a kit."

"You people." Paloma sighed. "I may look white, but like all persons of color, I am prepared for every circumstance. In the back cabinet in the situation room. Okay, now, like my grandpappy always said, I said what I have to say, and you need to let me get back to my business."

She turned back to her keyboard, dismissing the two officers as if she hadn't taken a break.

Ed pulled the file from Paloma's desk, while Clara headed to retrieve the gun residue kit. He was familiar with the kit's potential contents, such as adhesive stubs or swabs soaked with chemical solutions to collect possible residue from the dashboard, seats, or other surfaces. Each sample would be individually sealed and packaged for the forensic laboratory in Raleigh. Even if they found something, it might not prove that either of the twins had fired the gun—or any gun—but Ed was about order, caution, and step-by-step rules. Any link they found might be valuable in establishing possible connections between suspects (the twins), firearms (the pistol from the beach), and crime scenes (the actual beach); and it only counted if they observed, recorded, and verified it.

He intended to do this by the book.

The truck and bike keys were on a hook in a slim metal cabinet against the wall. The door had break-resistant glass and a lockable clasp which was left unlocked during the day. The keys were looped together with a large plastic strap and carried a tag with the vehicle's make and color.

Ed chuckled as he opened the door and removed the keys.

"What's funny?" Clara appeared with the test kit along with a zippered bag.

"It's the only key. I've got an idea." He felt silly for a moment. "Let's take off the tag and see if we forget which vehicle it goes to."

"Don't even think about it." Paloma didn't look up. Instead, she leaned into her work to peer at something.

"Busted." Clara laughed. "I got the fingerprint kit, too. We can compare them to the gun, if any are found on it."

"Are you familiar with the superglue trick?"

"Lots of times. Well, maybe a few times." Clara opened the door and held it, waiting for Ed. "Don't know that I'd do it first off, but if we need to. Absolutely."

"Okay. The interior of the truck is my best guess for finger-prints, but I expect we can pull some from the bikes, too. They might have worn gloves while riding them but likely not when loading and unloading them."

"How hard did it rain? Do you remember?"

It was a good question. Contrary to popular belief, light rain didn't affect fingerprints. The sweat and oils making up the print just sloughed the water off. Heavy rain was a different matter, as the friction of the water could scrub the oils off, much like a high-pressure car wash nozzle. It also meant that the gun, mostly buried in the sand and protected from the rain, had a good chance of retaining any fingerprints left by an unwary shooter.

Even the shell casings might contain enough material that the Currituck office could pull partial prints.

Ed considered the question seriously. "The worst of it was at the beach, I would think. That's why they were in Duck near the donut shop. A place a little less wet."

"So you think we'll get some prints from the outside of the truck?"

"And from the bikes. From the picture I got, they were on 'em when Wally and Nathan showed up."

"That's good. You hand me that, if you don't mind." She pointed to the kits. They were on the corner of the trailer where she had placed them while opening the truck door.

Inside the truck, they discovered that half their job was already done. Philippe Ballinger had been bleeding when the Dare County officers had gotten to the scene. He had clearly been inside while trying to stem the bleeding. Red fingerprints blanketed the console, the door posts, and the door cards. They had also left a full handprint on the dashboard just waiting on Ed and Clara to extract and send to Raleigh … or Barco … or to wherever it was needed.

And if they did run into trouble, there was always superglue. The chemical components in the glue, when heated, vaporized and were attracted to the oil in the fingerprints, meaning that even weak ones were easier to extract.

The gunshot residue was less obvious. They would need to spend hours swabbing, packaging, and labelling findings from different parts of the truck. Also, they were less likely to find any on the exterior of the truck or the bikes, as gunshot residue was less resistant to rain or any type of water. On a positive note, the corrosive salts in gunpowder residue could sometimes bind with the water and embed the gunpower on susceptible surfaces.

"Which do you want to do first?" Ed offered Clara both kits. It was the process that counted. One step at a time. If he didn't have a K9 companion to help solve this crime, then caution and procedure would have to stand in to get the job done.

It was something he enjoyed almost as much as working with dogs, but when Clara selected the fingerprint kit, he felt a niggle of regret.

A dog would be better. There was nothing a good dog couldn't help a competent officer get done.

—— Chapter 3 ——

Chest Deep

SERGEANT WALLY STYLES held the leash of A-District's new "mascot for a week" as he took in the fingerprint powder residue dusting the exterior of the impounded vehicles inside the sub-station's chain-link enclosure.

"Take your time, Roxie," he encouraged as the black-faced animal hunched on a small section of greenery. In his free hand, a black poo bag fluttered in the breeze. On the ocean side of the island, he was certain the wind was brutal, but here, among the trees, it offered a welcome respite to the sun. When the animal straightened and began to move away, he said, "Good girl. Those people in there will learn. You gotta go just like we do."

He bagged the refuse and tied it before dropping it in a covered trash bin, and found his protegee, Nathan, on the trailer with his hand on one of the bike grips. The man grinned at Wally and swung his leg over and positioned himself on the seat.

"You sure about that, Deputy? Might get your fingerprints mixed up with the lot."

"Clara said they're finished with it. Here's my plan. Since these are impounded, I suppose I need to test whether they might have been on the beach, you know, would they bog down in the sand, right?" The bikes were strapped down, so the one he was on remained fixed in place, but he leaned back as though doing a wheelie and wailed, "Rrrum, rrrum!"

"Man, we gotta wash some of the new off you. You need the captain's permission for that, and I expect she'll give you the same answer as me. No. Come down and take this dog inside. The potty break is over, and—"

"They found several rounds inside." Nathan stood, and he brushed at the back of his pants. The seat of the bike wasn't exactly clean.

"So I heard." Wally held the end of the leash the deputy's direction.

"I've got it worked out, Wally. If we had that gun Ed and Clara found, I could prove it. In my BLET training, I took a class on NIBIS protocols—"

"Protocols? Procedure, you mean."

"Procedure, then. Take the gun and compare the spent cartridges to the rifling pattern in the barrel. That would prove something."

"C'mon, wet pup. The dog's waiting."

"It would, though, wouldn't it? I've hunted all my life. I can tell my own cartridges just by looking." Nathan took the end of the leash and gave Roxie's neck a quick fluff.

"There might be a glitch in that reasoning." Wally was at the door, and he held it open for Nathan and the dog.

"No, just give me a second—"

"What caliber's the gun?" Maybe wash a lot of the new off

this boy.

"Um, a .44 maybe?"

"And the spent cartridges they found?"

Nathan blew out his cheeks. "Maybe I have some thinking to do still." As he entered the building, he had a hand with his thumb extended, and he was muttering, "One, the gun. What caliber? Two, is it the same—"

"You'll get there." Wally clasped the young deputy on the shoulder and released him. Inside, he paused at Paloma's desk. Nathan had unclipped the dog as they walked in, and Roxie was already on her bed. "She been good company, Paloma?"

Paloma cut her eyes to Diane's door and said, "Miz Turnip-seed's not done anything except be proper with me, Officer Styles."

"So, it's Officer Styles, is it?" Wally laughed. "I mean Roxie. She knows her commands, I'll give her that."

"I'll tell the captain you said so. She might not appreciate you comparing her to a dog." Paloma gave a teasing nod in the direction of Diane's office door. It was open but the light was off.

"That's harsh, Paloma. Maybe I should call Captain Le Grange and let him know I've recanted. I'm now on Team Le Grange, and I want to know if he has a spot for me."

Paloma snorted. "You, recant? Why, Wallace Styles, you and that man never got on a day in your life. He was as glad to be shut of you as you were of him. He's plenty happy with you right where you are."

"Then don't get me in hot water with the captain. If I'm moving onto Team Le Grange, I'm taking you with me."

"I don't mean to step on your toes, but I'm plenty happy here. You just get on and let me enjoy the dog. I might even get some work done."

A toilet in the building flushed, and Deputy Preston appeared, holding a brown paper towel and drying his hands. "It's free in there if anybody needs it."

The front door swung open, and Diane Turnipseed stepped through, slightly windblown, and with her phone to her ear. She said into the phone, "So that's a big no. Half of that beach is in Dare County. My officers called your officers, remember that. And I've got their truck in my impound lot. Kringlebach isn't here any longer, so work with me, William. Are we good with that?"

Diane looked up, saw the people in the room with her and sighed. She clicked off the phone and held it aside.

"How's Roxie doing, Paloma?" Diane seemed ill at ease at being overheard.

"Better'n you, if you're riling that sheriff from up north. I'm supposing that was *Sheriff* William Barnett you were talking to."

"I'm a big girl, so shush that. You, Wally, and you, Nathan, you got nothing to do except stand there and overhear everything I got to say?"

"Just waiting on orders, ma'am." Wally wasn't bothered. The captain was a pussycat next to the hardline Le Grange.

"Then let's see what the tide's turned up." Diane pulled a notepad from her shirt pocket, worked out a pint-sized pen, and wrote something before tearing off the page and holding it out to Wally. "I got an officer down in C-District with a new K9 she's been wanting to get on the sand. Name's Cynthia Ellison. You call that number and see if we can borrow her for the day."

"Yes, ma'am." Wally took the note, noted the phone number with no name, and realized the dog was focused on him. "Will Roxie present a problem? Some K9s don't work well with other dogs."

Roxie's ears perked up when Wally said K9, like she knew what he was saying.

"Roxie's doing us right. We'd be above our knees to call her a real K9, but to tell the story honest, she knows her commands."

Wally noted how the dog's ears responded to K9 again, this time shifting her attention to the captain. It was surely a glitch in the dog's behavior.

Nathan offered, "You want me to make the call?" He grasped the paper with two fingers but didn't pull it away.

"Nah, I'll do it." Louder, to the captain, he said, "Tide rolls out just like it rolls in. If this Sergeant Ellison is available, I'll get her up here."

"We're good then. Well, I'm off for a cuppa blackie." The captain moved towards the coffee pot, having dismissed the matter of the visiting K9 from her attention.

As they walked towards a phone, Nathan asked, "She didn't say sergeant. How'd you know?"

"Any K9 handler will be." He tapped the younger man's chest with his cap. "You try for the position someday, and you'll have sergeant on your nametag, too."

The young deputy grinned.

THE CALL TO CYNTHIA Ellison of C-District went smoothly enough. The K9 handler from down south answered on the third ring.

"Hold on a bit."

"Certainly," Wally began, as she called to someone in the background.

"Here, Lucy, now. This is the phone, and sometimes I need to answer it. I'm giving you some slack, but not for much longer, not with you doing that."

Wally knew of Cynthia, as they had both been with Dare County for years, but the A and C districts were literally miles and hours apart. He knew *of* her but had never spoken *with* her. He did know she was of a "grandmother" age, and he hoped she wasn't babysitting a granddaughter. The captain would not be happy about that.

The phone picked back up, and Wally heard, "Least that I can tell, we can talk now. Who is this?"

"I'm with the Dare County A-District—"

"You sure you're needing to tell me that?" A pause, and then, "My phone already loaded me up with your location. My old boss used to say not to fill her up with things she already knows. I could say the same. Now, who is this?"

"Sergeant Wally Styles." He waited, certain he didn't want to "fill her up with any more of what she already knew."

"Styles. Kin to Wallace?"

"Yes." Wally chuckled. "One and the same. So we both know of each other. Your old boss wants us to meet."

"I didn't hear her say that." Her final word faded out, likely her moving away from the phone, and Wally heard, "Not now, Lucy. Settle, girl."

"Grandbaby?" Wally hoped to hit on something the woman wanted him to say, rather than irritate her with every word.

"That's a good one. Might as well be. How can I help you, Wally?"

"The captain tells me you have a new K9 that needs some time on the sand, her words not mine." He paused, waiting for a response, and didn't get one. "Our K9 officer is waiting on a dog—"

"Five months out to get one. You got started yet?"

"No, ma'am. Ed just came on and hasn't had a chance to search yet. Anyways, we've had an incident at the northern edge of the county. I say it that way because the incident bleeds over into Currituck, so it's their incident, too. We're hoping you and your dog can be of assistance."

"How are you thinking I can help?"

"Good question." He was beginning to like this woman. She was on track and already focused on what mattered. "Let me lay it on you thick as molasses on toast. We pulled in two long-term rabble rousers from up in Currituck County, and one was all bloodied up. Normally that's just another rock to turn over, but up on the beach, we found blood, shell casings, and a gun. It might be that those connect to the truck and dirt bikes we impounded from them."

"You've processed those things, I suppose."

"There's part of our glitch. All that up there happened a little in Dare and a whole lot more in Currituck. Currituck has the evidence bags. We have the vehicles."

"And your rabble rousers?" The term carried amusement.

"We didn't know about the beach yet, so they were released."

"Big pitchers pour out milk everywhere. They'll be talking to everyone they know." She paused. "Currituck. I understand there's a feud up that direction. I suppose I do need to get on up there, maybe help you people out of your bind. I'll need to clear my calendar with Captain Burkhalter, so it'll be early afternoon. That's good with you?" Captain Lonnie Burkhalter was the new head in C-District.

"Yes, ma'am. I'll let the captain know." Wally grinned as he replaced the receiver, and he was surprised when his young protege knocked a fist against his arm. He'd forgotten he was there.

"I know her." Nathan grinned.

"Explain." Wally took his cap from beside the phone and

leaned back in the chair.

"A while back, a dead man was found on, um, Bodie Island, I think. Anyway, close to the lighthouse down there. I was a witness."

"You saw the dead man?" Wally sat up, interested.

"No, just a car that might have transported the body. I don't think it did, but my wife was questioned by the officers. It's what got me interested in a job out here."

Wally started to ask for more information, but the phone rang, and he lifted the receiver.

"Paloma here. You done with that call? I've got another caller on the line from the sheriff's office in Barco. I can have him hold."

"Put him through. Thank you, Paloma." He whispered to Nathan with a shrug, "The sheriff's office in Currituck County."

"My bad." He gave Wally two thumbs up.

The line clicked, and Wally said, "Hello?"

"Hey, this Deputy Johnson. I'm looking for Ed Walters or Clara Del Ray. Brannigan Calmont said to ask for them first, as they would be familiar with things. Are you Ed?"

"Not the last time I looked in the mirror." Wally chuckled. "Wally Styles speaking. What can I do for you, Deputy?"

"Brannigan said that Ed and Clara were with him, along with Sergeant Barker and Deputy Krazinski, this morning. I, um, well, I don't have the whole story, but Brannigan wants to meet someone at Corolla Beach, if that's possible. He says there's a dock in Sanders Bay. If you take a left at the Seaside Farm Market—"

"I know it." Wally cut him off. He teased, "Is there anything you do know, Deputy Johnson? This sounds sketchy."

"I like to go by Jared." He laughed and seemed to relax. "I do school resource, high school mostly, except for during Drug

Awareness Week with the lower grades. The boat that's available was only free for a few hours, so Brannigan had to head out. In a pinch, he might come to the Sanderling. There's a dock there on the Sound side, but he'd appreciate if you could drive up to Corolla Beach. I can call him on the radio if you can't make Corolla."

"Timing, timing." Wally blew out his cheeks. He looked at Nathan, covered the phone's mouthpiece, and asked, "You wanna go for a ride?"

"It's why I took this job." Nathan stood as he answered, prepared to move towards the door.

"We can do Corolla Beach," Wally said into the phone, and he hung up. He didn't ask for any additional information, as the deputy was clearly wet behind the ears and wouldn't be able to offer any up, even if Brannigan had shared it with him.

In the car, the same white cruiser he'd used for years, with the faded word POLICE down the side, Wally inserted his phone into an accessory holder on the dash and set it to guide them to the Seaside Farm Market.

"You said you knew—" Nathan began, frowning at the device.

"I do." Wally worked his cap onto his head before putting the car into gear. He often sunburned through his thinning hair, and he didn't always think about putting it on in the heat of the moment, so to speak. It was easier to keep it on—outside of when he was indoors. "Let me show you this. You see the arrival time? It also reroutes me if traffic ahead is slow. You young'uns will learn. Make technology work for you, not against you."

They met one oncoming car on Colington, a white truck with a work bed and Dominion Energy down the side, but otherwise, their drive to Hwy 12 was a clean shot. The highway north, unsurprisingly, was busier, still buzzing with late-season traffic. The truth was that the island chain was more than a vacation destination, although it seemed that way in July and August, with license plates from Virgina, Tennessee, and South Carolina filling the parking spaces of the restaurants along the roadway. Mild winter weather and cool summer breezes drew the crowds, and many of them never went home. Despite popular opinion, people lived here full time, and the roads were rarely vacant.

The minutes ticked off, with the Wright Brothers complex on the left quickly disappearing. Almost immediately, a large building housing a Lowe's appeared and vanished, giving way to a miniature golf course next to an emergency clinic. After passing a Target and movie theater on the right, the businesses and gaming opportunities either thinned out or simply became so routine as to no longer catch the men's attention.

Wally's phone indicated a right turn at the Kitty Hawk Visitor's Center, but neither the driver nor the passenger paid any attention. This was familiar territory even to Nathan, a Texan by birth, and only recently a North Carolinian by choice. It was Dare County, part of the A-District patrol area, and he and Wally had patrolled it numerous times since completing BLET training and donning a Dare County uniform.

The farther afield 12 took them, the less the commercial infrastructure invaded to distract them from the beauty of the island. Landscaped and often hidden residences—many only revealed by shrubbery-shrouded gates—were beautiful and suggested money in copious amounts.

Wally, however, was more interested in the views where the highway fronted the water.

"Let me show you this." They had reached Four Seasons Realty and Shane's Family Market just across from Cook Road, and a series of waterfront shops blanketed the Sound's shore.

Just past, the highway hugged the Sound so tightly that not even an ice cream stand had room to drop anchor. The water views towards the mainland reached into the car with open arms.

"You pointed that out last time." Nathan glanced but didn't really look.

"And it's still nice. Most of the shore is mixed up with shopping or homes, but this is one clear strip where everything opens up. You can't be blasé about that."

"Blasé?" Nathan laughed. "What's that?"

"You, right now. Anyway, it's gone now." The Sunset Grille had eaten the view, and the road turned back inland, passing a few houses before becoming trees and scrub.

"The Corps of Engineers!" Nathan perked up as the Corps complex appeared on the ocean side. It was the reason for the trees and scrub. They owned ocean to Sound, only granting access for 12 to carry passengers from south to north, and then possibly, if they behaved, back again.

Nestled in and surrounded by Corps land, the Duck Fire Department stood isolated in the scrub, and then the northern Duck suburbs crowded the roadway, channeling the men's focus back onto the road.

And they were only halfway there.

There was a reason the Dare County patrol districts were divided into three sections, with sub-stations at the northern and southern ends. It was a long drive anywhere on the Banks, and with the towns and villages along the way, you couldn't drive fast much of anywhere.

Corolla Beach eventually appeared out of the misty, salt-filled air whipped shoreward by the brisk ocean breezes. In town, Wally hit his blinker a good block before reaching the Farm Market. Orion's Way to the right led over a small bridge, and left took them into a shopping center.

"GPS says the next turn is the one we need." Nathan's attempt at being helpful.

"You sure about that?" Wally grinned. He jogged the vehicle left to circle the Outer Banks Boil Company and a Try My Nuts store before eventually reaching Corolla Watersports where he found a parking space and pulled in. "Both ways bring us in. Let's head out and see what our upstate brethren have for us."

"You don't need to tell me twice." Nathan grinned. He already had a hand on the door lever. He released it to the smell of ocean and grease, not surprising since the water was just in front of them and yet another restaurant, Mama Easley's, perched on the water next to Corolla Watersports.

Wally instructed Nathan to let the staff at the Watersports venue know they were here and were meeting Sergeant Brannigan Calmont from the Currituck Sheriff's Office on their dock. Nathan exited the building minutes later holding out a hand and a thumbs-up, and he jogged to catch up with Wally.

A lengthy boardwalk took them along the water's edge and transitioned to a strip of swampy scrubland that overshadowed the boardwalk. When the sky broke free, in front of them, needle-straight into the Sound, a lengthy dock lined with slips containing water sports equipment and dominated by a larger, open area at the end greeted them. To the southwest, Swan Island was a blip of greenery hugging the expansive Mossey Islands beyond. Northwest was open Sound for miles, with Monkey Island somewhere in the mist, even if Wally couldn't find it. Insects buzzed, and he brushed several from his neck.

"There!" Nathan pointed, and they could see a craft heading in their direction at high speed. "I bet that's him."

"Likely," Wally agreed.

In moments, they could define the bow of the inflatable, and as it angled to approach the dock, a broad strip of letters down the side said SHERIFF. Wally raised an arm and waved.

"Styles!" Calmont slipped the boat next to the dock, and threw out a line with an easy motion, as if this was by habit, and he knew the Dare County officer would automatically catch it.

"You tearing up our Dare County beaches in that Zodiac?" Wally wrapped the line around a cleat, and he moved to the stern of the boat to take a second line and tie it off, too. It was clear the two men knew each other well.

"Who, me?" Calmont gave his familiar half smile, and he adjusted his wire framed sunglasses. "I'm just trying to keep you people's business on your side of the county line. I didn't manage so well this morning, so I borrowed this boat for a second try."

"Tide rolls out like it rolls in. We got two of yours that we wish had stayed yours."

"And let them go. We got ears up north, too. Don't make us out to be the hicks we are."

"Don't have to try very hard. What'cha got for us?"

"This bag. Just need you to sign for it." Calmont lifted a black bag in thick nylon with POLICE stitched onto the side. He pulled himself out of the boat and onto the dock. "Your new chief's got a magnetic personality."

"Yeah." Wally smiled. "And that's an improvement. Ask anyone on my team. Oh, right, the rest left with Le Grange. I'm the only one who stuck around."

"Your chief thinks we're sharing the evidence we assembled this morning, and after she talked to my chief, my chief thinks so, too. I hear you got a K9 handler on the way up from the southern part of your county."

"We're hearing the same." Wally eyed the bag. "You're a delivery boy now?" He chuckled, certain the question would bring a laugh.

"I don't mind. I knew we wouldn't make any headway with this stuff, not quick headway, anyway. It all has to go to Raleigh, and you know how much importance they put on what we do. You guys rank higher in their estimation. So I told Barnett, if you insist, but I knew it wasn't a real choice." He chuckled. "Less work for us, I say."

Sheriff William Barnett headed the Currituck County Sheriff's Office, and both Calmont and Wally knew who he meant.

Nathan was off to the side, grinning and soaking in the repartee. Wally caught his enthusiasm and asked Calmont, "You in a big hurry to get that boat back?"

"Well," and Calmont glanced at his watch and considered the question. "What'cha got in mind?" He had fallen into Wally's casual cadence of offcut words.

Wally shared about his young protegee, his experience with Dare County on a previous case, and how it had sparked his interest in joining the Dare County law enforcement team. He also shared his BLET training schedule and that Wally was serving as Nathan's Field Training Officer under the FTO Program.

"So, the pup's still wet behind the ears." Calmont's words again reflected Wally's off-beat terminology, another indication of their relationship over the years. "And I'm guessing you two haven't had a visit to the crime scene, if it becomes that."

"I'd like to give the boy some exposure. You take your time deciding, Brannigan, but this will give the boy a whole slew of good training." When Calmont didn't answer immediately, Wally teased him. "Or are you afraid of my driving?'

"No more than you're afraid to get on that boat with me. Sure. I'm game. We've got time, just not too much time."

Calmont lifted the case, and he followed the two Dare County officers away from the inflatable Zodiac, along the boardwalk, and to their car. He did complain about the comfort level of the back seat, and as he climbed in, he remarked, "You're killing me, Calmont. You just wait 'til you need to get on the water with me. You'll think twice about asking me along next time."

It wasn't a seat at all, just a plastic bench with no padding.

Nathan was a lightbulb, and as he dropped into the front seat, he said, "This is better'n I thought it would be. Yahoo!"

Wally grinned. That must be the Texan coming out in him. Either way, the boy's enthusiasm was infectious. Now if Calmont would catch it, they could all have a good time.

HEADING BACK the way they'd come, the fifteen-minute drive was a good opportunity to expose the young deputy to Calmont's line of work.

"Brannigan, tell the deputy here something important about your job in your county." Wally turned his head just enough to see a frown flash across the back-seat passenger's face.

"Something? Okay, if you insist, but I'll have to talk fast. I've got a job that's the real deal, unlike you slackers down in Dare. When's the last time I saw a county ATV on the sand down in Dare? Oh, right, that was in Currituck. This morning by the way. And who was the good-looking officer driving it? Oh, right, Beach Detail Officer Brannigan Calmont. Say that with a sergeant when you address me, boys. Now for number two—"

"Enough!" Wally flipped his cap from his head, slammed it into the partition dividing the front seat from the back, and he laughed. He repositioned the cap on his head and said to Nathan, "You see what we get when we ask for inter-county cooperation? This schmuck back here. If his head wasn't filled up with good quality policing information, I'd stop and let him find his own way to his boat."

"You mean my rubber duck? The one that brought you the evidence bags from this morning? I'm hurt, Styles. Seriously hurt, like a knife in my chest." Calmont was adjusting his sunglasses and looking out the side window. He didn't look especially hurt or sound that way, either.

"You have ATVs?" Nathan twisted for as clear a view of the Currituck County officer as possible, his enthusiasm bleeding out. "We don't, um, in Dare County, do we, Wally?"

"No. Disappointed?" Wally grinned. "I'm sure the sergeant back there would love to have you on the Currituck team. Wouldn't you, Brannigan?"

"He'd learn more than with you, that's the real deal." When Wally gave a surprised snort, Calmont retorted, "Sorry, Wally, I call the cards as they fall."

They approached the pair of signs indicating the division between the two counties, and Wally slowed his cruiser. He hadn't paid attention to them on the way up, as this far north on the Banks was the limit of his patrol area, making them part of his knowledge base that fell into the background until he was required to access it.

He asked Calmont, "Dare County has no public beach access for miles. How did you people get across?" With the jog in the road, he didn't see any drives or access roads either direction, and he tried to recall the last access point they'd passed. It was a long time back. And his car wasn't driving on that beach, not unless he wanted a tow. He began mentally mapping out which private homes might offer the best options to get to the shore.

"Your people this morning were parked in Palmer's Island."

They were headed south, so it was just ahead on the left. "Me? I was on my ATV. My fellow officers arrived via boat."

"Ah, man!" Nathan's face fell. "Y'all have boats for the ocean, too? Next you'll be telling me you have jet skis."

"That's how they got home, so, sorry but yes. We don't have the Coast Guard to pick up the slack like you people down south." He shifted position as if trying to get comfortable—an impossible task on the plastic bench—said "here" at the left turn, and directed them left again to the last house in line.

Once on the beach, the wind had already swept a copious amount of sand over the lower half of the landscape fabric. The police tape had blown loose from one stake, leaving a lengthy section flapping wildly in the air. Calmont pointed to an approximate location of the county line, but he assured his companions that it could just as easily be a couple of yards north or south. The taped off area, while clearly reaching into both counties, mostly resided within Currituck County.

"There's something," Nathan pointed out. He leaned over the tape but didn't step inside.

"Yessir, I see it. Sharp eyes, Deputy." Calmont took off his sunglasses, stepped closer, then laughed as he returned his shades to his face. "Sharper than my team's eyes. We forgot one of our numbered tags. That's not crime scene material, unless you consider beach littering a crime. You can step over and get it. All this has been cleared."

They had about picked the area to death, including the compacted area where the out-of-character dips, divots, and troughs from that morning clashed with the rest of the undulating dune surface, when Nathan returned to the puzzling section of sand and asked, "How did you, I mean, what did you do here? In training they taught us—"

"I see what you mean. Photos." Calmont elaborated. "From

several angles. I watched my team snap them. Why?"

"I know these tracks. They're from a KTM 459XC-F." He said all the numbers and letters as if they mattered.

"You can tell from that?" Wally had joined them. He shared with Calmont, "That matches the bikes we impounded, KTM. I'm not familiar enough to remember the full designation, but the manufacturer is the same."

"So, Deputy." Calmont crossed his arms. "How can you be so specific?"

"It's the tire tread … well not just that." He frowned as if considering what had convinced him. "Other bikes could have this tread, but the KTM has a larger fuel tank, and that changes the tread pattern."

"And you know this how?" Calmont studied the imprint in the sand, and he realized the light from that morning had shifted, revealing the faintest of tread prints in the sand.

"I rode dirt bikes on my grandfather's farm back in high school. One was a KTM, so I'm familiar with them."

While there was every chance the forensics team could enhance the tread pattern from the images they'd acquired earlier, they were especially clear now. Wally was glad when Calmont pulled his phone out, leaned low towards the sand, and snapped pics from several angles. At one point, the sky brightened, the sun cast deeper shadows across the sand, emphasizing the tire tracks, and the Currituck County employee captured it on his phone.

As he stood, a robust, red-haired woman walking a dog headed toward them from the Dare side. As she approached, the dog shifted position to sniff something, and its thick leather harness revealed the stitched warning, DARE COUNTY K9, in all capital letters.

"Cynthia Ellison?" Wally was expecting the C-District K9

handler today, but he hadn't expected her here, not on the beach. There was no one else this could be, however.

"Would the sand dunes grow any taller if I weren't?" Cynthia pulled on the dog's leash, hissed, "Heel, Lucy," and paused until the animal obeyed.

"Just figured that must be you. I don't know if you know me, but I've heard of you. Wally Styles." He walked her way and offered his hand.

"And you survived Captain Le Grange." She chuckled. "Didn't get along too well I gather." She took his hand and released it.

"Not sure what you mean." His former captain had left the county choking on backwash, but Wally hadn't said a cross word. And nothing he'd done came to mind.

"Just figured you two would still be riding sidesaddle if you had. He left a lot of positions open up here, as I'm sure you can attest. A good man would have taken better care of the people he was hired to care for, and I mean the people of Dare County, not just you people working under him."

An alarm went off, and Calmont called to Wally, "Hey, Styles, my time's up. I need to get my boat back for the next guy. You ready to head on up?"

Cynthia said, "Not one of yours?"

"Wrong county. We're sharing this incident scene."

"Currituck, then."

"You're familiar." Wally had his keys out. Calmont was already waiting.

"Not really. It's a long drive from my place, and anywhere up here only ends in sand and Virginia. We've got enough sand down on Pea Island, and I've got no use for the devil's domain. You're needed." Cynthia indicated the Currituck County officer.

"Yes. He's on the clock with the police boat he came over on. I would like to stay and talk …"

"We're where we are. Go." She waved him away.

Wally called, "Nathan? You ready?"

Before the new deputy could answer, Cynthia said, "Nathan Preston? I'd heard you'd come home to roost."

"You know him?" Wally said to Calmont, "I'm on my way, Brannigan." To Cynthia, "Nathan knows everything from this morning, well, about this place. He can stay and show you around, and I'll be back in, oh, thirty minutes. Would that be helpful to you?"

"It won't hurt to have a knowledgeable second set of eyes. I can introduce him to Lucy."

Nathan agreed with enthusiasm, "Sergeant Ellison! Were you there when my wife was stranded on the ferry—"

Wally and Calmont were walking away by then and had tuned out the conversation, as it wasn't theirs and was remaining behind.

"Your new deputy's not too bad," Calmont offered, as he readjusted his cowboy hat. "He's a little green, but he was paying attention during BLET. How's he been for you?"

"Green like you say but enthusiastic as a squirrel in mating season. Today is good field training, and you coming out here has impressed him. All that knowhow in your head, I'm sure."

"Not as much as it might seem, but enough to impress a newbie. That tire track. I didn't expect him to come out with that. Might be good for the investigation, if that blood turns out to be human."

If. The Currituck County officer hadn't seen the face of the injured brother. Of course, Wally hadn't looked over the rest of the evidence to see what the blood was on. The men spent much of the drive back in silence, which suited Wally. His brain was churning over who was going to process the evidence. Calmont had been correct that the Banks often got bumped down in priority when Raleigh faced a backlog. However, Dare County didn't depend on Raleigh for everything. Currituck might not have a resident forensic investigator, but Manteo did. Emily Bryant served in that capacity for all three patrol districts and sometimes for Currituck, as the northern county didn't have one.

After dropping Calmont at his "rubber duck," Wally pulled out his phone. His radio was great for things that needed to be public, but for a question of permission to contact Manteo, that felt more like a phone call affair.

"Turnipseed. Yes?"

"My apologies, Captain—"

"Shush that, Wally." Diane let out a hard sigh as if she was quelling frustration, perhaps not as successfully as she wished. "To tell the story honest, you're on my phone ID, and if you call, it's not for a chat. So?"

"Yes, ma'am. I just met with Sergeant Calmont from Currituck. He was with Ed and Clara at the beach this morning, and I have the evidence they collected. I know you had a hand in that. Thank you."

"Dump the rest on me. I know this isn't the conversation."

"No, ma'am. Part of Calmont's reasoning for turning the evidence over to us is the timeframe for processing it. Dare County has someone who does just that. Can we bypass Raleigh and call her in?"

"For all sakes, why do you think I haggled with the sheriff up there, for my good health? Yes, I want Emily processing everything she can. Is that something you can handle?'

"Yes, ma'am. Just making sure I'm inside my lines." Wally sucked in a deep breath, expecting a Le Grange level tirade.

"Hold your taters, Sergeant. You're forgetting who you're talking to. If I didn't trust you to make good decisions, you would already be back in Manteo on a desk job. Now you be the man this job requires of you and make the decisions you know will move this investigation forward. Am I clear on that?"

"Crystal. Thank you, Captain."

The phone clicked off, and Wally wondered what he'd interrupted. It was no matter. What did matter was reaching Emily Bryant and hopefully finding her free.

His call went directly to her voicemail, and he left a skeletal description of what they had and a request for her to put them on her calendar, yesterday if possible, with the addendum that the request came directly from his new captain, Diane Turnip-seed. He finished up as he pulled off 12 and was puzzled to find another county car beside the rusty Jeep Cherokee Cynthia Ellison had arrived in.

Either Ed or Clara, as the captain had that black Explorer, rather than a squad car. Or both, as they had been assigned as a team that morning.

Then the lightbulb came on. Of course. If the K9 handler from the southern part of the county was here, Captain Turnip-seed would want someone present who knew where to search and what to look for. She would have no idea that Brannigan Calmont from up north had ridden down with Nathan and Wally to give the young trainee additional hours towards his mandatory field training.

Wally made his way down the drive, past the empty pool, and ducked behind the garage to reach the beach. Spray still danced from the tops of the waves, but the sun was brighter, and the light sparkling from the whitecaps had begun to fracture into miniature diamonds. He stood still for a moment, calculating the buffeting of his uniform around his shoulders and calves … his paunch kept the middle part taut … and judged that the wind was less. He determined that the weather would continue to clear and perhaps even turn into a beautiful day.

To the north, just about where Brannigan had decided the county line divided the beach, the redheaded Cynthia Ellison had her back to the water, with the wind forcing her curls around her face, and she used her left hand to pull them away. As soon as she released them, they were back where they wanted to be.

The petite Clara Del Ray faced Cynthia, not directly, but turned to where she could see the beach and the dunes. Her tightly tuned hair, pulled hard to the base of her neck, was impervious to each gust of wind. Her collar fluttered violently in the breeze, but that didn't transfer to her face or hair. Without interrupting her conversation with the C-District employee, she lifted a hand to indicate she had seen Wally appear on the beach.

The K9 at the end of Cynthia's leash enjoyed the attention of the two male officers, Ed Walters and Nathan Preston. Wally hadn't noticed before, but the dog appeared to be a Dutch Shepherd, a fairly small breed for a K9, but one he'd heard was proficient at the job. Nathan was on one knee giving the animal a fierce rub around the ears, and he said something, grinned, and looked toward Ed as if expecting a response. Ed, though, studied the animal with a wistful expression, the same one a former attendee at Wally's church used to have when the children's choir sang on Sunday nights. Her only child had died in a tragic accident, and he'd suspected she saw in other people's children the child she could no longer hug.

Wally didn't expect that Ed wanted to hug the dog, but he understood the feeling. The man didn't have one, and having a dog was his job. For the first time since Ed had come on board, Wally thought he understood something about the man. Ed was like a shrimp boat captain without a boat, watching the other captains head out to earn their living, then having to return to the warehouse to clean and package their hauls.

Despite his empathy, there was nothing he could do to help the big man, other than be supportive, which he would do in any case. He began to wade his way through the softening sand. The wind and the brightening sun would dry it rapidly, turn it into crystalline powder, and it would grow increasingly slippery to navigate. It was already more difficult than just an hour before.

Several shore birds scattered at his approach, with the majority of them running on tiny legs toward the leading edge of the waves rolling in from the ocean. As the water petered out and receded, the birds followed the shape of the waves up and down the sand as they scattered.

Wally's radio at his belt bleeped. When it crackled as if trying to come to life, he glanced in the direction of his car, before he paused and frowned. Why he had looked at his car, he didn't know. He reached to his collar and pressed talk.

"Wally Styles here. Who is this?"

"Oh, honey, there you are. Take this like I say it, but someone else should be on this radio. I'd be glad to be shut of it except Miz Turnipseed says it's part of my job."

"Certainly. Paloma, how can I help you?" Wally had worked with Paloma for years. No way would he say anything to criticize her or anything she did. The woman was the "e" in efficiency, even if she did sometimes come across as a bludgeon at the end of a pole.

"You want to come down here and see about your, um, *forensic investigator?* She says you called her, and there's no one home to give her directions."

"Emily's there already?" Wally racked his brain. He still had the evidence bags in his car. The K9 handler from C-District was with him, and he had Clara, Ed, and Nathan to consider.

"If that's Forensic Investigator Bryant, I suppose she is." Paloma's tone said she knew it was.

"I'm a good hour away, and I have the evidence bags. Ask her when and where she would like to meet."

"Me?" Paloma laughed. "I may look white, but I'm about to step on your toes, Wally Styles. You can ask her yourself."

"This is Emily, and I *am* white. Just where are you, Sergeant Styles?"

"Ah, Emily. I'm at the northern edge of the county. Two feet more in the sand, and I'm standing in Currituck County. The entire team is with me, except for Captain Turnipseed and our mutual friend Paloma, if you want to claim her."

"I do. Before we go any further, your Currituck friends did an initial survey of this morning's evidence, and they've already forwarded their survey to the office here. I have it in my hand. It's what I'd expect from a cursory overview. I really need to see the site. It's been a while since I've been to the Currituck Lighthouse. Can we meet there?"

"It's half an hour out of the way." And in the center of Currituck County. He'd have expected her to request a location inside Dare County.

"I know. But I like lighthouses, and it's an hour for me to come up for no reason. You've given me a reason. That's only an extra half hour each way. That'll give you and your team time to finish whatever you're up to by the time I get there. The lighthouse, then?"

Wally agreed and sank one foot after another into the increasingly soft surface of the dune as he moved forward to give the team the news.

"I WOULD like to climb it."

Wally and Nathan had left Ed and Clara with the C-District

K9 officer back at the beach. Their personal experience at the site made their input a perfect fit for the situation, and besides, Ed had been besotted with watching Cynthia Ellison work with her K9. No way was Wally tearing apart what could be a beautiful thing. "Thick as molasses on toast," he'd commented to Nathan as they'd made their way to their car.

"Them?" Nathan had looked back at the officers roaming the taped off crime scene, potential or otherwise.

"You sure you're on the same page as me?" Wally chuckled. "Ed and that dog."

The dog was searching, although it was hard to tell if the animal knew what it was looking for. Human remains, perhaps? Another weapon, one recently fired? Or still more drugs? Clara had mentioned the canvas bag that was ripped open and dribbling packets of powder onto the sand.

"Oh." Nathan's face reddened.

"That's harsh to put Ed onto another man's wife. Sergeant Ellison is married, if I tell it right. I don't expect she's looking for another man." Wally nudged Nathan's arm before separating to find his side of the car.

The drive up to the lighthouse was mostly a winding wall of greenery, with occasional buildings or water views. In Corolla, the street leading to the lighthouse was lined with rough parking spaces, many on the grass, with a wood rail fence forming an entrance to the lighthouse grounds. Inside, the tall brick structure was to the right, with a guest services building—the old lighthouse Keeper's House—and another small building around a grass courtyard. They matched in style and era and were connected by a walkway that circled the courtyard. The property was a cozy space enclosed by greenery and seemed oddly non-beachy.

"Emily!" Nathan waved. She held a lidded cup of coffee

while taking in the lighthouse thrusting up through canopy. She looked around at the sound of her name and recognized the new deputy.

"Where's the little woman?" Emily smiled. "Wait, Paytyne wasn't so little the last time I saw her, was she? On the ferry, she was about this big." She held her hands in front of her to indicate Paytyne's extreme pregnancy.

"We've got a little girl now. They're with my in-laws back in Texas until I get set up out here."

Wally teased, "Now who's thick as molasses on toast?"

"Molasses? Who said anything about molasses?" Emily tutted. She waved toward the lighthouse. "I would like to climb it. There's not much sense in coming all this direction and not. I spoke to the docent inside, and she said that if we're in our county uniforms, badges and all, we could likely get in for free. I don't have a county uniform, so I might have to pay, unless one of you wants to vouch for me and accompany me." She smiled sweetly. She held a handwritten pass for the docents admitting visitors into the lighthouse.

"I'll do it." Nathan had his eyes on the gallery encircling the lantern room, which from his angle could barely be seen.

"Sure," Wally said. He checked his watch. "It's an hour drive back to the sub-station, and Emily, you'll likely want to visit the crime scene." They were already calling it that, so he might as well. "I'll visit the restroom and check out the gift shop."

"You're not coming?" Nathan seemed incredulous.

"Been up there before. It's just another stair to climb. You young pups enjoy yourselves. Just mind the time."

Wally eyed the forensic investigator as she and Nathan approached the lighthouse entrance. Before going inside, she patted her purse as if looking for something. When Nathan paused to wait for her, she asked him to hold her coffee. Then, as if tripping, she seemed to stumble against the young deputy, and while trying to catch her fall, she smashed the coffee cup into his chest. The lid flew off, black showered everywhere, and Nathan jumped back while doing his best to not let Emily collapse to the ground.

Emily was laughing as she easily stood up. Nathan's panicked expression turned to laughter as he realized the cup had held black shredded tissue paper. He knelt, gathered what he could, and placed it back into the cup. The lid had rolled farther afield, but it was soon mated back to the cup, and they disappeared inside the lighthouse entrance.

Wally expected them to be at the top in ten minutes or so, depending on how much time Nathan wanted to spend checking out the views from the windows on the different levels. Emily had seen it before, so she would likely push him directly to the top. That's where the real views were, both towards the ocean, and especially over the Sound. The Whalehead Club with its boathouse, pond, and manicured grounds was the star of the show, with more distant views of the mainland on especially clear days. Wally didn't expect today counted as especially clear, although it was much better than it had been that morning.

He was about to enter the gift shop when the radio at his waist beeped at him. He frowned, looked down, and tried to imagine anyone from Dare County reaching him this far north. He turned up the volume knob when the speaker crackled.

"Wally, are you there?" The whisper sounded like the young deputy in training.

Wally activated the mic at his collar, keeping his voice down, and asked, "Yes, Nathan. Why are we whispering?"

"Emily and I are in the lighthouse—"

"I know. I watched you two head up." Wet pup, indeed!

"No, you don't get it. You dropped Sergeant Calmont off at the dock. Well, I don't know how it works, but I think he needs rescued."

"You sure about that? He seemed proficient at managing his boat when I last saw him."

"Well, Emily and I are watching him right now, or at least I think it's him. The man we're watching has on a cowboy hat and SHERIFF on the side of his boat."

"That's sounds like Brannigan. How do you know he needs rescuing?"

"He's in the middle of the Sound, and he looks like his boat won't start."

"You sure about that? Is he pulling at a rope starter or something?"

"Nah, he has the entire engine—"

Nathan's voice cut off, and Wally heard Emily in the background, "Let me have that."

"Emily, I've been trying to wash some of the new off the boy. I may not have gotten it all. Can you explain?"

"Wally, we'll be right down. I think the Zodiac's going under. I know the Sound's not all that deep, but this is about to test the good sergeant's swimming skills. We'll see you as soon as we can make it down."

Wally felt his senses thicken up for a moment. Brannigan was a good friend, and while he knew the Currituck Sound averaged only five feet, in places it could be twice that. Yes, a man might walk it if he knew exactly where to step, but the chances of doing it successfully?

This wasn't just another rock to turn over. This could be a friend's life at stake!

WALLY HAD OPTIONS for boats running through his brain.

There was nothing at the Whalehead. It was now a public park, and while it had a boathouse and boat slips, there were no boats in those slips that would carry them on a rescue mission into Currituck Sound. Corolla Watersports in Corolla Beach where he'd dropped off the Currituck County officer had plenty of boats. But to drive down and organize the use of one … then the time on the water to get to where Brannigan was might be just enough time for the tall, redheaded man to sink under the water for the final time.

Nathan and Emily appeared at the door of the lighthouse, and Emily located Wally and waved. Nathan expressed his concerns with more enthusiasm.

"We need one of them ferries—"

"Ferries?" Emily grasped his arm, pulling the young deputy up short. "Nathan, you may be new out here, but this isn't a general ferry land." She pronounced it like fairyland. "Those boats have work to do, and they take their time doing it. No ferry is taking the time to rescue that man, no matter how far underwater he goes."

"Right," Wally said. "Emily, um, I have an idea. How far out was Brannigan?"

"Nathan?" She released the younger man's arm and gave him a hard look. "Remember that island? You said something upstairs about him being a good rifle shot the other side of it." To Wally, she said, "He was out past Monkey Island. I can't calculate the distances over water that well."

"Monkey Island is a mile and a half out. Nathan, what's that you said about a good rifle shot?"

"Just that he was a good rifle shot or two the other side of that island that Emily pointed out. Monkey Island, you said?" Nathan grinned before remembering the seriousness of the situation and becoming serious again.

"Okay, that's likely a quarter to half a mile the other side of the island, so, two-and-a-half miles out." Wally began inputting a number into his phone. He caught Emily's eye as he lifted the phone to his ear. "There is a ferry. Give me a moment."

"I thought all the ferries were down south," Emily began as she turned to Nathan.

Wally was already focused on his phone, counting the rings, and hoping that the Knotts Island ferry wasn't refueling ... and that they would be amenable to helping one of their own. It was a big ask, but Brannigan was mixed up with the lot of them, so it was likely the ferry people knew him, as he could hardly be missed with his distinctive Irish appearance and that godawful cowboy hat.

The phone answered with, "Kylie, Knotts Island Ferry. How may I help you?"

"Hello, Kylie. I'm Wally Styles with the Dare County Sheriff's Office, and Brannigan Calmont from the Currituck County Sheriff's Office is in the sound, and his boat is sinking."

"Brannigan?" Kylie gasped. "How can I help? Do you need me to call 9-1-1 for you?"

"No time." Wally felt the panic rising again. He hadn't seen Brannigan in the Sound, wasn't sure of the exact situation, but he trusted Emily. Now he felt like he was wasting what little time Brannigan had on a wild goose call. "I suppose I was thinking ... the ferry ... I don't know of any other boats already out on the Sound—"

"Oh, that. Yes, I can help." Kylie's voice brightened. "Jerry, that's head of our maintenance crew, is down to Barco to retrieve a new replacement screw for one of our ferries. Where did you say Brannigan is?"

"Maybe a mile north of Monkey Island." Please be accurate, Nathan. This isn't just another rock to turn over. I need to trust your skills right now.

"Jerry's GPS locator says he's ... okay, let me refresh my screen ... oh, Jerry can probably see Brannigan if he knows where to look. Did Brannigan send you his GPS coordinates?"

"No, Kylie. We haven't talked to him. We saw the boat going down from the top of the lighthouse."

"Oh." She went silent as if trying to soak that in. "Let me contact Jerry with that information. Can you go back up the lighthouse for visual confirmation? If you stay on the phone, I can relay the information to Jerry."

"Yes, thank you, Kylie. I'll call you back when we're up there."

Nathan had followed the conversation well enough to understand where they were headed next. His eyes were on the top of the lighthouse, perhaps remembering what he and Emily had just observed ... a man he had met only recently and who had already earned his respect out on the beach.

Emily had her phone out, calling who, Wally couldn't say. When she pulled it from her purse, a whoopie cushion fell onto the sidewalk, and she didn't notice. Clearly, she was equally flustered.

Nathan saw the cushion and knelt to retrieve it, and Wally excused himself to speak to the docent in the gift shop, as trying to explain to the person working the lighthouse's entrance would take longer. He let her know that Emily and Nathan would be ascending the lighthouse once more and why and that he would be joining them. As he exited the gift shop, he was puzzled by the possible sinking of the Currituck County Zodiac. They were inflatable, but they were considered very difficult to puncture.

One boon from his side trip into the old Keeper's House was a pair of binoculars casually resting on a shelf behind the register. In bold white paint marker down the side, he read Currituck Light. While the docent was writing out a pass for the lighthouse, he studied the neck strap that dangled loosely off the shelf. It was clear they were regularly used.

"Your binoculars?" Wally indicated them with a nod of his head.

"Oh, those?" The docent smiled. "They belong to the shop. We have new ones just there—"

"May I borrow yours?" When she seemed hesitant, he said, "Just for spotting the sinking Zodiac."

"Oh." She paused, then said, "Oh, of course." She handed them to him, and he was out the door, with the strap wrapped around his wrist.

"How's our time?" he called to Nathan and Emily.

"How long does it take a man to drown?" Emily tapped her watch but didn't look at it, clearly a suggestion that time was slipping away entirely too fast.

"There's no sense in rushing just so's we can wait for Jerry to show up. We can't help Brannigan from here until then." Despite his calm words, he felt the same as Emily.

Still, a Zodiac sinking. He'd never heard of such a thing. Even with a punctured flotation chamber … it just didn't make sense.

Inside the lighthouse, despite the urgency of their mission, they were admonished to ascend methodically. The old building with its exposed red brick facing, constructed in the 1870s, was sturdy, but footsteps on each of the 220 steps to the top created vibrations that fed into the brick superstructure and could impact the overall stability of the brickwork.

So, no running or two-at-a-timers.

On their way to the lantern room, bubbling with the enthusiasm of a newly installed deputy, Nathan rattled on about his time with Cynthia Ellison at the beach "crime" scene. She had told Ed that Lucy was new to the district, as their previous K9 was injured in a shoot-out. He was okay now, she assured them, but she raised her eyebrows at A-District's new, if temporary, mascot, Roxie. "Didn't see that coming down the road, Diane babysitting someone else's dog."

Wally found the tale amusing, while Emily asked for more information about Roxie. Who did the animal belong to? Why was the A-District sub-station caring for it? And Diane baby-sitting a dog? Emily laughed, saying that Diane moved so fast, no dog would be able to keep up.

Poor Roxie.

The shift in topic away from Brannigan calmed their urgency. After all, Wally assured them, the Sound was big, and it would take some time for Jerry to reach Brannigan's location. They were likely to reach the lantern room long before the maintenance chief was even in view.

As they climbed higher, the staggered windows in the lighthouse's thick, masonry walls allowed glimpses of something other than foliage. The climbers were teased with water and island views, not all of which pointed towards Monkey Island and Brannigan. At the very top, they accessed the open-air walk around the lighthouse, and Wally uncapped the binoculars to search for Brannigan and his Zodiac. He dialed Kylie at the Knotts Island Ferry Terminal to let her know they were in place, and he was giving his phone to his associate.

The water sparkled with sharp pinpoints of hard, reflected light. The reflection of the blue sky contrasted against the dark surface of the inflatable, making Brannigan's boat easy to pick out amid the reflective clutter. In summer, a hundred boats of all sorts would be present to aid the stricken officer. Now, this late in the season, he was on the water alone. Then, to the north, wake churned, leaving a long trail of disturbed water. Wally lifted the glasses to his face, first landing on Jerry, as the long line of his boat's wake was more obvious. He was in a larger boat, but then that was expected as he was transporting a new propeller for the ferry. The boat had a wheelhouse, so Jerry wasn't in view, but the fact that it was there told the story of that.

Surprisingly, when he shifted the glasses to locate Brannigan, he found the Zodiac but no officer aboard.

"Here." He started to offer the binoculars to Nathan, but the younger man was giving directions to Kylie, so Wally handed the glasses to Emily. "I can't find Brannigan. The boat's there but no Brannigan."

"That's not welcome news." She adjusted the binoculars and began to search. "Found it. Where are you, Brannigan?"

"Can I try?" Nathan covered the phone with one hand, clearly anxious to look. This was exciting, even if it could end in disaster.

"Here." Emily handed him the glasses and took the phone. "I don't know where he went. I always say that saltwater cures all, but this is the cure no one wants. Then, all that's mostly fresh water, so maybe that's the problem."

She stepped away and began speaking to Kylie.

After only a moment of looking, Nathan pulled the glasses from his face. He grinned.

"What?" Emily said into the phone, "Hold on, Kylie," and she looked hard at Nathan for clarification.

"He's in the water. I think he must be in a shallow spot."

"In the water?" Emily spoke into the phone, then handed it to Wally. "Kylie said Jerry has him located, so we disconnected." She snatched the binoculars from Nathan and searched. "Ok, am I reading this right? He's standing beside the boat?"

"I think he's trying to fix something on the bottom. I saw him come up from underneath." Nathan started to reach for the binoculars once more, but Wally got to them first.

"Take your time, Brannigan." The tall, redheaded man disappeared back underwater. Studying the boat, Wally could see that one section of the hull was deflated, and the reflection of water in the interior told why the boat was now stranded.

Then ripples from Jerry's incoming craft shifted Wally's attention and apparently got Brannigan's as well. The redheaded man pulled his cowboy hat from inside the Zodiac, pressed it firmly onto his head, and began to wave at the incoming boat.

When Jerry was alongside and had the Zodiac tied to the stern of his larger boat, it became apparent why Brannigan was in the water. The wet man climbed into the inflatable to retrieve his things, and the deflated section of the hull collapsed enough to send a surge of liquid wet over the top. Brannigan was able to stem the surge by moving to the opposite side, but being inside the boat was not good for its stability on the water.

Eventually the men on the water had the situation sorted, and the Dare County employees at the top of the lighthouse were relieved to see Brannigan safely aboard Jerry's boat and the Zodiac securely in tow as the bigger craft began to motor northward.

As they started down, Nathan asked, "Couldn't he have walked to the shore? It only looked about chest deep."

Wally caught Emily's eye and laughed. It might be chest deep in that spot, but that didn't mean it was chest deep everywhere. People did drown in the Sound.

Just not today, and Wally was thankful for that.

Chapter 4

The Silt Stirs

FORENSIC INVESTIGATOR Emily Bryant draped the binoculars around her neck and worked the strap under her hair before starting down from the lantern room. Her fourth time traversing 220 steps ... she wanted her hands free to hold to the rail. Death by drowning would be bad enough—and she *was* glad the Currituck officer was only slightly drowned—but death by falling down the interior of a lighthouse would be an embarrassment, not only to her but to the entire Dare County Sheriff's Office.

And in Currituck County, of all places.

She would never be able to show her face again ... that was if it was still presentable after she hit the bottom.

At the second landing, she paused, held the handrail firmly, and said, "Bare feet and salty hair, what else do we need? An elevator!"

Wally laughed, stepped around her, nodded to the docent

monitoring that landing, and began down the next flight. Nathan seemed to be equally amused, but when he tried to follow on Wally's heels, the docent held out an arm and cautioned him.

"Just a moment, officer. Let him go a few steps ahead of you. Going down places more stress on the lighthouse. We want it to remain standing for another hundred years."

"See?" Emily leaned against him, placed her hand on his shoulder, and whispered into his ear. "Say it. An elevator would be nice."

"Here's my plan," Nathan quipped back. "No reason to hang back. Just one step at a time." He grinned, and when the docent gave him her okay, he began moving after Wally.

Emily fought a smile. On his shoulder, just where she had placed her hand, he now wore a sticky note that said, "Protest! All lighthouses should have elevators." Emily slipped her ink pen and sticky note pad back into her purse and waited for the docent to send her on her way.

HEADING BACK down Highway 12, Wally and Nathan led the way, with Emily following in her nondescript white sedan, the car she preferred over a county-issue version. Not only did the county reimburse her for mileage and fuel, when her job was done, no matter where she was on the islands, she could be off on a personal photo shoot, without wearing a county badge on her doors.

She called Nathan on his phone.

"Yes, Emily?"

"How did you know it was me?" She had hoped to tease him about the note. She wanted to pretend to be a mystery caller who wanted to join him in protest.

"Caller ID. You're on my phone."

"How? I've never called you."

"Wally gave it to me. He said if I was working for Dare County, yours was a number I needed."

"Two points in Wally's scorebook. Has anyone offered to join your protest yet?" She stifled a laugh.

"I haven't protested anything."

"Check your shoulder." Through the back window of their car, she could see him feeling of his left shoulder. "No, the other one."

His hands shifted, and he twisted to look at her through the back glass. "You stuck this on me?"

"You are as gullible as Sean Taylor. Oh, I'm going to enjoy working with you!"

Emily heard Wally in the background, "Emily, I've heard about you. This boy's pretty smart. Watch out."

"Hey, saltwater and all. Let's stop by where your Currituck officer took off in his little boat. I would like to see it if it's on the way."

"Done," Wally said from his side of the car.

"He said done, Emily."

"I got that, and I'll take a side of beach with it." Emily chuckled. "I'm following you."

She clicked off her phone and tossed it into the seat beside her. At the boardwalk, she carried her camera with her to document the area. The sinking boat didn't mean a crime had taken place, but evidence was best served up fresh. Her job as a forensic investigator was to collect forensic evidence. Her camera was her best friend, and she was wedded to it.

While under the trees, she pulled it from its case and twisted on a telephoto lens. She could change it when she reached the dock, but she wanted the long-distance view first. She would photograph the approach to the shore and what was off to each side after getting closer.

As she aimed her camera at the boat slips and the open dock just behind, she noticed a hooded figure beside one of the boats. She clicked the shutter, immobilizing the person as a dark shape against the brighter sky. He turned toward her—had he heard her shutter from this distance?—and she zoomed in, saw a glimpse of red under the hood, and clicked the shutter once more. And again and again, as he stared directly at her for a moment, then knelt to frantically search for something. She didn't know if he found it, but he suddenly stood, revealing a bodybuilder's shoulders, and gripped the handle of a black tote bag with a zippered top. Lifting it easily, he walked fast and hard in thick-soled boots past all three officers while trying very hard to hide his face.

"Excuse us," Nathan called to his retreating back.

"Some people," Wally murmured.

They hadn't seen what Emily had, and without telling them what she was doing, she powerwalked past them, changing her lens for close-up shots, all while keeping her eye on the spot the young man had been searching. When she arrived, she knelt and began snapping images.

"Take your time, Emily," Wally said with a laugh. "This place isn't going anywhere."

"Maybe." She looked up, searched the horizon across the Sound, and took in the trees back along the beginnings of the dock. "I didn't imagine that man, I know that. You two saw him, too."

"You think he was a drug mule?" Nathan said it with a tease.

"I think he was suspicious." She took a deep breath, working out why he stood out to her. The black hoodie, when it wasn't cold outside. The frantic searching, when there was no place for anything to hide. His sudden departure when they arrived. She glanced at Sean's shirt, with deputy all over it, and at Wally's, equally emblazoned with Dare County logos, and her gut told her there was something here that he hadn't found.

A call from the shore, where the boardwalk turned into the long, exposed dock, pulled their attention from the water.

"Hey, did you people see a person all in black anywhere about here?" The speaker was tall and thin, a weathered islander in rough jeans, a worn plaid button-up shirt with the sleeves rolled, and a cap with fold-up flaps. From under the cap, his thick black hair was shot with gray.

"With red hair?" Emily threw out something she had glimpsed in the second photograph.

"I knew it! I done told that boy to stay on his side of the Sound. You see what he was doing down there?" The man looked hot enough to spit fire at a pile of dry timber.

Emily looked first to Wally, then to Nathan, not sure this was a person they needed to share with. She asked, "Can we have your name, sir?"

"You people aren't from here, are you? Those uniforms, I can tell, you see. I don't guess it hurts much to tell you. Name's Samuel Knight. I live up Corolla way. I buried my wife in '87, just so's you know, name of Charlie, God rest her soul, and next to losing her, those danged Currituck cousins are the worst pain I've ever suffered. That one was Charles-Edouard, last name of Beaumarchais, and I guarantee you, he's up to no good."

The man turned on his heel without a word and left them to their business.

"Did I read that right? We've got a cousin conflict in the works?" Emily put her hand on her hip and shook her head. "Maybe they need a little beach time."

"Likely," Wally said.

"Hey, Emily, is this what you were looking for?" Nathan slipped a finger between two boards and withdrew a long screwdriver with the end filed to a point.

"Like molasses on toast. Freeze, Nathan." Wally withdrew a plastic evidence bag from a pocket, and he held it out for the sharpened tool. "We'll have to eliminate your fingerprints, of course, but something tells me Brannigan's Zodiac didn't spring a leak on its own."

"A picture, first," Emily commanded. *Best served up hot.* This was about as hot as it got, and if this proved to be anything, Samuel's battle between cousins was likely on.

When they reviewed Emily's images in her camera, Charles-Edouard was gloved, so that was no help; and as the docking material was weather-worn wood, it didn't seem there would be any purpose in looking for prints on the dock.

Along the boardwalk and the dirt portions of the path, they hoped for better success. They found a partial print that could have come from the heavy boots in Emily's photographs. It also could have come from a hundred other visitors to the Banks, but Emily photographed it from several angles and recorded the time and location.

There had been no reason to check on what the man got into when he ran from the dock, and the greenery would have prevented that, anyway, as the parking area was invisible from the boat slips. And in any case, there was still no proof that a crime had occurred, only a waterlogged Zodiac and an old screwdriver that now served as a makeshift awl. They couldn't even be certain why Brannigan's boat had tried to capsize.

Nathan did think to inquire of Wally and Emily why Brannigan didn't just call for help. Wally's phone had worked the entire time.

"Did you try to call him? Take your time, Deputy. Think about it." Wally gave him the space to work it out.

"Um, no. Emily?"

"Yes and no." Emily already saw what Wally was getting at. "When I heard he was from Currituck, I called the sheriff's office in Barco. They couldn't reach him by phone or radio."

"Turn this rock over and look at the other side. He didn't try to call any of us, either; and wasn't he in the water when we got back up the lighthouse?"

"Okay. You don't need to tell me twice. I got it." Nathan looked embarrassed, but he managed to shoot Wally two thumbs up, one from each hand.

"He may have to replace both his radio and his phone before we can get in touch with him." Wally seemed thoughtful for a moment. "The Sound is mostly fresh, but mostly means not completely. Likely, corrosion has already set in. Harsh, to tell it right, but that's likely God's truth."

"Okay," Emily said, to shift gears away from the Currituck County officer and his rescue. "While the sun shines, I'd still like to get to the beach and see what happened there. It's the reason I drove up, so the beach is calling!"

She lifted a hand into the air, with a finger pointed in the direction of her car, and she encouraged Wally and Nathan to follow her lead.

ACCESSING THE BEACH gave Emily the same experience as the other officers: parking on the court, then navigating the drive of the sprawling beachfront estate. She oohed and aahed over the extravagance and as quickly moved on to the beach when she exited behind the garage.

It wasn't the houses that counted. It was the beach they were attached to.

Emily went ahead, and to her surprise, a black, four-wheel-drive Toyota truck with heavily tinted windows and an unfamiliar business logo on the side was parked just on the water side of the taped-off crime scene. The tide was out, but if the truck remained there for any length of time, it would quickly become a boat anchor, much like Brannigan's phone and radio had. Salt was good for the soul but incredibly destructive to electronics and machines.

Something or someone moved in the taped-off area to her left. A familiar black hoodie appeared from behind a sandy rise, as an insistent voice yelled, "I need that bag, Creighton. I don't have the cash reserves to cover your brother's foul up, so find it!"

"Charles-Edouard?" Emily called out the name given them by Samuel Knight. She would bet the beach that the two were the same, although this time the hood was down, and coppery hair flashed in the sun and caught in the wind. The man grabbed the thick mane into a bundle at his neck and turned to see who had called him.

"Creighton, les flics!" In a clean motion, Charles-Edouard—if that was his name—pulled his hood back over his head, and in the action, becoming the person in Emily's photographs. He slapped at the shoulder of another person Emily just noticed. The second person, slim with thick hair, stood, revealing a shovel and biker's pants. His upper body touted a long-sleeved, white fitted shirt, now stained with beach and whatever else.

"C'mon, C-c-charles, it's the local g-g-gendarme. The bag has to wait." That must be Creighton, although he was unfamiliar to Emily. "Get in the t-t-truck. Let's go!"

"Hold on," Emily called. "I have a question—"

From behind her, she heard Wally and Nathan begin to yell, "Hey, you two! Stay where you are!" She turned to see them running—or attempting to, as the sand was eating their feet with every step.

The young men made it to their truck long before the two Dare County officers could reach them, and the vehicle, powered by a diesel powerplant, spit black smoke and rooster tails of sand as it did an about face and barreled northward.

Nathan held his cap in one hand and rubbed his hair. "I used to own a Tacoma. I didn't know they came in diesel."

"They don't." Wally stood beside him. "That's what Toyota sells to the rest of the world, a Hilux. Someone has had that imported. Did you get the tag number?"

"I did!" Emily held up her camera. "A good telephoto lens, a beach necessity for every occasion! Say thank you, everyone!"

"Les flics," Nathan remarked, with a puzzled expression. "Is that a beach term? I've not heard it."

"Brannigan's phone might be toast, but yours isn't. Look it up. I'm headed over to see what they were searching for. Whatever it was, I hope I already have it in my car."

Emily didn't follow any of that, but she knew how to tease information out of unwary deputies. She just needed a good enough prank to make him want to reveal all.

She glanced around the shell-encrusted beach, with her eyes landing just at the tideline where broken shells formed a painted strip of undulating white. Motion among the shells told her that life was happening, small beach creatures feeding on the residue of those that didn't survive the breakers as they tumbled ashore. She knelt, waited until a small crab scuttled from underneath an upturned shell, and she cupped it in her hand. It was so small she could barely feel it scrabbling for freedom. From her camera case, she pulled an old film cartridge—no longer used for film but handy because it sealed airtight—and dumped out the cleaning cloth it held. She worked the crab inside, snapped the lid on, and dropped it back inside the case.

She stood, took two steps away from the camera bag, and

called, "Does either of you see potential footprints? I'd like to match the one from near the dock. Evidence is only as good as the documentation we have."

"The sand's too soft in most areas, and half a dozen officers have canvassed the scene." Essentially, no, Wally seemed to say.

"There must be something." Emily walked halfway towards Wally, then stopped and called to Nathan, "Could you bring me that film cannister from my camera bag? I need to change rolls. This one is about full."

"Of course. It's why I got this job."

When he offered it to her, she said, "Thank you so much. I need your hands, though. Can you open it and hand me the film cartridge? If you'll cup your hand around it when you slide it out, it will protect it from sun exposure."

"I don't see no reason why not."

Emily watched, amused, as he wrapped one hand around the lidded end of the cannister, carefully popped the lid off, then turned it upside down to tap out the "film." The small crab saw its opportunity for freedom, and it scrambled up and onto Nathan's wrist before the deputy realized what was up and jerked away, sending both the crab and film cannister flying.

"That was great!" Emily laughed. "Wally, you should have seen the expression on this man's face. Nathan, I will need my film cannister back, thank you, but that was outstanding."

"You—" Nathan focused on her camera. "That's digital, isn't it?"

"Always has been."

"You got me good," he said, finally grinning, and he retrieved and handed her the empty cannister and lid. "What about the boot prints?"

"Unless you two see something, I agree with Wally. This

sand is soft, and it's covered with prints from you neanderthals tromping over every surface."

"My bad." Nathan lifted one shoe to study the sole. "I guess you could photograph mine to exclude it from the rest."

"I could, but I can do that later. I intended to get the scene as undisturbed as possible, but that shovel tells me that those two ruined undisturbed." She called, "Wally, you were here earlier. How much damage did they do?"

"All of it," he called back. "I think they were trying to dig to Virginia." He looked north, considering. "This beach takes you all the way to the border. This morning they found a bag of what could be drugs—"

"Drug smuggling! This is why I got this job, for sure." Nathan's eyes glowed. "Could have been one of them drug mules. Didn't they find blood, too? Here's what I think. They came down from Virginia to pick up a load of drugs, all the way down the beach on a four-wheeler. That'd be easy. Then, to avoid paying for the drugs, they just shot everybody."

"Okay, I give." Emily made as if to slip her camera in her bag. "I might as well go home. Nathan's already solved the crime. Oh, oh!" She looked around. "Dead bodies. I don't see any dead bodies. Nathan, where are the dead bodies?"

"Wally, they found blood, didn't they?" Nathan searched the taped off area with his eyes, as if he could find something if he looked hard enough.

"In the evidence bags. I'm not opening them."

"So," Emily said, hefting her camera back into her hands. "Blood, no body, and someone digging through the crime scene. Likely from Virginia, according to our deputy. Maybe it's time to do my job and get it all on film. Well, on my SD card." She caught Nathan's eye, grinned, and headed off to snap any images that might secure the scene for the investigation, if one was deemed necessary by Manteo.

Virginia indeed. It was boot prints she wanted, and she hoped she could find at least one good one.

EMILY PULLED into the A-District sub-station parking lot, surprised at the large truck and trailer filled with two bikes and taking up her favorite slice of gravel. The Bong overhead cut the lot into dark and light with shadow. This late in the year, parking in the sun was acceptable, but in summer, it was nice to claim the shade when possible.

Emily nestled her white sedan between a familiar truck, a maroon FTX that had Jason Romney's name on it, and an equally familiar black Ford Explorer. The black SUV didn't surprise her, but Jason now worked at Manteo with her, and his FTX did surprise her.

"Do I read this right? Diane Turnipseed transfers to A-District. Jason Romney transfers to Manteo. Both Diane and Jason's vehicles are at the A-District sub-station. They say salt-water cures all, but this is a different kind of cure in my book."

As she opened her door, she triggered the trunk release, and she gathered her camera bag and locked up before walking to the front door. Before she could enter, the gravel crunched, and Wally's patrol car joined all the rest. Emily waved and waited, and when Deputy Preston appeared first, she called, "You have that screwdriver, right?"

"Don't need to ask. Sealed and pristine." He lifted it into the air, holding the top of the evidence bag to show that it was fully sealed against any outside contaminants.

"I doubt it's pristine, but that's for someone else to deter-mine." Possibly Barco, with the Currituck County Sheriff's Office, as that's where it was uncovered, although if it proved to be part of a crime, maybe all the way to the Crime Lab in

Raleigh. "Are you bringing in those evidence bags from the beach, or does it all stay in the trunk?"

"Wally says inside. We can't process it all here, but it doesn't need to stay outside. They didn't send the drugs." He looked disappointed.

By then, Wally had appeared, and she asked, "Drugs, Wally? You mentioned that up on the beach, which I think correlates with what our intruder said to his accomplice. I'm sorry we disappointed them, but now Barco doesn't want to share?" She smiled.

"That's for sure. If they're smart, it's under lock and key and will stay that way. Our new boss did good to get all this." He popped the trunk lid to reveal the thick black nylon bag from Brannigan Calmont's Zodiac.

"Can I peek?"

When he nodded, she hitched her camera bag over her shoulder and joined him. He unzipped the bag and spread the opening to reveal the collected cloth, gun, and other paraphernalia from the sand. Each bag was labeled in the handwriting of the officer that retrieved it from the sand. An evidence sheet documented the handover from Brannigan to Wally. Emily pressed against one of the bags holding shell casings, taking in the shape of the cold metal. A cloth-filled bag boasted damaged fabric with darkened edges.

"Gunpowder residue?" She pushed the plastic tighter against the fabric to better tell.

"And blood," Nathan interjected. "That's what Ed and Clara said. There was blood everywhere."

"Oh, everywhere?" Emily teased the younger man.

"There was blood all over those bikes when they came in, too." He waved a hand in that direction. "You should have seen the man Wally and I took to Urgent Care. He could barely see with all the blood."

"It wasn't as bad as the young pup makes it sound." Wally chuckled. "It was the other one that tried to do a runner."

"You got their names, right?" The story was getting more interesting with every tidbit she squeezed out of them.

"Philippe and Creighton, um, Ballinger, I think, from Currituck, the town, not the county." Nathan stopped, frowned, then smiled again. "Well, it is in the county, so both, I suppose. Captain Turnipseed delivered them home."

"Oh, those two." Emily should have figured, what with the bikes and the truck. The trouble was that she didn't often get this far north, and they were Currituck County troublemakers, not Dare County residents. Only the times they bled their trouble into Dare County did they come up on Manteo's radar.

That was more often than Manteo wanted, she knew that. The cousins from Corolla had shown up in Manteo, angry that Dare County was poking their fingers into Corolla's business when it wasn't Dare County's business and insisting that Dare County wasn't allowed to poke and prod into anything in Currituck County.

The new Dare County sheriff, Ollie Glynne, had stepped in with, "What stays in Currituck County is Currituck County's to deal with, but let it cross that county line, and it becomes ours. I'll check on this if you'll give me some breathing room. It might take me a minute, so if you can provide your contact information, I'll see that you're kept informed."

"You know of 'em?" Wally closed the bag and lifted it to sit on the fender.

"Yes. Now I better understand Samuel from the dock. He mentioned cousins, and seeing this, I can feel for him. Nathan said one of the men you had at Urgent Care was named Creighton. Was that our Creighton from this morning?"

"I didn't get a good look, but mixed up with that lot, I'd say yes. He had the right build and the stutter." Wally lifted the bag from the fender, closed the trunk, and motioned inside. "This needs to be indoors."

"Of course." Emily found Nathan already holding the door open. She smiled as she stepped past, while pausing to tap him on the arm with her knuckle and whisper, "Until the next prank, my friend."

He called after her, "What? Wait, there's more?"

She laughed, greeted Paloma, and headed towards the situation room. She placed her bag on a table, retrieved her camera and headed to the metal cabinet holding the keys to the impounded vehicles.

"Paloma, may I?" Emily indicated the glass door.

"It's unlocked. All I do is turn the key every morning. The rest of it is up to you people."

"I'll take that for a yes. Thank you."

Emily knew the vehicles had been gone over, but part of her title was *investigator*. What she couldn't document didn't count as evidence. Blood and blood. There had to be a link some-where, and she and her camera were going to go head-to-head with the Currituck cousins. If they were bringing their nonsense to Dare County, she would do whatever was within her power to ensure that they regretted it one hundred percent.

As she opened the glass door, the reflection of a brown dog on a dog bed caught her attention.

"Paloma, what's that?" Emily pushed the cabinet door closed without accessing the keys and knelt before the animal. "You are beautiful. When I say the Banks are calling, what I really mean is you. Paloma?"

"Well, honey, take this like I say it. If you don't know what a dog is, I don't know why you have that fancy title before your name." Paloma sat before an old-fashioned typewriter, and she inserted a sheet of fresh paper and turned a wheel on the side to roll it forward. It clicked rapidly as it rolled through, and she adjusted a paper guide to hold it in place. "I'd be happy to answer any other questions you have, but as my grandpappy always said, if you can't come in out of the rain, don't be asking for dry clothes."

"Point made. You have work to do." Emily was rubbing the dog's head by then.

"Thank you. If you don't want the truth, don't start the conversation. That's also something my grandpappy said."

"Wally?" Emily called the name loud enough to carry. "I've set Paloma off. Can you come in here?"

"What?" Paloma rolled her chair away from her typewriter and gave Emily a long look. "Are you trying to get shut of me? I may look white, but there are two ways about this—"

"I've got it, Paloma." Wally interrupted with a laugh. "Roxie is our new mascot, but only until the new sheriff gets back in town."

"She's a Belgian Malinois, correct?" With that dark face and those intelligent eyes, who wouldn't love her? "I've heard that they're used in the military, which means she likely has the chops. You people have a new dog handler up here. Is she on a trial run?"

"Ed wishes, I think, but she's a rescue from out west, either Kentucky or West Virginia. She's too old for the training program or I think Ed would already have her enrolled."

"Then she wouldn't be in my office," Paloma said under her breath.

Emily noted the temporary nature of her assigned corner. "She doesn't stay here at night. Who takes her home?"

"Captain Turnipseed." Nathan reappeared. "She's really just

been here today. My solution is to build her a dog run out the back of the building. Then when a drug mule comes down from Virginia, we pull her out, and we got 'em!"

"Outside? Never, don't even think that." Emily noticed a bag of treats on a table, and she stood and opened them. The dog's eyes followed her, but she didn't move from her spot on the bed. Emily patted her leg and said, "Here, Roxie."

In a smooth and quick motion, the brown dog was on her feet and at Emily's side. Wally and Nathan had seen the dog respond earlier, but Emily laughed. She removed a treat from the bag and said, "Sit."

The dog did, while keeping her eyes focused on the treat.

"This is fun!" Emily twirled the treat in a circle and said, "Roll."

Roxie did, returning to the same location with the same stance as before, while maintaining her attention on the treat. Wally pulled it from Emily's hand and held it to the dog. Roxie still stared at it, once lifting her eyes to Wally's face, then to Emily's, before zeroing back in on the treat.

"Okay," Wally said, and Roxie snapped it up. "Good girl." He patted her head. "Bad girl," he said to Emily and wagged a finger at her.

"Me? That was fun. She's adorable. I might want one—"

"You do not. I hear the stories from Manteo. You'd prank the poor animal to death."

"I would not—"

Paloma ended the conversation. "I don't mean to step on your toes, but you wanted those keys for something. You gonna take them or not?"

"Busted," Emily said with a grin. "Bye, Roxie. Who wants to join me to take pictures of that truck and those bikes out there?"

Wally and Nathan followed her, with Wally giving Nathan the preferential slot for involvement. "He needs exposure to what you do and how you work."

"I'm not going to prank him, not while I'm working."

"I hear stories—"

"Okay, I give. I likely will but I have some real questions, so only after that."

"Only after the real questions. I can live with that." Wally motioned Nathan forward. "She's got some questions for you, young pup. Get over here and get busy. You're the one that went over all this, so put yourself to good use."

"Yessir." Nathan grinned. "It's why I took this job. What do you want to know?"

"First, unlock." Emily handed him the keys.

"I've got all the documentation on this inside. Pictures, prints, everything." He held the keys but didn't move towards the truck. "I went over everything, although it was this morning and not last night. We didn't know it had a connection to a crime scene until then."

"So it sat outside overnight." Oh, well. She was here when she was here. "Tell me everything from then to now, just not from when I was with you. I already know all that."

Nathan narrated, with Wally occasionally backing him up to fill in details or guiding him back onto the topic when he took a side trip. Emily had sensed the connection between the impounded vehicles and the beach when Samuel Knight had run across their path in Corolla Beach, but when the same black-cloaked figure had appeared on the beach along with someone she learned was directly associated with this truck, well that was a bucket of sand poured all over her.

"So, last night, Diane delivered two brothers back to Currituck, the town, not the county, except that one is in the other—" She looked hard at Nathan when she said that. "—and we only saw one of those brothers on the beach this afternoon, the one without the damage to his head. Open the door and let me inside."

Some blood remained on the exterior of the truck, but with the door open, more was inside. Emily retrieved her camera while the story was being told, and she was letting the patterns of the events work themselves out in her thoughts. She was a forensic investigator, someone assigned to deal with facts after-the-fact, as in dead bodies that were already dead. Yet there weren't always hard crimes on the islands. Often, for months on end, she fulfilled other duties, did other things, involved herself in other aspects of investigations. It was the reason she relished opportunities like this. Take pictures, record the details, gather evidence. She dealt with the hard facts.

The why was for the detectives.

Today, it was the pattern of events that had hooked her attention ... two men last night, two men today, one of them the same, one of them missing.

And the blood on the beach. She had seen the evidence bags in Wally's trunk. She had taken enough pictures on enough crime scenes, and she would agree with anyone who asked that the clothing contained blood, and it likely matched what was in the truck, even if the final determination wasn't hers.

Blood here, blood there. Two men here, two men there, one man missing. Or was he? Like a good investigator, she allowed that there was a second possibility. Perhaps his injuries had been worse than originally thought, and he was at home recovering.

The real question was ... where would the forensic evidence say the blood on the beach was from? From the man missing from last night's run to Urgent Care ... or from a person truly missing, one taken out by a gun, someone who had abandoned a bag of drugs, and who had vanished without a trace except for the blood he had left behind?

EMILY WAS INSIDE the truck snapping photos, and Wally was helping Nathan with something underneath the vehicle when Wally's radio beeped and said, "You people about done out there?"

The man didn't immediately respond, and Emily encouraged him with, "Paloma's keeping track. She might expect an answer."

"Just another rock to turn over. Hold this, Nathan." After a pause, "Wally here. Yes, Paloma?"

Emily tuned out the conversation. She was disappointed with what she was finding. Blood, yes, but mostly smeared. Where there might be prints, the area was already dusted with fingerprint powder. What she needed was to have the items from the beach processed. A good set of prints directly from the men picked up and released the day before would be good, but without probable cause—and with them residing in a different county—that was a sand dune yet to be topped.

How did Diane say it? She would be in the collards for certain if she attempted to match fingerprints without having comparison prints; and to get them from people unlikely to willingly provide them was like setting out tomorrow's breakfast before the sun went down.

Okay, Diane might not say exactly that, but it was close.

She noticed Nathan at the door waiting for permission to speak.

"Yes?" She was on her back under the dashboard, hopefully capturing a bloody print that hadn't yet been dusted with powder. Sometimes people who were in pain used obscure handholds to maneuver while getting in or out, and she suspected this was from that. She snapped the picture before giving the new deputy her full attention.

"Wally's taking a call. He thinks we may be headed up to Knotts Island."

"As in Currituck County. Isn't that where the rescue boat from earlier was headed?"

"I believe so. Wally's inside and still on the phone, with Brannigan, I think."

"Lots of thinking, not much knowing." Emily extricated herself from the truck. "Why didn't he call Wally's phone? I assume that's why Paloma pulled him inside, to take the call."

Nathan broke into a grin. "Wally's number got drowned with Brannigan's phone. Brannigan said his phone and radio both went underwater before he realized the boat was compromised. That's why he couldn't call for help."

"I get that. What does he need you two up there for? Can't he find a ride home on his own?" She was certain he could catch the ferry back to Currituck, and the county had additional officers that could ferry him back to his car, wherever he had left it.

"I'm not sure. Wally's still on the line with him."

"Okay, I give. Change of topic. Your boss's car is here but I haven't seen her. What's that about? And that's Jason Romney's truck. Is there a connection no one's told me about?"

"I don't—"

The door to the sub-station opened, interrupting Nathan's reply, and Wally exited, calling, "Young pup, you ready to head out?"

"Of course. That's why I took—"

"Can I interrupt this tete-a-tete?" Emily closed the truck door.

"Oh, Emily." Wally seemed surprised to see her still there.

"Did you forget about me? I know I like being on the beach even more than spending time on county business, but I haven't abandoned you yet. If you want, I can do that now."

"Nah, just a glitch. This cousin thing—"

"This Currituck cousin thing. And aren't half of them from Corolla? Both of those places are half an hour north of our jurisdiction. I know this is bleeding over the county line, but isn't Knotts Island very out of the way?"

The fact was, the only access point to Knotts Island directly from the eastern side of the Banks was by boat, and that didn't mean by ferry. The Knotts Island Ferry only traveled from Currituck, the village, to Knotts Island, which barely counted as an island. On a satellite map, it was more like a peninsula pointing south into the Sound, with water on both sides and attached directly to Virginia. Access to North Carolina was solely by ferry, and that was directly from Currituck.

It was *very* out of the way.

"We're mixed up with the lot of them up there, what with that truck you're processing and all those evidence bags we just dropped off. So, yes, Knotts Island is a long ways, but we're working with Brannigan already, so there it is."

"Where does that leave me? I drove all the way up here—"

"There's that." Wally removed his cap and readjusted it over his thinning hair and grinned at Nathan. "Brannigan did ask who all were in the lighthouse directing his rescue. I told him me and the young pup there, and maybe a pretty forensic investigator, so if you want to tag along, help show the deputy the ropes, you're welcome."

"That's better." Emily smiled, and she began to disassemble her camera. "Let's head that way while the sun still shines. I'm expecting we're riding the ferry there and back, so hours to go. Dark comes early in the fall, and—"

"Don't say it." Wally closed his eyes.

"What?" Emily acted innocent.

"That it gives you plenty of time for pranks." He let out a sigh, while in the background, Nathan grinned.

"What? I would never!" A shocked expression blasted her indignation. Then she grinned. "But now that you've brought it up, that's not a bad idea at all. But seriously, what's the real reason I'm invited? Does Brannigan require an admiring female so he can boast of his swimming skills? Or how well he can keep a boat afloat? I don't know that I can sing his praises on either count."

"He might want both of those, but on the way to the ferry landing, he and Jerry had time to talk, and Jerry told him a few things that might link Knotts Island to our crime scene on the beach. Brannigan suggested we might ought to come check it out, maybe talk to Jerry and see what we think."

Emily laughed. "Why don't I spend more time up here? I had no idea this place was so lively. Yes, I want to come. Am I going to be stuck in the back seat of your car?"

Wally shrugged. "You and Nathan can duke it out."

Nathan's look of dismay tweaked Emily's compassion, and she said, "Let me get a blanket from my car. Nathan, here's the keys to this truck. You take them back inside."

When Nathan disappeared, Wally chuckled. "You're giving in that easily?"

"Are you kidding? I'll be up front before he comes back out of that door. The blanket's for him."

And she would. Bet on it.

IT TURNED OUT that Monkey Island wasn't the only point of social demarcation between the Corolla clan living on the ocean side of the Outer Banks and the interlopers who had claimed a foothold on the mainland side of Currituck Sound. Knotts Island served at one point or another as a battleground, a place for truces, an occasional redoubt from the ongoing conflict, and at times, all of these. It was also an overnight destination, especially when leaving on an afternoon ferry.

The landing at Currituck was little more than a pullout from the main roadway, with wooden overhead beams to drive under. The sign by the gate said more than any human voice could. The last ferry from Currituck would be theirs, and to catch the return ferry meant they couldn't disembark on the other side.

"No feet on the sand this trip," Emily quipped when she read the sign.

"How do you mean?" Nathan was out of the car, and he was stretching to relieve the pain of riding in the plastic seat.

"The ferry times. It's a forty-minute ride, and the final ferry back only gives us fifteen minutes on the island. I hope Jerry is a fast talker."

"Oh, I don't guess I said." Wally looked sheepish. "You people are from down south, and I assumed you were aware."

"Aware of what?" Emily didn't like the word, not used in the context of taking a ferry that squeezed the time on the other end into a tighter package than freeze dried cod.

"Afternoon ferries are always overnighters up here. Jerry's got a couple extra rooms he said he can loan us." Wally shrugged. "Done it like this once before, not with Jerry, but the islanders are welcoming and will do us right."

"And if I have other plans?" She didn't, but she might have had.

"Well, Nathan and I need this over there." Wally's door was open, and he patted the top of his cruiser. The ferry, a very small one, could be seen in the distance. "That boat's about to board, so if you want to stay, that's your choice. Uber, maybe?"

"Nathan?" She turned her attention on the younger man. "You knew this?"

"My bad." He shrugged. "Wally warned me that the ferries don't always run on our schedule. I don't mind, really, as my wife's in Texas and I got no one waiting on me at my apartment." He pointed to the incoming ferry. "This is cool. No reason to hang back. It'll be fun."

Two other cars had joined them, one an older truck with rust-stained wheel wells, and the other a smaller SUV with an older couple visible through the windows. Wally's cruiser was now trapped, and that said what it said about Emily having any real choice.

"I get it," she said to Wally once they were aboard. "This is payback."

"For what?" He had his cap off against the stiff breeze coming off the water. They had exited the car as the ferry moved forward, and the wind had threatened to toss it into the Sound. His hair quivered against his scalp but didn't dance so much as hunkered. Nathan was in the front seat of the car with his head back and his eyes closed.

"The ultimate practical joke. I was put off at first, but now I'm into it. Spend some time on an unfamiliar island, a bit of salt water—just not too salty—time on the sand ..."

"I can see you've not been to Knotts." Wally placed his hat back on his head, covering his thin hair, and he worked it down tight. "Not much sand out there."

"Rats." Emily laughed. "Wishful thinking. Still, while the sun shines."

"Not much more of that, either." Wally pointed behind them where the late afternoon clouds to the west were already taking on color.

The landing at Knotts Island was little more than a chain-link waterfront lot in a residential-type neighborhood, with neatly trimmed grass and a small block-construction restroom. Once off the boat, there weren't even any attendants to ensure correct ferry etiquette when exiting the landing.

They were greeted by a familiar face.

"Hey, you people over there with Dare County on your car!" Brannigan Calmont stood beside a middle-aged man with a bit of a belly in blue, stained coveralls. "Meet Jerry Fordham, my lifeline this morning and your host for the night. He's working to get my Zodiac patched so I can head back home tomorrow."

"Hey y'all, folks." Jerry nodded at them. "That's a right nice car you got there. I hate that the boss's boat got mammucked, but we'll have a nice sit down on my pizer, maybe shotgun a beer or two, and have a real field party. Then we'll get the lot of you back to the ferry in the morning. Unless'n you'd rather visit a joint for a quick bite to eat first."

Brannigan laughed. "You catch all that? Jerry's from Ocracoke originally, so you gotta wade through his words from time to time. I'm just now starting to understand what he's saying."

Jerry shook his head and grinned before he turned to the vehicle he and Brannigan had arrived in, a step-side Chevy square cab from the seventies in baby blue and rust.

Emily pulled Brannigan aside, introduced herself as the county forensic investigator, and asked him to clarify why he'd requested her presence if it wasn't to brag on his boating skills. She'd seen him floundering in the water when his inflatable was half submerged, so she hoped he had a better reason.

"If you insist." He looked like he really wanted to share. "I hoped to save it for later, but I see that's not making any headway. Unlike you slackers down in Dare, I've been busy with our new shared case."

"Oh, so it's finally official? We're sharing now?" Emily was warming up to their conversation.

"Your head honcho thinks so." He was grinning.

"Sheriff Glynne? I thought he was out of town."

"Oh?" He didn't act as if that was news. "Maybe that's the reason your Captain Turnipseed is in cahoots with our Sheriff Barnett. Here's the deal. According to Jerry over there, there's a bit of family drama unfolding on the island, and I expect it to impact our investigation significantly."

"Don't do this to me." She put on a pouty look. "Say what you mean."

"I'll let Jerry tell it later, but the warring cousins? Are you familiar with them?"

"From Corolla and Currituck, those?"

"Ha!" Brannigan laughed. "It's a Romeo and Juliette story if I ever heard one. Just wait until you hear Jerry's version."

Emily was aghast when the man refused to reveal more, and instead, climbed into Jerry's truck and closed the door.

"Emily?" Wally was getting in his car, and Nathan stood with the back door open.

"Coming," she called, but she did take time to glare at the tailgate of the blue Chevy. Romeo and Juliette. They both died for love. What did that mean? Did she have another dead body on her hands? And this wasn't even in her jurisdiction.

One thing she couldn't put aside. Brannigan had piqued her interest. She really did want to learn what Jerry had to say.

"THEM KNIGHTS over on Corolla, them's not really Knights either, you know."

The five of them had driven the couple of miles up South End Road to Knotts Island Market, which was, from the lack of infrastructure along the roadway, their only option for food. The place did have a full-service deli with take-out options, but the officers and their host were at an inside table. It held a fresh roll of paper towels on a holder complemented by free salt and pepper.

"I need to work this out." Nathan frowned. "Samuel Knight? We met him today. That's not his real name?"

"That it is. Old Samuel Knight." Jerry nodded confidently. "But then it's not, either."

"What—" Before he could finish, a hand on his arm caught Nathan's attention.

Brannigan grinned. He'd spent the day with Jerry, and he was enjoying the conversation—at the expense of the Dare County officers.

After Brannigan released Nathan's arm, Emily pushed her hair behind one ear. "Jerry, your story fascinates me. I love finding out about the Knights. Aren't they the people that built the Whalehead in Corolla?"

"Aye, missus. Some of us hoi toiders from down to Ocracoke come up to help 'em build it. What a place it were! Every fancy thing they could install back then. Them folks built a warehouse over on the mainland for storing their materials. It were converted to condos, called them lofts, back in the seventies, if memory serves, at which time they added a big pizer overlooking the Sound."

"Interesting." Emily rested her chin in her hand. "Pizer, please explain what that is."

"One of them covered things to get you out of the weather." Jerry didn't seem to mind talking, and he was open and quick to explain anything that seemed confusing to others.

"A porch, right?"

"That's about right, little lady." Jerry's eyes twinkled. "My grandpappy used to get up to some meehonkey over to that warehouse when it were abandoned. Fireworks, that's what he liked. He told me how they sounded in that big, hollow place. He was quamished when that company come up to make it into condos."

Brannigan filled in, "That's where the Currituck Knights live now, only they aren't Knights, either."

Emily laughed. "You know this story?"

"Just parts. Jerry's been chatting me up. That's why I knew y'all guys would be interested."

"I want to know how these people aren't Knights."

"Jerry?" Brannigan opened the floor to the maintenance man.

"No one knows the whole story, but I got more of it than most. Now, hold on before you toss in your questions. I'll get to that in a bit." Jerry had green tomatoes and cheese from the deli, and he put the two together and took a bite. He chewed and swallowed before going on. "Juno Brayboy, you heard'a her?"

Nathan started to answer, as Diane had mentioned her just the day before, but Emily cut him off. She wanted to hear Jerry's version.

"No, I haven't. Please tell me, Jerry." She smiled sweetly.

"Worked for the Knights in the big house, likely late twenties. That's last century twenties. Turned up with a baby, called Old Man Knight the daddy. Don't know if he was, maybe Juno couldn't say who the real daddy was. Well, when the old man died in the thirties, t'weren't a way to know after that, and it was Knight Juno put on the boy's birth certificate, so Knight he was. His name were Creighton. Samuel were Creighton and Sally's son, along with Gippy and Lucie. You'd know Gippy if you seen him."

Jerry paused and Brannigan added, "He drives an old yellow Corolla. He's all over the Upper Banks." He pronounced it the Toyota way, Co-*roll*-la, rather than the town way, Co-*rahl*-la.

"Old Gippy likes to shotgun some moonshine when he comes to visit." Jerry nodded with a grin.

"Real moonshine?" Nathan's enthusiasm overruled Emily's attempts to hush him.

"Shush. I'm interested." To Jerry, "Besides Gippy, is Samuel the only Knight left from Juno's family?"

"That'd be taking us down Tobacco Road, now wouldn't it?" Jerry chuckled and took up the story again. "Gippy and Bette had Ruthie and the twins, Lavie and Sukie. Sister Lucie married a Cadillac salesman in Trent. Their two live out of town, the boy, John, in New York. Their daughter, she's a looker. Nearly won a beauty pageant and now teaches in Goldsboro."

"And Samuel's children? Where are they?"

"Charlie died of breast cancer in the eighties." Jerry shook his head mournfully. "Likely the reason the old man is like he is today. God playing meehonkey with the old fella's life, leaving him in a pinch without a good woman."

"No children then."

"Said that, now, didn't I?" Jerry didn't seem irritated. Instead, he grinned. "It's them French cousins that had too many. Whatever moonshine they been drinking makes for twins, that's sure as hoi toid on the sound soid."

"We just dealt with two of your twins." Wally had been enjoying his sandwich and listening at the same time. "Creighton and Philippe."

"It's a slickcam day when those two don't stir the sand." Jerry nodded. "Give me a good O'Cocker any occasion, and I'll see you a better man. What's them boys up to now?"

Wally sketched a loose version of the recent events, while leaving out any incriminating details. Jerry nodded, grinned with appreciation a few times, and laughed at Creighton trying to do a "runner" when they came out of the clinic. The rest dug into their food during Wally's tale, and for a time afterwards, the "field party" inside the market was focused on the food and not the reason they were there.

Finally, Emily couldn't contain her questions any longer, and she asked Jerry, "You said twins. Besides Creighton and Philippe, there are others?"

"Go visit that warehouse up to Currituck. You'll see. Colford and Marie, them has two normal kids, though one of 'em is in school in France. Then there's Collie, Colford's half-brother, and his four siblings: Jean-Paul and Charles-Edouard—them's the boys—and then there's Marie Louise and Dorthea, both pretty as can be but not a nice one among the lot of 'em."

"Charles-Edouard. Samuel mentioned him. He asked if we had seen him at the dock in Corolla Beach." Emily's interest perked up.

"Wasn't he one of the two men we saw at the beach? He called the other one Creighton." Nathan was paying special attention now, revealing his newfound excitement at the possible connection.

"You know 'em." Jerry's eyes narrowed, and he pursed his lips in thought. "Might not know this."

To Jerry's side, Brannigan fought a smile. Clearly, this was why he had requested their attendance.

"Okay, Jerry." Emily prepared herself. "Shoot."

"Shoot. That's a good'n. I like you." Jerry's eyes flicked from officer to officer. "That ferry to Currituck, sometimes I ride along. Seen some things. Might see some more things, things no good hoi toider oughta see."

"Tell me, Jerry." Emily leaned forward, giving the man her complete attention, hoping to drag it from him before her curiosity killed her.

"Drug mules. Seen some, come down from up to Virginia the overland way. Ride the ferry, once in the boot of a car. Sometimes they come back, sometimes not. One of 'em stayed. Be right nice to her, and she might help you out in your investigation."

Emily wasn't sure it was an investigation. The jury was out on that. She wasn't even sure they had confirmed the crime. And she had completely lost track while following Jerry's rendition of the family tree, but she *was* interested.

This was a woman she wanted to meet. She burned with anticipation.

ON THE RETURN ferry to Currituck, Emily's head swam with the Knotts Island tidepool from the evening before. Jerry had been just the hors d'oeuvres among the sharks, with stories of fish swimming in ponds that she never imagined fish in.

Amanda Sargeant linked both the Corolla Knights and the Currituck branch of the family. She didn't belong to either, but she had made herself a part of both as a survival mechanism. She agreed to meet with the officers but not at her home. Would Jerry please pick her up?

"I'm glad to meet you people." Amanda was a waif, slim with long blonde hair and a clear complexion, but the shadows under her eyes suggested more. She seemed hesitant to sit at the table as if unsure of her welcome, either that or she was frightened of something.

"Hello, Amanda." Emily spoke brightly. "Come sit here. My friend, Nathan, won't mind standing, will you, Nathan?" Nathan hesitated until Emily moved sideways on the bench, hissed, "Now, Nathan," and forced him aside.

"You people been eatin'." Amanda took the spot but looked longingly at the deli counter.

"Would you like something?" Emily pulled out a twenty and offered it to Nathan. "What would you like?"

"I reckon … nah, just an apple. That's all."

"Roast beef, Nathan. And a bag of chips, oh, a soda. What flavor, Amanda?" When Amanda shrugged, Emily motioned for Nathan to head to the counter.

Jerry watched the interchange protectively but allowed the officers to steer the conversation. Amanda was from a holler up in Apple-ATCH-uh; she'd left her favorite hound dog behind when she'd headed out to the coast; and her momma, a widow woman since Amanda was five, had died the previous year. She'd been on the streets when she met up with Charles-Edouard, who'd offered her an opportunity to make some money.

The money had come with strings, and Amanda figured she was now entangled for life. Leastways, it seemed that way.

She quit talking when the roast beef arrived, and for a time, Emily watched the poor thing eat. The first half of the sandwich evaporated before the woman slowed, pushed the rest away, and pressed her hand against her stomach, claiming that she hadn't eaten like that in weeks, but it was as fine as grits on toast, and thank you.

"We've met Charles-Edouard." Emily smiled to encourage a connection.

"What's he gone and done now?" Amanda closed her eyes and seemed to cringe.

"We were on the shore, and he was with Creighton." Emily didn't have much else, so she offered her final tidbit.

"I might expect." Amanda wilted more and then seemed to gather herself together. "DeDe, Charles' niece, came to stay with me once. Charles wasn't happy."

"Oh? Why was that?" Emily again.

"He says I should go there, to The Wharf, but it gives me the shivers. I like Corolla better."

"Oh?" Emily caught Brannigan's grin. She realized Amanda was about to reveal something the Currituck County officer wanted her to hear. "Why is that, Amanda?"

"Lavie." The blonde-haired waif smiled, even as she refused to look at anyone in the group. The silence swelled as the team allowed the young woman to proceed at her own comfort level.

"Who's Lavie?" Nathan broke the ice.

Emily rolled her eyes and wanted to throttle the man, but Jerry stepped in and asked, "Amanda, may I?" She shrugged, and he encouraged her with, "I was telling a right nice story about Suki and Lavie before you got here. I can continue? You won't mind, will you?"

At a second shrug, Jerry began to fill them in. Suki and Lavie were younger twin daughters to Gippy and Bette Knight. They were born Suzanne and Laverne, but no one knew them by those names any longer. Both Suki and Lavie lived down to Corolla. "Auntie Lavie," as she preferred, painted island scenes for the tourist trade. She liked the beach but maintained a small place on Knotts Island, with a powered motor skiff for going back and forth.

The motor skiff was important, he clarified, as the ferry didn't go to the shore side of the Sound, only between Currituck and Knotts.

During their conversation and while Amanda ate, Emily noted the tracks on the young woman's arms; and recalling Charles' demand to "find that bag" while on the beach, she began to fill in the blanks. Romeo and Juliette were Lavie and Amanda. The young woman's involvement with Charles was likely one of drug-fueled necessity, although Emily doubted Charles knew about Lavie. Most importantly, Jerry had said one of Charles' drug mules had stayed, and he had obviously brought her to meet them.

On the ferry, Nathan joined Emily at the railing, with the breeze on their faces pushing away the slightly sour aroma from the watery spray. He leaned in on his elbows and asked, "You think Amanda was one of them drug mules? If so, did she carry them, um, you know, inside?"

"I don't know but likely." Emily kept her face into the wind to keep from crying at the young deputy's question. She couldn't even bring herself to prank him after learning Amanda's story. "Brannigan gave me two contacts. I've got their names here."

She pulled out a slip of paper from her pocket and handed it to him. In what must be Brannigan's blocky print, it listed two people: NARC Officers Willis Washington and Kenneth Contras.

As he returned it to her, Wally called from the car, "Hey, you two. Been on the radio with the captain. She told us to take our time but things seem to be getting thick as molasses on toast—"

"She said what?" Emily had never heard Diane Turnipseed say such a thing.

"Sure." Wally tipped his cap to her censure. "Let me tell it like she said it. According to the captain, her words, not mine, she was about at high tide, and her waders were about to be swamped." He grinned.

"That sounds like her. What else did she say?"

"She's called in the cavalry. Someone from C-District she said you might know."

"I know everyone from C-District." At least the old crew. Some spots had been filled with people she hadn't met. She called out those she knew were still there. "Mary? Cynthia?"

"Nah, someone named Taylor."

"Sean Taylor?" Emily laughed, and in that name, the Sound smelled fresher, and she found herself anticipating arriving in Currituck. "She hates the man. Why's he on the way up here?"

Sean was the former "new guy" down in C-District, a tailor-made poster boy for every recruitment pamphlet ever produced. He had become enthralled with drone pilot Deputy Clifton Magruder from Carteret County and had immersed himself in training to set up a dedicated drone operator's position in Dare County. He had transferred to Manteo and was available for callout anywhere needed in the county. Emily ran into him occasionally at the main Manteo facility. She still pranked him when she could, but he was growing wise to her shenanigans.

Still, new location, new opportunities for fun!

Wally interrupted her plans by pointing skyward. "Look there, missy. That's why."

Overhead, towards the shore near Currituck, a speck in the sky buzzed. It seemed to recognize that it had been located, and it appeared to pause. Emily remembered that when a drone didn't appear to be moving, it was coming directly at them.

"Yikes," she said, and she grabbed Nathan's arm and said, "Inside the car, now!"

They got inside just as the drone dove at the car and released a water balloon that hit the windshield square and sent water flying. The ferry horn sounded, whether because they were approaching the landing or because of the drone, who knew? By the time Wally had the wipers on and the windshield cleared, the drone was already away and over the trees.

"Paybacks?" Wally grinned.

"You know me too well, but likely," Emily said. Her window hadn't been closed all the way, and she used her blanket to dry her arm. "Just wait until he sees what's coming."

"You sure about that?" Wally laughed and lowered his window to prepare for offloading the ferry.

Emily caught sight of Sean Taylor, now wearing a sergeant's insignia as the official Dare County Drone Operator. The man still preferred his lifted Jeep, even on calls, and had the tailgate with its massive offroad spare swung sideways and was sitting on the short cargo ledge with his feet up and resting on the chromed bumpers. His arms were on his knees, and he held the drone's controller in his hands. He waved at Wally's patrol car and glanced up to where the drone hovered overhead. The small machine dropped to the ground, where it landed, and the fans jerked to a stop. Sean stood, put the controller in the Jeep, and knelt to lift the drone and inspect it.

Inside the Jeep, a basket overfilled with water balloons sparked Emily's imagination. She could use the man's own pranks against him. "You don't know who you're dealing with, Sean Taylor," she muttered.

"What's that?" Nathan pulled himself forward to be heard through the barrier between the two compartments.

"Better said, *who's* that?" Wally pointed to two men walking toward them wielding baseball bats, and he pulled the car to the side of the road. The first one was familiar from the day before, both at the dock and then on the beach while disturbing the taped-off crime scene. The man at his side was twin-similar, although with a strikingly slender build and reddish-blond hair past his shoulders rather than copper.

Both men glared at the faded logo on the side of the white cruiser.

Emily said, "Charles-Edouard and Jean-Paul."

Nathan knocked on the dividing barrier. "You know them?"

"I just walk in the sand and soak up my information from there." She snorted with impatience. "I listened to Jerry. He mentioned their names together. Twins, remember, lots of 'em?"

"I don't like the looks of this." Wally's voice matched his words.

"No need to ask. I got me the solution." Nathan began searching the doors for exit handles, and there were none. "Wally, let me out."

"Hold up." She caught sight of Brannigan's Currituck County vehicle tucked in an out-of-the-way location, and for a moment, she thought someone would get out and set the two men on their ears. The she noted the trailer for the Zodiac and knew that if the brothers did mean trouble, she might as well throw handfuls of sand at them.

She pulled up the radio mic. "Emily Bryant with Dare County. We are at the Currituck ferry landing and are being approached by two men, likely Charles-Edouard and Jean-Paul—" She covered the mic and looked at Wally. "Did you catch their last names?"

"Beaumarchais."

"Beaumarchais," she said into the mic. "They are carrying baseball bats. Anyone? Emily over."

"Sheriff Barnett here, Emily. Glad to hear our southern cousins are up and giving us a shout. It might take me a minute to provide assistance. How urgent is your situation? Over."

"Unsure, Sheriff. We had a run-in with Charles-Edouard yesterday—" Wally held up two fingers, and Emily amended her count. "—and then another at a crime scene we were reviewing."

"Yah, the one Turnipseed contacted me about. Brannigan's got himself cocked up on that. You got an escort there with you?"

"I'm with Wally Styles in his patrol car. Deputy Nathan

Preston is in the back seat. We met with Brannigan on Knotts Island, and he's on his way back. I think his car is directly in front of us."

"I know the two men. Good thinking radioing in. I'll be there to bail you out. Watch your back until I arrive."

Emily replaced the mic onto its holder and glanced back at Nathan. He was focused on the approaching men. A tap on the front fender pulled her attention forward. Jean-Paul had the end of his bat resting on the car as he glared through the windshield, while the bigger, more muscular Charles-Edourard walked towards the driver's side. His face tensed in a scowl, and he grasped the bat's handle in both hands and tossed it back over his shoulder as he prepared to swing.

His scowl turned to fury when the bat was yanked out of his hands. He twisted his head around and spat, "Do you want a slap on the he—" before freezing.

"Didn't expect me, did you, Charles?" Brannigan tossed the bat up, caught it on the handle, and did two practice swings. "Thanks for the new bat. Hey, Jean-Paul, I need that one, too. It's my Christmas present for my nephew. He told me to tell you thanks."

"That's a good one," Jean-Paul retorted. "Such a silly boy."

"I'm not the one who was a fashion model back in France. Pretty boy indeed." Brannigan laughed. "Hand it over."

Emily breathed easier with Brannigan in control. She was no longer sure Currituck County was for her, especially when she pictured Amanda Sargent, "girlfriend" to these men's brother.

Drug mule.

That's what the man had forced on her, and seeing these two in action, she had no doubt these two minnows didn't swim too far from the tidepool.

Thank you, Jerry, she thought. Thank you for the heads-up. Now if she could just find some sand to scrub the residue of these people from her day …

But that wasn't happening right then. She opened the door, asked Brannigan what she could do to help, and then faced the ultimate surprise.

A motorcycle officer, helmeted and in leathers, pulled up, stood, and slipped off his helmet to reveal a tall, fit man with thick, cropped hair gone prematurely gray.

"Sheriff William Barnett. I promised you I'd be here." He saw her taking in the bike and explained. "I used to be a motor-man. It's in my blood. You must be Emily, and you, Wally, and the man locked in the back seat?"

"Oh, my word, Wally. We forgot Nathan." Emily released Nathan using the outside handle. "I'm so sorry, Nathan."

"She was pranking you," Sean Taylor called from the back of his Jeep.

"I was not. You could have come and helped, Sean."

"My fault." Sheriff Barnett. "He was on the radio to me, too, just after you. I told him to hold back."

"Why? If Brannigan hadn't showed up just in time, they could have smashed the car window." Emily was amazed at the arrogance of some men.

"But he did show up, and I had a good excuse to get out on my bike. To change the topic, how's that new sheriff down there? Glynne, isn't it? Ollie Glynne?"

Emily didn't know if her opinion of the Currituck County sheriff had just gone up or down. Whichever, she thought, *Yes, Sheriff Barnett, I will watch my back. Thank you for the warning.*

The Beaumarchais twins were soon sent packing, both batless and with a warning; Brannigan backed his trailer to load the Zodiac; and Emily once again claimed the front seat for the ride back to Kitty Hawk. When Wally drove away, Sean was deep in discussion with Sheriff Barnett at the back of Sean's Jeep.

The sand? Who cared about the sand?

What she looked forward to was a long, hot shower. No dead bodies. No women used as drug mules. No men carrying baseball bats. Just her and her shower head and all the hot water in the world.

It didn't occur to her to wonder why Sean Taylor was in Currituck County about as far away from his old haunts in C-District as he could get and still remain south of the Virginia border.

And in conversation with the local sheriff.

But then, bare feet and salty hair on an overnight to Knotts Island had become too much even for a beach-loving girl like Emily Bryant.

Chapter 5

Sabotage on the Sound

CAPTAIN DIANE TURNIPSEED braced against the offshore breeze. Her hair fought her hand and refused to stay behind her ear, and the fabric of her uniform whipped and snapped around her. She muttered, "Might could be a gale if the weatherman chooses to call it such."

She was meeting with Currituck County Marine Patrol Officers Barker and Krazinski—at Sheriff Barnett's request—on the beach where the bag of drugs had been recovered. They knew that now. Testing had verified the contents.

The other items collected from the area were on their way to Raleigh for further processing. She had put a rush on them, but then, everything that went to Raleigh fell into a bottomless fish basket. Retrieval was by chance, not design, she sometimes thought.

"I bet tomorrow's breakfast we can do this from my car."

Diane fought against the soft sand as she approached Sergeant Scotty Barker. "You done seen all this before. You might be above your knees to think you'll get anything new from this today."

Between the two officers, Barker was her number one choice for interaction. His solid waistline and ruddy complexion lent him an aura of experience in comparison to Deputy Dillon Krazinski's fresh face, freckles, and strawberry hair. A stickler for procedure versus an eager beaver. There was no comparison to Diane.

To substantiate her claim about the crime scene, one section of police tape, already flapping from two days of buffeting wind, lost its grip on one wooden stake, broke, and began flailing like an octopus having a conniption fit.

"Your forensic investigator's lead yesterday—" Barker continued to talk, but a gust of wind whipped his words away.

"For all sakes, tell me that again." Diane had her back to the water, and her hair fought against her face, becoming a torrent of unwelcome irritation on top of being on this beach when she had better things to do. She used both hands to pull it to the back of her neck and held it with one to leave the other free.

"The license plate." Barker grinned. "Krazinski and I wanted to quit jawing and step in and get involved."

"How does me being out here help?" The wind blasted again, and Diane fought to stay standing. The strawberry Krazinski was a good distance away, trying to rescue the snapped tape and wiping sand from his face.

"Inter-county cooperation." Barker knelt at a place where the wind had peeled away the top of a small dune, and he brushed at it, then pushed his hand inside and pulled up. He revealed a brass shell cartridge. He looked at her and grinned. "Missed one!"

"You might could retrieve it then."

"Plan on it." He pulled a bag from his pocket. Using a sliver of driftwood, he inserted it into the cartridge and transferred it to the bag, folding the top over and slipping it into his pocket.

"You're not going to mark anything on that bag?" Maybe not a stickler for procedure.

"No pen." He stood.

"Hold your taters." Diane worked hers from her shirt pocket and offered it to him. "What's Krazinski doing over there?"

Her question was valid. The man had knelt beside the wooden stake and had a multitool out and was picking at the end. He had the loose end of one-half of the tape in his other hand.

"God knows." He shook his head, marked the bag, offered the pen back to Diane, and returned the bag to his pocket. "Dillon, we need to hustle. What'cha doing?"

"Putting the tape back. It came loose." He held up the multitool to show he was prepared and meant business.

"The captain and I know that. Leave it and get over here."

The younger man stood, holding both the multitool and the tape. He looked from one to the other, closed the multitool with his thumb, slipped it into a pocket, and seemed disappointed to release the tape before heading their direction.

Despite her protests, Diane knew why Sheriff Barnett had requested her to meet with the two Marine Patrol officers. With her own sheriff off to a family reunion in West Virginia, she had reached her hand into Currituck County's fish basket and hauled in the evidence retrieved from the crime scene. Her request wasn't untoward. Dare County did carry greater influence with Raleigh, and that would get the processing done quicker, despite Diane feeling like she had dumped the material into a bottomless hole. More importantly, events were transpiring in Dare

County, not only in Currituck. She'd be no better'n a leaf peeper if she looked and left, expecting someone else to clean up after her.

Having exhausted the scene with only one shell cartridge to show for it, the three people retreated to the road and out of the onslaught of sand and wind. Back with their cars, she quizzed Barker.

"Why the license plate? Brayboy nonsense has been bleeding into my county for a long time. You know all the participants." She had put it together already, but she wanted to make sure Currituck was on her page.

"You know Washington and Contras've been looking for a link between the Wharf bunch and several drug busts."

Diane followed him fine. She had met with the NARC officers from the neighboring county, Willis Washington and Kenneth Contras. Willis' badge touted him as Wilson but everyone knew him by his nickname, so that was fine with her. The Wharf bunch had to be the Currituck branch of the Brayboy feud. She'd dropped off Philippe and Creighton just two nights before.

Diane said, "We've not busted anyone." Not yet, not with Raleigh lagging behind.

"Why do you think this *situation* happened on the *beach*?" The "situation" was the bag of drugs, the clothing, and the gun and shell casings.

"To tell the story honest, it seems you already know. You tell me, Sergeant Barker."

The thing was, Diane did already know. It had happened in C-District when a family was abducted from their yacht by drug smugglers and nearly killed on Ocracoke Island. Intercoastal waters, the Currituck Sound, even Pamlico Sound were easy to monitor. There might be a lot of territory in those waters, but they were self-contained with limited entry and exit points.

The Atlantic Ocean was a big fish to wrestle into your net. Storms could take you out and waves could batter your landing craft, but once you were on the shore ... no one could monitor a hundred miles of open beach one hundred percent of the time. Not with the horizon unbroken for three thousand miles to the African continent.

Of course, the Caribbean was closer, and that's where the drugs likely originated, but still, you find a fish head in a raccoon's paws, and it's still a fish head, no matter where it comes from.

Yes, Barker, dump it on her, all of it, but she was already on his page. Dare County and Currituck County might be in cooperation to find the raccoon, but this needed something more. The only question was whether the Coast Guard might be interested. Multiple Agency Cooperation? She felt she was about to put her spoon into their pot, and she wondered what she would stir up when she did.

"FOR ALL SAKES, Deputy Taylor! Dump it on me. You here to see what the slack tide's turned up, or is there another reason for you to come all this way to put your spoon into our pot?"

He was crouched behind Paloma's desk and engaged with Roxie, but like a flea on a ship's cat, when it bites, you recognize it immediately. He stood, grinned, and said, "It's lieutenant now, ma'am."

"Just keeping you on your toes—"

"Or Sean," he said with a grin. "That would do."

"And you could make a change and become the man your parents wisht you would be." She said that quieter and caught Paloma shaking her head but very intentionally not involving herself in the conversation.

"How'd you know it was me?" His bright expression had yet to fade. He kept his hand on Roxie's neck and worked his fingers into her coat.

"I can't miss that car you drive, now can I?'

"Jeep, ma'am. I mean, it's a car, sure, but it's really a Jeep. Sheriff Glynne offered me a new one like yours, and I said to let Jason have it, if that was okay with him. I didn't see the new car, but Jason's truck is outside. I guess I'm saying I've got no regrets giving it up, but I thought Jason would be driving it. Have you seen—"

"It's not like I weren't listening now, was it, Taylor? Am I just now walking in the door? Did you see me open it and step through? Oh, right, you were here and watched Paloma call me on the radio and tell me Jason's exact location. That's a big no because it didn't happen. We're good?"

"Yes, ma'am, we're good." Sean's enthusiasm continued to leak through, and his grin broke out once more. "And it's not all that far. I live in Kill Devil Hills. I can stop by any time. Now about Jason's truck—"

"Don't you worry yourself about it, Taylor."

"Sorry, ma'am. I might better." He gave Roxie a final pat and stood. "Good dog. She reminds me of Toby." Toby was the C-District K9 until he retired after being injured in a shootout.

"I wisht ..." Diane muttered before admitting that some things weren't hers to wish away. "Dump it on me, Taylor. What are you saying?"

"I have a new apartment, and Jason's taking my spare bedroom. He wasn't in Manteo, so when I saw his truck here, I thought I could drop off his new keys."

"Good. You can take his truck with you. We picked up his new Explorer yesterday, and he's having the lights and sirens installed. Thought you might know that, what with being bosom buddies now, or am I getting above my knees?"

"We're not living together *yet*." Sean pulled out the set of keys. "He needs these first."

"Say the rest of it." Paloma finally decided to enter the conversation, and she looked up at him from her keyboard. "Some people can't come in out of the rain without gettin' soaked. You, boy, tell her about that helicopter you're so excited about."

"Helicopter." The one word was all Diane could get out. Then, "Coast Guard?" She cringed when Sean's grin grew into a full smile. "I bet tomorrow's breakfast I'm not gonna like what I hear."

"Sheriff Barnett asked me to come up to help out, since they don't yet have one of me." Sean's chest puffed in pride. "I wasn't busy, so the guys at Manteo sent me on up."

"For?" Dump it on me, Taylor, and do it quick.

"Shoot, I'm doing nothing except showing 'em they can count on me. The sheriff up there's been searching for some missing boats. I said, what's a drone for except to fly about searching for missing things? Only, when I got there, Sheriff Barnett showed me where he wanted to search, and no regrets, cause like I said, they can depend on me, but Currituck Sound is big."

He paused to take a breath, and Paloma muttered, "Like my grandpappy always said, sardines in a can know everyone's business. Now I'm knowing everything."

"For all sakes, Taylor, even the help's tired of hearing the story. You're above your knees if you don't wrap this up." Diane still hadn't made it past the reception room, and she did have work to get done.

"Sheriff Barnett said all he needed from me was—"

Sean was interrupted when the door attempted to open, only

to find Captain Turnipseed standing in the way.

"Hey, Paloma, what the—" Clearly Jason's voice.

"Hold your taters, Jason," Diane chided him as she moved out of the way and let him enter.

"Sean, perfect." Jason grinned. "Good afternoon, Paloma. How's the best front desk operator in the district doing today?"

"I'm doing, Jason, and it's better'n you be doing if you doan finish up and get on outta here." She cut her eyes to Diane and back again.

"Oh, hello, Diane. Can I borrow Sean for a while? I'll get him back before you miss him. Oh, and Roxie, too."

"I was trying to hoggletie a tall tale before it grew tall as a beanstalk." She dropped her things into a chair. "Thank you for rescuing me. You can have Roxie if you promise to keep the deputy."

Jason laughed. "I should'a expected that. Roxie! Come, girl. You, too, *Sergeant* Taylor."

The dog stood, paused to look at Diane, and waited until she nodded her head before leaping forward to join Jason.

As they clicked Roxie's leash to her harness and exited the building, Diane overheard Sean, "I'm a hundred percent here a hundred percent of the time for you, Jason, whatever you have planned. What are we doing now?"

Jason replied just before the door closed, "I got the new Explorer's lights hooked up …"

The door closed behind them, and Diane muttered, "Them men don't got the sense that God gave a minnow."

"Yes'm, I suppose you're right about that. Now you head on into your office, 'cause I got me some work to do."

As Diane closed the door behind her, she remembered that she still didn't know what the helicopter was for … or what division it was from. The Coast Guard seemed most probable, but for what reason?

One thing was certain, Sean Taylor hadn't changed. Be positive for a positive life ... better, before the sun comes up, pull up your pants and become the man your parents wisht you'd be, Sean Taylor, then get on back to Manteo and leave A-District in peace.

She knew better. If Taylor was teaming up with Jason Romney, there was no peace to be found. She closed her eyes, thought of a good cuppa blackie, and tried to decide if it was worth braving Paloma to reach the coffee pot.

She eventually decided it was, and she opened the door and headed out.

WITH HER CUP of coffee steaming—her "cuppa blackie"—and her office door closed, the staccato tapping of Paloma's old-fashioned and outdated typewriter was the only sound that invaded Diane's peace. She closed her eyes and tried to remember why she had run from C-District so hard.

Right. Jason Romney, and he hadn't stayed where he belonged.

He hadn't exactly followed her to A-District, but the Manteo office was just around the corner, so to speak, and as the new district-wide detention officer assigned to the county lockup in Manteo, the entire county was his new playground. She had run as far as she could, and he had ensured that she had no escape.

Then there was Sean Taylor. To tell the story honest, his hands were always digging in the bait bucket and stirring up the muck. Just when she thought she had his nose to the grindstone, he thought up another way to break her focus. She admitted that he showed moments of brilliance, but she wisht his spoon would stir someone else's pot.

And then that helicopter.

Just that morning, she had faced the prospect of calling in the Coast Guard to cover the coastline for signs of possible drug smuggling, and she returned to the sub-station only to learn that Taylor had beat her to it. What he'd *done* she didn't mind. It was one more fish off her line. It was that *Taylor* had done it that loaded up her thoughts with frustration and, yes, guilt. It seemed the man just needed some space to run, only she wisht it was someone else's space the man was running in.

She opened her door to find Paloma's hands above the keys on her typewriter and her eyes watching Diane. "I'm heading to the radio room. Don't let me disturb you."

"You never do."

"By all sakes, then why'd you stop typing?" It seemed everyone was above their knees today.

"Just lettin' you get on about your business. Then I can get on about mine. Two ways about this. You can stand there talking and neither of us getting anything done. Or you can go do what you're planning to do, and we both get everything done."

"It t'weren't like I wasn't fixing to," Diane muttered as she moved past Paloma's desk and toward the radio room.

"I may look white, but some people ..." and Paloma faded into the background of the general office machines as they hummed, buzzed, and cycled to do their respective duties.

Diane pulled out the chair and flipped a switch to engage with the wireless, and light background chatter hummed from the speaker. Sean and Jason were, thankfully, fully occupied, and anyway, they weren't assigned to the A-District patrol area. By rank, she had command over them, but in practice, they weren't hers and could be where they wanted without Diane's say so. She had hoped to offer Roxie to Ed to babysit until Sheriff Glynne returned from his wife's family reunion. Dogs were his thing, and he would at least have one, even if it was no more than a rescue. Jason had just put a hole in that bucket. Wally and Nathan, along with Emily Bryant, had survived a night out to Knotts Island, a place Diane had never dreamed of wanting to visit. There was nothing there except houses and fields, unless you counted the one road that took you all the way into Virginia, and who cared about Virginia?

That left Clara Del Ray. The woman was at deputy status, meaning she was still working her way up the ladder, but she seemed to have her head about her. Her references from Brunswick County glowed brighter than a full moon on a calm sea. Whatever her reasons for coming to Dare County, work here was slow compared to the woman's former position in Brunswick, and Diane could see that she wanted more do to.

She pressed the talk button and said, "Captain Diane Turnipseed calling Deputy Clara Del Ray. You out there, Clara? Diane over."

When Clara responded with, "Clara here, Captain," Diane was surprised to hear the distinctive chop of helicopter rotors in the background.

"Clara, Ed there with you?"

"No, ma'am. Two officers from Manteo and half of Currituck County, though."

"What are y'all doing?" The helicopter, she meant. Earlier, Sean had started to tell her, but Jason had appeared. She guessed they had sorted out Jason's truck, because she hadn't seen them since.

"The county drone operator—" *Taylor!* "—and his companion—" *Likely Jason!* "—are using a drone to help direct the Coast Guard in searching for a damaged boat. I don't know all the details, ma'am, as there's a lot going on right now, but I think the sheriff requested the use of our drone operator to cover places the helicopter can't easily see."

It sounded like Taylor. "Exactly where are you?"

"On the shore of Currituck Sound ... um ... I'm looking around for a good landmark. There's a big building on the water—"

"The Wharf in big letters?"

"You know it, then."

"Better than I want. If you think it'll be another half hour, I'll coming up."

"Yes, ma'am. I expect so. I'll see you then."

She was surprised to see Paloma standing at the coffee machine filling her thermos. When the woman handed it to her, she didn't question how she knew, just said thanks and headed out the door.

Jason Romney and Sean Taylor. They had better not be embarrassing her with the Currituck County sheriff. If so, they were so far above their knees that they might never make it back to the shore.

The drive to The Wharf was a repeat of two days before, the same as to and from her home in Elizabeth City. Diane backed out of the sub-station lot, headed out past the Wright Brothers National Monument, and turned north out of Kill Devil Hills and through Kitty Hawk, where she hooked left across the entrance to Currituck Sound. The route took her across the Wright Memorial Bridge to Point Harbor and on up along the North River to Barco. There, her normal route changed, taking 168 north to Currituck, the village, but cutting right out to Bells Island, which thrust deep into Currituck Sound, before actually reaching Currituck.

The tip of Bell's Island, a giant arrowhead of landscaped leaf peepers' houses, many of which she was certain were seasonal, wasn't her goal. Neither was the campground at the very tip. She, instead, aimed her harpoon at the parcel of county cars schooling near the old Knight warehouse facing the Sound. Its faded words across the back side looked even more tired in the daylight than they had two evenings earlier.

"To tell the story honest," Diane muttered, "I don't see Clara's car."

Clara would be in one of the old county sedans, still perfectly functional, the same model as the ones still in use in C-District, but up for replacement, as vouched for by Jason Romney's new SUV.

The tide pool of cars near the old warehouse included a black SUV with the Currituck County logo and a stripe that wrapped up and across the hood. It nosed in next to a white sedan with "Sheriff" in large letters and Currituck just above it. No logo, suggesting it had been in service for a while.

Unlike Diane's Explorer, the black Currituck SUV boasted a Chevy Tahoe badge, while the sedan appeared to be a Ford Crown Vic of an era when they were all the rage for law enforcement entities. Light rust around the window frames suggested it might not be in use much longer.

Closer, Diane searched for good parking. Only then did she see Jason's new Explorer, and just on the other side, the Dare County sedan assigned to Clara. She gave up on a sensible parking location and pulled longways behind them both.

"I'll move my car, Jason," she growled to herself as she opened her door. "You might could just ask."

One additional Currituck County car surprised her. A black Chevrolet Camaro, striped to match the black Tahoe, with tinted windows, a concealed lightbar in the front window, and auxiliary lights in the grille. It boasted fancy chrome wheels to match.

"They're above their knees if they take that to the beach," she said, before dismissing it from her notice. Closer to the water, Clara waved and walked in her direction. She held Roxie's leash, and the dog seemed on high alert, heeling properly and responding to Clara's every motion.

Diane called, "I know I weren't imagining things. I heard a helicopter over the radio. Where is it?"

"Up towards the northern end of the Sound. Jason joined them, and since no one was left to take care of Roxie, she's mine."

"Jason was with Sean Taylor. They both had the dog. So tell the story honest. Did Taylor abandon the animal, too?"

"Oh, nobody's abandoned Roxie." Clara knelt and wrapped an arm around the neck of the brown and black Belgian Malinois and gave her a quick ruffle behind her ears. "I volunteered. Sean's working the drone for the sheriff and couldn't do both at the same time."

"Who else is here?" Diane knew many of the people working in the Currituck County office, though not as well as she might wish. Her house in Elizabeth City was in Pasquotank County, but she drove through Currituck County to work each day. She knew them well enough to wave, even if she didn't know their children and significant others.

"Jason and Sean, and there's Sheriff Barnett. He came on that motorcycle." As she stood, she pointed to a bulky black bike in the Currituck County livery that matched the one on the Tahoe and the Camaro. "The sheriff is on the radio with the helicopter. It hasn't landed since taking off, and I wasn't here then, so I haven't met the operators. Oh, and the Camaro. That belongs to School Resource Officer Jared Johnson. He's here."

"Hold your taters. I know of Johnson. He's likely a deputy to be a school resource officer. They gave him that to drive?" Diane knew Sheriff Barnett well enough that she wouldn't expect that of him. Besides, let Taylor get wind, and no telling what he'd be asking Manteo for next.

"That's what I thought." Clara smiled. "Jared said it was confiscated from a drug bust. The sheriff allocated it to him for public relations with the school system."

"I bet tomorrow's breakfast the deputy didn't think to say no."

"No, I don't suppose he would." Roxie was sitting attentively at Clara's feet, and Clara asked, "You want to head down, Captain, and see what's going on?"

"Yes. You might could fill me in while we walk."

After the news of Brannigan Calmont's boat being sabotaged and creating a bit of excitement the day before, Diane expected something of the sort. If they wanted clues to the likely culprits, they only needed to look to that big building on the water. She knew two of the men who lived there, and she'd also learned that one of them might have been involved with Brannigan's misadventure. That was enough to paint guilty on them, for all she was concerned.

Clara shared that they weren't looking for a police boat. This was a suspected drug runner, one that had damaged a smaller boat and hit a dock, causing the boat house at the end to collapse.

"For all sakes, they can't find the boat that done all that with a helicopter?" Diane wondered at the minnows at the rudder of the helicopter if they couldn't find a damaged boat after it had mutilated someone's dock. About that time, a faint whop-whop echoed across the water.

"There they are!" Clara pointed, and Roxie faced the direction of the hand, focused and ready for whatever Clara told her to do. "They aren't looking for the boat. Sean found that. It was rammed up on the bank, abandoned. They're looking for the men who were driving it."

"They might could do better with a good K9 unit." In that

moment, she thought of Toby, Cynthia Ellison's dog from C-District. The memory of his injuries in a gunfight hit her hard. She was unfamiliar with Cynthia's new animal, though she trusted that if Cynthia was available, she would drive up to help.

"The sheriff wanted to call in his team, but his K9 officers are tied up on the Northwest River Marsh on the game preserve. That's up on the Virginia bor—"

"It's not like I don't know the game preserve."

"Yes, ma'am." Clara self-consciously reached with her free hand to tuck imaginary stray hair back into the knot at the nape of her neck.

"Don't mind me, Deputy. Go on."

Diane was processing the drive time and whether Cynthia would think Diane was above her knees asking her to come up two days in a row. The county would cover her expenses—fuel, whatnot—but the woman would have to be free.

In any case, Cynthia was now under the command of Captain Burkhalter, the new lead officer over the C-District sub-station. He was a shore person but not from the Banks, and with his toffee skin and bleached hair, he seemed to her a fish caught in a tide pool not of his own making. His tide pool was of the Hawaii sort, not the down-to-earth Bankerism of the North Carolina barrier islands.

Clara continued to fill her in, and Diane took note of both: her thoughts and the situation as the deputy knew it. Roxie was another notch on the stringer, and Diane decided that two for one was the best ratio of all.

"You heard from Ed recently?" They were almost to the covey of officers on the shore, and Diane slowed her pace. Sean Taylor was on an upended bucket, with his drone controller on his knees and his attention on the screen. The bucketing of the surrounding air suggested the helicopter was landing. Any louder or windier, and Diane and Clara would no longer be able to converse.

"Yes." Clara brightened up with good news. She was close to yelling. "He's on the way back from the canine academy in Sanford—"

"Hold your taters. Tarhill? To tell the story honest, he musta left at the crack of dawn."

"Yes'm, I suppose he did. You thinking he could join us?"

"Call him up and let him know I want his spoon in our pot soon's he can get here. I'm calling the C-District sub-station to check on Cynthia Ellison. You met her yesterday."

"With Lucy, yes! I didn't even think to offer the sheriff—"

"You mighta been above your knees if you had, but me, that's different. Before we head down there, you see where Ed is, and I'll check with C-District to see if we can borrow their new K9."

"And her handler." Clara grinned.

"I thought I just said that." Diane already had her phone out, and she stepped away and tapped the icon for Lonnie Burk-halter. She was pleased when it picked up almost immediately.

"Lonnie. Howzit goin'? What can I do for ya'?"

"Captain Burkhalter, Lonnie, this is Diane Turnipseed up in A-District."

"How are you, Captain? You missing us yet? Well, not me, as I wasn't here, but you know what I mean. Sergeant Ellison said she was up there yesterday. By the way, thanks for givin' her some sand time with the new pup. Lucy's been out of sorts with nothin' much to do since things calmed down after you left."

After I left? Was that a sideways critique? Diane shook her head and got to her request. "Lonnie, I'm up here in Currituck County with the sheriff and the Coast Guard. We're looking for two suspected smugglers who hit another boat, took out a dock, and beached their craft before disappearing into the scrub. The Currituck K9 unit is unavailable. I'm pulling in my K9 officer, but you might have heard that new pups are in short supply. Is Cynthia free this afternoon?"

"No problem, Captain. She's been in Manteo all morning and is on a late lunch now. I can give her a call if you want. Where are you exactly?"

"Bells Island."

"That's all? No rights or lefts or anything?"

"She'll know. She needs Lucy with her."

"No problem. So, half an hour? An hour? I'm not sure of the distance."

"About that. Thank you, Lonnie."

"Slippahs on the sand. Later!"

Clara was waiting on her when Diane tucked her phone away, with Roxie squatting patiently at her side.

"You handled a dog before?" Diane thought of Toby. He was all dog, doing dog things except when Cynthia put him to work. This one? Much different. Seeing her in the field with someone else made that apparent.

"Nah, she's just a good one. I didn't even ask her to sit. Ed said he can come the north route through Elizabeth City. He's about three-quarters of an hour out."

"Cynthia's about the same. Let's head down and offer our services to Sheriff Barnett. He might be appreciative that we showed up."

The helicopter was down in a clear spot just off the shore, and Jason Romney was the first to leap out. He waved at Diane and Clara, ran to Sean and clapped him on the shoulder, and leaned down to say something to him. Sean laughed and pointed to the drone coming down a few feet away.

Jason shifted his focus and headed in Diane's direction, calling, "Diane, Clara! You guys here for the fun?"

"Jason, for all sakes—" Diane began.

"Ah, let it go this time, Diane." He was still smiling, and he turned to hold out his arm in Sean's direction. "You see that man? He's found his niche. Everyone up here's loving him. Manteo might be challenged to keep him in Dare County after this."

"That's how it's going, is it?" Diane studied the young deputy, now promoted to sergeant. She tried to see success in the pretty face, the immaculate uniform, and the irritatingly upbeat personality. She needed down to earth and focused, the reason she had called in Cynthia Ellison. "I need to speak with Sheriff Barnett. Jason, you keep Clara and Roxie company. Oh, and Jason, Cynthia's on the way with her new K9, and Clara's called Ed Walters, my new K9 handler. They should both be here in a bit over half an hour. You keep an eye out for 'em, if you don't mind."

"I don't know, Diane. I am the County Detention Officer now." He broke into a grin and said, "Of course. Anything for you. Happy?"

"You are above your knees, Jason. You just do what I ask, and I'll be happy enough."

Diane turned her back on the man. Maybe she needed to be the one to transfer to Currituck County. Even then, he would find a way to harass her. He was hopeless, and that's all she had to say about that.

K9 HANDLER Cynthia Ellison arrived first in an old Jeep Cherokee decorated with rust. Her thick rash of red curls announced her presence as soon as she opened the truck door to move to the back of the vehicle, where her new K9 eagerly waited for her. She flipped up the back gate and said, "Hello, Lucy. Hold a bit, and I'll let you out to do your business."

"Thank you, Cynthia, for giving up part of your day for me." Diane had been watching for her.

"Afternoon, Diane." Cynthia didn't turn around but instead belted the dog's harness around its chest. "The good Lord knows there's not enough good dogs around. Lucy's one of 'em, but like Richie says, a good day's practice is always appreciated."

Cynthia finally turned and smiled at Diane, and she invited the Dutch Shepherd to jump from the bed of the truck. The dog was smaller than Cynthia's previous K9, a German Shepherd named Toby, with short black hair interwoven with brown, and large ears accented by a pinkish-red tongue. She stood for a moment, at attention, with her ears pointed sharply skyward, before moving to the side to squat.

"That's it, Lucy," Cynthia prompted. "We got work to do, and this is step one. Now, Diane." She gave her attention to her former boss. "I know you're dead as a dandelion without a dog up there in A-District, but you know I'm willing to step in any time. How can Lucy and I help today?"

"Two men ..." and Diane went on to describe the situation as she knew it, including that Ed, the A-District's new handler, was on the way, although he wouldn't be with a dog. She hoped Cynthia didn't mind him tagging along, as it would likely be a good experience. *Plug a few holes in his drain bucket to keep him focused on why I put him into our bait bucket.*

Cynthia laughed.

"I spoke with Sheriff Barnett. He said he'd have his K9 team here, but they're at the game preserve up north—"

"No cell service." Cynthia nodded knowingly.

"—and he's willing to compensate Dare County for your

services."

"Least that I can tell, Dare County done took care of that, but tell him thank you anyway. Who's dog is that?" She nodded toward Clara and Jason who stood with Roxie in between them.

"Sheriff Glynne's. I'm babysitting for a few days."

"Good-looking dog. Belgian Malinois, if I'm not riding sidesaddle. He in training for the new position?"

"She and no. Her name's Roxie, and she's a good'un, but she's a rescue from West Virginia, I believe. Excuse me, Cynthia. I see Ed's car."

An older style cruiser approached, and watching it, Diane was newly aware that while it didn't have the rust of the Currituck County car, the shocks and the way the tires rocked the body over the rough surface suggested it was long in the tooth. Anyway, that was Manteo's bait bucket, so she let it go. When Ed pulled his lanky body from the passenger compartment, he seemed to spread out like a newly hatched butterfly unfurling its wings. The helicopter was heading back aloft, and the buffeting from the blades whipped Ed's loose clothing, revealing him to be thinner than his uniform suggested.

"Ed," Diane called over the sound of the aircraft's throbbing rotors. "Let me introduce Cynthia—"

"Yes, ma'am, we've met."

Diane turned her attention to Cynthia, to see her nod.

"In Manteo just before Lucy arrived. I hope you've referred him to Tarheel Academy."

"It's on our radar." Diane nodded, and she began to fill Ed in. They headed towards the water, and Ed stopped beside Roxie, knelt, and greeted the animal. At the sound of her name, Roxie went full attention before accepting his caress around her ears.

Cynthia said, "You said that dog's a rescue. You catch that?

Richie says that when a dog acts like a police dog, it's likely a police dog."

"We only have her until the sheriff returns, but you're welcome to take her along. To tell the story honest, Ed might could prove you right or wrong."

Sheriff Barnett approached and asked, "This the celebrated C-District handler I've heard about?"

"Hardly celebrated." Cynthia laughed.

"Aren't we all Bankers at heart? Never accept a pat on the back." The sheriff grinned. "Did Diane fill you in, or do you need an update?"

A man with black, tightly woven dreadlocks walked up to the sheriff and stood at his elbow. He was dressed in street clothes, a black hoodie and well-worn black jeans over black trainers.

"Willis?" Sheriff Barnett gave him his full attention.

"Change of situation, Sheriff. That boat Calmont brought back in? Whoever did the repairs might need to be shot."

"It got Calmont home." The sheriff tightened his jaw, thinking. He shifted his attention to Diane. "Diane, this is Sergeant Willis Washington, one of our NARC officers. His pal, Kenneth, is out there somewhere. Willis, this is Diane from Dare County with Cynthia Ellison and?" He indicated Ed and waited.

"Ed Styles." Ed nodded but didn't offer a hand.

"So, Willis, a little lane-splitting might be called for." Or, maneuverability, his comment suggested. "How does this change things, and what do we need to do?"

"We don't have our missing suspects yet, but the heli just went up to locate Barker and Krazinski. We're hoping to divert our resources to finding our men, sir."

"This won't be as easy as a flyover. Has anyone been in

touch with Calmont?" Barnett seemed to be lining his ducks up, possibly to give himself some breathing room to decide on how to best play his hand.

Willis cleared his throat. "I would really like to move on this, sir. You see that sky?" Overhead, a black wall had formed in the direction of the ocean, cutting out all light on the east side of the Sound. Already the water was forming a chop. "I'm in the thick of this, along with the rest of the team, and we don't plan for any one of our men to be left behind."

Barnett turned to Diane. "Captain, do I have the use of your people? Anything you can do to help will be appreciated."

Diane took in the helicopter overhead, gleaming against the bank of clouds. When that wall hit, the machine would have to ground itself. And Sean Taylor was above his knees if he thought he could fly that drone better'n the pilot could manage a machine a hundred times the size.

"Cynthia, Ed," she said, shifting into action mode. "You got something waterproof in your cars? This is gonna swamp our waders before we're done."

"Yes, ma'am," Ed said and nodded. "A second set, too, if someone needs it." He watched her for a moment, and when she nodded at him, he took off to his car.

Diane donned his second set, and she took Lucy's leash while Cynthia retrieved hers from her Jeep. She sorted out Ed's new responsibility with Roxie, telling him that she knew the dog wasn't qualified, but that Cynthia had seen something in her, and that she was confident that with Ed on the other end of her leash, the dog would prove itself or not. Either way, today they would find out.

The rain had started by the time Clara was suited up in protective gear, a clear raincoat with a hood and a short bill that extended over the woman's face. When Diane frowned at her, the younger woman laughed and explained that her other one was in her locker at the sub-station.

Sheriff Barnett's team was doing the same and likely glad to be protected, as the helicopter came down blowing wet everywhere. The door on one side opened, water dripped, and Barnett ducked his head and ran towards the chopper to speak to the pilot. He then gave him a thumbs up, the pilot slammed the door and was airborne once Barnett was out of the way.

Diane wasn't surprised to see Willis Washington in a leather duster with a flat-brimmed leather hat that reminded her of one she had seen in an Australian documentary. Another man, Hispanic, short, and round, had joined him. He was laughing at something Willis was saying, so Diane assumed this was the other half of the NARC team that Sheriff Barnett had mentioned.

"Jason," she called, heading his direction. Water dripped from his shirt, and she was certain his boots would fill up before long. "For all sakes, can't you see the water falling from the sky? Here on the Banks, we call that rain, and we try to stay out of it."

"Are you offering me your raincoat?" He grinned but had to wipe water from his face.

"I'm trying to keep you fit enough to perform your job. This' un's from Ed. Mine's in my truck. You get up there and get it on. No sense one of our officers standing around making himself sick just because he can't remember to bring along a raincoat."

"I'll take you up on that. Thanks, Diane."

Diane watched him make his way to her Explorer, his wet pants already clinging to his long legs. She shook that thought away and found Cynthia, Ed, and the dogs. Good, she thought. Cynthia had provided waterproofs for the animals, also, something a thoughtful—meaning experienced—K9 handler would know to do.

Sean Taylor eventually had to give up on his drone. By that time, the Sound was erupting with white water, and large raindrops were pounding the surface. The wind continued to increase, pushing around anything not firmly secured to the ground.

"Don't know that we're doing any good." All engaged personnel had disbursed in the search, and Diane caught the sheriff with his hands in his pockets and his shoulders huddled against the wind.

"I think a break is coming." He nodded towards the east where the black wall had begun to reveal blue sky. "That there might give us some breathing room." His radio chirped, and he reached toward his collar and triggered his mic. "Barnett here. Yeah?"

The voice came across loud and clear. "Zodiac located. Barker and Krazinski still missing. Coast Guard says they will continue the search when the weather passes. Will keep you posted."

"Not good." Diane took a deep breath and studied the horizon. The rain was already lighter but still coming at a good clip. "What are you thinking?"

"That I've got a good team, and your Dare County K9 teams are spot on. I'm getting reports on the box, and my people say they're impressed."

Diane understood the box to be the radio, but she wanted to clarify one thing. "I've only got one K9 team out there, and that's Sergeant Ellison with Lucy. That Malinois is just filling a leash for the day."

"You know I used to be a motorman." He looked at her sideways with a grin.

"You done said that, so yes." Motorman. Motorcycle officer. "Dump it on me. What's your meaning?"

"A motorman is as close to the action as he can get. He can't afford to get cocked up, and that means he has to watch his back all the time. My people know me and what I look for in people and animals. They're telling me that little escort is a K9 we need on our team. You said your man's not got a dog. Maybe he does now. It wouldn't be as easy as a flyover but check into the dog's background. She's offering up some call signs my officers can't miss."

"You're not above your knees to say all that. Cynthia said something the same just a bit ago." Jason, now waterproofed, was with Sean, and she wanted that drone back into the air. If Dare County was paying that man, she wanted him doing what he was paid to do. "Even if your men went overboard, they could likely find footing, right?"

"There's a chance. Rough water might cock that up."

"Still, a chance. I'll see if my man can get that drone back into the air and be the eyeballs the county pays him to be."

Diane touched the bill of her hood and moved in the direction of the men. With the storm and that wind, the inflatable Zodiac could have dumped them anywhere. And she wanted them found.

"Taylor," she called. "Tell it like it is. Can you have that thing back in the air before tomorrow's breakfast? We've got two men to find."

As if in response to her question, sunshine shot through the clouds, illuminating the surrounding area, a bright, gleaming flash that made Diane wince. Water sparkled on everything. The sun as quickly disappeared, but it took the remaining rain with it. But before Sean could get the drone back into the air, the distant whop-whop of the copter began to beat the sky. It occurred to Diane that they also needed to bring in the boat.

"Jason," she called, "I got a request for you. Sheriff Barnett received a message that they located the Zodiac empty. You get with the sheriff and see if you can coordinate getting that boat retrieved. Is that something you think you can do?"

It irritated her that the two men shared a grin before Jason nodded and headed Barnett's way. She muttered, "Doesn't got the sense that God gave a minnow." Then she let it go and headed out to locate where her K9 officer had gotten to. Roxie was Sheriff Glynne's, and it wouldn't do to let her come to any harm, least not if she wanted to keep being the captain over A-District. She'd be so far above her knees if she did, she might never make it back to shore.

DIANE LOCATED Clara in a conversation with the young school resource officer, Deputy Jared Johnson. He had his cap in his hand, exposing a short mop of sandy hair that jutted out at various angles, making him look barely older than the high school students he likely befriended. Camaro indeed. With the rain having moved on, Clara had her clear hood thrown back, revealing her tight blonde bun at the nape of her neck, but she had her cap on her head. Her bright red lipstick accentuated her conversation, with occasional pauses to allow the Currituck County deputy to reply or add information to what Clara was saying.

When Diane approached, Clara touched Jared on the arm and motioned toward her boss. Diane's radio beeped, and she held up one finger. "Hold your taters, Deputy." Into her mic, she said, "Turnipseed here. Dump it on me and tell the story honest." She noticed both deputies giving her their full attention as her radio came on with Jason's voice.

"Diane, Jason—"

"Don't load me up, Jason. I know your voice."

"Man!" He took an audible breath on the other end. "Okay, here's the thing. We've located Brannigan. He's heading over. He said the Zodiac felt fine when he brought it in, but after yesterday, he doesn't put anything past The Wharf bunch. He's coming down in a Whaler. He says it's hard to punch a hole in one of those."

"He planning on towing the Zodiac in?" She focused on Jared, as it was a Currituck boat. When Jason said yes, the younger man's face relaxed. "Let me know soon's you hear about the two men driving it."

"Done. Out."

"I hear this was drugs." Diane thought about the family that had been forced from their sailboat down to Ocracoke Island. That had been drug smugglers. People had died, and more would have except for Shelby, Cynthia Ellison's daughter, who had been living rough on the island.

"Yes, ma'am. Jared Johnson. Glad to meet you." He held out a hand and smiled, ducking his head slightly in a modest gesture of deference. When Diane shook and released it, he seemed to want to open up. "I spend a lot of time at Currituck County High in Barco. Red and black, rah, rah." His smile grew wider, and his eyes lit up. "You might'a seen my Camaro over there, the county's, exactly, but it's assigned to me. High school, all that." This time he shrugged.

"And your point?" Diane's focus was on the missing men, not on his car or where the man was assigned.

"Captain," Clara said. "Jared's how we got here. You might want to hear this."

"For all sakes, Clara—" Diane quelled her frustration. She recalled how Sean Taylor's enthusiasm had frustrated her, and now he seemed loved by everyone in two counties. This man was likely the same. "My apologies. I'm above my knees. Go on, Jared."

"Tell the Captain about Ricky."

"Sure," Jared agreed. "Ricky's a chef, and sometimes he brings food to the sheriff's office. He travels to private gigs, so he needs to be picked up when he gets in town—"

"You know him how?" Diane was searching for the line that connected the two men and why Ricky was important to the wrecked boat and the two missing officers out on the Sound.

Jared seemed puzzled by the question, when Clara jumped in. "Jared and Ricky live together. They're roommates."

"Hey, not exactly—"

"Exactly enough," Clara insisted. "Tell the rest of it."

"There's this kid at school, he has this vibe where he's always flexing at the girls. I was out to pick up Ricky in Ricky's car, and I saw Rhys with one of the Ballinger twins. I don't know if it was Philippe or Creighton, as they look too much alike, but Rhys was acting a little sus around the twin—"

"Does Rhys have a last name?" Diane had her note pad out, and she was jotting as Jared talked.

"Sure. Rhys Naughton." He spelled out Rhys' name. "The next day I took Rhys in the Camaro to the McDonald's for a soda and quizzed him. That's how I knew about this." He grinned.

"You think this Rhys is involved?"

"Maybe." He shrugged. "The Ballingers are in all sorts of things. I'm meeting with Rhys and some of his friends to find out more. Sheriff Barnett has requested help from the State Marine Patrol Office, but the man there, Rodger Landry, says he'll send in help if needed, but he prefers our local office to handle this if possible."

"So that was a big no." Diane considered the implications.

She couldn't shake the smugglers from Ocracoke. Overhead, the chop-chop of the helicopter rotors increased in volume, and she looked up to see it taking off due southeast. Her radio beeped, and she keyed her mic. "Turnipseed. Dump it on me."

"Our man's done it." Jason again.

"That you, Jason?"

"Oh, you want to know now? You said not to—"

"For all sakes, Jason! What is it now?"

"Taylor's all hero down here."

"Sean? How?" She said it hard and unbelieving. Hero? "Tell it like it is, Jason."

"That man's found our boys. Barker and Krazinski are on Goosecastle Point. That squall flipped the Zodiac. They righted it but it waterlogged the engine, and the wind pushed them all the way down. They lost the boat but managed to get ashore. Brannigan's headed that way instead of for the Zodiac."

Diane zeroed in on Jared. "Goosecastle Point. How far's that?"

"A mile and a half, maybe two. You pass it on the way down to Monkey Island."

"Could that squall've blown that Zodiac that far?"

"Hey, easy, touch grass." He shifted one foot to tap at a patch of the green stuff.

She leaned back into her mic. "Okay, Jason, let me report to Sheriff Barnett."

"He already knows, Diane. He's down here giving Sean high-fives."

Diane clicked off the connection, and as she turned away from the two deputies, Jared's black car, impossibly shiny, reflected the sun into her eyes, and she squinted. She headed towards the other members of the conjoined county team, muttering, "Then why am I here at all? I might oughta go on back down south to Dare County, better, catch the ferry to Morehead. Might find something to do down there where it's appreciated."

She had her head back on by the time she reached the celebratory party on the shore. Still, The Wharf hunkered just over their shoulders, and the memory of the abandoned sailboat hovered just on the other side of the sandy embankment she could see across Currituck Sound.

She was distracted from her thoughts when Sean Taylor noticed her, raised his arms to wave, and called, "Captain Turnipseed! We found them, and I owe it all to you!"

Don't load me up, she wanted to say. Instead, she smiled and called, "Congratulations! You did this on your own."

As he turned around and threw his arms around Jason and began shaking hands with the other team members, a blip of a thought skittered through her head. *Don't got the sense God gave a minnow.* She as quickly let that off her line and joined in to celebrate the retrieval of two valued members of the Currituck County team.

"CAN WE CALL this an Impact Team?" Sergeant Sean Taylor's face glowed with excitement. "Shoot, y'all, this is the best thing ever! You know you can count on me!"

Diane refrained from rolling her eyes. She remembered the applause the man had received the day before, but she didn't see it. He wore his uniform well, but sure as taters in a bag, his minnows weren't all swimming in the same pond.

But yes, this was likely an Impact Team. They were gathered at the A-District sub-station and crowded into the situation room. Sean Taylor, as he was the county Drone Operator, and he would be instrumental in flyovers to determine where the physical officers needed to head, stood at a narrow smorgasbord of prepackaged breakfast treats, and he was chatting up everyone who approached.

Jason was present, although Diane didn't know why. Sheriff Glynne was still out of town, or she would call the man and ask him why his Detention Officer wasn't off detentioning somewhere besides in her A-District sub-station. When she'd confronted him, he'd placed the onus on Sean, saying they were roomies, and Jason had wanted to tag along to see what he was getting up to in A-District.

Likely not, but Jason wasn't a fish she could toss out of her fish basket, so she had to let it go.

Of course, Wally, Clara, and Ed were in the room. Diane breathed a sigh of relief that Ed had volunteered to take over Roxie. She was at his side, her eyes attentively taking in the room, but alert to Ed's every change in motion. To tell the story honest, if any man could make that dog into a good K9 officer, Diane was about convinced Ed might be in the running.

Nathan Preston was off to the side showing off his new sidearm to the equally fresh-looking Currituck County deputy that Sheriff Barnett had assigned to facilitate communication between the two counties. The previous day, Nathan had been off to Lawmen's in Raleigh for his new weapon, hence missing the excitement from out on the Sound.

Jared Johnson had his cap rolled and tucked inside his belt, his sandy mat exposed and as tousled as yesterday. Diane had thought to lay the blame on yesterday's weather, but this morning, she decided it was just Jared. Nathan was fresh-faced, but he could be a seasoned officer next to the baby-faced Jared.

The room seemed incomplete without Emily Bryant and Cynthia Ellison. Yet, they were off to their respective duties. Today, there were no images needed from the forensic investigator, nothing specific to investigate, so Manteo had her filling in other areas. They weren't Diane's areas, so she was not in that loop. When the tide turned, Emily would be back, she was certain.

Cynthia had praised Roxie, the Belgian Malinois, the day before, remarking on the animal's responses to Ed's commands. The search for the drivers of the wrecked boat had been occluded by the search for the missing officers, but Lucy and Roxie had given Sheriff Barnett a step up in determining the direction he intended to take. His K9 teams would be available today, and he had thanked the Dare County teams for their quick response and active participation in an investigation that had already embroiled both counties.

Yet, even as Diane appreciated Cynthia's willingness to help out when she called, the C-District K9 handler was now under Lonnie Burkhalter's oversight. She had come to help only with the new C-District captain's permission, so Diane couldn't make Cynthia's help a command performance, nor would she. Even so, she could miss the familiarity of a woman who understood how Diane thought and slotted in next to her like a high-quality reel on an offshore rod.

She lifted her most anticipated object from the morning, a steaming "cuppa blackie" from beside her, and sipped it before calling to the room, "We might oughta pull ourselves together and get started. Chairs, please."

The hubbub shifted, not quite going silent, as Ed adjusted his chair to angle more towards Diane; Nathan indicated two chairs for him and the Currituck County deputy; and the others worked their way through the menagerie of seating surfaces. The space was adequate for five but crowded with eight, nine counting Roxie. The markerboard was small—though it fit the space—and Diane printed three words stacked in a column up and down.

Sailboat.

Avon Pier.

Springer's Point.

She closed her marker, turned around, and faced her Impact Team. "To tell the story honest, these three things have been on my mind. I don't think I'm above my knees to say they're connected to what we saw up on the Sound yesterday." She started to ask, "Any thoughts?" but Taylor already had his arm in the air, and he was shaking his hand back and forth as though he might be lost in the crowd, and she wouldn't notice.

She said it anyway. "Any thoughts? Taylor?"

"Yes, ma'am. Shelby Ellison."

"For all sakes, Taylor …" She heard her words trail off. He wasn't correcting her use of his last name, and that threw her. "I give up. Dump it on me, Sean. What are your thoughts?"

"Thank you, Captain." He grinned.

"For?" She might snap at him anyway, just for old times, if he didn't get to the point.

"For my name. Anyway, here's what I say. That sailboat, Shelby saw it that night. And we saw it, too, the same one, off Avon Pier." He grinned, glad to be sharing what he surely thought was Diane's reason for combining the three items on the markerboard.

"And?" Diane couldn't miss Jason's approving grin and Jared's puzzled look. She tended to side with Jared, but Jason wasn't often wrong. She pulled from her limited reservoir of patience and gave Taylor permission to continue.

"Springer Point, Captain. That's where Blackbeard met his end. And that's where Shelby led us to that family that was abducted. It all fits."

Diane was reminded of the race from the previous spring, the Blackbeard's Revenge 100, and the two men who had been killed. She caught Jason's eye and pleaded with him to step in. He was clearly following Taylor's logic, but it was a closed fish basket to her. She had intended to connect to the abandoned Zodiac, the beach crime scene, and Goosecastle Point. How he had managed to drag Shelby into the tidepool was beyond her.

"Jason, I'd be above my knees to steal Sergeant Taylor's thunder. The floor is yours to get these three things on the markerboard stringed together with the sergeant's observations. While you're coming up, thank you for seeing about releasing the truck and those bikes from our parking area. Those boys might not have the sense God gave a minnow, but without an indictment or any real evidence for criminal mischief—" She shrugged rather than finish, as her team would understand just what she meant. The law sometimes said to open your hand and let go, even if what you were letting go of was bound to cause more trouble in the future.

Jason stepped to the lectern and took over the discussion. He caught Sean's eye and winked before beginning. "Sergeant Taylor's observational skills pick up on everything, often in ways that amaze me. He links together events that wouldn't occur to me. For example, these items on the markerboard. Some of you aren't familiar with them, so let me fill you in ..."

Old news, Diane thought, not really having considered that not everyone present was there when the events happened. That was part of the trouble of transferring to a new location. In C-District, she had hand-assembled her team, people she knew and liked, and who understood her as well as she understood them, Taylor excepted, although he had done well enough since transferring to Manteo as the County Drone Operator. Arriving in A-District had been like beginning from scratch, with people so green they might just be putting out their first shoots.

Okay, she was willing to make an exception for Wally

Styles, who was an old hand. He'd taken Nathan Preston under his wing, and for that, he couldn't be faulted.

A light knock on the door, and Paloma peeked through, motioning for Diane to join her outside. Diane caught Jason's eye, held up one finger, and pointed towards Paloma to let him know she would be outside and to continue until she returned.

"Dump it on me, Paloma. The last three days have had me wading in the collards. What's so important to pull me from my Impact Team meeting?"

"Well, honey, you all in there like sardines in a can, how was I to know you were having an *Impact Team* meeting?" She hit the words Impact Team hard. "Thought you might be glad to be shut of that bunch and catch a little fresh air." She pursed her lips and didn't go on.

"For all sakes, Paloma—"

"If you're trying to rile me up, it won't work. I'm just making my point. Just because I'm not white don't mean I can be pushed around. Now you, on that phone on my desk, got a call waiting that says one of those bikes you cleared out of our lot just got someone into a pounding of trouble. Dead-type trouble, so don't go getting uppity with me when I call you out of a meeting no one told me was an *Impact Team* meeting. You want to see about that phone call, or should I just ask them which'n's dead and let it go at that?"

"Thank you, Paloma. I'll take the call."

"Then I'm going to the lady's room to give you some privacy." She disappeared down the hallway.

"Diane Turnipseed. With whom am I speaking?" She had wanted to bark, "Dump it on me," but Paloma's reaction had stung, and she couldn't go wrong with the more formal phrasing.

"You know I used to be a motorman, and details are what

kept me alive. I know this isn't Diane Turnipseed. She would never say that—" The speaker was Sheriff William Barnett, surprising but not surprising. He was in a different county, but they had worked a rescue together yesterday.

"For all sakes, William." Diane couldn't restrain herself. "I just got my nose carpet burned by my front desk. I didn't know but what you would do the same."

"Okay, then. That's the Diane I know." He chuckled. "I would'a called you on the box but this is something I want just you to know. You might should'a kept that truck and those bikes in your impound lot a few days longer."

"They weren't in my impound lot. They were taking up valuable parking space outside my office that I didn't have to give. Besides, Manteo says no warrant, no impound. T'weren't much I could do about that." And with Sheriff Glynne out of town, there had been no one to argue her side, though she was relieved to see them gone.

"I'm guessing you know about the Brayboy problem." He paused, letting Diane know this was the crux of his call. Diane was a true Banker, but the north and south portions were a hundred miles of sand apart. Someone could scream bloody murder in Corolla, and no one would know in Hatteras.

"Better'n some, not as well as you. What's happened now?"

"The two we were searching for who slipped the noose?"

"You said your K9 team could handle it."

"Which they did. They found those two dirt bikes."

"Those two the ones dead?" Diane's heart hit her chest wall hard. She was here to protect, even if people didn't want or deserve her protection. Death, even of someone who might deserve it, always stung.

"Nah, just bloodied. It's their uncle, someone named Charles-Edouard Beaumarchais. Our K9 team found him floating face down in the Sound this morning. I think several of your people met him on the beach the other day."

"It's in their reports. Connect him to Philippe and Creighton for me." And the dirt bikes led to this how?

"Here's what you don't know about the Currituck branch of the Brayboys. They just showed up a few years back but started flashing money like they pulled it from the Sound. A few of them, at least. Charles-Edouard was one. I've seen his gym set up at The Wharf. There's more money in that one room than in most of Currituck. And those bikes you impounded? Not cheap. Deputy Johnson has been pursuing a drug connection through his high school contacts, one we think links to France."

"You thinking this is a drug deal gone wrong?"

"Unsure. Not enough information."

"Connect the bikes to the uncle."

"There's a bit of swamp land off Tulls Creek Road. The boys were left tied up, gagged, and beaten in the mud. Their truck is gone, but the bikes were still on the trailer. Creighton's not talking, but Philippe was just conscious enough before being airlifted to Norfolk to learn that the three of them were taking the bikes out, as he said, to ensure that those Corolla-loving deputies hadn't messed them up, and Charles wanted to drive. He got the truck stuck, and that's when they were attacked."

"By their Corolla cousins? And this is connected to the missing men from that boat?" To Diane, it didn't make sense, because if it did, that netted a whole school of sharks into her waters.

"If so, they weren't drug runners. The Corolla bunch are vehemently opposed to anything the Currituck side does, especially any suspicion of drugs."

"Then you don't have them."

"That's just it. We do. Only one, though. The one that was

impaled by a board from the dock they plowed through. I guess his partner didn't think highly enough of him to not leave him behind."

"We don't have the reports back from Raleigh, but are you thinking that evidence from the beach the other day is connected?"

"I'm a motorman, Diane. I'd bet my reputation on it. Still, this is right in the middle of Brayboy country. This won't be so easy as a flyover."

Diane noticed Paloma hovering down the hallway, and she thanked the sheriff and disconnected the line. She heard laughter from the incident room and made out Jason's voice telling them a story.

"Well, Jason," she muttered. "You're hitting a home run."

She didn't know what made her think of baseball, except that three strikes meant you were out. As Sergeant Mary Wilson from her old haunts used to say, "Things come in threes ..."

She didn't know if that even applied, but to tell the story honest, it left her unnerved and wanting to find the answers.

Samuel Knight. His name was in several of the reports. That's where she would begin first.

Chapter 6

A Hidden Deed Revealed

COROLLA NATIVE SON SAMUEL KNIGHT stood on his porch and looked toward the ocean. The porch was uncovered, a concession to the wind that could batter Corolla like a truncheon. While he enjoyed the warmth of the sun, he squinted against the incessant glare making the light in the air sharp and brittle.

Inside, coffee simmered on the cooker, but today, he needed something besides four walls and wallpaper that should have been replaced three decades ago. Because he was tall, he could just catch the water over the tops of the houses that had grown up between the old home place and the shore. Because he was thin, the stiff offshore breeze whipped his rough jeans and worn, plaid button-up shirt against muscles that were deceptively strong despite his age. Because the sun was out, his sleeves were rolled up, and because his thick black hair couldn't warm his ears, he wore a cap with fold-up, fur-lined flaps.

The flaps were down, and still he shivered.

It was the memories, not the breeze that did it. Charlie, his wife, gone back in '87 after only fifteen years together, with no children to show for it. Gippy had his three: Ruthie, Lavie, and Suki, all girls; but that was that, so there was nothing to be done about it. Anyway, Ruthie was married and with her boys down in Tallahassee, while Lavie and Sukie had no designs on children.

It was a shame, but Samuel couldn't choose for them. He hadn't been able to choose when Charlie took ill, and he couldn't choose for Gippy's bunch.

No children around, however, that was hard.

To the side of the house, his green Dodge pickup with its worn clutch had seen better days, but today, last night's teardrops still littered the paint and sparkled like jewels in the sun. He'd kept the old truck after Charlie died because it reminded him of her, but now he kept it because his papa's legacy was all he had. The Knight money that had built the Whalehead hadn't stuck around long enough to come to them. He chuckled at a memory of his father's way of seeing a fancy truck drive by and saying, "Get me one of those, that'll be all right." Yet, he never did get one, not that Samuel knew.

Mama died with Lucie, likely the reason Lucie was born with only three fingers on her left hand. She did well enough marrying Marc Collier, living in that fancy house in New Bern; and their two: John in New York driving a fancy Corvette; and Sissy, once a finalist in the Miss North Carolina pageant, now divorced and teaching in Goldsboro. That was a shame, but it was what it was. Samuel wondered at times if Lucie missed not having grandchildren, with John's string of girlfriends and Sissy with no interest in marriage anymore; but Lucie and Mark seemed happy enough, so he guessed maybe not so much.

Mama's death was likely why Gippy had coveted so many girls, filling in the hollow in his heart from losing her at such a young age. Samuel was three, and he still had his mama in his memories, but Gippy at two remembered suckling but not much else. It was a heavy blow, so Samuel had to give him that.

The sun glinted off a windshield in the distance, and Samuel followed it, his face growing tighter when it paused at the entrance to his and Charlie's place. Fancy paint, fancy shine, tall like a truck but not truck. Then the black vehicle no longer seemed to move, sure as a Lamborghini was his favorite car, meaning it was coming directly down the driveway.

It pulled up, and behind the grille, he could see the law enforcement lights of a car someone didn't want to look like a law enforcement car. He noticed things like that. Cars … well, he might drive his old Dodge, but that was because of Charlie. Other than Charlie, he might well have his Lamborghini; and he might yet, get his hands on some money.

The door opened, and an attractive lady with dark hair emerged. Her clothing and belt with all its accessories told the rest of her story. Her eyes, a little hard and a little tired, took him in, wrapped him and his house and his Dodge all up in a tight little package, then she took a deep breath and closed her door.

"Samuel Knight?" She remained beside her car with its unmarked doors, like it was a real car and not a law enforcement one.

"Might be. Depends on who's asking. Shiny car you got there. Saw them police lights in the grille." No children, his view of the ocean stolen, and not a dime from that Whalehouse-joint-turned-park. He wanted to draw a line, but he wasn't sure a line needed to be drawn yet, so he bided his time and patience.

"Diane Turnipseed with Dare County, and yes, this is my county car." She paused and waited, having set the hook in Samuel's turf. It was up to him to bite.

"You took Le Grange's spot, I hear. Didn't think much of Le Grange. The man was too quick to make judgement calls and wouldn't back down when he was wrong."

"I've been told that. Can I join you on your porch?"

My porch. With those words, Samuel softened. She had recognized his home, his autonomy, and his rights. He'd not interacted with Le Grange any more than need be, but with Brayboy business spilling over down south, at times it couldn't be helped.

"I've got some coffee on the cooker. If you don't mind joining me inside, a cup might put you right."

"A cuppa blackie?" Diane smiled. "To tell the story honest, that's the one thing you could'a offered that I wouldn't refuse."

Samuel held the door for her, as a gentleman should, shucking his cap as he entered the house. He ran long fingers through his hair to tame it, and in a mirror, he noted the gray shot through the black and thought, Charlie gone now about forty years. I suppose it has a right, too. Two cups from the hooks under the upper cabinet, a quick pour, and the refusal of anything to soften the bitterness upped his estimate of the Dare County officer, and he invited her to sit at a wooden table underneath a wide window facing the ocean.

"Use'ta could see the water from here." He nodded the direction of the sea.

"And them houses yonder stole it." She lifted the cup, and steam writhed around her face and into her hair.

"Yep." He let the preliminaries expire. "You're a bit above your jurisdiction. What's got you up this direction?"

"We had to rescue two officers yesterday." She worked her

lips as if thinking how much to share. "From the Sound."

"Saw the helicopter. About the time that squall blew across, right?" Cat and mouse. Tease a little information to bring the other person out.

"I'll tell you what I can, Mr. Knight. Two men died, one of them related to you."

"Not to me. I know all my people, and unless that Sound goes up to New York or down to Tallahassee, not likely any of mine was out there yesterday."

"You know Charles-Edouard Beaumarchais, I'm told."

"Know of him. Not so sure I'm related to him." His heart tightened, though. He did know him, knew how much he disliked him, or at least what he believed the man was doing to the family, the honest, Corolla side of the family. John up in New York, he was bound to be in this if Charles-Edouard was. Poor Lucie. "Am I pushing too much to ask how?"

"We don't know. He was found face down in the Sound. He has two nephews, Philippe—"

"And Creighton. What have those two done now?"

"They rode in an air ambulance to Norfolk. They were found tied up and beaten."

"Not dead, then. You said two." Samuel realized he hadn't taken a drink from his cup, and he lifted it and used it to distract himself, forcing a long sip before setting it back on the table.

"It gets complicated. I came to see you because two days ago, you talked to two of my deputies at Corolla Watersports. Charles was there, and you asked about him. Then, later they were certain he was also at a crime scene that Currituck and Dare County were jointly investigating.'

"The one by the county line."

"For all sakes! You know that how?" It was the first time the woman had broken her professionalism.

"Gippy, well, Gerald, but we've always called him Gippy, he's my baby brother. He talked to your officers. You see a yellow Corolla—" pronounced Co-*roll*-la, like the car "—up and down the Banks, and that's Gippy. He told me what he knew, which wasn't much, I must say." Samuel took another drink from his cup.

"I might oughta keep this to myself, but since you people seem to be a grapevine up here, I'll tell you this. We're waiting on Raleigh, but there's reason to believe there might have been a third victim on the beach there."

"Reason to believe means no body, am I correct?"

She didn't answer him, just lifted her cup, looked out the window, and took a longer drink than strictly necessary.

Ah, Lucie, he thought. You poor, poor girl.

If there was blood, he suspected he knew exactly whose it was and why it was there. Especially since he'd heard from Lucie just that morning asking if he'd heard from John.

He didn't expect to now, not if Philippe and Creighton were in Norfolk, Charles-Edouard was face-down, and John was nowhere to be found.

One thing made him grateful. The boys' bad deeds had bled down into Dare County, and now they had two law enforcement teams after them. Maybe this woman could shake the net and put things right. Like his papa would always ask him when they were on the water, "Not afraid of drowning, are you, boy?" Samuel couldn't always answer that honestly, but he suspected this woman wasn't afraid of anything. Perhaps she should be, but from her looks, that wouldn't slow her down, and that was all right with him.

"You done with that cup?" Samuel stood and pointed. When she pushed it in his directions, he carried it and his to the sink, rinsed them, and turned them upside down to drain. Before turning around, he said, "My papa always said that grown up is as grown up does. I best be grown up with you. Lucie, that's my sister Lucille, rang me up this morning asking about her boy, John. You might best know that John's up in New York, working in finance, so he says, with a shiny red Corvette car. He's a good-looking boy, slim like his daddy, and likes to bring down a new girlfriend time-to-time. You may wonder why I'm telling you all this, but I know for a fact that John's been shoulder to shoulder with Charles-Edouard. Well, Lucie can't seem to locate John. Don't know that it's anything, but with that crime scene on the beach, just saying, 'cause that's about when we saw him last."

"If Raleigh can pull DNA …" Diane let her suggestion trail off.

"I might can get you something." Samuel paused, let out a deep breath. Saying it was to make it real. "To compare, you understand. Lucie would be glad to know it's not John."

"Then we're good." The chair legs on the floor scraped. "I'll bet tomorrow's breakfast you got things to do. I appreciate you giving me part of your day."

"You able to let yourself out, I suppose." He didn't turn. He was offering up John, and it didn't suit well with him. The Currituck bunch? Them didn't matter. His family, even if John might prove a ne'er-do-well, well, it weren't right, was it? It just weren't.

He heard the door close, and he stepped to the back stoop. From the rear of the house, he could see the Sound if he imagined the trees all gone. His land went all the way back, even if it was a maze of booby traps for the unwary.

That was the entire Sound, life or death, who could tell?

Was he afraid of drowning? Just ask Charles-Edouard. And that was the telling of that.

SAMUEL REACHED to the dash and turned his key to the off position. Once his old pickup's engine sputtered to a stop, he let out the tired clutch, set the parking brake, and removed the key. The crack in the laminated windshield glass was so old, it was a jagged lightning gash of dirt that could never be cleaned away. Just past the crack, Gippy and Bette's place, fifty years old if it was a day, hunkered in the island undergrowth, amid trees that were hardly higher than the rooftop and still obscuring every bit of light that might consent to enter the dusty windows.

Gippy and Bette weren't showy people, not house proud, anyways. Gippy liked to shotgun moonshine from time to time, and Bette, well, what could he say? She did like her manicures, always waggling her fingers to show off her latest creations. She could tie her blond hair into a ponytail with a twist of her wrist and never mar a nail. She tried to buy skinny jeans but couldn't keep up the weight to keep 'em tight so wore frothy button-up shirts and heeled sandals to distract.

Bette appeared through the screen door, looking as if she was searching, when she opened her hands wide in excitement and knelt to retrieve a pair of heeled sandals. When she stood, she noticed Samuel's truck and waved.

"Samuel, come on in. I found my sandals." She held them up as if he couldn't see them already. With her free hand, she waggled the backs of her fingers his direction. "Yvette at the nail shop. I have to show you. Don't just sit there." She smiled, then disappeared back through the screen door.

Gippy was the second son. He'd married first, but the home place would go to Samuel, so Papa had helped him and Bette buy something of their own. Ruthie, their oldest, visited with her husband from Tallahassee once a year, but their two boys always had sports practice or a new job or something to keep them away. Lavie and Sukie, the twins, were in as much as out, though Lavie had that little place on Knotts and Sukie was sometimes in her old bedroom and sometimes with her latest boyfriend.

The house rested on low pylons, hardly enough to be elevated, but it had never flooded, not in fifty years. The drive, yes, but never the house. The driveway disappeared around to the back, where Gippy had a garage and parked his old, yellow Toyota. Samuel couldn't see the garage so didn't know if the Toyota was home. He allowed he could have called, but then that wasn't family, was it? After fifty years of Gippy and Bette living here, if Samuel didn't feel at home to just drop over, then when would he?

He unlatched his door and worked a thick folder of paperwork from the seat at his side. The trees kept the wind at bay when it blew from the ocean, and he made it to the door without any of his papers getting away. He didn't knock, just opened it and made his way to the kitchen.

"You got coffee?" He asked it like a question but intended it as a statement. She already said she did.

"On the table." Sure enough, a cup had steam rising. "Gerry's in the garage. You want I should call him?"

"Nah. In a minute. I'd like a bit of coffee before it gets cold."

"Suit yourself. I'm headed up to put a fresh topcoat on my nails." As she walked by, she held out her fingers and waggled them a foot from his face. She laughed and soon he heard her feet on the stairs.

The back screen squeaked, and Gippy and his moustache appeared. "Thought I heard that old Dodge. I may be a Banker, but I know my engines."

"And the sound of my door slamming." Samuel held the cup in both hands, soaking up its warmth.

"That, too. I might have me one of those. Bette makes a good cup, you follow me?" He laughed, moved to the coffee pot, and reached into the cabinet just above to pull down a half-empty bottle of whiskey.

"That'll make even my coffee pot taste good as Bette's."

"Like I said, I'm a Corolla Banker." He looked at Samuel with an amused expression, then eyed his cup and poured it half full before resealing the bottle and topping the cup off with coffee. When he approached the table, he set his cup down and studied the file folder. "Thought maybe the tide'd come up and eaten what's in that folder."

"Might be time to revisit it." Samuel studied his younger brother. Ruthie didn't care about what was in this folder. She'd run to Tallahassee decades before. *Let 'em have it,* she'd said when their French cousins had come over to claim The Wharf. And Samuel's thoughts hadn't been too far from that. That's why this file'd stayed in his office drawer the past five years. Now, with the Dare County captain telling him two deaths had alighted on the Banks and maybe a third, a finger was pointing to what needed to be done.

"Papa should'a filed to take it before it went to that developer." Gippy still stood, with his coffee steaming on the table. With the whiskey, it didn't steam quite so actively as Samuel's, but there it was.

"Ah, sit, Gippy. You know why. The place was a wreck. Papa didn't have money for both the back taxes and to fix it up."

"You mean he spent all his money on this place." For Gippy and Bette, his remark suggested. He did sit, and he suddenly took up the cup and threw back half the contents.

"Slow down, Gippy. I didn't say that." Samuel opened the top of the file folder, revealing old legal files, court documents, and whatnot else that applied to the family's history in Corolla and across Currituck Sound.

"You ain't got to say it. Lucie did often enough."

"Let Lucie go. She walked away. This is me and you. I want those people out of there. Don't know how. Just thought this might be a place to start." He pushed the stack of papers in his brother's direction.

The creak of the stairs warned of Bette's return, although neither man paid it much attention. She appeared at the door and stepped through, pausing to blow on her nails.

"Sukie must'a been here last night." Bette held her hand at arm's length to evaluate her polish job. "She left the bathroom a mess."

"Sukie's a mess." Gippy fought a grin and caught Samuel's eye. He leaned towards his brother and whispered, "She brought a boyfriend over last week. Weren't that ever the fireworks show."

"She ought to marry one of 'em." Samuel was back browsing the folder. Sukie was an ongoing soap opera in real life.

"She says she can kick out a boyfriend but a husband's too sticky." Bette decided her polish job was fine and walked to Gippy's side, placed a hand on his shoulder, and kissed him on the forehead. She was careful to hold her hand so the polished nails didn't connect with his shirt. "With you, I like sticky just fine. That what I think it is? I thought you boys gave up on that years back."

Samuel looked up and locked eyes with Gippy, warning him that this was serious. He was certain his brother read his intent just fine. Gippy nodded, patted his wife's hand—also careful with her polished nails—and stood to give her a hug.

"Bette," Samuel said, "there's a policewoman visited me this morning. She brought me some news, some of it maybe bad."

Gippy frowned, took a longer look at the paperwork, then offered Bette his chair. He pulled one up from across the room and turned it backwards before sitting, using the back to rest his arms.

"I wanted to tell Gippy first, but I can tell you both just as easy." He pushed the paperwork slightly aside, enough to show that his story wasn't directly about that. "Mostly it's about that bunch over in Currituck ..."

He explained what Captain Turnipseed from the Dare County Sheriff's Office had said about Charles-Edouard and his two nephews, and that a second man was dead, with another they weren't sure of. Yes, he said, it was confusing to him also, but sometimes life was, wasn't it?

"Why would she come see you?" Bette said the one thing Samuel hoped she wouldn't.

"Say it, Samuel." Gippy sighed heavily. "I did it, so say it."

"You did what?" Bette slapped his arm, thought not hard enough to leave a mark.

Samuel intervened. "Something happened a few days back down on the county line. Gippy stopped to talk to the officers, so that led to me."

"You!" Bette stood, and she adjusted her frothy shirt. She turned her back to her husband. "Did you ask if they wanted a ride in your car? Or tell them a story about your daddy? Oh, I know how this went. You and your whiskey, Gerry. You will get yourself in real trouble one day." She turned to glare at him with red eyes.

"It's okay, Bette." Samuel needed to keep to the matter at hand, not Gippy's weakness for his whiskey. "No one in this room's in trouble. You heard from John the past few days?"

"Why would I?" She was back focused on one nail, giving her attention to her fresh topcoat. "He lives up there in fancysmancy New York. I only ever see him at Lucie's over to New Bern."

"John in trouble?" Gippy was tapping one fingernail on the table, a clear sign of either worry or impatience. His face didn't reveal which. John was the golden child, with a job in finance in the city, a fancy sports car, and pretty girls on his arms. The fingernail said John didn't fit into this conversation.

"You do know he's been shoulder-to-shoulder with Charles-Edouard." Samuel let that air out for a time. Gippy's eyes closed, and he let out a sigh, telling him yes. "I promised that officer I'd get her something with John's DNA on it."

"Oh!" The light seemed to come on for Bette. "Lucie will be horrified. What was it, underage girls? No," and she sat and her eyes sparkled, "drugs. Everybody does drugs these days. That car—" Her eyes went wide. "No, and we thought he was so successful—"

"Samuel didn't say that, Bette." Gippy placed his hand on her forearm. "Let's let the man talk, you follow me? No jumping into the Sound just because the wind picks up." He turned his attention to Samuel. "I heard some about John and Charles-Edouard, him running with those Currituck folk. Nothing good can come from crossing the Sound with people like that. I only stopped because Bette talked to the Calmont officer on the way back from down south. You know him, Samuel."

Samuel nodded that he did, a man by the name of Brannigan, with freckles, red hair, and a cowboy hat. He understood Gippy's reference to Brannigan was his way of shifting some of the blame back to his wife.

"That's him. I only stopped to tell them I'd seen something suspicious the previous night but didn't place it as being John. They didn't seem much interested."

"I guess this can wait." Samuel closed the file folder and

pushed it to the back of the table. It could stay here as well as at his house. "I need to see what Lucie's got that will help with identifying John. I should give her a call."

"Identifying?" Bette's eyes went wide again.

"Wrong word, Bette. My apologies. I need to put my manners on. Clearing, not identifying." Samuel berated himself at the slipup.

"Thought maybe you weren't gonna tell us, Samuel. You follow me? If you're going to Lucie ..." He let his words die away.

"Blood, that's all. They found a little blood, nothing more, lest not that that officer told me."

Samuel stood. It was time to go before fingers started pointing at him. He sure hated breaking the news to Lucie, but a grown-up man does what a grown-up man needs to do, even when it means you're crossing water that's over your head. If any accusations were made, he wanted them aimed directly at Currituck.

He remembered something else his papa used to say when they were out on the Sound: "Just keep outta the deep spots, stroll right across." This was one deep spot Samuel suspected he might not be able to avoid.

SAMUEL, SIX at the time, and wearing a light jacket over a tee shirt and shorts, sat at the same kitchen table under the same window that he would one day look out of and bemoan the houses that blocked his view of the sea. His mama was three years gone, and while he remembered her, there was less of her to fill his imagination with each passing Christmas and birthday.

Gippy, just a year younger, sat across from him, with a plate of grits and gravy. He pushed the yellowed mash around with a spoon before reaching to lift a cloth from a bowl of scratch biscuits.

"No, Gippy," Samuel whispered. "Those are Mama Juno's."

Lucie, or Lucille by her birthname, nestled in Juno's lap in an old-fashioned Early American-style rocker in the living room. Since the passing of their mother, Sally Lady, in '54, their grandmother, Juno Brayboy, had taken over much of the mothering of the three children. Lucie was no longer a toddler, but as the baby of the family—and the spitting image of her mother—she was catered to more often than was right or proper.

Mama Juno would have it no other way.

The front screen opened and slammed, and Samuel jumped. He held a finger to his lips and stared hard at Gippy. It didn't stop what he dreaded.

"Why, boy, just you wait—"

Samuel felt his daddy's presence over his shoulder. The man was bigger than life, bigger than any other man on the Banks, and bigger than God when he was angry.

"You want to keep your two front teeth, you'll finish that breakfast and get out the door to find something to do."

"Yes, Papa." Samuel didn't dare look but remained frozen.

"Don't you make me say this twice. I don't see no spoon in that hand. Get to it, boy. You, too, Gerald."

Then the oppressive presence of Creighton Knight and the black cloud of his wife lost to childbirth eased, the air in the kitchen cleared, and the world outside flooded the window once more.

"You want mine?" Gippy stared at his grits, but his attention was clearly on the biscuits.

Samuel glanced over his shoulder, saw his papa standing over Mama Juno and Lucie, heard him mutter, "If Sally was still here ..." and pulled a paper napkin from a stack.

"Dump it on this, Gippy. I'll put it in my pocket, and we'll toss it into the sea."

When it was done, he rolled it and put the package into his jacket pocket. He took a risk and called, "Mama Juno, Gippy's through. Can he have a biscuit?"

He listened for an answer, heard his papa say to his grandmother, "There's money can be had from the Sound ..." and pretended he heard her say yes.

"Gippy, okay," Samuel said with a smile.

"Didn't hear her say." Gippy's eyes were on the bowl.

"I did. Go ahead." Samuel shoveled his final bits of grits and gravy into his mouth, whispered, "Hide the biscuit and come with me," and stood.

"You boys finished?" His papa.

"Yes, Papa. We're going outside now."

"Don't shadow this door 'til the sun goes down. You hear me, boy?" He always spoke to Samuel, never to Gippy, even when he meant both. He held a surprisingly thick stack of greenbacks in his hand, money which sometimes appeared without explanation but kept them fed and sometimes provided new clothes.

"Yes, Papa." He took Gippy's hand, pulled him from the chair, and disappeared though the screen door, slam, slam, into the broader world of Corolla, the sand, and the sea.

They could head behind the house to explore, but the Sound was hard to reach, although the two boys had done it often enough. Too young to prowl on their own? Their papa said they weren't too young to die on their own, so they's best get to learning to survive what life had to offer. The seashore was a hike the other direction through the sand, the undergrowth, and across the sandy driving path that some liked to call a road. It wasn't unusual to find cars abandoned for days or even weeks, their wheels half buried, and their door sills resting on the sand.

Sometimes boards were scattered alongside the driving path, useful for under the wheels of stuck cars, but also for pretend rescue surf boats when the wind calmed and the waves weren't too rough.

"I want to throw it," Gippy called to Samuel. They no longer held hands, and the smaller boy ran to keep up with his brother. The biscuit was long gone into the boy's tummy, although a crumb or two still littered his face.

"If you want. Papa can't find it, so you have to toss it hard." Samuel pulled the rolled package from his pocket. The gravy was seeping through, but it was a small price to pay. He offered it to his brother. "Far into the water, Gippy. The fish will have a good snack."

"Yuck," Gippy said with a shudder. "I don't like grits and gravy."

"The fish do. Now, throw hard as you can!" Samuel stood erect and glanced over the sand, not expecting to find anyone, as this far north on the Banks there was no one to see, not outside of the summer people who made their way up to stay in the cabins and houses erratically scattered up and down the sand.

Something did catch his eye. A sign in the sand. He called to Gippy, "Tide's coming in. Stay out the water. I'll be right back."

When he reached "the sign," he took in four regular imprints, these from real surf boats. He looked behind him, west towards his home, where the roof of his house was just visible through the scruffy dune grass. Someone had come and gone, but what for? There was nothing to come and go *to*. Just sand, scrub, and trees along the Sound side. Back out to sea, he scanned the horizon. Only one boat, too far to make out much.

At his feet, the rising tide had begun to eat the bow imprints in the sand, making them as though they never were. Many years later he would connect his papa's money with the imprints from the four "surf" boats, but just then, Gippy called, "Samuel, look at this shell!"

Samuel tore his direction. He wanted to see. He really did.

SAMUEL PULLED his green Dodge off Hwy 12, noting the airbrushed New Beetle outside his door. The airbrushing extended down the sides of the car, an "artsy" version of a middle-aged woman painting an island scene, with her name in almost unreadable cursive underneath.

Lavie. Or, as she liked to be called, Auntie Lavie. Older sister Ruthie hadn't been able to pronounce Laverne, and so Baby Laverne became Lavie to her family and eventually everyone else. One of Gippy and Bette's two youngest, Lavie was the twin to sister Sukie, though they were twins in looks only. Lavie aimed for a motherly vibe but had no designs on marriage or children of her own.

She mostly lived in Corolla and painted island scenes in the summer, hoping tourists who visited snapped them up as unique and valuable. They were neither, but they kept Lavie's lights on and gas in her car, and she was able to maintain a getaway on Knotts Island and a little skiff to motor back and forth.

He had no idea why she was waiting for him to return home.

He parked the old truck, setting the parking brake before releasing the clutch and opening the door. He noted Lavie's door opening at the same time. She must be impatient. Or in desperate need. Lavie never moved faster than people's demands allowed.

"Lavie," he called when he could fully see her face. "Been at your parents. I've some coffee on the cooker, but it might need a bit of warming. You thinking of coming in?"

"Uncle Samuel, this has been a day! Oh, but what you don't

know." She placed her hand to her face and she shivered, her head first, and it followed to her feet before she grabbed the top of the car door to steady herself.

"Coffee then. Come on in, girl."

He did note that she wasn't in her painting gear, rather wearing thick dungarees, a knit beanie with a rainbow tassel, and wellies. Lavie wasn't a wellies-type girl except when she was in her little boat and headed over to Knotts.

As she entered, she worked the heavy, rubber gumboots off to expose equally heavy socks underneath.

"I don't have any other shoes. I hope you don't mind my socks." The socks *were* Sukie, in bright rainbow colors.

"No so much as I would mind you wearing your wellies inside. You been on your boat?"

"Oh, Uncle!" She fell onto a chair at the table and forced her fingers into her hair. Then she pulled the beanie from her head, tossed it on the table, and did the hair thing once more.

"Trouble, I assume." It might as well be. There was enough of it going around. Just ask Charles-Edouard. "Is that old motor giving you fits again?"

"No, worse." She glanced around her, looking for something. "I didn't bring it in. I'll be right back."

She stood, headed for the door, stopped to slip her feet into the gumboots, and let the screen slam on the way out. Through the window, he watched her lean into the back seat and emerge with a brown paper shopping bag. She clutched it to her like it would get away if she didn't hold it tight. She reversed the process upon reentering the house and dropped the bag on the table.

"You want coffee now, or is that our focus?"

"You are so sweet, Uncle Samuel. Coffee, please."

"Let me put you right, then." He took the cup the police

officer had used earlier, checked the inside to see that it was clean, and he poured Lavie a cup. He made an extra for himself, using his same cup from the morning.

"Thank you." She lifted the cup to her face, and the coffee inside tried to slosh out. She was still shaking.

"I know you got your manners on, Lavie. It's the reason you're trying to drink that coffee instead of telling me what's on your mind. Grown up is as grown up does, so spit it out."

"Amanda—" She choked on the name and set down the coffee cup.

"I know about Amanda. This isn't the wide world up here, Niece. What about her?"

"Then you know she's at my place on the island. And why."

"Maybe more than you think I do but go on." Lavie might refuse to talk about her "private" lifestyle, but it was no secret to those that knew her. As far as Amanda, with the news from this morning, it was like hauling in a crab net to find a crab hanging there, and the crab's name was Charles-Edouard. It would be no surprise to see him involved.

"Collie claims to be her boyfriend—" Collie was Collins Beaumarchais, from the side of the family living at The Wharf in Currituck, and the eldest brother of twin brothers, Jean-Paul and Charles-Edouard; and twin sisters, Marie Louise and Dorthea.

"So I hear." Samuel sipped his coffee to give his niece time to get this out. She was struggling, but he couldn't help her without telling her that her secrets were less secret than she hoped.

"He's not her boyfriend, really." She locked onto Samuel's face. "Really, Uncle Samuel. Not like romantically. He says he is to get Charles-Edouard to leave her alone."

"Not a bad idea. Being left alone by Charles-Edouard, I

mean. What's turned things around?" She hadn't mentioned the man's death, and Samuel wasn't certain the policewoman would want him to tell every person in Corolla, even if he had told his brother and his wife.

"Collie called Amanda. They found Charles in the Sound."

"I heard." Samuel breathed easier. It was no longer his secret to keep. "That's good for Amanda, right?"

"I don't know, Uncle Samuel." Tears began to stream down her cheeks. Without explaining, she stood, pulled a black leather satchel from the shopping bag, unzipped the top, and dumped out the contents onto the table.

Cash tumbled everywhere, more than Samuel had ever seen in one location before.

"This is the Lamborghini of surprises ..." He looked at Lavie hard as he let his words trail off.

"I know, Uncle Samuel. When Amanda called, I motored over there. Charles-Edouard left this with her and told her to never open it. When she heard about him being found, she cut the lock off and discovered what was inside. She didn't want it in the house with her."

"You've told no one about this." The old gears in Samuel's head were unlocking and beginning to turn. Charles-Edouard gone, face-down in the Sound; the bag of money, unclaimed and undocumented; the lawyer's fee to boot out their French cousins and reclaim The Wharf as their legacy and their right.

"Of course not, Uncle Samuel. Amanda's frightened, and I want nothing to do with it." Many of the bills were loose, but most were banded in stacks of twenties and fifties. She picked up a stack, glared at it with disdain, then tossed it back on the pile and headed to the sink to wash her hands. "I feel filthy even touching it."

"Let me put this right. We don't want to implicate Amanda

in anything, now do we? Like my papa used to say—" He cut off his words. He had intended to finish with "—there's money to be made in the Sound," but he looked up to see Lavie's full attention on him.

"What, Uncle Samuel? What did Grampa used to say?"

"When you're in the Sound, just keep outta the deep spots, stroll right across. Amanda could be in a deep spot if anyone knew about this." He pushed the pile of money tighter, containing the spread, as if it would contaminate anything else it touched.

"I would take this to Mama and Daddy, but Mama, she likes fancy too much. She could never not tell everyone." Lavie's face crumpled. "Daddy would ask about Amanda and why Charles left the money with her, and I don't have it in me to share that with him."

"Lavie, come sit." Samuel indicated a chair but not the one next to the money. He took her hands in his and looked into her face. "I can take care of this. Do you need some of it for anything? Your car or for paint supplies? Maybe to do work on your Knotts Island place?"

"I live poorer than I really am, Uncle, but you know me well enough for that. I might like Daddy to have a new car, but he loves that old Corolla—" pronounced Co-*roll*-la "—and Mama … she would only brag. No, make it disappear. If only Amanda hadn't opened it." Tears appeared and began to run down her cheeks.

"With Charles gone, no one will know—" at least he hoped not "—and if someone comes around, I'll tell them what Papa used to say to people who wanted to cause him trouble."

"What's that, Uncle?" Lavie's face was clearing up, and she wiped an eye and tried to smile.

Samuel balled his fist and growled like an old-time Banker,

which of course he was, "You want to keep your two front teeth?"

"You are so good for me, Uncle Samuel. I'm glad I came straight to you. Let me help you put this away—"

"No, no, Lavie. You don't need to think about this again. You get outta here and head back to check on Amanda if you think she needs you. Grown up is as grown up does, and that means I got this."

"Thank you. I love you, Uncle Samuel." She searched for her keys, then let out a nervous giggle and said, "Oh, I left my keys in the ignition. Why would I have brought them in? I never do."

As she started up her car and turned around to head out of the driveway, Samuel stepped inside the house and evaluated the pile of money. He was glad she hadn't reloaded the bills into the bag and that she had washed her hands after touching the one stack. He glanced at his hands. He had, though, before he touched her hands, but that couldn't be undone. From under the sink, he pulled out a pair of latex gloves, slipped them on, and returned the cash to the leather satchel, which he carefully returned to the paper shopping bag before folding over the top and setting it on the floor beside the table. He then pulled off the latex gloves while keeping them inside out, slipped them into a used zipper baggie, squeezed the air out, and sealed it. Then, with a bottle of bleach, he wiped down the entire tabletop and his hands before rinsing them with water from the sink.

He walked to the front door and took in the sky and the bank of dark clouds over the ocean and decided that there might be another squall blowing in today. He held up the baggie, evaluated it and what it might mean if the gloves were ever tested for drug residue, and decided that if he was burning trash, he might need to get to it.

He hadn't forgot that he had promised that Dare County officer a DNA sample from John, yet it was the lawyer on his mind; and this sudden, God-given influx of cash; and Lavie's tears; and wanting those Currituck folks out of that Currituck property that should rightfully belong to the Knights. This was just taking back a shingle-full of what they had stolen from his people. It was only right, tit-for-tat, the Banker way. You get in my face, and I take your two front teeth. Anyways, they had decided to wade the Sound and forgot there were deep spots just where they least expected. If you can't keep your head above water, you best keep outta the Sound.

With his mind made up, Samuel made his way to the burn barrel, tossed the baggie inside, added some cardboard and wood scraps, and doused it with lighter fluid. A lighted match ensured the baggie and the gloves inside would never see the light of day.

He did need to head off to see Lucie. She had moved on from Papa's stories of the wealthy Knights from whom they'd descended—and who'd forgotten about them—but she bristled at the Currituck interlopers with their verifiable but distant bloodlines.

Verifiable! Samuel spat into the burn barrel and listened to it sizzle. They were no kin of his!

He pulled his old cell phone from a back pocket and checked the signal. One bar. He might could make the call to see if Lucie had something and could perhaps meet him halfway, maybe in Roper. Yeah, Roper would be good. He clicked to call.

"Samuel, that you? Any news about John?" Lucie was like that, to the point.

"Nothing yet but still checking. Listen, Lucie, you got something with John's DNA on it? I had a police officer stop by—"

"What are you saying, Samuel?" Even over the phone, Lucie puffed up. "This something to do with those Currituck fools? How dare they! I'm glad the county has the Club rather than that bunch of foreign braggarts! Better a museum than belonging to that crowd! Why, they are not even Knights! By rights it's ours, and once we have the house back—"

"I never said anything about the Whalehead, Lucie. Just something of John's, a hairbrush or comb, anything. The officer wants to eliminate him from something. She assured me it's all routine." Now he felt he was lying, but Lucie was like that. You had to test the water, and if it churned, you best backpaddle to the edge.

"I might have a clip of his baby hair. I could give you some of that. He's okay, though? I haven't heard in a couple days."

"I'm checking on it, Lucie. Can you meet me in Roper? I want to get the hair to the officer today. To clear John, you see. Then you can know he's safe."

"I'll need gas in my car, and Marc might need to ride along—"

"That's fine, Lucie. It's a long ways, so I'm gonna get outta here. I'll see you and Marc in a couple hours."

He hung up, poked the coals in the barrel, and decided the gloves were gone. Inside, he lifted the floorboards in the closet, set the paper bag inside, locked the door—which he rarely did—and started his truck up to head to Roper. He could go north from Kitty Hawk, through Elizabeth City, and across the Albemarle Sound Bridge; or head on down to Kill Devil Hills, back through Manteo, and along the southern shores of the Albemarle.

Currituck had him irritated, and the northern route would pass nearly in sight of The Wharf; so he chose the southern route. Besides, it would save him a quarter hour, and he wanted to be there before Lucie. With Marc working at the Cadillac house in New Bern, there was no telling what car they might be in, but they knew his Dodge. They could find him easier than he could find them.

It turned out to be an easy decision after all, unlike the money under his floorboards. But he had several hours to think on that, whatever he decided he wanted to do.

SAMUEL KNIGHT pushed in his clutch, forced his old column shifter into first despite a slight grinding of gears, and eased out from the Beaufort Community College parking area towards Newland Road. It would take him under Hwy 64 and rejoin the highway fifteen minutes later in Creswell and give him the opportunity to stop by Maitland's. He'd gotten onto that idea from what Lucie had handed him when they met up at the college.

"Marc," Samuel had called from his truck when the new Cadillac pulled in, and the driver's window disappeared into the door. "Thank you for being company to Lucie for the drive out."

"He had to come by rights." Lucie leaned over the center console and called out Marc's window. "It's the price of being married to me." Her hair, once dark, had gone fully gray years before and now sported a light auburn wash. She wore it short with curls. She liked stylish, modern clothing that hid the extra pounds she could no longer keep off.

Marc laughed, let himself out, and opened the back door. The wind had picked up even this far from the coast, and he held on to keep the door from flying out of his hand.

Lucie called to Samuel, "I'm not getting out. We're meeting Sissy at Texas Roadhouse in Goldsboro this evening, and we can just barely make it if we do a quick turnaround. Thank you for looking into John's whereabouts, Samuel. I don't think

Gippy's even noticed. That brother of mine—" She pushed her hair back from the left side of her face, revealing the congenital deformity that had left her with only three "fingers." No one who knew her very long thought about it anymore, but there it was, out and on display, proof that it no longer defined Lucie's self-image.

Marc offered him a decorative cardboard box with a lid. Before he passed it through Samuel's window, he adjusted his position to block the wind as best as he could and pulled the lid free.

"Here's what Lucie says. This on top is John's baby book. He has several locks of hair inside, and she wasn't sure if it matters how old he was when they were cut. The rest of it is some old family papers she's been meaning to send your direction and hasn't gotten around to. She said you'll know what it is when you look through it."

"Thank you, Marc." Samuel pulled the box through the window and placed it on the seat. "I'll be heading back then."

"Trying to avoid, what do you call this, a blow coming up?" Marc's clothes whipped against him.

"Come on out and enjoy it." Samuel knew better, but he liked to offer.

Marc grinned. "I'd love a place on the Banks, not likely up to Corolla, though. It'd be a hard drive back to the Cadillac house each day."

"On the Banks we call it retirement." Another tease.

"I don't decide anything without Lucie, and she's not given me permission yet. I think she likes the free cars."

"Maybe she's right. You take care, Marc." He called and waved to Lucie as Marc returned to his car, "Thank you, Lucie. I appreciate you and Marc taking part of your day to bring this up."

"You just let me know about John. Don't forget." She wagged a finger at him, a real one from her right hand, before settling back into her seat and pulling out a magazine.

As Samuel pulled out, the box got him to thinking. The funeral home had handled his papa's details back in '07, and while Robbie Cranwell handled the business now, his papa, Frank, had known his grandmama, Juno Brayboy, back in the day. He didn't have Maitland's number, but he hadn't forgotten how to find it.

The fifteen-minute drive gave him time to pull the lid free, set the baby book aside, and browse the family papers. A few were filled with legalese, some water-stained and faded, and a number were newspaper clippings brittle with age. He'd leave those until he got home. He found a few old photos, one of him in his mother's arms at two. She was likely pregnant with Gippy, but in the old image, it was hard to tell.

By the time he reached Maitland's, he could hear the wind whistling though the nooks and slippery places every old truck has. Beside him, one file, containing papers in a brown sleeve, had one word scrawled across the edge in pencil, Juno, with the year 1935 underneath. That one he really wanted to look through. He glanced up at the building, which looked the same as always, a shoebox by New Bern standards, but large enough to do the job. The Juno file had his attention, so he put it under his arm and headed inside.

"Robbie," he said as he closed the door. "Expected to see Lark at the desk."

"With the storm, she headed home early—"

"That Samuel Knight I hear?" A man closer to Samuel in age appeared from a side office. "What's it been, twenty years since we saw your daddy to the other side?"

"If you call it that way. How are you, Frank?" Samuel held

the brown packet in one hand and reached the other to shake.

"Better'n you folks out on the Banks. I seem to hear sad news from out to the Sound. You bringing me paperwork on your cousin?"

Samuel laughed. "Let me put you right, Frank. Only one person I know of you could be talking about, and I don't lay claim to the man. This? I picked up some family papers from my sister—"

"Lucie? How's Lucie getting along these days?"

"She and Marc are meeting up with Sissy in Goldsboro this evening, so I suppose just fine."

"She still driving those new Cadillacs?"

"For as long as Marc has a job at Trent. Listen, Frank, you mentioned my folder. I was wondering—"

"Juno Brayboy." When Samuel gave him a puzzled expression, he explained, "I can read as well as the next man. Your grannie and the name she put on your daddy's birthing certificate. I was about to give you a call, anyways. Come join me in my office."

In Frank's line of work, no whispers went unrequited or ignored. It's what drove business, kept people coming in and out … in a casket or otherwise. Lark lived toward Elizabeth City, across the Albemarle but right close to the highway leading to Currituck and the Sound. It was the reason she'd gone on home early, having to cross the Albemarle Bridge in heavy weather. It didn't suit her none. Lark's cousin lived in Currituck, and she'd called Lark to see what she knew about the county cars all over the place, even a Coast Guard helicopter flying overhead.

Frank hesitated for a moment before telling Samuel that people knew about the feud between the cousins, if Samuel wanted to name it that. People did, like it or not, so that's what

Frank had taken to calling it. Frank continued and explained that his daughter lived in Dare County, and she'd seen the truck and those bikes impounded in the county's A-District lot. Everybody knew who those bikes belonged to, and when somebody turns up like Charles-Edouard did …

Frank trailed off about then, and he waited expectantly on Samuel, opening the floor, willing to accept any whispers the man might be willing to share.

"You know what you know, Frank, I give you that." Samuel set the folder on Frank's desk with his grandmother's name exposed. "The feud's real, at least on my part, but no one in my family's done anything to Charles-Edouard. If he's dead—" Samuel didn't want word to get out that he was sharing what he shouldn't be sharing. "—he's dead by his own doing, not from me or mine."

"You would like them gone, though." Frank sat back in his chair, calm in his certainty. "What about the deed your daddy used to crow about? Your people still can't get hold of that?"

"I'm working a way." He thought of the money under the floorboards and the lawyer fees it would pay.

"May I?" Frank pointed to the folder.

Samuel shrugged and pushed it toward him. "I was collecting some things from Lucie, and she wanted this out of her house. I haven't opened it yet."

"But you saw the name, thought it might be good." Frank had slipped out the paperwork and was glancing through it.

"Well, yes." And Frank was doing what Samuel couldn't easily do, linking the dots together. It was the reason he'd taken his paperwork to Gippy's earlier, knowing it would take the two of them to work out what this man could do alone.

Gilt edges made one form stand out, and Frank worked it out from the rest. He opened it, read the words to himself, then looked hard at Samuel.

"Juno always said your daddy was a Knight to the bone. A lawyer would need to say, but I believe this here paper is signed by none other than Edward Knight." He turned it towards Samuel and pointed to a signature at the bottom of the page.

Samuel let his eyes climb to the top where, under two gold seals, words in oversized script spelled out in gold lettering, "This day, in the State of North Carolina, it is hereby certified that the Waterfront Warehouse Complex with Ten Acres fronting the Currituck Sound, hereafter referred to as The Property, bounded by ..." At those words, he skimmed the rest, looking for his grandmother's name.

"There." Frank pointed. The majority of the document was in smaller, faded type, unlike the pristine gold. But there it was, Juno Brayboy, good as gold. "I'd be taking care of this, Samuel. Don't know that it's good for anything, but it might be."

"Thank you, Frank." After all these years, Samuel's heart was pounding with excitement, and he could hardly speak.

"You'd best get on home. This wind's gonna fight you all the way. If it works out that you can, let those Currituck folk know it's not too far for me to drive out to help them in their time of sorrow."

"Thank you, Frank." Samuel shook hands with Robbie on the way out and was still surprised when he exited the front door. The darkening sky tore at his clothes before subsiding enough he could make it to his truck.

He debated whether it would do him any good to stop by to deliver John's baby book to the Dare County offices. As he pulled out and aimed for Hwy 64, he hit his first rainsquall and flipped on the truck's wipers. He let the baby book go. He had time to think on it before he got there, and by then, who knew what the storm might become.

THERE ARE WORSE things than an island storm. Samuel learned that at three. He didn't remember much of his mama, and only tidbits around her death, but he remembered that it was the greatest loss of his life at the time. On the drive back, crossing the Virginia Dare Bridge and on across Roanoke Island with the Manteo turnoff coming and then going, the box at his side consumed him. The deed—it looked so real and official—was a gift of life made good again.

If it proved good in court. He reminded himself of that more than once.

But "if" didn't ride along with him in his truck. This and the money under his floorboards … well, with those, the storm didn't matter much. Even as the wind whistled through the cracks in his weatherstripping, and the hard-driving rain occasionally dripped from the top of his windshield, the idea of redeeming his papa's name and kicking those Currituck people off The Wharf and back to France overrode any sense of dread the weather could possibly inflict.

Heading north on the Croatan Highway, water was taking out low-slung cars where it pooled in congested spots. A two-door sportster half off the shoulder had its flashers flashing, and inside, a business-type person glowed in the light from their phone. The water on the glass created a modernist scene as Samuel passed, with the person's image flickering in the streaks of water, changing him from funny to freakish and then back to funny again.

Samuel's real surprise came after taking the 12 turnoff at the Visitor's Bureau, crossing Virginia Dare Trail, and passing Southern Shores Realty on the left. The road was mostly lined with houses for a good ways, and as he approached the Dare County EMS Station at Dogwood Trail, several rugged, specialty vehicles pulled out with lights flashing, heading the same direction as him.

There wasn't much to think of it, just to get out of the way and not hinder them. The weather had turned on the Banks, and who knew what people might get themselves into. Like he always said, grownup is as grownup does, unlike that off islander back on the highway, driving a low-slung car on high-water days.

His surprise shifted to disbelief and then dismay when the road was completely blocked just before he reached Hickory Trail. There wasn't much at Hickory Trail except trees and houses, and mostly what you saw was trees when you drove by, that and two pedestrian crosswalks painted on the asphalt. Today, in the spattering rain that had become driving sheets of irritation, several Southern Shores patrol cars had the lanes blocked, their lights flashing, and a patrol officer in a slicker was directing traffic down to one lane, which was partially off the roadway, and then, just barely allowing them room to squeeze by. To Samuel's left, a woman in thick dungarees, a cable knit sweater, and a knit beanie with a rainbow tassel huddled under a blanket with a female officer at her side attempting to keep her dry.

The dots connected when he saw the Beetle with its rear tire blown out and the back bumper fifty feet away and blackened like it had come from a fire. Part of Lavie's face had been torn from the Beetle with the rear tire, leaving her gaping oddly as if amazed that part of her was gone. He found a spot he could pull completely off the road, opened his door, and started to head back to check on his niece.

A patrol officer in a car with fogged up windows decided otherwise. He threw open his door and emerged, calling, "You! Get back in your truck. There's nothing for you to see here."

Samuel responded in the same manner. "I'll talk with you when you get your manners on. That's my niece back there, so let me put you right. I intend to check on her. You can follow me or get outta my way."

Samuel didn't wait on the man but headed towards Lavie, now mostly soaked and dripping, and knelt before her and took one of her hands in his.

"Uncle." Her eyes were fuller than might be expected by the rain. Her face crumpled.

"Are you okay, Lavie? That's all I want to know."

"I think so. Did you see my car? The officers say it was an explosive device. Do you think …" She grasped his hand with both of hers.

He put his fingers to her mouth to quiet her question and looked at the car just down the road. The trouble was, he did think. Charles-Edouard, the satchel of money, Amanda calling Lavie, and Lavie carting it away. He shivered, and not from the rain. If they had wanted to take Lavie out, they would have placed the explosives in a more opportune location. Clearly this was a warning.

We want our money back. Or else.

Samuel tried to remember if anyone might have seen Lavie heading to his house, either coming or going. His house wasn't hidden, or else he wouldn't be able to glimpse the ocean from his porch, even if he had to stand to do so.

Or else. What would that mean? With Charles gone … and another dot connected for Samuel. It became obvious that Charles had never been the kingpin in whatever that bunch was running from The Wharf. Someone somewhere was still alive and making tracks in the sand. For no good reason, he remembered being six and seeing his papa with a wad of greenbacks with no job and no explanation for why.

He felt an insane loss for Lavie's satchel with its money and all the good it could do. The lawyers, the gold-encrusted deed, and The Wharf began slipping away, like those long-ago surfboat imprints in the sand being washed away by the rising tide.

Chapter 7

Overwash

DEPUTY NATHAN PRESTON perched on a stool just behind Paloma Ronson's desk at the A-District sub-station. Bursts of noise from down the hallway and out of various rooms told of unseen activity in the building.

"I don't like to criticize white folks, but that new gun you're wearing, you even fired it? My grandpappy always said that if you introduce a gun in the first act, it better go off by the final scene." Paloma had out an old-fashioned jar of correction fluid, and she was leaning into her typewriter and dabbing at a misspelled word.

"I don't even know what that means." The keys from the impounded truck were long gone, and the empty metal cabinet at Nathan's side had his attention. He opened the glass door and then clicked it shut.

"It's good I unlocked that cabinet." Paloma resealed the

correction fluid and dropped it in her drawer. She fanned the correction with her free hand.

"Why is that?" Nathan put his hands between his knees and gave Paloma his attention.

"Cause it seems like you got nothing else to do 'cept fiddle with that door."

"Paloma, here's my plan." Now that she had broken the ice, he had to let this out. "My wife, that's Paytyne, is in Texas with our daughter. I've been so busy with Wally doing my field training that I've hardly had time to think of anything else. I want to invite her out to see where I work and to meet all y'all."

"You've not looked out the window this morning?" She swiveled her chair and looked him long in the face.

"It's just a little rain." He dropped off the stool, walked to a small window that opened on the parking lot, and pulled a curtain aside. The sun was up, but that didn't mean it was bright. Everything gleamed with wet, and bands of light rain danced across the lot like a choreographed music video.

"It seems to me you gotta know it's raining to come in out of the rain."

"What?" Nathan dropped the curtain and gave Paloma a puzzled expression.

"This heap of calls says some people might get washed off the beach before this blow is over." Paloma held up a stack of phone messages jotted down on official forms. "You take these. You'll have something to do."

"Just this morning?" He took them and flipped through the stack. "Some are from last night. Isn't someone already assigned to—"

"You seen Ed or Clara this morning?"

Nathan handed the messages back to Paloma and peeked through the window again. "I don't see their cars."

"Now, we're getting somewhere. You might want to wait a few days on your missus." She tapped the stack of messages. "I don't need to take any more of these. Someone has to transcribe them into the computer, and that someone's me."

"In Texas, this isn't even real rain. We grill out in stuff like this." However, Nathan recalled that there *was* thunder overnight, and the rain *had* been incessant. Even so, Paytyne was used to worse. More to the point, anyone who lived in Texas was used to worse. Nathan had come to describe the difference as being gently reminded that the weather was changing versus being hit with a sledgehammer to let you know it was already here. Of course, North Carolina was the reminder while Texas was the sledgehammer.

"And we're on a sandbar. A flat sandbar."

"But when it stops, all the water runs into the ocean. How deep can it get?" It made sense, no matter how hard it rained.

"Don't be riling me up, now, you and that Texas nonsense. Even white people might be glad to be shut of this rain by the time it goes away."

He could see that Paloma had concluded their conversation as she began typing once more. He was just starting to twiddle his thumbs when the captain's door opened, and Jason Romney appeared. With the weather, he was in heavyweight jeans, cowboy boots, and a standard-issue county shirt with county labels, multiple pockets, and all. He held a small spiral notebook and finished writing something before closing it and slipping it into his shirt pocket. He noticed Nathan and called out his name.

"Deputy Preston, I'm glad you're still here." Jason moved forward, and a neatly dressed man followed him out of the office. "Have you met Sergeant Taylor? He's our county drone operator."

"Not likely today," Sean Taylor quipped. "Have you seen

the skies?"

"That's what I've been saying," Paloma interjected without pausing at her keyboard. "But who am I to criticize you white folks?"

"Nathan, you two been having a discussion?"

"He calls this a Texas sprinkle shower, and while I don't want to step on the man's toes, Texas is a world away from North Carolina." Paloma paused, pointed to something on the page in her typewriter, retrieved the correction fluid from her desk, and said, "You people need to get on about your business and quit messing me up."

Jason motioned to Nathan, and he joined them as they headed down the hallway. "So, you two met?"

"You were at the meeting yesterday." Nathan acknowledged Sean. "I wanted to talk with you, then we got that report of that man floating in the Sound. You think he was one of them drug mules?"

Sean glanced at Jason before answering. "That's what we're hoping to find out."

The three men filed into the small office shared by Nathan and his field training officer, Wally Styles. Two desks on opposite walls provided just enough room to allow them to work at the same time if they didn't take up too much space. Nathan quickly learned that his field training officer liked to lean back in his chair with one foot cocked over his knee, so a spare chair was wedged next to a filing cabinet for Nathan when Wally was in full work mode.

The room was empty, and Nathan fell into his desk chair. He leaned forward with his hands on the knees, and as soon as Jason and Sean were settled, his thoughts burst from him. "What I really wanted to ask about yesterday was Springer Point and Blackbeard. That's all down on Ocracoke Island, isn't it? My wife and I were on a ferry that got stranded on a sandbar a while back. Paytyne was pregnant with our daughter, and she was given a lift on a fishing boat. I stayed in the car, but I remember some of your faces. That might have been about …" He left the question hanging.

"A year ago?" Sean looked at Jason for confirmation. When Jason nodded, the neatly turned-out young sergeant admitted sheepishly, "I was really seasick, but I remember sitting next to a pregnant woman we picked up. That was your wife? Didn't Emily Bryant meet with you at the Bodie Island lighthouse?"

"Right, but that was on a previous visit. Paytyne and I had come out for my cousin's wedding. That's why I wanted this job." He grinned broadly. "No reason to hang back, I say—"

The walk down memory lane was abruptly cut off when the lights in the building flickered and died, and the heating went silent. In the silence, only Paloma's typing punctured the darkness with staccato clicks, until even they went quiet. Wind-driven water pummeled the outside of the frame building, and a long gust began to whistle until the building vibrated.

It finally settled, and the lights flickered. Small things in the building began to rouse back to life with clicks and buzzing noises, until everything came fully alive. From down the hall, Paloma said, "About time," and the clicking from her typewriter started up again.

Wally Styles appeared at the door drying his hands with a brown paper towel. "At least the water works when the power's out. You people are thick as molasses on toast in there. Before I get stuck in with you, I might check to see if the captain's free."

"Anything I should know?" Nathan.

"A car bomb up to Southern Shores yesterday. It showed up on the inter-agency database this morning. I recognized a name

I know."

"You need my help?" Again, Nathan.

"Nah, just a glitch. I'll let you know if anything comes of it." Wally leaned in, dropped the paper towel in the trash, and headed towards the main desk and Diane Turnipseed's office.

"Like Texas yet?" Jason grinned.

"The lights came back on." Nathan was enjoying this. "So, close but not quite."

Jason and Sean laughed.

"No drones this morning." Jason stood and tapped Sean's shoulder with a loose fist. "How about checking to see if any evacuations are possible today? It might keep us out of trouble."

Sean nodded. "You got that right, Jason. Nathan, you joining us?"

"That's why I got this job. Just give me a second." He scribbled a note to Wally, put it on the man's desk, and exited the room.

As they headed back down the hallway, Sean shared about Paytyne's rescue from the ferry. "That boat that rescued your wife? I hated being on that thing. I mean, I want to serve, commitment and respect and all that, but being on the water doesn't agree with me. I tried to think not seasick, and it didn't help at all."

"Paytyne told me."

"What? Everybody knows?" Sean stopped walking and let out a hard sigh. "Shoot, y'all, I'll never be able to board a boat again."

Nathan couldn't picture not wanting to be aboard a boat, and they had the big Coast Guard ones out here. How he hoped! That would be more fun than almost anything, and it'd be great if Paytyne was here to watch.

As they approached Paloma's desk, Wally appeared from

Diane's office, with a spiral notebook he was just sliding in his shirt pocket. A weather radio behind Paloma's desk kicked on with a piercing warning siren. After the required eight seconds of the high-pitched tone, a voice began, "This is the National Weather Service. Rising winds and possible tornado conditions from Kill Devil Hills to Corolla in Currituck County will likely create life threatening surf conditions. Anyone living in this area—"

Phones from everyone in the room began dinging. Jason had his out first. On the screen, a text titled OBXAlert scrolled across the screen revealing a very similar message to the one from the National Weather Service.

Diane Turnipseed appeared at her office door with her phone in hand. "Who has an Explorer available?" The clear meaning was that with the conditions just outside, a low-slung patrol car wasn't likely to suffice. She raised an eyebrow and aimed her question directly at Jason.

"Ah, Diane. It's brand new." Jason had his hand halfway into the air.

"And you're above your knees if you forget it's the county's and not yours. Dump on me what you four men have swimming in your bait bucket that you can't toss over the side."

The building shivered, the lights blinked off without even a flicker of a warning, and thunder jarred the windows as they strobed with a lightning flash.

"That's harsh. That was a water tower hit." Wally. The water tower literally overshadowed the A-District building at its feet.

The radios on each person's belt kicked into life. "Manteo for Diane Turnipseed. Are you available, Diane?"

Diane retrieved her radio from her belt on the back of her door, and she stepped back into her office and partially closed her door to talk. With the building's power off, the sounds of the storm leaned in until a generator burped and began to hum, and the building shook off the distraction and began to return to life.

Diane appeared back at her door. She paused, closed her eyes and took a deep breath and let it out before speaking. "Some people don't got the sense that God gave a minnow."

"Not us, I hope." Jason, grinning.

"Shush that, Jason. I'm working out a plan." She gritted her jaw for a short time, then said, "Ed and Clara are out doing traffic calls. I hoped to send Wally and Nathan to notify people who might not have their weather radios on, but now that's a big no."

"I'm willing to help, Diane." Jason.

"Don't you worry yourself about it, Jason Romney." She frowned, then shifted her line of thinking. "To tell the story honest, you can. Boats have been sighted offshore—" and at looks of dismay from everyone except Nathan, she held up a hand. "Hold your taters. Like I said, some people don't got the sense that God gave a minnow, but that don't change our job none. We're here to make sure they survive this even if they are above their knees to be out on the water today. You people get on your foul weather gear—oilskins if you got 'em—and Jason, you chauffeur these other three down and see what there's to see."

"No evacuations?" Jason grinned.

"You don't got a radio on?" Diane blew out her cheeks in frustration. "Why do you call yourself a sheriff's deputy if you don't know how to deputy?" She closed her door hard and sealed herself inside.

"Because I'm a sergeant, Diane. Did you forget? I got promoted." Jason seemed pleased with himself.

His answer was something hitting the door from the other side.

Paloma inserted a fresh sheet of paper into her typewriter and muttered, "I'm just repeating, mind you, but it seems the captain just said that some people don't got the sense God gave a minnow. What people, I'm asking, cause I 'bout think maybe she's right."

All of this made Nathan happy. He was right in the middle of it, part of the team, and he could hardly wait to get Paytyne here so she could see his dream playing itself out in the real world.

WITH JASON'S Explorer not being a "patrol car," it had real back seats. Nathan breathed easier when he opened the door to see vinyl rather than hard plastic. The wind rocked the vehicle, gusting with angry hammerfists, and bands of stinging rain pelted the glass while trying to get inside. After several minutes, Jason and Sean joined them just as an especially strong gust hit the parking area, and they fought to hold on.

Wally took the back seat with him, and with both doors open at the same time, the center of the seat was wet before they could seal themselves in.

"Man," Jason said after closing the door, while pushing the hood of his waterproofs back from his head. "This wind must be causing crazy swells. It's caterwauling like a seasoned seaman after too many beers."

"Think positive for a positive life." Sean was buckling his seatbelt. He paused, undid the clasp, felt inside his waterproofs to ensure all his attachments were firmly attached, and let out a deep breath before buckling up again. "All good."

"Here's the thing," Jason said, looking into the backseat via his rearview mirror as he started the truck. "Counting Currituck

County and Hyde County, there's a hundred miles or more of beach on the Outer Banks. I've got one pair of binoculars in the glove box. The captain wants us to check on boats offshore. Any ideas where to start?"

"I've been to Jeanette's Pier," Nathan offered. "It's close to the turnoff to Manteo—"

"Nah, too far south." Wally had put on his cap as soon as his hood went down, and he had an arm on the windowsill absently tapping the inside of the glass.

Sean grinned. "Shoot, the Nag's Head Pier is just down the road. If we're going to a pier, why not that one?"

"Done it like this once before," Wally drawled, with an *I've got a story for you guys* tone. "Most of this place, you can't see the shore 'cepting you're on top of the dunes, and mostly, the houses have all that claimed. We so much as twitch onto their property without a warrant, and they'll call the city cops on us. You think the piers are a good option, but in this wind? This is a gale, and don't bet it can't become a nor'easter if it wants to decide it that way."

"Tie it up for me, Wally. You have advice you want to share with us, then give it to us." Jason's eyes were still in the mirror, and he had yet to shift into gear.

"First of all, this is seeming like just another rock to turn over, and an unnecessary one at that." The rainbands outside were lashing the windows harder. "I trust the captain, but this sounds like she wants to wash the new off the lot of you."

"Serve no matter what, right, Jason?" Sean found something funny. "You got on the captain's last nerve this morning, so can we say wild goose chase?" He punched Jason on the shoulder with a fist. "On the double, boss. Of course, I can do that. Please."

"I deserve that." Jason shook his head but chuckled. "I do

get like that around her. And you're right. She likely just wanted me out of the office."

"What happened?" Nathan had been banished to Paloma's section of the tidepool while Jason and Sean were in their meeting with Captain Turnipseed, and Wally had abandoned everyone for the restroom.

"You want me to tell it, Jason?" Sean snickered.

"It should be illegal for you to do this but go ahead. I'm headed to 12 while you tell your wild tales." He shifted into reverse, and the vehicle began to move.

"There's no one in detention at Manteo, and I can't fly my drone in this weather, so we're filling in at A-District—"

"And Diane doesn't think A-District needs anyone to be filling in—" Jason added his view. They were crossing the small bridge at Blount Bay, and to the left, rows of small whitecaps were being beaten down by curtains of driving rain. The tires on the Explorer thumped as he entered the bridge and again as he exited the far side.

"So, anyway, Jason was telling her that he works for the whole county, not just A-District, so he can serve anywhere the county needs him. Isn't that right, Jason?" Sean was almost beside himself with his story.

"Okay, I'll say it. She said I was above my knees if I was forgetting that I'm a sergeant and she's a captain. Anywhere in the county, she ranks me and can tell me what to do." Jason seemed to slump in his seat with the admission.

They did try the Nag's Head Pier. The parking lot was mostly empty, with water flooding the area ankle deep in places. They removed their galoshes before entering the building, and once inside the colorful but rustic interior, they let the employees know why they were present and that they would be heading out onto the pier. Stepping back into their galoshes and outside, Wally was proven right. As they made their way along the pier, they were completely exposed, the wind tore at them, and underneath the pier, the water churned. Jason had his binoculars, which he tried to use and finally offered to anyone else who wanted to try.

Nathan took him up with, "You don't need to offer it to me twice." Jason had him secure the strap in case the glasses slipped, and Nathan put them to his face and tried scanning the horizon. Rain spattered the lens, requiring him to continually wipe them, and finally he settled into searching through a water-soaked, shifting image, deciding he could see well enough to determine whether he had located a boat or not.

The rain grew heavier, and eventually even Jason called the visit to the pier a failure. As they plodded back to the Explorer through the waterlogged parking lot, Wally said, "Seen it once like this before. Back in '06, had over a foot of rain. Flooded out the northern Banks. Might have an overwash if this keeps up."

"Overwash?" Nathan climbed in the truck and asked the question as he pulled off his gummies.

"In 1962, the Ash Wednesday storm took out Hwy 12 and upwards of eighteen hundred houses." That was from Sean, and Wally raised his eyebrows skeptically. "It happened down south between Avon and Buxton. I swear."

"You're a young pup to know that."

"Shoot," Sean said, looking exceptionally pleased. "I studied up before taking a job here, so if you want facts, you can count on me."

The car's radio went off. The connection crackled but the words could be understood clearly. "This is Coast Guard MH-60U *To-The-Rescue*, Pilot Martin Wyman calling Jackie Powers at Station Hatteras Inlet. The windshear up here is atrocious. I need to bring my bird in and come back out when this clears."

The helicopter pilot went on to give his current location, say that he had located the struggling boats, and requested additional help from the station. He laughed and said, "Tell Gaskill and Farrow that if they're not on that boat you send out, I'm loading them up and dropping them in the water beside the ship, windshear or no."

"That's where we need to head. Wally, how do we tell where they are?" Nathan.

Jason reached to the glovebox and pulled out a paper map. He handed it over the seat. "Sean, did you get those coordinates?"

"On the double." He pulled out his spiral notebook from his shirt pocket, and he clicked to open his pen. He thought for a moment, mouthing the pilot's words as if remembering them exactly, then eagerly wrote down the numbers. He tore the page out and passed it over the seat also.

Wally offered Nathan the map. "Can you read longitude and latitude on one of these?"

"Let me see." Nathan opened the map to find the southern end of the Outer Banks on one side, and the north end on the other. He traced his fingers down the ruler guides at the edges and nodded affirmatively. "I've got it worked out. Let me see the numbers."

He found the approximate points on the X and Y axis and pulled his fingers down and across until they met. He frowned, leaned in to read the fine print, then announced, "Either Currituck County or Dare County, just offshore. That's where he's at."

"So, north. Do you want to pick a county?" Jason was in reverse. He backed into an empty space, shifted gears, and headed out of the parking area towards 12 and the northern

Outer Banks.

"Try the county line," Wally said. "Are we all tagging along?"

"Captain's orders," Sean quipped, grinning at Jason.

"That's where we found the gun and the bloody clothes, right?" Nathan was growing more excited by the minute. "At least one of them's gotta have a drug mule on board, don't you think?"

"A drug mule?" Jason was accelerating north along 12, and the highway had turned into a virtual river. He flipped the HVAC controls to defrost as he said, "A drug mule is for when you're trying to hide the drugs to get past security."

"Then it must be an attempted drop-off, right? This would be the best time for one, because no one would be out there to see them."

"He's got a point, if they could brave the surf, which is clearly giving them trouble." Wally pointed out something else that substantiated Nathan's evaluation. "Ed and Clara did find a cache of drugs with that gun and the bloody clothes. Might find another one." He gave Nathan a thumbs up and grinned.

The rain was blinding by the time they reached the turnoff into the Palmer's Island residential area. The big houses were shrouded in wet, and water flowed from the roofs like icicles. The circle where they'd previously parked was an inland tide-pool, and the lights from the Explorer gleamed off every beam, board, and piece of landscaping.

"Gummies on," Jason commanded, "if we are of a mind."

"You can be sure about that." Wally stamped one foot to force the lumpy, waterproof boot around his heel and thick socks. "Let me get my second shoe on."

"Here's the thing." Jason cracked his window slightly, and wind-whipped spray hit him in the face. He closed it without hesitation. "It's brutal out there. Anyone volunteering to stay behind?"

Nathan glanced in Wally's direction to gauge the man's reaction to Jason's question. Wally was his field training officer, which meant he controlled many of the choices Nathan could make. He had on his waterproof boots, but that didn't mean he wanted to fight his way through this weather. Even for Nathan, who was enthused just to be here, imagining an overwash with nearly two thousand houses lost had worked its magic in his brain. He almost hoped Wally would suggest that they remain in the car, while he would be exceptionally disappointed if they did.

"This is just another rock to turn over. The wet pup next to me needs to experience this. He may not agree, but I'm in charge, so we're tagging along."

"Tagging?" Sean looked back at Wally with surprise. "That's Jason and me. You guys are the bosses here."

Wally winked at Nathan. "We're the bosses, Nathan. You got your wellies ready?"

On the beach, the waves grabbed at the sand and tried to claw the Banks back into the sea, leaving the officers a tiny sliver of dune to stand on. Each time a roller hit, the vibration of the tons of water on the sand was a sledgehammer under their feet, telling them that their safety was temporary, and the sea could reclaim it at any time. The wash from the breaking waves tumbled up the shore and over where Ed and Clara had staked the possible crime scene, truly stealing any evidence that might have been left behind.

Without even trying them, Jason handed Nathan the binoculars. With the wind, the men could barely stand upright, and Sean wrapped the cord around his wrist just in case and put them to his eyes. Water already coated the lenses, and what missed the binoculars forced its way into his waterproofs and tickled his breastbone with icy fingers. Towards the sea, the rain and spray from the surf formed a blanket of haze, but in the distance, three sportfishing boats danced in the grayness, obscure except for the lights from their sterns. One rolled more violently than the others as a wave swept past, and Nathan held his breath longer than he thought possible until the boat reappeared from behind a massive swell. The image through the binoculars blurred, and Nathan couldn't keep his eyes focused. He pulled the glasses from his face and shook his head.

"Let me show you this." Wally offered to take the binoculars. "It's got image stabilization, but you can adjust the eyepieces separately. See if that helps."

Suddenly, a bigger ship appeared alongside the sportfishing boats. Nathan pointed, "The Coast Guard!"

Jason and Sean took his thunder, however, when they picked out the one boat that had rolled excessively. "They're losing that one," Jason called, his voice yelling.

Nathan searched for the boat he had seen rolling earlier and found it closer to shore than he expected. Men in orange immersion suits were dumping crates and boxes over the side, likely to lighten the load, which he considered smart. One large crate was trailed by a long line, and just before the line fed all the way out, the man tossed a smaller package after it. It gave off a red flash before hitting the water and disappearing behind a rising swell. Then the man threw out his arms to catch himself; the boat was lifted partially into the air; and the starboard side went underwater. It attempted to right itself but couldn't, and three men in orange leaped from the capsizing boat to take their chances in the sea. Then a swell obscured any additional action.

"They jumped," Nathan called. "Why did they—"

The boat reappeared, struggled for a moment as if it just

might make it, rolled bottom up, and was totally gone. He could just catch flashes of orange from the escaping fishermen. Farther out, had he also seen the other boats dumping items? If so, the example set by the sunken boat had saved them, as the larger Coast Guard ship was affixing long tow lines to hopefully get them out of harm's way.

The waves from the storm continued to break high up the beach as the stranded seamen struggled to find their way onto the shore. One was continually washed back into the sea. The three men didn't try to help one another, as it would have been useless, but still. Eventually, they saw the four Dare County officers, and the man closest lifted his arms to wave. As he fought his way up the beach, followed by a second man, Jason and Wally helped pull them to the top of the dune. Inside the bulky immersion suits, their faces were haggard but alive.

"I can no longer see your friend." Jason yelled to be heard. The first man who had arrived looked out to sea, also didn't locate him, and turned from the water and shrugged.

The boat, being pushed by the waves, was now visible with its port side to the sky, as it was forced onto the sand. Items that hadn't been thrown overboard—including ice chests and fishing gear—had washed free and were now tumbling dangerously in the surf. An especially large wave lifted the boat, rolled it completely over, and when it was done, the water retreated and pulled the vessel back the other direction. The wheelhouse was now missing, and broken bits of boat swirled around the hull before being carried off by the next round of crashing waves.

The third man finally washed up close enough for Jason to grab his immersion suit and work him onto a section of sand that wasn't constantly underwater. He rolled him to his side to clear his mouth, but even with chest compressions, there was no hint of life. He felt inside the immersion suit for ID but came up empty.

Quizzing the two survivors didn't yield much. They were shivering, didn't seem interested in any of the events they had just experienced, and kept asking for a phone. The one thing Jason did get from them could be summed up in one word.

"Fishermen. Just fishermen. Nothing else. We out fishing, and boom, sky fall, and now we on the shore. Just fishermen." Then they sank into their immersion suits and seemed to fade into themselves, taking no interest in the dead man who had been their companion on the boat.

Jason offered Wally the key to his truck and requested that he and Nathan radio the situation in. He didn't know what help they might get with the storm hitting so hard, but someone needed to know.

The surf was overwashing the path behind the garage, and as they moved into the street, the water was to the rims on the Explorer's wheels. Inside the truck, they pulled the doors to, and relative silence overtook them.

"They didn't even care about the dead man." Nathan shook his head disgustedly.

"Describe what you saw through the binoculars." Wally had the mic in his hand, but he hesitated before calling in.

It was the red blinking light that caught Wally's attention. He had Nathan repeat that part of the story, quizzing him on several points, before making his assessment.

"You think it was drugs, don't you?" Nathan was once more interested in the three boats and their occupants. "Should we go back and search that boat?"

"Now? You sure about that?" Wally still held the mic and chuckled. He cracked the window to reveal the howling wind and raised it immediately. "Perhaps at low tide. We won't find anything, though."

"But if they had drugs—"

"I don't doubt that's a possibility. Those crates you saw going overboard? That's a common technique. The red light you saw is likely a lighted buoy. When law enforcement arrives, they dump the drugs for later retrieval and become a fishing boat, no harm done. The Coast Guard can even inspect the boat and won't find anything. Then, later, they return, drop a line, and retrieve the drugs."

"So, they really are fishermen." Nathan grinned.

"Did you even listen—"

"Fishing for drugs." Nathan did two fist punches, like in a boxing ring and offering a light's out jab to an unwary opponent.

"Got it." Wally shook his head, hit the talk switch, and said, "Sergeant Wally Styles calling Manteo. Capsized boat with two survivors and one deceased person at the Dare County-Currituck County line. Is there any way we can get assistance at this time? Over."

"Karen here, Wally. Say again. At the county line? You're on the beach? Didn't expect you to be going for a swim on a day like today." The surprise in her voice came through clearly.

Nathan let their conversation go and focused on one word. Deceased. That brought home to him that someone had died. He looked at the surroundings outside and the tidal pool in the court that was keen on becoming one with the ocean. As the incoming surf crashed onto the sand just outside his field of view, it sent spray high into the air, the water found every opening, and a new flood surged past the buildings lining the beach, turning the court into a miniature version of the raging expanse on the other side.

So, overwash.

Yeah. It seemed like it was a thing. He closed his eyes and did his best not to imagine how bad this storm might get if it didn't end soon.

DURING THE TIME it took for additional help to arrive, the four Dare County employees settled the two rescued men as high as possible to avoid the constant overwashing of the dunes and walkways. The third man was pulled onto a slight rise that was occasionally battered with heavy spray but otherwise seemed unlikely to drag him into the sea. Nathan cringed at the battering rainfall continually refilling the suit around the man's face, soaking him in a private flood in an eerie but inescapable way. His skin was unnaturally pale with dark undertones, and thick shoulders under the survival suit said he should have had the strength and power to get ashore. Dark, curly hair escaped from the hood of the suit and matched his eyebrows. Full lips and clear skin suggested he was fairly young.

Wally assured Nathan that the life that had been there was already gone, but there were two other men they could help. Jason began giving instructions, first to check on the deceased man regularly to make sure the rising water didn't take the body before help arrived, and for one of them to head to the highway to wave down any approaching vehicles. He didn't know what their help would arrive in, but something tall enough to wade the deep water.

While gathering a spare tarp and other things out of the truck, they caught chatter from Manteo. Highway 12 just north of Buxton was experiencing full overwash. Although the county always kept a team of earthmovers at the Hwy 12 location to rebuild the sand dunes that protected the highway in situations like this, even they had given up to the ocean and could only wait for the winds and waves to subside, isolating Hatteras Island from the rest of the Outer Banks. The ferry on the south side of the island was inoperable during heavy storms, so anyone on the island had to hunker in place.

The stranded boat on the beach continued to suffer the pummeling of the waves. It had dug into the sand, and while it rocked with each hammer hit, it remained upright and in the same place. Much of the debris from the battered upper portion of the craft swirled and tumbled in the onslaught, but some of it had washed over the dunes to where it could no longer be pulled back into the sea.

Help came in the form of a large red firetruck with the Duck Fire Department logo consisting of a duck in flight on the side. Nathan stood at the entrance to the neighborhood, his feet gratefully out of the water, when the flashing lights appeared through the rain. He waved and started towards the highway but backed away from the waves of water coming from each side of the truck—a storm of its own, a type of personal overwash that trailed it wherever it went. Once off the highway, the big machine was more cautious. When the truck pulled forward and rolled down a window, Nathan pointed north. "Take a left down to a court, that way."

"I know this neighborhood," the man replied. "It's likely flooded with this weather. Where are the men we're to pick up?"

"I'll walk with you and show you."

"Nah, hitch a ride. We'll save you the walk."

Nathan leaped on a running board along the side of the truck. Initially, the neighborhood roadway had little water, allowing him an easy ride on the running board. But the court at the north end of Baum Trail containing Jason's Explorer was daunting and dropped the firetruck's forward motion to a crawl. The water swirled just under Nathan's feet, meaning the truck's wake could easily flood the attached yards as well as Jason's Explorer.

Nathan dropped back into the water and knocked on the

driver's door of the firetruck. When the window came down, he called, "You'll have to follow me. They're on the beach side of this house."

"You couldn't find a better spot for us to pick them up?" The man peered through the windshield, wiped away moisture beading on the inside, and jumped when a strong gust of wind-blown spray filled with sand and seafoam splattered the truck. "Okay, I give. At the back. Give us a moment."

Once the men from the boat were packaged up and off for medical treatment, and the dead man was sorted for the morgue, Jason, Sean, Wally, and Nathan waded back to their truck and shut the storm outside.

"Do we follow them?" Nathan tried to clear a window in the direction of the departing firetruck. The Explorer shivered with the wind, and the bashing rain meant that even with the windows cleared on the inside, they could hardly see past the edge of the street outside.

"Nah," Wally said. He rummaged in the back and called, "Jason, you got any towels back here?"

"Paper in the glove box." He directed Sean, "Look in there and hand me a wad." He passed them back for Wally and Nathan to use.

The radio kicked in again, this time from the A-District sub-station. "This is Paloma." The connection went silent, then it came on again. "Uh-hem, Paloma with A-District calling—" She could be heard talking to someone with her. "Two ways about this. You can come do this or let me get on with it." Then she returned to the mic. "Paloma for Wally Styles. Are you out there, Wally?"

Jason lifted the mic. "Jason Romney here, Paloma. Wally's with me. Do I need to hand him the mic, or will I do?"

"Don't go getting uppity with me, Jason Romney. Sardines

in a can know everybody's business, and I know a bit of yours. If you and that bunch that left here earlier are all together, Miz Turnipseed wants you to know everybody on this island can read this radio as well as we can. I don't mean to step on your toes, but you just upset some people up in Currituck County."

"Okay. I don't—" He hesitated and glanced around the interior of the truck at the men with him. "—I mean, here's the thing. We rescued two men, and the third, well, we tried. Who's upset about that?"

"What was his name, Miz Turnipseed?" Diane could be heard in the background, paper rustled, and Paloma muttered, "I may look white, but us Black folks say what we mean. On the paper and not even underlined. How am I supposed to know it was on the back side—"

"Paloma?" Jason waited for her to acknowledge him.

"Some people can't get out of the rain. Here, I have it. Samuel Knight."

"I know the name. What's his complaint?"

"Now we're getting somewhere." Paloma sounded pleased. "He said he wanted to put all of us people right, that we had done let all those drug runners off scot-free. I told him I did nothing of the sort—"

"Thank you, Paloma." He overrode her this time. "Tell Miz Turnipseed we'll be more careful what we say over the airways after this."

He released the mic back to the dash and laughed.

"You people will learn." Wally was finishing up with the paper towels.

"How's that, Wally?" Jason turned to give him his attention.

"If it's Samuel Knight, we're back into the Brayboy feud. If it's stirring again, and I suppose we can make that call, what with everything that's stirred up the past few days, we might need to see if the captain wants to keep Sheriff Barnett in the loop about this complaint. Samuel's a tough cookie, but he usually knows what he's talking about."

Nathan grinned. Drug mules. He had worked it out and called it. He could barely believe he'd just helped bring in a whole trio of drug mules, albeit with one dead. He called into the car, "No reason to hang back now. Do we go north first or to the hospital to arrest those guys?"

"Whoa, wet pup." Wally chuckled. "Samuel's accusation isn't probable cause just yet. Let the storm settle, and we'll get back out here and look that boat over."

"No, no, you don't understand. What about those other two boats? What if they have drugs too and don't get searched?" Nathan couldn't see why they didn't sense his urgency.

Sean grinned and said to Jason, "Was I like that?"

"Pretty much. Nathan, the Coast Guard has those boats. They have the authority to inspect them for drugs or other paraphernalia. If they're running drugs, well, I wouldn't want to be aboard when they reach Station Hatteras."

Nathan felt relief, but it came with disappointment. Someone else would find the drugs, meaning, not him. Then, Jason moved onto the highway, the water swirled around them, and they headed south back towards the A-District sub-station to check in.

The wind buffeting the truck and the layers of spray from over the houses on the shore took his attention away from everything else.

Overwash! It filled his head with dread, but he wasn't given much time to paddle down that creek.

"So, young pup. What did we fulfill on your field training schedule today?" Wally had his cap in one hand and watched Nathan from slitted eyes. The feeling was one of critical evaluation.

"Um," and Nathan tried to leap from the tidepool of *over-wash* into one called *performance review*. "Um, we got really wet ..." His voice died, and he noticed the drone operator in the front seat turned to look his direction. He remembered his question to Jason: *Was I like that?*

"Sure. Then I can call you wet pup instead of young pup. You must have learned something, techniques, interpersonal communication—"

"That, yes." Nathan sat up. "I directed the fire truck driver to the men from the boat."

"So, explain the skill. Giving directions is something most people learn naturally. How was this different?"

"You don't need to tell me twice." He frowned, gave it a moment, and grinned. "I've got it worked out. They wanted the men from the boat to be on the street. The driver wasn't happy when he didn't immediately see them. I saw no reason to hang back, so I just led them to the beach, and they were good with that."

"Then, what about with us?" Wally motioned around the truck's interior.

"Us? There's been nothing to work on." He paused. "Has there? This is police work. Of course we get along. That's how it's done."

"That's how it's done?" Sean Taylor laughed. "Don't put this guy in a room alone with Captain Turnipseed. One or the other will come out scaled and filleted."

"Does that mean you're glad to be mixed up with the lot of us?" Wally seemed to approve.

"You don't need to ask. That's why I got this job."

Nathan settled into his seat, heard Jason on the radio with the A-District sub-station, and knew he was requesting permission to return to base. The wind still whipped the surface of Blount Bay as they crossed the bridge, but the rain no longer rattled the windows like octopus tentacles searching for an evening meal. Walking in, Paloma was at her typewriter, but she had her fingers frozen in midair, and she was clearly listening to a conversation coming from Captain Turnipseed's office. When she saw the men, she slipped her chair back, stepped to the door, and knocked.

From inside came, "For all sakes, hold your taters." Then louder, "Yes, Paloma?"

"I'll be glad to be shut of these men out here if you want to see 'em in your office."

"Hold on," Diane said.

"I thought I was—"

The door yanked open. "Not you, Paloma. The phone. You four, get in here." She turned away and began talking into the phone. "Yes, Sheriff Barnett. I understand. My team is here now. I'm putting you on speaker phone so everyone can hear. If you don't mind starting again at the beginning."

Diane clicked her phone's speaker button and placed it on her desk. She pulled a full-size sheet of lined paper from inside her desk, along with a pencil that was freshly sharpened.

"Present are Captain Diane Turnipseed, Sergeant Jason Romney from the Manteo office, Sergeant Sean Taylor, also from Manteo, Wally Styles from here, and Nathan Preston, also from here. You may start, Sheriff."

"Thank you, Diane. I know this is abrupt, what with the travel conditions outside, but I've been following the updates on the radio about the status of the boats just offshore. My congratulations on choosing to notify the Coast Guard. Good move, all of you. Here's where my phone call comes in. Everyone in Currituck County who's interested can also follow the same updates on the radio. I've got a frantic young woman outside of my office by the name of Marie Louise Beaumarchais who is convinced that her boyfriend might be the dead man from your overturned boat."

Diane Turnipseed looked up from her notes and smiled. She pointed to Jason before asking, "Sheriff, does he have a name?"

"Yes. It might take me a minute." They could hear papers shuffling. "Ah, not as easy as a flyover, but I've got it. Alain Valois, possibly on a student or work visa from France. He goes back and forth, so she's not sure exactly what his status is."

Sheriff Barnett went on to reveal that Marie Louise said Alain had been out of the country but was due to arrive today. He often flew into Norfork and caught a ride down on a fishing boat. His phone started giving her a "no longer available" message. Now she feared it was in the sea, and Alain was with it.

"Did she describe his appearance?"

"Oh, yes. I have that, too." Paper rustled, and he said, "Thick shoulders, dark, curly hair, with full lips. Also, his ethnicity is white. I don't suppose you need his birthdate or country of origin?"

"Perhaps later, Sheriff. Jason, can you speak to this?" Diane gave him the floor, since he was there when it happened.

"I can. Sheriff, I gave the man CPR with no success. He was already gone when we pulled him in. However, the description is spot on. We didn't get an ID. The men he was with didn't seem interested in him or to know him. We checked him for identification once we couldn't get a response from him but didn't remove his survival suit, as we could barely stand in the wind. We were fighting to keep the body from washing away."

"I understand. But you do feel that the description matches."

"Yessir, absolutely." Jason paused, looked at Diane, and said, "In my opinion, sir."

"Diane, do you have any thoughts on whether this might be connected to four days ago? As a motorman, I was trained to pay attention to the details. There's a lot of details that I can't help but line up together. It also concerns me that we've had a feud going on, and this might be a flareup. Marie Louise's family line goes back to the Brayboys."

From her expression, she understood exactly what he meant.

Nathan wanted to mention Samuel Knight and his accusations. If this was a part of the Brayboy feud, Samuel's comments had to count for something. He was the main Brayboy, the way Nathan saw it.

The phone conversation continued, however, and Nathan had to shift gears just to keep up. Samuel Knight slipped into the background of his thoughts, and his pen kept scribbling away.

Then he noticed that the rain had picked up again. *Overwash.* He gritted his teeth, put his pen to the paper, and tried to put it completely out of his thoughts. He was successful more or less, except for when the frame building shivered, and it seemed the storm might lift it completely from its foundation and launch it into the sky.

THE SUN ROSE over the distant ocean in a pink-tinged sky with just enough clouds to define where land met the sea. The surf still tore at the sand, exposing gouges where the incoming waves had devoured the beach only to spit it out far down the shore.

The stranded boat, now unlikely ever to float again, rested at an angle, with the bow protruding out of the sand like a divining rod aimed at the sky, while the stern was awash and trailing waves. Sand ate at the inside, carving a path that invited creatures and people alike to come in and explore.

Some distance from the boat, the scattered residue from the battered superstructure and the fishing gear from inside dirtied the beach. Long fishing rods, one snapped in half, lay scattered, with several still loaded with fishing line. Already, the metal parts were fighting rust. Sitting in the sea wasn't a good plan for survival, even for metals that claimed to be rust-resistant.

The most interesting thing on the beach had been last seen going overboard just before the boat turned belly up. Almost covered in the sand and attached to a buoy, a light flashed. A long cable snaked from the buoy through the sand, curled, turned straight, then twisted into curls again, until it reached the waterline where it was affixed to a perforated shipping crate. Just visible inside the crate, plastic bags shimmered, revealing white powder inside. On the other side of the crate, a chain led to an anchor half buried in the sand. During the fury of the storm, the boat had been tossed wildly in the waves. Either the chain had dragged or the occupants of the boat had been closer to the shore than they thought.

Perhaps that was why the boat went belly up, or maybe sabotage was the culprit. Either way, it didn't change what was on the beach this morning.

Then, one side of the shipping crate cracked, sagged, and a gap appeared. The first bag fell, floated for a moment, then eventually found its way to a permanent nest on the beach, where the water scooped away the sand underlayment and trapped it, captive to the forces of nature.

More of the packets followed suit, enough that soon there were small plastic packets up and down the beach, many digging into the sand, with a few free souls refusing to bed down, determined to remain free, free, free.

MANTEO CAME calling for Jason Romney and Sean Taylor.

While they weren't needed for their official duties, the North Carolina State Crime Laboratory at Raleigh had the results of the evidence found on the beach five days earlier and needed someone from the county to retrieve the results and the evidentiary material. With Sheriff Glynne still at his reunion (and missing the fun of the nor'easter pummeling the coast), the main offices at Manteo were short staffed, and the Crime Lab had placed a fifteen-day window on Dare County to reclaim their evidence from the crime scene.

Meaning that it was now officially a crime scene.

It had been one before—the drugs—but the stains on the clothing being identified as human blood moved everything to a whole new level. They were able to pull a DNA profile, and they thanked the Dare County team for collecting the evidence before the storm. With the rain and surf battering the coast, another day might have degraded the samples too much to be useful. They also encouraged Dare County to be patient. Finding a match in the system might take longer, and if the person didn't have a DNA profile on the books, then it might become a dead end, literally.

"Don't know why we have to do this." Jason read Paloma's notes from the call. "Four hours to Raleigh to retrieve the evidence … I don't guess it matters that Currituck County is sharing this crime scene with us. They could pick it up as well." As Jason and Sean were hitched at the hip for the day, the younger man stood over Jason's shoulder while he tried to read ahead.

"Shoot, Jason, we did send the goods to them." Sean had his customary grin and an enthusiastic expression on display.

"Most of it." He folded the message and slipped it into his shirt pocket. "Currituck County kept the drugs. It should be illegal for them to keep the exciting stuff and give us all the footwork." He pulled his keys from his pocket and smirked at Sean. "If I'm driving to Raleigh, you're going with me."

"But I—"

"No buts, Sean." He shifted his next question to Paloma. "If they've determined this to be a crime scene, are they requesting the satchel of drugs from up north?"

"What?" Paloma's eyebrows jumped. "It's you people that got rained off that beach up in Corolla. I just take phone calls and enter information into the system. Now if you want to sit down c'here and work this typewriter, I'll take your keys and sort out all that stuff out there you claim to do. Other'n that, you take care of your business, and I'll take care of mine." She turned to her typewriter, searched for a sheet of paper to insert into the paper feed, and tried to look as busy as possible.

Jason laughed and gave a hard look in Nathan's direction. "You interested in going with us?"

"To Raleigh to pick up the evidence?" *Yes*, but before Nathan could agree, Wally cleared his throat.

"Field training, young pup. That's you. Mentor, that's me. Sorry." Wally addressed Jason. "It'd be good exposure, but not today. Besides, if he gets mixed up with you lot, he'll never be satisfied working with us out here."

"What?" Nathan protested. "No, Wally. I would never—"

"You sure about that?" Wally winked at Jason.

A ruckus just outside ended the banter. Paloma stopped fiddling with her blank sheet of paper as the front door rattled, and it abruptly opened. Two figures in waterproofs with hoods dripping rainwater forced themselves through, shoving one another on the shoulder to be first in. Outside, the wind still howled, but the rain now fell in sheets rather than bucketfuls. Wally stepped up behind them to close the door and seal the rain and wind outside.

"How may I help you?" Paloma stood, and her voice commanded the small space's attention.

Instead of answering, the two cloaked figures swept their hoods back and grinned. One was plumper than the other, with dark, spiky hair, and his shirt collar looked like it had been tumbled in a dryer and left for a week before he decided to put it on. The other boasted a rangier build, with an orange fireball for hair and more freckles than any person had a right to wear. Jason's face fell. Sean laughed, and Wally gave them both a puzzled look.

Nathan said, "I remember you two from down south. Aren't you from near the Bodie Lighthouse?"

"Maybe," the two said in chorus. The spiky-haired one said, "My dogs are outside in the bed of the truck. You might recognize them, if we were. We strung a tarp over the bed—"

"Nubbin and Carrot!" Jason interrupted, and the talking ceased. "Why aren't you down in your home territory?" Meaning Manteo or farther south on Ocracoke Island. It was where the two normally spent their time and pulled their teenage pranks.

"That's just it, Mr. Romney." The dark-haired one, which Nathan now thought must be Nubbin, as he had been talking, and Jason had said his name first, beamed. "It's all overwashed down there. The highway is the beach now. Nobody can get through."

"Yeah," the other boy agreed. He broke character and giggled. "Nubbin's mom don't need to know, but we tried to drive across. We nearly got washed off the beach."

"But you didn't," Jason said. He wasn't cutting them much slack, not today. "Why does the road overwashing there mean you have to be here?"

"You got beaches up here, and Nubbin and I want to see

what the storm's doing. We heard there was a boat washed up on the beach, and we wanted to find it."

"Yeah, find it, Officer Romney." Carrot broke into another giggle, like he'd said something amazingly funny.

"Well, did you?" Jason glanced at his fellow Dare County employees before turning back to the boys, and he crossed his arms over his chest and leaned back on his heels.

"Did we?" The boys answered in chorus. They reached in their pockets and began to pull out packet after packet of white powder in clear bags. They piled them on Paloma's desk. "And there's lots more. We thought you should know before someone else finds it."

Nathan was excited and crushed at the same time. More drugs. He had been out there when the boat went aground, and someone else found the drugs.

It wasn't fair at all!

BY THE TIME Nathan and Wally made it to the county line and onto the beach, the rain was down to leftover mist, and the skies had started to clear over the ocean. While on the drive, Wally put in a call to the Currituck County Sheriff's Office, as they would want to coordinate with Dare County. Both teams were part of the Outer Banks-Dare Narcotics Task Force, and help from Currituck's NARC Officers Willis Washington and Kenneth Contras would be helpful, appreciated, and a show of inter-agency cooperation on an investigation that was becoming more complex by the day.

Time and distance were the issue. The Sound essentially separated Currituck County into two separate worlds. On the northern side, the county rubbed shoulders with Virigina in an almost unbroken stretch, but access was nonexistent. The only other approach was by boat or to head south through the northern reaches of Dare County, which was cumbersome and time-consuming. Travel from Barco on the west side of the Sound to anywhere on the ocean side was double that from the A-District sub-station in Kitty Hawk.

Wally waited as the phone rang. Shannon Baylink at the Currituck County Sheriff's Office's front desk picked up.

"Sheriff's Office. This is Shannon. How can I help?"

"Shannon, this is Wally Styles with Dare County. I believe we met before at a state conference."

"Let me think … yes, two years back. How are you, Wally? You keeping out of trouble?"

"Only when it keeps out of my way. Then the tide rolls in, and you know how that goes. Let me get to this. We've been working with your people on a beach investigation on the county line. Are you aware?"

"Let me think." It sounded like she already knew. "Just this morning, we sent a satchel of drugs to Raleigh, and that was at Dare County's request, thank you, Dare County. Nancy's running it in. Do you know Nancy?"

Wally did, Nancy Griffin, a good-looking officer in the Criminal Investigations Division, always in a skirt, but with a gun at her fingertips, even when you couldn't see it. He'd never figured out where she kept it, but he'd seen it come out of thin air, and he knew she was never without it.

"Nancy's on her way there now, leaving us short-handed, again thank you, Dare County."

"That's good." Wally moved on to the people he really wanted. "Washington and Contras, are they available? We have more drugs on the same beach."

"I thought you were keeping out of trouble. It seems not." Shannon went on to tell Wally that Washington and Contras were at Currituck County High School along with School

Resource Officer Deputy Jared Johnson. The three were involved in a school-sponsored presentation on the wisdom of not doing drugs, and Shannon would let them know. Was this an active event that required backup? She could try to sort out more deputies if Dare County thought they weren't up to the task. She laughed, and when Wally clarified that a boat had grounded on the beach during the storm and the drugs were likely from that, after a moment of thought and another "Let me think," Shannon announced that the two NARC officers would likely want to join the Dare County team, so would Dare County please begin the operation? The Currituck County officers would be in touch.

"I think she runs that office." Nathan grinned.

"That's sure." Wally picked up the mic to the car's radio, and he began with, "Wally Styles calling Ed Walters. You out there, Ed? Over."

Ed came back with a quick response. A dog barked twice in the background.

Wally looked at Nathan and grinned. "Ed, I understand you might have a working dog with you. Is that her I hear?"

"You hear her, but she'd not officially anything." He spoke off the mic, "Good girl, Roxie. You're familiar with police radio." He returned to Wally. "I dunno but what she's done this before. I'm not hoping the sheriff takes her back anytime soon."

"Listen, Ed. The captain's out of the office, and Nathan and I are headed back to the beach up on the county line. I'm not sure where Clara is. Drugs are washing up on the sand, likely from that capsized fishing boat. Are you and Roxie available to meet up with us?"

"You hoping Clara can be there also?" Ed seemed to be processing the idea as a possibility.

"No. I'm heading up to determine what the situation is. The

report we received said the beach is devoid of action, just that it's littered with drugs. I done it like this once before and nearly lost the evidence to the tide. To tell it right, I don't want to miss out on this one. Besides, the young pup needs to see this, learn what it's like to be a deputy on the Banks. You take your time if you need, but I'd appreciate your help. Roxie's, too, if you think she'd be of any use."

"It'll be a minute, but we'll be there. Ed out."

Wally looked at Nathan and said, "Just another rock to turn over, eh, Nathan? Are you still enjoying this?"

"It's exactly what I got this job for. Do you think this is connected to those people up in Corolla?"

"More to the ones in Currituck in that Wharf building, but likely to both. If that woman's missing boyfriend was on this boat, and he was the one we pulled from the water; well, if he was involved with drugs, there'll be a lot of anger simmering between the two branches of the family."

Nathan felt a chill and shivered. Nervousness or excitement? Lots of people were dying, a thing likely connected to the ongoing family feud between the Brayboys on the Banks and those on the Sound, but all in all, it was exactly what he'd hoped for.

It was excitement, he decided, and yes, he was still enjoying his job with the Dare County Sheriff's Office more than he ever thought possible.

Chapter 8

Currituck Beach Light

COLFORD SEREYS, great-grandson of Baron Philippe de Rothschild of French winery fame and Pauline Potter de Rothschild, the influential New York interior designer, sat in a wide-armed lounging chair facing a glass wall looking out over Currituck Sound. One arm dangled from the side of the chair carelessly grasping a black smoking stick with a Gitane cigarette protruding from the end. Smoke curled lazily toward the ceiling, but the reason for lighting it was long forgotten.

He and his wife, Marie, occupied the penthouse at The Wharf, their due as the elders in the family. The interior of the room shimmered with the best of French furniture, although from a design era long out of fashion. Through the expanse of glass, the balcony facing the Sound told the truth of Colford and Marie's current state of financial affairs. Peeling paint, rotten wood, and a sliding screen that flapped in every strong breeze revealed the level of the family's fall from grace. Grand-mère Philippine, the stepdaughter of Philippe and Pauline, had rolled in more cash than the French government paid all its workers, but it had not trickled down to Colford's father, Philippe Sereys, or to his stepfather, Julien de Beaumarchais, whose five children now lived under the same roof.

Colford was glad to have a roof under which to live after he and his sister's families were banished from the Rothschild estate that had been their home for so many years. While Mémé Philippine had still lived, the de Rothschilds had felt the social pressure to fund her grandchildren's lifestyles, but with her death a decade before, the efforts had begun to push them out and out and all the way out to this abandoned condominium building far across the sea.

Of their two children, John and Louise, only John had joined them in the banishment. Louise was in Europe at school on the Rothschilds' dime. John had refused the opportunity when offered, saying there were too many strings and too high a price to pay. The Rothschilds could not buy his soul at any price. Now he mocked his uncle, Creighton, when he bemoaned the money that had vanished with their split from the Rothschild hoard.

A glob of ash from Colford's French cigarette fell soundlessly onto the Persian carpet underfoot. He lifted the smoking stick to his lips only to realize the cigarette had become cold.

"Marie!" Colford ran his free hand through his thick, dark hair. The mass sprouted from his head in exuberant waves, matching his equally thick eyebrows and the mane curling from inside his shirt, along his thick forearms, and likely everywhere else. "Marie!" he called again. "Where is my cigarettes? Be sensible and bring me some."

"Here, Colford." Marie appeared silently in a patterned silk robe. She wore her dark hair in a bun at the base of her neck.

Chewed nails appeared as she placed a fresh pack of Gitanes on the arm of his chair. She stepped away without additional words and began moving items on a large console on a nearby wall.

"Be sensible and sit down for a moment, Marie. Did you bring me a match? I cannot light my cigarette without a match." To be sure, he had the new pack open, and he was working a stick of paper-wrapped tobacco into the end of his smoking stick.

"You be sensible, Colford. Do you even smoke them?" She held three books in one hand and looked in his direction. "You constantly leave them to burn out, smoking up the ceilings, but you never seem to inhale. Look there. Ash on the floor. Please, my dear Colford. Clean up after yourself. Have you seen my novel? I just had it ..." Her voice faded as she turned her attention back to her search.

"You are taking John's car this afternoon?" He didn't mention what for, as they disagreed on her "volunteerism" at that lighthouse on the far shore. He hated that place, as it overlooked the Whalehead, the home they should be occupying, rather than this dismal makeover of a shipping warehouse.

"Not this afternoon, Colford." She paused her search to give him a condescending look. "I will be leaving about eleven. I am signed up to start my docent duties at noon. And what other car should I take? It's the only one in the family."

"Marie Louise's boys have that truck. No one is using it now." Marie Louise was his sister, as compared to Marie, his wife. The truck belonged to Philippe and Creighton, Marie Louise and Creighton Ballinger's sons. Philippe was named after his grandfather, and Creighton after his father, although they were twins in everything else.

As soon as he said it, Colford realized his comment was a non sequitur. The whole matter of what had happened to

Philippe and Creighton—now in Norfolk in the hospital—and Charles-Edouard … the truck had been located and retrieved but was again impounded. Its return was imminent, but it remained unavailable. Marie had refused to discuss any of it or listen to anyone else discuss it.

"I will do this my way, Colford." She set the books down and held a long breath before seeming to come back to life. "Oh, is there any place worse than this room? I do miss the estate in France. John has assured me his car is free for my use. Our son will be our salvation. Then we will have a larger car and hire a driver, too. He has assured me so."

He watched her walk out the door, still without a match for his cigarette. He pictured John's car, a small Japanese one, with room only for two. They would need a larger car if they were to hire a driver. They could not close the doors if they all attempted to travel at once in the small convertible.

He stood, holding his cigarette and smoking stick in his hand, to look for a match. He let his nephews and his half-brother fade from his thoughts. They lived on a lower floor, and he had little to do with them. Besides, it was only sensible to think of what was at hand, and that was his need for a match. He opened a gilt, Louis IV box, and inside, he found the match he was certain must be there.

Colford returned to the chair, struck the match, lit his Gitane, and loosely held the smoking stick while he dangled his arm to the side. He let his eyes roam past the rotted wood on the balcony and across the shallow Sound beyond. He pictured the distant half of the family living on the far side of the water. If only they'd stood up and claimed what was theirs, he and his family would be living at the Whalehead today. He sighed, packaged that up, and put it away, closing his eyes and imagining Marie climbing the steps to the upper reaches of the

Currituck Beach Light tower. She always liked to be at the top, though he had never understood that. She could not be sensible, not even for a moment. He blamed it on not growing up under the auspices of Grand-mère Philippine. There was a woman with the good sense to marry money and keep it flowing for her entire life.

The sad part was that she had to die, and the flow of money died with her. Even Colford couldn't find the sense in that, but he recognized fully that it was the reason that they were here and not in their house on the Rothschild estate back home.

Where Marie wanted to be.

Where she always wanted to be, even when she was at the top of that senseless lighthouse doing what made no sense to Colford at all.

"PAPA, YOU MUST come down. The police have questions." John Sereys, Colford's son, spoke over the phone handset with a bored, mocking tone. "One is perhaps a gendarme, so it must be important. They insist that they speak with you."

Colford had walked across the room to answer the house phone, only to realize he still held his smoking stick, and the cigarette had burned without being smoked at all. Perhaps Marie was right. Why light them when he rarely smoked them?

"Your mother must have romance, and I must have a visit with the police. What would Mémé think of that, John? They are sensible people. You deal with the matter and leave me be."

"No, Papa. The policeman says someone new is dead. They have questions. He will not condescend to tell me more."

"Besides Charles-Edouard? How tiresome."

"He did not say."

"Collie, perhaps? Can he not handle this?" Collie was Collins Beaumarchais, John's uncle and the de facto head of the

Beaumarchais half of the family living at The Wharf.

"Ah, Papa. Collie feels we have fallen too far to recover, and that we are Rothschild by name only and no longer by fortune. He will not present our family in the light we deserve. Besides, they are asking for you."

"Then I suppose I must. Your mother is at the lighthouse today. Did you see her headed out?"

"I had to give her my keys, so yes. You are on the way down?"

"Be sensible and give me a moment. I need to find my cigarette, and I will be there."

Colford glanced around the room for his smoking stick and realized it was in his hand. He noted the pile of ashes on the floor by the chair and considered leaving it behind but decided a walk would encourage him to inhale and take what pleasure he could from the tobacco. He took the time to load a new cigarette into the stick.

Stepping out of the apartment was striding back into the world of reduced lifestyle, limited finances, and a building that had stood abandoned for years. Paint, carpets, and their things from France had made his and Marie's apartment bearable, but the rest ... no one could be sensible about faded wallpaper and broken elevators. The stairs took him to a lobby that had once boasted the latest in style but now was dark and worn. Three policemen awaited him, two men wearing the sheriff's office logo, and the third a woman in all blue with USGC on her cap.

All three carried weapons.

Two civilian policemen and a military gendarme. Colford took a draw on his cigarette, and he let the smoke escape as he introduced himself.

"Colford Sereys." He offered a hand. "You have met my son, John. How may I help?"

The civilian officers introduced themselves as Sergeant Scotty Barker and Deputy Dillon Krazinski. Barker was solid like Colford, and Krazinski was a rash of red, hair to freckles, and as fresh-faced. The gendarme was Marine Enforcement Specialist Connie Underwood. Colford made the connection. She was not truly military police, but he also understood that there was little difference in the distinction. She served in a policeman's role, and for that, John was correct.

After the introductions, Scotty Barker spoke first. "Mr. Sereys—"

"Colford, please." Colford noticed he hadn't taken a puff of his cigarette in some time, and he lifted it to his lips.

"Of course." Barker paused, frowned, and didn't repeat Colford's name. "You are aware of our presence in this area over the past few days."

"During a recent stormy spell, yes. Something about a boat, I believe." He frowned. "Why the military presence?"

"Our helicopter was involved." Underwood, diminutive with dark hair pulled back hard under her cap, gave a quick nod. "That makes the Coast Guard part of all this."

"And I can help you how?" Colford still wasn't seeing it. He returned Underwood's nod and then gave his attention to the two men.

"Philippe and Creighton Ballinger." Barker had a notebook out and read the names before looking up. "They live here, correct?"

"Not in my apartment, but yes. My sister's boys. What is this to do with me?"

"You have heard they were airlifted to Norfolk."

"Yes." He shrugged. The boys were always needing money from his sister but accepted little responsibility. It was good to be rid of them for a time.

"And that a third man was found deceased."

"Ah, Charles-Edouard. His father, Julien, is still in France. He refuses to be notified, so there's nothing to be done about that."

"Refuses?" The word burst from the fresh-faced Krazinski. "Man, my dad would want to know."

"Julien works the Rothschild vinery and cannot be bothered with America. I had heard about Charles-Edouard and thank you for your confirmation."

"Has this Charles-Edouard associated with a man named Alain Valois?"

"Alain? You will need to ask my half-sister, Marie Louise, about that. He is her boyfriend."

"Then you don't know—"

"I have already said. John mentioned that another man is now deceased. I assume Alain is that man?"

Barker cut a look at John and frowned. "The identity of the body has not been confirmed, but yes. It is possible."

"Then it has nothing to do with me, and I already knew of Charles-Edouard. Will that be all?"

"I gotcha." Barker frowned again, took a deep breath, and pulled an envelope from a shirt pocket. "We're here to do more than notify you of Charles-Edouard's death or of the possible death of Alain Valois. I have a search warrant for Charles-Edouard's possessions, his apartment, and any vehicles he might have owned, used, or operated."

Colford glanced at his son. The boy rolled his eyes and shrugged. John had plans for rescuing the family from their reduced circumstances, but only their family. He mocked his uncle Creighton, who had no head for business and had lost his manufacturing venture in France; and John frequently spoke of wanting Collie and his bunch of Beaumarchais half-relations out of his way. They were a drain on the family and added little to the family's bottom line.

One thing John didn't understand. While Collie was the eldest and therefore the head of the Beaumarchais branch of the family in America, once the Rothschild money had passed him by, he had given up, yet there were Philippe and Creighton's bikes. They had come from somewhere, and Charles-Edouard had outfitted one of the lofts with expensive gym equipment.

Money from some dark and unknown source had been filtering into that part of the family. Colford had his suspicions, and now, with a search warrant in hand, these police might very well prove him right or wrong.

He pushed that away and blinked rapidly to refocus his thoughts. He cleared his throat, only to find it raspy. "John, my cigarette. Where is my cigarette?"

"In your hand, Papa." John tilted his head just enough to indicate where to look.

"In my hand." He realized both hands were in the air, a reflexive habit he had when he was confused or simply didn't want to move forward. He placed his smoking stick to his lips and closed his eyes as he drew in a deep breath. He let the smoke out as he turned to the ruddy Barker. "I am a sensible man, Sergeant. What do you need from me to help move your search forward?"

"I don't normally do searches, so I appreciate your patience and help. Dillon and me are normally on marine patrol, but with that storm, everyone's filling in where they can. With your permission, two officers from Dare County are on their way for assistance."

"Dare County." Colford considered the information and shrugged. "From the west, perhaps?"

"From south, Papa." John. "Philippe and Creighton drive

through it when they go to the beach."

"Yes, yes, the impounding the other day." The truck had been released to them, and then with the attack on his nephews, it had gone missing ... and had been hours before it was recovered. "The truck is due to be returned. Have you any information about that?" Colford waved the hand with the smoking stick. He took a drag and paused to enjoy the sensation before letting out a slight cough.

"We followed it in, so yes. Even though it just arrived from the impound yard, it's included in our search warrant. Hopefully we can clear it by tomorrow."

"Yes, that will be good. They are my nephews, you see ... John, my son, is a fine boy, but those two, God love them, they cannot survive without their truck."

Krazinski nudged Barker. "Remind him of the keys, Scotty. We need those to get inside."

"Quit jawing, Dillon." Barker shook his head and drew a finger across his throat. He whispered, "If this could be drugs, we need a dog here first."

As if by magic, his radio blipped, and he unclipped it and held it to his mouth.

"Sergeant Barker here. You people find the place?"

"Never lost it." A man's voice. "I've got an idea. You tell me how to get inside the building, and we'll get this show on the road."

"Sergeant Walters?"

"I dunno. I was when I looked in the mirror this morning. Let's try this one on. You call me Ed, and I'll let you use my dog to help you with that warrant."

"Papa," John called, "I'll take care of letting him in."

John headed toward the front door and disappeared outside. Colford apologized to the officers that he didn't have ready keys to each apartment, but his half-brother, Collie Beaumarchais, might very well have one. Charles-Edouard was, er, had been Collie's younger brother. And if not, Charles-Edouard's twin, Jean-Paul, might be somewhere about.

They located Collie in the basement of the large warehouse-turned-condo building, a room that served as the mechanical room and fronted a concrete wharf directly on the Sound. Uninsulated steel ductwork, round industrial lighting, and workbenches along the perimeter said this was the beating heart of the structure. Wide, arched doorways to the wharf were sealed with brick, but small windows punched through the tops of the walls, adding natural lighting, and an older furnace had the side removed, with parts and tools scattered nearby.

"Collie? I have a question for you. Are you in here?"

A tall man in his thirties with receding red hair and wearing stained coveralls over a thick waistline appeared from a door wiping a wrench with a red cloth. "If you must know, yes. Who are these people, Colford?"

"They are here about Charles-Edouard." Colford heard additional feet, and he turned to find John leading in a rangy man with a dog and a younger woman. He returned his attention to his half-brother. "They've confirmed the dead man is Charles, and there is another, perhaps Alain."

"There's no point in that. We already knew. Marie Louise told me about Alain. So, what do they need?" He spoke only to Colford and had yet to acknowledge the officers.

"They have a warrant for Charles-Edouard's apartment. Do you have a key?"

"It is not locked. If you must, go through it all. Take it all, I do not care." He turned away, still wiping the wrench with the cloth, and muttering, "I only thought we could go no lower, and now Charles has proven me wrong once again."

As they headed upstairs, Colford noted the breed of dog, one he recognized, and he remarked, "A Belgian Malinois. Do you have many on your force?"

"My first," Ed said, as he rubbed his eyes. "Sergeant Ed Walters," he offered, and he held out a hand.

"Of course," Colford replied. He shifted his smoking stick and took the hand. "Your partner?"

"Deputy Clara Del Ray," she inserted cheerfully. "I understand your family is descended from Juno Brayboy." When Colford didn't immediately reply, she clarified, "I'm just filling in the blank spaces and don't mean to intrude."

John Sereys answered. "We are from the line of Grand-mère Philippine de Rothschild. When you speak of Juno Brayboy, that name does not apply to us. Ms. Brayboy was a house servant when my family owned the Whalehead in Corolla. Any connection is speculation only."

"But they carry the Knight name. How does that work—"

Colford took a draw on his smoking stick and tuned out the conversation between his son and the attractive female deputy. It was an old discussion that had been explained too many times, and he was no longer interested. When they reached Charles-Edouard's apartment, the door was indeed unlocked and partially opened. Colford pushed it wider and noted the dirt and water spatter just inside. He frowned, stepped farther in, and that was when he was made aware that things weren't as they should be. Large windows opened to the Sound, and expensive exercise equipment littered the room. Literally. The apartment was a wreck, and Colford had no idea why.

Sergeant Barker stopped him before he had gone more than a few steps. "Mr. Sereys, you need to let us enter first. It seems that someone has been in here already. If this is a break in, we don't want to further contaminate the scene."

"Yes, yes, only sensible." Colford's feet seemed frozen even as he said his words. Things overturned, holes punched in the walls ... Charles-Edouard hadn't been the best of brothers, but he took pride in his things and bragged about his accomplishments. He would never leave his apartment in this condition.

"Mr. Sereys." Barker's hand gently grasped his elbow.

"Yes, yes. I must sit down for a moment. Pardon, if you will. My apologies."

Colford stepped outside and was grateful to see John bringing up a chair. He offered his arm to his son and let himself be lowered into a seating position. John informed him that his cigarette was cold and offered to take the smoking stick, which Colford released to him.

Around Colford, the policemen talked among themselves, coordinating, while the gendarme removed herself to her vehicle to gather additional supplies. The blonde woman, Deputy Del Ray, stood to the side with the dog handler in a discussion about whether they should request another dog rather than use the Belgian Malinois.

"Your dog," Colford asked. "What is her name?"

"Roxie." Sergeant Walters, the tall man, answered.

"Is this search—" Colford cleared his throat and waved his hand to indicate the commotion that had taken over the area outside Charles' apartment. "—about drugs? I have had my suspicions, you see."

"Papa, no. Never say such a thing." John's eyes were wide with dismay.

"For all the sand on the shore, John. Consider your Grand-mère Philippine. If such a thing had ever happened under her roof—"

"Such things did happen under her roof," the young man

muttered.

Colford frowned at the interruption, paused, and nodded. "Which is why we must face what is before us. Why else would the police bring a dog, if not for that? Officer Walters, this is your dog, you said, but she is new to you. Is this correct?"

"Yes."

"She is still in training?"

"Yes."

"Then we must give her the chance. I wish you to explore what is inside. If my brother, God rest his soul, was into something that caused this, we must know. Please, go in."

The young blonde officer asked the dog handler, "Should I call Cynthia to bring up Lucy anyway?"

The handler gave Roxie a searching look, as if trying to read something about her, then he nodded and knelt before the Belgian Malinois and began talking to her quietly. The Coast Guard deputy had returned with gear to prepare for a search of the room, and the people began slipping on thin gloves and plastic booties over their shoes. A case of additional supplies—includeing a camera—sat to the side.

Colford was distracted from the events by John's phone. His son pulled out the device, glanced at his father, and clicked to talk. He put the phone to his ear and stepped away for privacy. After a few minutes, the phone disappeared back into his pocket, and he knelt at his father's side.

"The storm, Papa. It seems there is damage everywhere." John smiled apologetically.

"That was ta mère on the phone?" *Your mother*, he asked, the familiar French spilling out. "She is okay? The car is okay?" Without the truck, there was no additional transportation.

"All is okay. With all this—" John waved to indicate the disruption. "—I can hardly ask to leave, but this is my chance,

Papa."

"Chance? For what? Be sensible, John. You must be here. The police may need answers. Mémé would not think highly of you abandoning the family at a time like this."

"To be seen, Papa. I have always said that if Collie would just get out of my way, I could become someone. I could turn the family around."

"To be seen doing what?"

"The cleanup, Papa. Maman says the lighthouse is closed with the storm damage—"

"Non, it cannot be!"

"It can be, Papa."

"The lighthouse is damaged? It is of brick. Surely, John, non."

"Not the lighthouse, of course, Papa, but tree limbs do come down in storms. Power lines get tangled."

"Then ta mère must return. If it is closed—"

"Maman says she will work in the Visitor Center for the day. People are volunteering already to clear the grounds, and media people are on the way. Perhaps I will have my picture in the paper."

Colford sighed and wished for his cigarette. So much was happening in just one day. John always had plans, hoped for something better, and Colford was glad for it. Sometimes, however—

"Papa," John said, focusing his father's attention. "I will need a ride. May I have a small amount of Mémé Philippine's money? Without my car …" His sentence died away, the explanation unspoken. After all, it wasn't his fault he didn't have a ride to the lighthouse. His father must step up and provide the money.

"Yes, yes. My bankcard is on my desk. Be sensible, John,

and only spend what you need. When it is gone—"

"I know, I know. When it is gone, there is no more. I will call for a ride now." John grinned, stood, pulled out his phone, and stepped away to begin his call.

THE OFFICERS with the search warrant were long gone by the time Marie Sereys and her son, John, returned from Currituck Beach Light. Marie stepped inside the apartment, put a hand on her hip as if modeling for the cover of a romance novel, and addressed her husband.

"You should have seen John, Colford. Everyone at the light-house had such nice things to say about him." She moved to the side as John lugged in a large wooden propeller. "There, John. Above the console. It will be something of this place in our apartment, perhaps a breath of fresh air."

"What is that?" Colford noted his cold cigarette, and he put his smoking stick aside and stood from his lounge chair.

"An airplane prop, Papa." John wore a thick sweater over jeans and seemed as fresh as when he had left earlier in the day.

"You went to clean up, this is correct?"

"Yes, Papa."

"How do you not look like you cleaned up?"

"Please, my dear Colford. The newspapers were present. John could not look a mess for the cameras." Marie stood back to judge John's positioning of the propeller against the wall. "Yes, John. Right there. It will be something new in this room."

The ride back with John had brightened his wife's mood, and for that, Colford was grateful. John had his own apartment, as did each of the family, and on some days, they didn't see him at all. Marie looked forward to the days that they did.

As John went in search of a hammer to hang the propeller, Marie regaled Colford with the roof shingles that were missing from houses, one fence that had blown down, and the tree branches! They were everywhere.

"You found the propeller in a tree?" Colford shook his head. "Was it still attached to an aircraft?"

"Please, Colford. You do not need to be ridiculous."

"How am I ridiculous? John, am I being ridiculous?"

"Papa, I didn't want to say, but Maman has been eyeing this for some time." John seemed to lose some of his excitement over the propeller with the admission.

"Marie?"

"It was only a little money, Colford."

"You bought it?" He imagined the wallpaper and the elevator that didn't work.

"You did give John your card. What else was I to do? You tell me to be sensible. Now, you be sensible." She gave him a brief kiss on the cheek before heading over to supervise John. She turned back to Colford. "John tells me some men were by today."

"And a woman, Maman," John inserted. "A dog also, a Malinois, wasn't it, Papa?"

"Yes." Colford had moved to the window wall overlooking the Sound, and he inserted a fresh cigarette in his smoking stick. He didn't light it. Outside, the water glittered, with the afternoon sun catching on just the tips of the startled ripples running from the wind. "Marie, the storm damage on the Banks. It was bad, was it?"

"I've already said. It doesn't change in the retelling." The propeller now rested on the console, and John had completely disappeared. With her distraction gone, she browsed a stack of books.

"The lighthouse must be closed then. You will no longer be volunteering." He had tried to dissuade her in the past. Philippe and Creighton had refused to stay on this side of the Sound, and now, look at them. And Charles-Edouard. If they had shown some sense … but then, that was why they were where they were now.

"Don't be ridiculous. Of course I'll continue to volunteer. Docents will still be manning the Visitor Center, and that's where I'll be. I already let them know I will gladly take on any extra duties they require. What did the men want today?"

"Nothing to do with us. It was Charles-Edouard they came to see."

"Not funny, Colford. You did not like Charles. That was clear to everyone in the family, but to tease about what has happened? It is cruel." She had located her book and was searching for her place, and when she found it, she smiled and sank into her favorite reading chair. "What did they want with Charles?"

"Someone had been in Charles' apartment." Colford made the remark as a distraction. They hadn't said anything explicit about drugs, although Colford was convinced it was the reason for the dogs. The second animal, smaller and blacker, had arrived, with an officer named Cynthia Ellison, someone Colford had learned was also from Dare County.

"Was anything disturbed?"

"All of it. They didn't let me inside as my feet might contaminate the scene, but I saw from the door. Everything was topsy-turvy. The door is now blocked with crime scene tape, or I would take you to see."

"That sounds very serious." She was growing disinterested in the story, and her eyes were already on her novel.

"Maman, a call for you." John reentered the room with a hammer and a bracket for attaching the propeller to the wall. He held out his phone. He was the only one of the three that maintained one.

"I am just starting my novel. Can I call them back?"

"It's Jackye from across the Sound. You have forgotten something." John placed the hammer and the bracket on the console and carried his phone to his mother.

"Jackye, Marie speaking—"

As Marie's voice blurred into the phone conversation, Colford stepped from the window to offer help to his son. He pointed to the bracket and asked, "Does that attach to the propeller or to the wall?"

"The wall, Papa." John flipped the propeller over to show a similar but slightly different bracket already on the back side.

"And you already had this how?" He lifted the unused bracket, unsure how this worked to hang the propeller.

"I got it from the shop. It fits like this." He showed his father how it inserted into the other half to hold the decorative item securely on the wall.

"Ah, very good. Did they say how long the lighthouse will be closed? Is it very damaged?"

"Non, Papa." John seemed amused. "It is all well. It's the grounds that were impacted. I think perhaps a couple of days, maybe a week. Mark this for me." He offered his father a pencil and held the propeller to the wall.

"John, your phone." Marie held it in the air.

"In a moment, Maman."

"Someone must go back to the lighthouse. My purse. It needs retrieved. You must go for me."

"Maman! I'm hanging your propeller. Can your purse not wait?" He looked to his father for assistance, both exasperated and amused.

"It is your mother's request. Be sensible, John. How can we not? I will accompany you." Colford smiled, shrugged, and placed the pencil on the console.

On the way to John's apartment, they rounded a corner to discover Marie Louise Ballinger, Colford's sister and the mother of the two young men recently airlifted to Norfolk. She was here and not there as transportation was difficult without a dedicated vehicle.

"Where are you two men headed?" Marie Louise leaned casually against the faded wallpaper and held a tumbler of golden brandy in one hand. The slender woman tended towards a moustache, and it was unbleached. Her voice was slightly slurred, and the long, thick braid down her back showed her careless attention to her looks.

"Marie Louise." Colford blinked. "Marie was volunteering today, and Jackye Sallinger phoned from the lighthouse. We must run over."

"And your son is with you. How sweet." Marie Louise took a sip from her glass, unsteadily stood, and held her hands to John for a hug. She wrapped her arms around him. "We all know Creighton would have lost his business eventually, but to lose my boys too? It is too much. I'm so glad Colford and Marie still have you." She released him and began to straighten her clothing.

"They are not lost, Tante Marie Louise. Can you not—" John glanced at his father for help. "—arrange transportation to visit them?"

"The phone." She wiped a tear from under one eye. "I have called, and they cannot be seen. It is so sad. And I must be here for my dear sisters, Mary Louise and Dorthea. They have lost their brother." Then tears truly began to flow.

"Ah, Marie Louise," Colford said, putting an arm around her.

"Creighton refuses to see the state we're in. Even Mémé Philippine advised me not to marry him. Now I cannot even travel to see my boys in the hospital." She pulled away, laughed, and patted her face. "Oh, oh, I must stop this. Oh, look! My brandy is gone. Is it five yet? I told Creighton I would wait until five for a refill."

When her tears threatened to erupt once more, Colford gave her a kiss on the cheek and said, "I'm sure it is five o'clock somewhere. Why don't you head back inside?"

"In a moment. Creighton is out of cigarillos and is smoking a Pall Mall. The apartment must air first. You two, go. I will be fine." She found the wall again, leaned her head back, and closed her eyes. Moisture brimmed but not enough to dampen her cheeks.

At his apartment, it took John a moment to gather his keys and sunglasses, and he took the time for a fresh change of clothing. When he rejoined his father, he said softly, "Poor Tante Marie Louise. My uncle was once truly rich, wasn't he?"

"Mémé would not think highly of this discussion, John." The talk of one's own money was acceptable, but to discuss another's was a gross breach of etiquette.

"He was, wasn't he?"

"Very, even more than your maman and I."

"I will turn the family around, Papa. All I need is my chance. It should have been Collie who was found—"

"Non!" Colford stopped the two of them in their tracks. He spoke in a hushed voice. "Never, my son, let anyone in this family hear those words."

"I only meant that if Collie will get out of my way—"

"Non. Not a word. Am I clear?" Colford looked hard into his son's face.

"Oui, Papa. Not a word."

Passing Charles-Edouard's apartment, crime scene tape spoke to the police presence from earlier, and once outside the residential portion of the building, additional tape suggested each location that had been searched.

Once on the far side of the Sound, as usual, the rough parking up and down the short road leading to the lighthouse was mostly filled with cars, even with the storm debris scattered about. It was still early evening, but the sky was quickly losing the light. Walking through the wall of shrubs and through the tidy gates from the street onto the grounds, the lighthouse to the right looked as it always did, and the two men ignored it. Across the open quadrangle, an accessory building was closed, but to the left, the old keeper's quarters was open and bright. Signs along the walk directed them that direction, with the notice that the Visitor Center was open but due to the recent storm, the lighthouse was temporarily closed.

Inside the Visitor Center, John spoke to a woman with "Macie" on her name tag and asked for Jackye.

"You were here earlier." Macie smiled. "John, right? The news crew loved you."

"I don't know—" John's face flushed.

"Don't be humble. Marie's your mom, right? And this is your dad?"

"I am. Colford Sereys." Colford smiled and offered his hand. "We are proud of John."

"Marie couldn't stop talking about him today." Macie smiled. "Let me get Jackye."

When the docent appeared, she grasped John's shoulders and said, "Back so soon!" Then she turned to Colford. "And your father. We've not met. I'm Jackye. We love having your wife here. Thank you for allowing her to volunteer her time at the lighthouse. Without her, we'd all be lost. But you're here for the purse. Marie's not normally forgetful, but with the change today … you know she normally works at the top of the

lighthouse. Then with the news crews ... too many modifi-
cations in the schedule, I guess. It messes everyone up."

From behind a counter, she lifted a clutch with a long,
leather strap, offered it to them with a smile, and asked if there
was much storm damage across the Sound. Colford started to
answer when two teen girls stepped inside and asked loudly,
"Your sign says the lighthouse is closed, but the doors are open.
Can we go inside?"

"It should be padlocked." Jackye frowned, reached behind
the counter again, and pulled out a thick set of keys.

"Well, it's *not*." The girls seemed offended that their words
weren't taken at face value.

"Dears, I'll check and see. But, no, it's been closed all day
and likely through next week. I apologize for the inconven-
ience."

She turned to Colford and John. "I wouldn't normally ask,
but we're shorthanded today. Do you mind accompanying me?
I locked it myself after checking on the lighthouse this
morning—" She held up the keyring and dangled it. "—so I
can't imagine, but to be safe."

"Of course," Colford assured her. "We are sensible people,
and it is a small thing for us to do."

When they stepped outside, he took in the storm-ravaged
condition of the grounds. With the sunset, lights on the property
automatically came on, and at this time of the year, they were
already glowing, normally giving the grounds a romantic old-
world feel, one of tropical ambience and well-maintained
charm. On an average evening, it was warm and welcoming, but
the blowdown from the storm had shifted that. Much of the
ambient lighting was choked by debris, and already, within the
encroaching canopy of branches, shadows were winding omi-
nous fingers toward anyone within their reach. Across the

quadrangle, the padlock that prevented entry into the lighthouse was still secure, but the chain that twisted through the door handles had been cut. A sturdy bolt cutter rested against the side of the tall building, with the business side up. One of the two doors was thrown wide, creating a chasm of blackness into the interior.

"I'm afraid I don't have a flashlight. John, do you carry one in your car?" Colford patted his pockets. Alas, his actions suggested, there was no light to be found. "Perhaps you have one from inside?" He turned the question to Jackye, and he motioned to the brightly lit Visitor Center.

Jackye glanced at the darkening sky overhead and nodded, her expression revealing her relief at the suggestion. "I have one inside. I should have thought of that. Do you mind waiting? It'll take me just a moment." She smiled and headed back to the Visitor Center.

"Papa, what do you think?" John studied the upper part of the lighthouse.

"About?" Colford was a sensible man. He was here because of Marie and for John. He easily accepted that this wasn't his problem, even as he was willing to help.

"Charles, Papa. Remember, his apartment was discovered ransacked today. Then there's Philippe and Creighton. And Alain. It is sad, though I didn't know him well. And you do know two policemen nearly drowned only days ago. Some people are saying it was sabotage." He whispered his next words. "By Charles-Edouard."

"Charles was your uncle, but there's much about him you do not know—"

Jackye interrupted with, "I found it!" She flicked a powerful flashlight on, and it created a bright circle on the sidewalk. She aimed it at the building, and the light leaped through the open door and revealed the decorative floors and the stone steps just inside.

"Does the lighthouse own a bolt cutter such as this one?" Colford thought this important. If so, one of Jackye's coworkers might have a reason for entering, although the reason why they would not ask for a key escaped him.

"The shed has numerous tools, but that?" Jackye aimed her flashlight at it. The daylight was still sufficient for normal vision, but now that she had the flashlight, it seemed she was determined to use it. "I don't recall it."

"John has his phone. I suggest we contact the sheriff's office." John's reminder of Charles' apartment had touched a nerve. He motioned to John who lifted his phone from his pocket as if ready to tap in the numbers.

Jackye looked at her watch. "We close in thirty minutes. They would have to come from Barco. That's on the other side of the Sound. It would be properly dark by the time they arrived," she explained as she glanced around the property.

"Perhaps they can send someone who is closer already?" He hoped she got what he meant. If no one was available, then they could go in.

"Yes, that might be a good idea. The number is …"

THE "SOMEONE WHO IS CLOSER" went by the name of Sergeant Brannigan Calmont. He stepped out of the passenger's door of an unmarked lifted Jeep. Its only clue to its department connection was the flashing lights on top as they strobed into the surrounding trees.

As the red-haired officer hooked his belt around his waist, he glanced around, then reached back into the off-road vehicle and removed a cowboy hat and adjusted it on his head. He leaned into the Jeep to speak with the driver, then the flashing lights went dark, and the Jeep's engine died. A second officer emerged from the driver's side. Rather than a cowboy hat, he pulled out a cap with DARE in bold letters and Sheriff's Office underneath.

"Jackye, you out here?" Brannigan Calmont stepped through the picturesque gate leading to the lighthouse. "I like to call the cards as they fall, and this is a mess."

"Hey, Brannigan. Thank you for coming. You must have been close." Jackye, with her flashlight aimed at the ground, walked his direction. The flashlight wasn't really necessary, as there was enough ambient light, but now that she had it on, it was going to be in use.

"It's all in the title, Beach Duty Detail Officer, and you people are where the beach is. I have Sergeant Sean Taylor with me from that wastrel county just to the south of us. Is it all right if he joins us?"

"I look forward to it." She was close enough that she held out her hand to Sean. "I'm surprised you're hanging out with this bum. I've known him since he was knee-high, and he's not grown out of his little boy pants yet, not that I can tell."

Sean laughed and shook her hand. "Good to meet you, Jackye. Our two counties are on an inter-agency investigation, and that's got us teamed up tonight. I'll be mostly out of the way, but like I always say, I'm a hundred percent here a hundred percent of the time, and I'm willing to help in any way."

"Wonderful." Jackye nodded.

"So, a little break in, Jackye?" Brannigan scanned the area. The light was enough to make out each building in the compound, but the doors and windows were black rectangles, except for the Visitor Center. The lights there were on, but it was clearly closing.

"We don't know yet. Let me introduce you to my two

helpers. This is Colford Sereys and his son, John. They offered to wait with me until someone arrived. Colford's wife, Marie, volunteers with us, and John was here this afternoon to help with the clean-up from the storm. The paper was here, also, for media coverage, and as you can see, that slowed our progress some."

"Colford, John." Brannigan shook, then Sean did the same.

Jackye continued. "Marie accidentally left her purse. With the storm and the lighthouse closure, she worked inside the Visitor Center, and with John here for the day, I suppose she overlooked it. I called, and Colford and John are here to retrieve it."

"No one would think otherwise, Jackye. Now about the break in. What happened?"

"I checked the lighthouse this morning. I have the key, and I usually unlock it each morning. It was locked as usual when I arrived, and when I locked it back, I added the chain and padlock, with a sign to say it is closed for the day. I know it disappoints people, but that's the way it is. I was inside getting Marie's purse for her husband when two teen girls came in and wanted to go up in the lighthouse. When I tried to tell them it was closed today, they said the door was open."

"Sure, I'm with you. You didn't go in?"

"Well, I would have, but when Colford suggested we call, I was relieved. If someone's in there—" She shivered rather than finish her thought.

On the other side of the wall of greenery separating the lighthouse grounds from the street and road-side parking, a car started up and headlights snapped on. The car could be heard shifting into gear, then the headlights dipped and swung in an arc as the car backed up onto the roadway and turned around to head to the highway.

The last of the visitors were exiting the Visitor Center, and

Macie appeared in the doorway and called, "Jackye, are you going to be much longer?"

"Just a bit, Macie." Jackye excused herself to take a few steps towards the lighted doorway. "I have my keys with me, so when you're ready to head out, lock the doors, and I'll close down when I get back in there."

"Okay, then. I've got one more person to check out, then I'll be leaving."

"Then good night. I'll see you in the morning." Macie waved, and when she disappeared back inside, Jackye rejoined the officers and Marie's family. She said brightly, "Shall we see what's inside the dark tower of gloom and death?"

Sean Taylor muttered, "At least I know I'm not in this alone." He felt of his equipment belt and said, "I think my flashlight came off in the car. I might need it for this. I'll be right back," and he headed to the Jeep.

"I might need mine, too." Brannigan snapped his off his belt and had it shining. He called to Colford and John, "You two have lights? If you're with us, it might make it easier."

Colford chuckled. "I will be sensible and stay behind you." His son, John, had his phone out and clicked on the light on the back. He held it up and frowned when the small device hardly revealed more than he could see without it.

They heard Sean's door close, and the sergeant appeared with his light bobbing along the ground at his feet. "Shoot, y'all, you people waiting on me? Let's get to it."

"Yessir, if you think it best." Brannigan chuckled. "Unlike you slackers, I'm taking lead. Jackye, if you want to fall in behind me, and Colford and John after that. Sean, I'd like you to cover our retreat."

"On the double, boss." The young man's voice bled relief.

Above them, a noise caught their attention, and everyone

looked up. The lighthouse, which had been dark, flashed on for three seconds before fading away.

Jackye shared, "It will do that every twenty seconds. It turns on at dusk and off at sunrise."

"Just the one flash, right?" Brannigan.

"For three seconds, yes," Jackye.

"That noise? Is that part of it turning on?"

"I don't recall it, but I can't say for sure. I'm usually gone by now."

"We have to call the cards as they fall."

"You already said that." Jackye teased him.

"That doesn't mean it's not true." Brannigan took the outside steps up to the dark void where the door should be, and he paused and lifted the chain with the attached padlock. "They cut the chain, not the lock. That'll save the lighthouse a few dollars." He felt the lock more closely. "They tried, though."

"It *is* hardened. We do attempt to keep the old place safe." Jackye aimed her light at it as she passed, and the cut marks gleamed. "The lights for the building are just—"

"No," Brannigan said. He held out his hand for the others to hold back. "If their eyes are night adjusted, we can blind them temporarily by catching them in the face. Also, let me do the talking unless you find something vital." Everyone understood what he meant: someone inside. "If we all talk, we won't make any headway. I'll keep my talking to the minimum, then if something important happens, and someone calls out, we'll all be together. Everyone on board?"

Jackye quietly reminded them that lighthouse policy was to be gentle on the steps and only one person per level at a time. It was a very old building, after all.

Inside, there were doors to the left and right, and Brannigan shone his light into one, and he motioned for Sean to take the other. When he was satisfied they were both empty, he motioned once more for them to follow him as he began ascending the stairs. At each landing and window, Brannigan moved his light across each surface to ensure that no brick or metal step was left unchecked. At about the halfway point, noise overhead caught their attention, and Brannigan stopped everyone. Metal clanged, and Jackye said, "That's the door to the gallery."

"Could it have been left unlocked?" Brannigan again.

The muffled sound of a voice rained down. Sean said, "That's not an unlocked door."

"An animal, perhaps?" John's voice quivered.

"Let's keep going." Brannigan moved his light partially up the lighthouse walls, but with the steps and the multiple half-landings up and down the cylindrical structure, it created a confusing series of jumping shadows that were less than helpful.

At the top, just below the lantern room, where the door opened to the outside gallery that encircled the top of the lighthouse, outside air flooded the inside of the structure. When Brannigan arrived, the door was partially open. He turned to say something to Jackye when a scream pierced the night and then cut off. Before anyone could react, a male figure in a black hoodie wearing a balaclava, black jeans, and gloves and athletic shoes slammed into the door and into the upper room in the lighthouse. He froze when he saw Brannigan's light, then slammed into the red-headed man, knocking his light onto the floor, where it rolled away, dragging shadows everywhere across the interior of the lighthouse. He leaped for the steps, hitting at flashlights as he passed, taking two and three steps at a time, not caring if he tripped those trying to get out of his way. Sean Taylor grabbed for the man, and had his arms around him, when the black-suited figure elbowed him in the face and smashed his head into the masonry wall, sending him sliding headfirst down the steps to the next landing.

Brannigan had retrieved his flashlight, and he aimed it down. Catching Sean's final slide down the steps and his awkward landing with his head twisted against the wall, he called, "Sean, are you okay?"

When there was no answer or movement, he completely ignored Jackye's caution to be gentle on the steps, and he dodged everyone as he flew as fast as he could to check on the injured officer.

SEAN REGAINED consciousness as the Emergency Response Team from the Corolla Fire Station settled him on an emergency stretcher in preparation for carrying him down the stairs. The interior lights were now on, and they were strapping him firmly in, as the stretcher would be at a severe angle all the way down the lighthouse.

"No regrets, I always say." Sean's eyes didn't quite focus, and he tried to smile. One hand was free, and he attempted to touch the face of the nearest paramedic. "Grant, is that you?"

"I can be, if you'll put your hand down." The paramedic gently lowered his arm to his side and continued to secure him to the stretcher. "You're pretty banged up, buddy. That bump on your head isn't likely going to feel good on the way down, but I'd like you to stay awake if you can."

The medical team took to the steps first, taking their time on the way down, so that they didn't miss any. The paramedic kept up a conversation with Sean as they progressed, but Sean's responses were all over the place, and he kept repeating, "Where are we? Why am I strapped down?"

Colford remarked to everyone who would listen, "Anyone sensible can see that was one of the Knight bunch." He snorted his disgust. "Always making trouble for us. What would Mémé think of being attacked in a lighthouse—"

"Papa, it's not for us to say." John held up a hand to hush his father's remarks. "And you forget, Mémé Philippine is a Knight by all rights."

"Not by blood." Colford was tired, needed a cigarette, and found all this very frustrating.

"But by rights. Otherwise, we would not be here." John used both hands to indicate that the matter was settled for the time being.

"Why do you blame the Knights?" Brannigan had slotted Colford and John into what he knew of the Brayboy feud and had his interest piqued.

"Papa is just frustrated. My uncle was recently found dead, and—"

"Charles-Edouard." Brannigan nodded. "The other two were airlifted to Norfolk."

"Yes. Two of my cousins." John seemed surprised at the officer's quick response.

"But why would your father blame the Knights? There's no indication this has any connection." It didn't seem to be a true question but rather one the man already suspected an answer to.

They had reached the bottom of the stairs, however, ending the conversation before the question could be resolved. The paramedics loaded Sean into the ambulance, and with lights blaring, they pulled down the road towards the highway, took a right, and disappeared into the night. Only then did the discussion turn to what had happened and what each person had noticed during the series of events.

Jackye was the first to bring up the obvious.

"Brannigan, that was a man we saw upstairs." She said it as a statement but one she needed verified. She studied his face hopefully.

"I thought so." He adjusted his broad-brimmed hat. However he had managed it, it had remained on his head the entire time. "Colford, John, y'all give me your thoughts. Our intruder, man or woman?"

Colford said, "I only saw them in passing. I felt it was sensible to hold to the railing rather than focus on their appearance. I am very sorry." He shrugged. It was hardly his business, as he was only here to collect his wife's purse. And it seemed nothing was damaged, except for the cut chain. That could be easily replaced. "John, did you get a look?"

John was more confident. "I was watching the door when it was thrown back. I'm certain the person carried a man's build, especially with the wide shoulders. No woman would have that. Did anyone else see the eyes? Blue, very vivid." He turned to his father. "Papa, you must have noticed his eyes. No one could miss them."

Colford shrugged again. "As I said, only in passing."

Jackye returned to her question, this time with a different focus, and she directed her attention to John. "You asked if we heard an animal."

"I did," he quickly agreed. "But it was the door, obviously. Or a bird, perhaps."

"Brannigan?" This time, her voice shook. "I don't want to think this, but I can't help my imagination. Nothing inside appeared damaged, so why would he cut the chain and be outside on the gallery at night? What if—" Her voice choked.

"What if what, Jackye?"

"If he wasn't the only one that climbed the stairs?"

"But we were on the gallery." John frowned hard. "You, too, Papa, right? We saw no one."

"As John says," Colford agreed, "our intruder was the only person inside. The sergeant inspected every possible place to conceal oneself on the way up. Where else was there to hide?"

"The scream, though. Brannigan, it wasn't a man's scream."

"Slow down," the tall sergeant cautioned. "We won't make any headway with speculation. If someone else was up there, and we didn't find them, are you suggesting ..." He didn't say but waited on Jackye to confirm her suspicions.

"I don't know. Maybe not." Her shoulders sagged, and she wiped at her face with open palms as though fighting tears.

"But you would feel better if we checked." He touched her shoulder to get her to give him her full attention.

"Thank you. Yes, I would."

"I would say if you insist, but you don't need to do that. I agree. If we even suspect that something went down—" He froze with his words and hit himself on the temple with the flat of his hand, pushing his hat up and leaving it crooked. "Let me reword that—"

"No need." Jackye laughed, but she was close to tears.

"Where do you want to start, Jackye? There's tons of brush outside, and we just came from inside. We can go back to the top and inspect the gallery for clues, or we can begin searching the grounds for, um—"

"I get it." She held her hand to cover her mouth, and she kept looking into the darkness.

"Do you want to start upstairs? We didn't suspect a second person earlier."

"No. We were focused on getting help for your friend." She smiled, but it was forced. "If we start here, we might need an additional flashlight for Colford."

"Good thought." Brannigan paused, gave Colford his attention, and asked, "You are still willing to help? If not, I understand."

"We are here. It makes sense to do what we can." Colford

looked at his son, and John nodded his head in agreement.

"Good. I have my partner's flashlight but not a second one for your son. If you think it best, I can try to locate one for John."

"I likely have another one in the Visitor Center. I think I still have my keys with me." Jackye felt of her pockets, and when one jangled, she pulled them out triumphantly.

"Then you get those, and we'll start when you return. John, do you mind accompanying her?"

"Certainly. I will let nothing get in my way."

As Jackye and John made their way toward the Visitor Center, Colford stepped to Brannigan and asked, "Do you think, perhaps, it is sensible for a person to climb a lighthouse to toss another person off?"

"No." Brannigan rubbed his forehead and realized his hat was cocked. He straightened it before continuing. "I was on the Sound about a week ago, and someone punctured several chambers in my Zodiac. That wasn't sensible, either. Three days ago, we nearly lost two officers in the same Zodiac. Was the repair done improperly, or was it sabotage again? There are too many things that don't feel good about this. I'm willing to trust Jackye's instinct."

"You heard the scream, oui?"

"I had other things on my mind, but yes. I heard the scream."

"And it was a man or animal to you?"

"Like I said, I had other things on my mind. If you insist, though, it could have been either."

"So," and Colford knew he was pressing the question, but this man seemed to have a mind that thought of these things. "An animal could have been thrown off the top." When Brannigan frowned at him, Colford said, "People do what they will do. It is not up to me to approve or disapprove."

"If you insist, possibly. I don't think so, however."

"Then, not a man that went off the top, but a woman. Am I correct?" Colford smiled, pleased at his deductive reasoning.

"You're forcing me to admit this, aren't you?"

"Only if you wish. My Grand-mère Philippine would say that when something is reasonable, then that is the only choice possible."

John and Jackye were headed back along the walk, and John now held a bright flashlight.

"Colford and I have been talking, Jackye." Brannigan was already aiming his light to reveal the foundations of the tall brick structure. "I suggest we cover this area." He moved the light to let it sweep over the debris scattered around the lighthouse's foundation. "If, and I mean if, something did go over, how far away do you feel it would land?"

"How far could they throw it, do you mean?" John.

"If you insist." Brannigan.

"Not far. A person is heavy, and the lighthouse is wider at the base."

"Oh!" Jackye put a fist to her mouth and gasped. "I can't bear to think of something so horrible."

"You can wait and let the men search." Brannigan.

"No, I'm okay, or I will be. I want to do this."

Most of the storm debris, even where it was thick, was a loose assemblage of snapped limbs and thick foliage. The flashlights, however bright, seemed to reveal more shadows than information. Towards the backside of the brick structure, John called to the others.

"Look there." He aimed his light at an especially high mound of brush, one that would be slow to dismantle to search underneath. Much of it was bathed in shadow, but the top of the pile was especially dark, as if something had hollowed it out from the top down. When John moved his light back and forth, the outside edges of the mound formed the rim of a bowl filled with shadows and dread.

"Good job, John. I think you found the real deal. Let me head in first." Brannigan began pulling branches from the mound and dragging them to the side, and within moments, John and Colford were helping. Jackye held her light to illuminate their activities as best as possible.

Jackye's light caught the blonde hair first, causing Brannigan to freeze and hold up a hand for the others to stop. He fought his way over a final branch and used his light to illuminate the discovery. A slender woman lay on green needles attached to branches now crushed in the aftermath of her fall. Her long, blonde hair was splayed around her head, and her clear complexion glowed in the light.

"Amanda Sargeant," Colford breathed, when he was close enough to see her face.

"You know her?" Brannigan had recognized her from his visit to Knotts Island less than a week before.

"Collie's girlfriend," John answered. "Well, not anymore." He must have realized how that sounded, and he quickly rephrased his comment. "Not because of this, mind you. Amanda was involved in some stuff with Charles-Edouard, and I think Collie wanted to rescue her. Amanda was more interested in one of the Knights, though."

"Lavie Knight," Brannigan let out before he could cut off his revelation.

"You know?" John seemed stunned. "Hardly anyone knows about Amanda and Lavie."

"Not even Collie?"

"I guess Collie must, but I've never told him, I assure you. Can I ask how you know? Lavie would never tell anyone. It was a secret she thought she kept from everyone."

"From Amanda. She requested to meet with us up on Knotts Island a few days ago."

"I wish I'd known." John seemed distressed.

"You mentioned Collie. He's your uncle, right? Do you think, perhaps ... if he had found out about Lavie?" Brannigan seemed to once again be testing the waters.

"For sure that wasn't Collie we saw." John let out a laugh. "My uncle hates the Knight branch of the family as much as we all do, but he would have done well to make it to the top of the lighthouse, and he would have been out of breath if he had."

"Okay," Brannigan said with a sense of relief. "Everyone, I'll check for vitals, but no one else is to touch the body. Just keep back, and I'll call this in when I determine who I need to contact. Jackye, if you'll shine your light this direction, that will be a big help."

Jackye's light found him, and Brannigan began to navigate the best branches to reach Amanda while not disturbing the crime scene ... and it was a crime scene, whether she was alive or dead.

Dead seemed the obvious choice, but that would be the coroner's decision, if that was who Brannigan determined he needed to call.

AS THE CURRITUCK COUNTY Sheriff's Office didn't maintain a forensic investigator but relied instead on inter-county cooperation with her southern sister, Barco notified Manteo, and two hours later, Emily Bryant arrived at the scene.

"Do I read this right? Sergeant Brannigan Calmont? I saw Sean Taylor's Jeep out there. What are you doing here?" Emily had her white clean suit on, with her camera around her neck, and a case of extra materials in her hand.

"Emily." Brannigan greeted her and pointed to the two men

sitting on a low fence to the side. "I tried to send these two home, but they wanted to meet you. They knew our deceased woman. You do, too."

"Okay, I give. Who do I know up here?"

"From Knotts Island."

She frowned, then her eyes went wide with understanding. "Amanda Sargeant? No! Then, this is drug related? Was it that boyfriend over in Currituck?"

"Too many questions, not enough answers."

"Who are the men?"

"A nephew and half-brother of the boyfriend. I've taken their information, as they are possible witnesses to the crime. The nephew assures me the boyfriend couldn't have made it to the top of the lighthouse."

"Oh, my word. I hoped I misunderstood. So, she was really thrown off and fell to her death?"

"That's the way I read it. Can I introduce you?"

Emily glanced at the men, shook her head, and said, "They're a distraction to me right now. Do I need pictures from the top, also?"

"Your call, but that's where we were when we heard her scream. We saw her assailant, but he was covered head to toe. I'd be surprised if he left any fingerprints or other evidence. He's the one that put Sean in the hospital."

"Sean Taylor?" This time, Emily froze and looked hard at Brannigan. "Oh, my word! I heard the ambulance. Sean! Who would have thought? Is he going to die a hero?"

"Hopefully not die." Brannigan chuckled. "A hero, we can always hope there."

"And he was up here for?"

"Our investigation. Inter-county business. Now he's part of the investigation."

"So, you think this is connected?"

"That is Amanda, and those men are up to their knees in the Brayboy feud. They're even suggesting possible suspects, all on the Knight side of the family, of course."

"Two points in your scorebook, Brannigan. I'm liking Currituck County more and more. If this was a drug deal gone south, you'll be the one to prove it."

"Not my job. I'm here to collect evidence."

"And get me a medical examiner? I don't know if he's available, but Steven Hill's the best."

"I didn't know you could request."

"You can't, but I always do. Sometimes it works. I'm getting busy now. I'll need all this cordoned off with tape, and I'll let you know if I need anything else."

Brannigan nodded and headed towards the two men who had waited with Jackye throughout the whole ordeal, although she had claimed exhaustion, closed up shop, and abandoned them an hour earlier. They stood as he approached.

"That's your medical examiner?" Colford was surprised to see someone so pretty.

"Forensic investigator, and she's from Dare County. We don't have one. I have worked with her before."

"I see. From a different county. Then John and I are finished here?" Colford had wanted to watch the events play themselves out and to be able to tell his wife the end of the story. He had seen the woman's dismissal of them, however, and remaining here would only keep supper waiting until long past bedtime.

"I'll be in touch. I have your information." Brannigan patted his chest pocket and the spiral that could just be seen.

Colford gathered up John and his wife's purse, and they clambered into John's small car. The dead woman he did not care about, but still, in his mind, this was the work of the

Knights attempting to discredit his side of the family. If it was drugs, and it could be with her connection to Charles-Edouard, things could get very ugly indeed. He didn't know how he would need to handle it, but when he got to The Wharf, he would have a serious talk with Collie. His brother had to know something, and it was about time that Colford learned what it was.

Chapter 9

Fireworks in the Darkness

DEPUTY CLARA DEL RAY processed what she knew of Sean Taylor, the young drone operator from Manteo. She recalled his dark eyes, the way he wore his uniform, and the care he took with his appearance. At The Wharf, when the two Currituck County officers were blown off course all the way to Goosecastle Point, he had been instrumental in locating them.

Being relatively new to Dare County, Clara didn't *really* know the man, but at the Team Impact meeting, he had known about Shelby Ellison, Blackbeard, and Springer Point, as if they were links in a very important chain of events in a monumental case.

Solved? Resolved? Or still pending? It had caught her attention, and she had done some research. Now she knew that Shelby was Cynthia Ellison's granddaughter from Ocracoke Island, and that Blackbeard had been killed on Springer Point.

More details of the case involved a family that had been abducted and held captive during a drug operation gone bad.

She had also uncovered the reason Cynthia Ellison had a freshly assigned K9. Her previous dog had been injured in a firefight and retired from service. The records showed his name was Toby and that he now lived with Cynthia and her husband.

Doing her research had ramped up Clara's enthusiasm for working with her team in Dare County. Those cases had been under the auspices of Diane Turnipseed. While the captain could come across as brusque and even distant, clearly her previous team had worked to earn her respect, with numerous resolved cases on record revealing their success. Captain Turnipseed's success. Her team's, also, but the top person carried the ultimate responsibility and by default received the ultimate glory.

When she was first hired, Clara had thought A-District was slow compared to her previous position in Brunswick County, but when she totaled the dead or potentially dead people piling up in just the past week, this place was firing on all cylinders. Now, though, her duties were taking on a darker tone. She knew Sean Taylor, had admired his obvious enthusiasm for his job, and it didn't hurt that she also admired his Jeep and had hoped they could get together on an off-duty day to take in some four-wheeling time on the sand. Sand, surf … it was the reason she had transferred to Dare County.

When her radio first lit up, she'd thought nothing of it. She was in the old patrol car she shared with Ed, and she lifted the mic from the dash.

"Clara here. Getting my feet wet. What can I do for you?"

"How much do you know about the events up at the lighthouse in Corolla?" The caller was Emily Bryant.

"It's been a busy week, but I recall a sergeant from Barco going down in the Sound. Wasn't he sighted from the lighthouse? I think you were there, so you know about that. Is there something else?"

"Yes." The radio went quiet as though Emily had released the transmit button. Then it lit up again. "Tonight. Do you know about tonight?"

"No. I've been on traffic duty. What should I know?"

"You've met Sean Taylor?"

"Yes. We are on an Impact Team together. Why?"

Emily began describing the events from the lighthouse, the suspect who had run down the staircase, and the disastrous outcome of that. She touched on the woman who had been found but more importantly, she said, the story was that Sean Taylor had attempted to restrain the suspect on his way down the stairs, and when Emily climbed up the lighthouse to photograph the scene, she had found traces of blood just where she calculated that Sean's hand might have brushed the stairs and the walls. She and Brannigan Calmont from Currituck County had contacted the Outer Banks Health Hospital where Sean was taken by the paramedic team to let them know that they needed his fingernails checked for DNA evidence. Was Clara close enough to see to that?

She was, and now she was headed to the hospital with a DNA collection case, fully kitted out with swabs and vials to use on Sean's hands. The darkness seemed to be chasing her, pressing in, hounding her. Occasionally catching sight of the beach, the light was just enough to define the horizon between sky and sea, with silhouettes of houses and buildings occasionally testifying to the life inside by bright squares of curtainless windows. Taking a left into the hospital parking lot, she found the space reserved for law enforcement, parked, and headed inside. At the desk, she identified herself and asked for the location of Sergeant Sean Taylor, explaining that he had just been brought in with a possible head injury.

The walk to the Emergency Department was under a cloud of worry. The front desk had known exactly who she was here to see, and they had immediately expressed their sympathy for what had happened to him. Inside the ward, one nurse was setting up fluids on a rack attached to the bed, and the other was organizing fresh bandaging and tape. The young officer was bare to the waist, and already, bruising was showing up as bright red marks along his side. An arm revealed torn skin, but the real damage was from his neck up. His hair was catastrophically matted with blood, and one eye was completely red and nearly swollen shut. His arms boasted tubes and needles, and his neck was firmly encased in a full brace, although his hands were relatively injury free with dark stains under several of his nails. For a moment, Clara wasn't sure it was the man she had come to see. Then she noted his county-issue pants and took control of her emotions.

"Excuse me, but hello. I'm Deputy Clara Del Ray with the Dare County Sheriff's Office. Is this Sean Taylor?" As much as she hated to see him in this condition, she was glad he was still a mess, and his hands and nails hadn't been cleaned.

The nurses gave her a quick glance, but the man called out with a muffled, "Clara?"

"May I?" she asked one of the nurses, and she stepped to Sean's side when the woman gave her room. "Sean, I heard what happened—"

"Where am I?" His words were slurred. "I was … I was … Jason, is Jason here? No, I was with, um, that man from that other county … why can't I move my neck …"

"Clara, right?" The nurse pulled her aside. "We're about to head down for a scan. There's a possibility of a bleed on his brain. We'll know more then."

"Then let me ask you. Have you cleaned his hands?"

"Well, no. He just arrived, and his head injuries have been top priority."

"Okay, then. Do I have time for this?" She held up the kit, gave a brief explanation of what had occurred, and said that collecting possible blood samples from under his fingernails was vital to a pending murder investigation.

The nurse asked her co-worker, "Julie, how long until the scan?"

"Someone is in now, so as soon as they are finished. Five minutes, perhaps? Ten at the most."

"Is that enough time?"

Clara nodded. "It will be. Where can I set up?"

This affected part of her team. This was something she couldn't get wrong.

PULLING THE SAMPLES from underneath Sean's fingernails seemed like it would be over and done in Clara's mind, but the practice of it in training wasn't like working on a man who was suffering from confusion and, at one point, what must have been a mild seizure. She kept working, however, and the medical team gave her the time she needed, even after they were ready to go.

At one point, he flailed at her and called out with slurred speech, "I don't like being held down. Leave my hands alone."

"I'm sorry, Sean," she whispered as she placed her final samples in the collection kit.

"It's the brain bleed," the nurses assured her. "I'm sure he would never say such things if he was in his right mind."

She still felt his privacy had been invaded, and that she had done something to him without his permission. She remained in the area as they disconnected him enough to roll his bed out and start towards wherever he was being scanned. She stepped past the curtain that had given him some privacy, only to find the ward quiet, except for the occasional buzz of various machines and the whir of the fan as the HVAC clicked on.

"Well then," she said to no one. "You get your feet wet, and that's when you find you're no longer wet behind the ears, so to speak. I need to get my samples under ice." This might be her first sample collection for Dare County, but she had worked in Brunswick County long enough to know that DNA samples didn't stay in the local districts but were shot straight to the big boys. They would need to go to Manteo, where they would likely have a courier transport them to the State Crime Lab at the Department of Justice in Raleigh.

Back in the car, she picked up the radio. "Deputy Clara Del Ray calling Emily Bryant. Are you out there, Emily? Over."

"Emily here. How did your samples go?"

"Please and thank you goes a long way. I said please, and when I was through, I said thank you. I don't think they'll mind seeing me again."

"His hands were still pristine?"

"Absolutely, though if I have someone over for dinner, that's not the pristine I want. I'm guessing they'll want these in Manteo tonight."

"I'm glad you contacted me. I have more samples from the lighthouse—"

"That's out of county, isn't it?" Clara knew about "inter-county cooperation" and all, but she expected some separation. She had seen some of that when she and Ed had discovered the gun and bloody clothes up on the county line.

"I serve as forensic investigator for both counties when needed. Besides, whichever county claims the samples, they are all going to Raleigh. It looks like I'm running them in tonight.

Do you want to meet up and sign those over to me? I can pick up cooling packs and transport them for you. It might save the county some hefty courier fees."

They decided on the Home Depot parking lot where the N Croatan Highway hooked west to head onto the mainland. Thankfully Clara knew where that was, and she patted the sample case on the front seat beside her, trusting that this would provide the information they needed to catch whoever had committed this double crime. She was the first to arrive, and she pulled into the lot and found a broad, empty section of parking spaces and pulled up, leaving the car running and her lights on.

She watched the people coming and going, unsure what Emily would be in except that it was a white sedan. The roads weren't especially busy, so when a brightly painted New Beetle with an airbrushed face and name scrawled down the side pulled out of the Crumbl cookie shop just across the highway, it caught her attention. The back bumper was missing, and the image of the face was partially torn away. She realized she had seen the car up and down the northern beaches on the Banks, and if she remembered correctly, the driver was an artist who painted and sold her pictures to the tourist crowd.

Something seemed odd about how the car was behaving, and Clara realized the Crumbl shop was closed, and likely had been for hours. What was the car doing emerging from there? It passed the Home Depot lot where Clara waited on Emily, although on the opposite side of the highway; and it pulled off to the right into the TowneBank parking lot, where it parked and the driver emerged, a woman wearing thick dungarees and wellies. She seemed to be looking for an ATM. However, she didn't look to be in distress and wasn't acting panicky, so Clara turned her attention back to the roadway for other points of interest.

A full-size pickup truck with a blazing lightbar across the top of the cab came barreling in from the Sound side at far over the speed limit. Clara sat up, checked her surroundings for city police, and made the judgement call to initiate pursuit. Before she could shift from park to drive, her radio bleeped, and she heard: "White truck, license plate BALLIN II, headed east on 159. Repeated calls of reckless speed. Any local cars initiate pursuit if able."

"I see him." Clara spoke into her mic and returned it to the dash. She didn't take the time to identify herself, but flipped on her lights and siren, released the parking brake, and dropped the transmission into drive. The heavy vehicle didn't have the quick, neck-snapping launch of smaller, lighter sports cars, but the big engine had torque to spare. The tires squealed as the massive tonnage atop the axles fought to maintain its stationary momentum and then built speed quickly. The car sloshed out of the parking lot onto Croatan, forcing her to head east, the direction of the oncoming truck with its blinding lightbar.

As she slowed to intercept the big truck, she remembered why the tags seemed so familiar. This truck had been impounded in the A-District sub-station parking lot for multiple days. She didn't know what it had been up to since then, except that it was reported missing from the scene when the Ballinger twins were airlifted to Norfolk. She would have heard if they were back; and their cousin, Charles-Edouard, was in the morgue.

Then it came to her. At The Wharf up in Currituck! That was the last time she'd seen this truck, when they were serving the warrants to search Charles-Edouard's belongings. She could check off the names of two people who had been at The Wharf who wouldn't be in the driver's seat. Emily had validated that Colford and John Sereys were at Currituck Light until well into the evening. The only other person they'd met was the man in the mechanical room, Collie Beaumarchais.

All that took up little more than a second in Clara's head, and when she looked for the truck coming up alongside her, she was astonished to see him slam on his brakes, and with squealing tires, jerk the vehicle over the median, through three lanes of oncoming traffic, and across the sidewalk into the Townebank parking lot. The driver leaped from the truck—definitely Collie Beaumarchais, with his thick waistline and receding red hair, leaving the door open, and he lifted his fist in a threatening manner as he walked hard towards the woman in dungarees. He seemed to be yelling, although Clara couldn't hear what was being said.

Clara grabbed her mic, clicked it to talk, and said, "Clara Del Ray with Dare County. The driver of the white truck has pulled into the TowneBank parking lot at N Croatan and Juniper Trail. He is exhibiting threatening behavior toward a woman in a Beetle with a logo and name on the side. I'm across the highway and in pursuit, heading that direction."

She had two options: continue east on Croatan to the 12 interchange and circle back to head west on Croatan, or follow the truck's example and jump the median. She pictured the woman in the Beetle and the emotions that must be running through her, and she made the only reasonable choice. She checked for on-coming cars, saw that she was clear, and with her lights and siren blazing, she cut across the eastbound lanes, felt the car rock as she crossed the median, and slammed the gas to reach the TowneBank parking lot as quickly as possible. She did make the choice to take Juniper Trail rather than cut across the sidewalk. The white truck might have the clearance to do so undamaged, but she was in an aging patrol car, and it offered her no such assurances.

As she pulled up to the couple, the situation seemed less volatile than she had previously thought. The red-headed Collie still gesticulated threateningly, but he didn't have a weapon that Clara could see, and he wasn't within striking distance. He also looked woefully out of shape, although Clara knew that adrenalin could drive even poor physical specimens to commit unbelievable atrocities. She left them centered in her headlights, placed her hand on her weapon, and opened her car door. In the distance, a backup siren wailed that it was on the way.

She stood and called out, "Collie, this is Clara Del Ray. We met earlier at your place across the Sound. You were working on the furnace in the basement. How are you doing tonight?"

He had a fist raised, not to hit, Clara thought, but to express his anger. He paused, looked at the cruiser with its flashing lights, and back to the woman with the dungarees. Clara could now read the name on the side of the car. Lavie Knight. The confrontation was beginning to make sense.

"Collie, is it okay if Lavie steps over here so that I can get some information from her? Do you think that will be okay with you?" Diffuse, Clara kept telling herself. Get them apart, give them time to cool off, and then she could find out what had triggered this.

"That woman!" Collie shook with anger. "It's her fault, all her fault!"

"I hear you and understand." Clara could see that Lavie was broken, and she didn't think it was from Collie's abusive tirade. She had been acting lost even before the man had appeared on the scene. "I would like to talk with her and with you. I'm sure we can work this out so that we can all get on home before it's too late." They could file reports for harassment in the morning if they wished, but on a public roadway wasn't the place to settle their differences.

"She killed Amanda. She was my girlfriend. I loved her. This … this …" He broke and began to sob. He sank back against his truck and pressed his hands to his eyes and let out a wail of despair.

"Lavie, this way." Clara motioned to the woman, and when she began to trudge Clara's direction, Clara opened her back door and help her sit on the edge of the seat. "Are you okay?"

"I tried to save Amanda." Lavie was barely coherent, and her voice shook. "When she told me about the money, I knew it was a bad thing. I didn't know it would come to this. I couldn't have known, could I? What am I to do now?" She looked into Clara's face, and her cheeks gleamed with her tears.

The additional police car was there by then, and a group of tourists carrying Jersey Mike's cups paused on the sidewalk to see what was going on. When the local police approached Collie, he turned his back to them, noticed the group on the sidewalk, and yelled, "What are you hoping to see? I may not have the Rothschild fortune any longer, but I'm still one by name." He dropped his head to his truck and sobbed, saying, "America. We have fallen too far to recover."

"Sir," one of the policemen at Collie's side said. "Sir, if you could look at me so that I can ask you some questions."

"If you must." He raised his head and turned his back to the tourists. However, the look he gave Lavie said his hurt and anger hadn't dissipated at all.

THE WHUP-WHUP of a helicopter overhead caught Clara's attention. She searched the sky to locate it and, when she did, she followed it as it arced out and over the Sound. Once fully over the water, a searchlight formed a cone of illumination from the aircraft to the surface. It jumped around before going dark, and as the sound faded, she focused back on the disturbance between Collie and Lavie. She explained to the local personnel that she was meeting with a colleague to sign over crime scene evidence for delivery to the Crime Lab in Raleigh, and did they require her presence any longer? She could come back if they needed her, as she would be in the parking lot just across the street.

With Lavie situated in another car, Clara backed her cruiser out of the way and headed to the Home Depot lot, and just in time, too. She recognized Emily in a white sedan as it turned into the lot and pulled up in a nearby spot. Emily opened her door, stood, and looked over the top of her car at the lights still flashing across the street.

"I like to say that saltwater cures all. It seems someone didn't get the message." Emily shook her head and turned back to Clara. "Do you know what that's about?"

"I was part of it."

"Oh?" Emily's eyebrows shot up. "What part? The good part or the bad part?"

"Mostly just filling in until the city cops could step in. I was waiting here when a call came in about that truck, and I was closest, so—" Clara smiled and shrugged.

"Ah, the BALLIN II tags. Wasn't that at the A-District sub-station a week or so back?"

"Towing two off-road bikes on a trailer. I saw it this morning over in Currituck at The Wharf."

"Am I reading this right? Those kids that got airlifted to Virginia, it was theirs, correct?" Emily rubbed her arms. "They called me in for pictures when they found the drowned man. Now that was a sad one. Still, you can never tell. When those French people took over The Wharf, they sure stirred up their cousins over on the Banks. It's all beach to me, but they need to get their priorities in order. Do it while the sun shines or the wind's gonna be blowing a whale-load of sand right down their gullets."

"That's a beach-ism?" Clara knew most of them, as her parents had maintained a house on the Banks as long as she remembered, but she'd never heard that one.

"Nah." Emily laughed. "My granny owned a chicken farm. My mixed metaphor is from her side of the family. Well, Raleigh's calling. You got those samples from Sean's fingernails?"

While Clara gathered the samples, Emily opened her trunk to reveal a chest with several fresh freezer packs. Before taking the samples, she pulled out a metal folder with a flip top that formed a stand when folded all the way to the back, and she sorted out a form on top before filling in several blanks. She asked Clara, "Uppercase D or lowercase?"

"Upper." She appreciated her asking.

"Then sign here, and I'll be on my way."

Clara signed, added the time, and she handed off the samples to Emily who positioned them in the chest. She sealed the top and closed the trunk lid.

"Are you heading back over there?" Emily nodded towards the bank. Despite her question, it looked like the party was breaking up.

"They have my number. Do you know anything about a helicopter that just flew overhead?" As if to support Clara's question, a distant whup-whup from the south broke the silence, and within a few minutes, a second aircraft was passing overhead.

"That's Coast Guard," Emily observed. "None of the rest of us have choppers. If they're headed over the Sound, it's likely a report of a missing boater. People stay out too late, batteries go dead, engines won't restart. Especially this time of the year. It gets dark surprisingly early, and it catches people off guard. I expect we'll read of an amazing rescue in the morning, and the Coast Guard will all be heroes."

"I hope so." Clara pictured Charles-Edouard and the man pulled in from the boat that had capsized on the beach.

"Count on it. I left Brannigan Calmont with the lighthouse up in Corolla. As long as he doesn't figure out how to turn off the light, I think everyone on the Sound will find their way home tonight. You be safe, girl."

"You, too." They hugged briefly, and Emily started up her car and was gone.

Clara thought of the Coast Guard Enforcement Specialist, Connie Underwood, that she had met that morning in Currituck. Connie would know, surely, about the helicopter and what it might be looking for. Only, Clara had no way of contacting her without going through Manteo or directly to the Coast Guard station. That might be a little too familiar for a freshly hired Dare County newbie with only one fingernail extraction on her resume.

As Clara watched the last of the participants drive away from the bank, she couldn't keep her thoughts from playing with the events from the past week. Drugs in the sand, then more on the shore. Two dead men, a dead woman, and another one if they could locate a body. A warrant to search a dead man's possessions. As she tried to match up the facts as she knew them, she hummed a little ditty to herself. Drug here, drugs there, there could be drugs anywhere.

She scanned the sky in the direction of the Sound. No helicopters, and too much city noise, even if they did happen to be close enough for her to hear. Would the Coast Guard break out two helicopters to search for missing boaters in a brackish body of water that was rarely deeper than five feet? She didn't know, so she dropped into her car, started it up, and headed south towards the sub-station to fill out her daily report.

IT WAS LONG after dark, and Clara was surprised to discover Diane Turnipseed's Ford Explorer in the sub-station parking lot. The underside of the Colington Road Water Tower glowed with reflected light. As Clara pulled in and killed her engine, the door burst open, and a wall of brilliance cut across the shallow porch and illuminated the railing leading up to the elevated building.

Clara opened her door and climbed out. "Captain? Is everything all right?"

"You just come from the hospital?" Diane was a black silhouette against the brightly lit interior.

"Yes, ma'am. I met with Emily—"

"She done told me. She said you saw Officer Taylor. Dump it on me. How bad is it?"

"I was able to pull the blood samples from his hands just fine—" Clara felt on her left foot, unsure what answers the captain wanted to hear.

"I weren't asking—" Diane cut off her rebuttal and softened her tone. "Is the man alive and breathing?"

"Yes, ma'am. They were taking him for a scan. They suggested he might have a bleed on the brain."

Diane laughed. "Shush that. I bet before tomorrow's breakfast he's back at the station to make my life miserable."

"A brain bleed's serious, Captain."

"Only if you got a brain to bleed. If you knew Taylor like I do, you'd know, sure as taters in a bag, he's empty-headed as they come. Now, I just got a call. You ready for one more outing tonight?"

"Absolutely. Where are we headed?"

At Clara's "absolutely," Diane slammed the door and headed down the steps. "Get in the car, and I'll fill you in on the way."

"Yes, ma'am."

Clara only had to toss two coffee cups out of the seat, as Diane had shifted her thermos by her side as soon as Clara opened her door. As soon as both doors were closed and they had their seat belts hooked up, the captain started the engine, and the headlights flared. She reversed and stopped with a squeal of the tires, and then the big machine surged through the gate and onto Colington Road. They were near the Wright Brothers Monument before she began to fill Clara in.

"To tell the story honest, I should'a expected something like this. I wisht—" and Diane hit the steering wheel to finish her sentence.

"Yes, ma'am?" Clara played the scene gingerly. She had no clue what this could be about.

"We had those bikes and that truck in our yard, didn't we? Impounded and out of those people's hands. I thought that with those boys up in Norfolk, things might settle down, and now, one varmint's attracted a whole nest of 'em."

"I'm not following you, ma'am."

"They just picked up that truck west of the bridge over the mouth of Currituck Sound."

"The white truck with the Ballin II plates? No. Collie and Lavie were both released with a warning. I was there. And it was at TowneBank in Kitty Hawk."

By now, Diane had taken a left to head north up 12 toward Currituck County. The engine in the truck sucked gasoline, not paying attention to anything except Diane's foot.

"You were there?" She gave Clara her hard attention.

"I was waiting at Home Depot for Emily. That's where we were meeting up for her to collect the samples from Sean. When the call came in about the truck, it was right in front of me. I intercepted, but then a Kitty Hawk police car arrived, and they took over. I had to get back to my meeting with Emily."

"This happened afterwards, then. You said it was Collie driving?"

"Yes. He saw Lavie Knight's car and chased her down. They were having an argument."

"And he was heading west?"

"No, east."

"Did he have the trailer on the back, or anything in the back of the truck?"

"No."

"What you're telling me's got me in the collards for sure. If he had already delivered the bikes, why was he heading back out to the beach—"

"I'm lost, ma'am. Can you fill me in, please?"

"Hold your taters for a second." A car was tootling along in front of them, and Diane flashed her brights, hit her blinker, and pushed the Explorer into the oncoming lane and around the slower car. "Sheriff Barnett gave me a call and asked me to bring up as many officers as I had available. And yes, he said a deputy would do."

"Thank you, ma'am."

"You don't worry, Clara. I've had a look-see at your record in Brunswick, and I'm glad you put your spoon into our pot. Those motorcycles are out there tearing up the beach out of hours, and to tell the story honest, I don't expect to find those two boys from last week on them."

"How do we know they're the same bikes?"

"The trailer's parked up there, and it's empty of bikes."

"The same trailer?"

Diane didn't respond, as Clara hadn't really asked a question, rather was taking the time to process. The truck and trailer had been searched under the warrant earlier that day. They had both been secured with police tape before leaving The Wharf. It hadn't occurred to Clara that the truck likely hadn't been released to be back on the road. She berated herself, but then, other things had been on her mind, like a fellow officer in the hospital with a possible brain bleed … and a dead woman who had been thrown from the top of a lighthouse.

"Captain, when I responded to the truck in Kitty Hawk, I spoke with the other party, Lavie Knight. She said something unusual. She told me that she had tried to save Amanda, and that when Amanda told her about the money, she knew it was a bad thing. I got the impression she thought Amanda was killed because of the money."

"What money?"

"She didn't say, and then the Kitty Hawk officers showed up, and they took over."

"How much do you know about Lavie Knight and Amanda?"

"Just what Emily updated me on, that Amanda was likely thrown from the lighthouse."

"I might as well throw it all at you, knickers and all. Emily was up on Knotts Island last week and learned that Amanda and Lavie were romantically involved. Now, Amanda didn't say that, but everything she said suggested it, to take that like you want. The bigger twist is that Amanda was used as a drug mule, we think by Charles-Edouard, and Collie, his older brother, took Amanda under his wing. He considered her his girlfriend, even if I doubt she reciprocated his feelings. For her, it was protection, I'm sure."

"So why would anyone kill her?"

"Lavie said that she shouldn't have told anyone about the money. Here's new information for you. Lavie was in a wreck just the other day. An explosion of some sort. With what we know now, I don't think it was accidental."

"If Charles ..." Clara let her thoughts run. "If you think it's okay, can I tell you what's in my head?"

"Dump it on me. I want to hear what's in that head of yours."

"Charles is dead, killed by all accounts. He was using Amanda as a drug mule. And we know the beach was a landing spot for drugs coming into the county. Am I on track so far?"

"No holes in your bucket that I can tell."

"Okay, and we're pretty certain that Amanda and Lavie were romantically involved. In order, we accidently uncover a stash of drugs on the beach, Lavie's car is likely rigged with an explosive device, Charles is taken out and his two companions tied up and severely beaten, Amanda travels to Corolla, and she is thrown off the lighthouse. All these must be tied together. The thread is there if we can find it. Oh, and one other thing. Collie said all this is Lavie's fault."

"Then he must know something we don't."

They were nearly to the sign welcoming them to Currituck County when a school of headlights blinded them. Diane's intention was to head deeper into the county to meet with Willis Washington and Kenneth Contras, the NARC officers that had located the trailer. They had been monitoring the location of the boat that had washed ashore in the hopes that if more drugs were somewhere in the water, they could be retrieved before anyone else got to them. A diving team had attempted to search, but the surf was still unsettled, and the best they had been able to do was to continue to monitor the area. Blinded by the lights, Diane braked hard and swerved to an empty place in the grass. She rolled down her window and located a man in the highway.

"For all sakes, what's going on here? This is a highway, not a parking lot."

"Thinking maybe you're lost. Why'dn't you head on back the other way and let us to our business?"

"That's a big no. I've got business just the other side of here. You people need to clear the road." Diane's frustration was clearly building.

A different voice spoke. "That you, Officer Turnipseed? I think I recognize your voice."

"Samuel Knight?" Diane growled to Clara, "These people don't got the sense that God gave a minnow."

"Yes'm," Samuel said. "Let me put you right. Our people are out here to handle some business. Gippy's correct. It might be best if you turn around and head on back into Dare County. You can come by my place tomorrow if you want to know what we done."

"You can dump it on me now, and I won't have to come back tomorrow."

"Well, now, that wouldn't do anybody any good, now would it? You'd best let this be and let us get on about our business."

In the distance, the surf could be heard battering the shoreline. Just audible over that, the high-pitched whine of dirt bikes tearing across the sand revealed something happening on the beach.

"It's time to quit talking, Samuel." Gippy came up to stand behind his brother. "I may be a Banker, but I'm a Corolla Banker. We've been here since this was a bare strip of sand, and we're not letting anyone take that from us."

Through the windshield, Clara could see additional figures, some of them women, and all equally agitated. In the glow of the dash lights, Clara saw Diane cut her eyes her direction.

"What are you thinking, Captain?"

The sound of the bikes had grown louder, and before Diane could answer, Samuel called, "Everybody, I'm moving my truck. We can pick 'em off if we stand in the bed. Everyone get ready." He turned to Diane. "Ma'am, I might back up if I were you."

The crowd began cheering, and without anyone giving any additional instructions, they began returning to their cars and trucks, while Samuel opened his truck door, hit the starter, and when it jerked to life, backed up—barely missing Diane's Explorer—and onto the grassy area beside the highway as close to the beach as possible. It was tilted at an angle, but he killed the engine, loudly ratcheted the parking brake, and climbed out. Before closing the door, he leaned the seat forward, pulled out two boxes, which he sat on the top of the cab, then pulled out a long case. He carried it to the back of the truck, dropped the tailgate, and set the case down. With the flip of two catches, he raised the top half, gently caressed the contents, and seemed startled when his younger brother called from the trunk of his yellow Toyota Corolla.

"That's it, Samuel. We got 'em to rights tonight. Make 'em think the tide reached out and ate 'em up." He cackled like he thought this was the best night of his life.

"Captain, I'm not sure this is going to be a good situation. Back in Brunswick County—"

"We're big girls," Diane said. "Not nothing illegal happening yet, 'cept blocking the road. Everybody's been polite and everything. So, hold your taters, Deputy. Our time's coming."

"Hold my weapon, you mean." Clara knew exactly what Samuel Knight had been caressing in that case in the back of his truck. She was certain Captain Turnipseed knew, too.

"It's not like I'm not listening. You do that, Clara, and we'll all be better prepared for what I expect's about to happen. Hush now while I radio Sheriff Barnett to apprise him of what the slack tide's about to turn up."

Clara noted that the captain already had her weapon's holster unlatched. That chilled her and excited her at the same time. Police work in Dare County wasn't slow at all. She was in the thick of it, and it seemed things were just getting started.

THE SHERIFF DESCRIBED a similar situation playing out farther up Hwy 12 and advised Diane to take care on the Dare County side. He would try to send Washington or Contras down for additional support, but he wasn't sure they would get through. Things were getting rowdy, and if he had to start issuing arrests, he'd soon run out of space to put them.

Diane said she understood the situation and that she and her deputy would jump into it, knickers and all. Her conversation was interrupted when the people scattered along the highway began to chant, "Not in our county!"

"You ready, Clara?" Diane returned the mic to the dash and placed her left hand on the door latch.

"My sidearm says I am." Clara grinned.

"Then let's hoggletie this situation once and for all." Diane flipped the latch, the door snapped open, and she stood.

Clara repeated the action on her side of the truck. The wind from off the water swept over her, cool and filled with sand and salt. Already the grit coated her neck inside her collar, and she could taste the sea on her lips. The slap of the waves on the beach just over the wall of greenery reminded her of being here with Ed and discovering that the shore sometimes held more than just sun and fun. It could also contain blood and guns and stashes of drugs that someone had overlooked … and then maybe returned to claim only to find them missing.

Diane marched to an old green Dodge truck, the one Samuel Knight had moved and the one on which he had opened the case from earlier. The case was now back in the cab and on the seat, and Samuel, his brother, and several other people were standing in the bed. The lights from Diane's Explorer were still on, and they illuminated the scene while casting dark shadows that hid as much as the headlights revealed.

Diane interrupted the chanting fury with, "You people are sure keeping me on my toes. You inviting me up there for a look-see? Or are women not allowed?"

The chanting continued further down the road, but the voices in the truck died away.

"That's better." Diane placed her hand on the corner of the bed, lifted one foot to the end of the bumper, and she hauled herself aloft. "I'm sure hoping I don't need to check permits for any concealed weapons tonight. You people all look old enough to have a gun or two out, that is if you don't plan on doing something illegal with them. To tell the story honest, I don't see nothing much to shoot at, so this must be a simple meet and greet, right?"

The whine of the motorcycles on the beach was louder, and Gippy hissed to Samuel, "Thought you told her to go on home. I'm not no coward, but with *her* here, that changes things." Gippy held a firearm in one hand, as did everyone in the truck.

One man had a scope with a laser sight, and he held it aimed toward the beach. Diane forced her way to him, grasped the barrel of the rifle, and said, "Won't find any feral swine or coyotes out there, and I can't imagine you might be planning to point this at a human."

Clara followed what the captain was saying. Laser sights were legal in some situations, but this wasn't one of them, and these men must know that. The captain was attempting to diffuse this situation before something happened that couldn't be undone.

A petite blonde woman wearing slim jeans that weren't slim enough and a bland but frothy button up top swayed up in heeled sandals that clopped against the pavement. She held a wrapped package over the side of the truck bed and said, "Gippy, you want this?"

"Bette," he growled in a low voice. The intensity of his words meant they carried to everyone near the truck. "Them Currituck folk are coming. Now's not the time."

"Suit yourself," she said and pulled the wrapped package away. "I thought you might be hungry. You were earlier. How'm I to know when you don't tell me? Any of you other boys want this?"

The man with the scope started to reach for it but Diane refused to let go of the barrel of the rifle, and he hesitated.

"Suit yourselves," Bette said, and as she turned away, she called out, "My sandal! It's caught in the sand. Oh, someone help me!"

Gippy handed his brother his firearm, jumped down from the bed of the truck, took the wrapped package, placed it on the tailgate, and knelt to rescue his wife's sandal. He muttered, "Acorn don't fall too far from the tree, does it, Bette? Why you wear these sandals everywhere you go is beside me."

"Just help me to the car. Oh, Gippy, what if there are crabs? I don't want crabs to bite my toes."

"Then don't wear sandals—"

Their voices faded in the night, but the distraction was just enough that Samuel was able to bypass Diane Turnipseed's cautions, raise his gun, point it towards the beach, and call, "I don't take nothing from a lowlife like you people," and the end of his weapon flashed as the report of the shell leaving the barrel shattered the calm.

"You better think twice," Diane started to say, but even

Clara knew that the moment had passed. Even the man with the scope jerked his gun from the officer's grip, clambered onto the cab of the truck, and took two potshots at whatever he had discovered on the beach.

Clara was quickly overwhelmed. This had become mob rule: those with the might ignoring those who were in the right. In the distance, Bette was letting out yelps of alarm and running with her hands over her head while ignoring her injured sandal. Several other women had dropped beside their vehicles, with one laughing as she swigged at a longneck. Men who must have started firing without thinking what they would do when their stock of shells was exhausted leaped from their perches to sort out new shells or to reload before they stood up to pop out yet another round of death.

Rat-a-tat, rat-a-tat. It wasn't at all like Clara's training.

A man yelled from the truck, "Hey, that's too close to my ear. You want me to go deaf?"

The man next to him laughed. "Not my fault! Where's your ear protection?"

Diane removed herself from the truck bed and indicated that Clara should join her back in the car. Inside, with the windows up, the noise was less, and Clara asked, "What now?"

"We sit here."

"And if someone gets killed?"

"It won't be us." The lights from the dash revealed the anger on the captain's face. "To tell the truth, I don't expect I'd grieve much if one of them out on that beach swims with the fishes. Don't you tell anyone I'm saying this, but these people are doing a good thing, just not in the right way. I might have to arrest all of 'em, but I won't tell 'em they was wrong."

FLASHING LIGHTS eventually appeared on the northern side

of the impromptu shooting range. Two Currituck County cars with sirens blazing finally got the attention of the Corolla posse who were defending their rights and land along this sandy stretch of the northern Outer Banks. NARC agents Willis Washington and Kenneth Contras climbed out of the first one, leaving their lights and siren tearing into the darkness. Contras looked around, amazed, and called out, "Really?" He shook his head and said to his partner, "Washington, let's ramp it up. Let's get some names and addresses."

"No cap!" As in *sure* or *no lie*. He called to a nearby offender who was holding a recently fired weapon and checking the chamber to ensure that it was empty, "What's up? All out?"

The rounding up took a while, with weapons confiscated, names and addresses taken, and all possible details sorted out to be resorted in the morning. Sheriff Barnett took control of the process and made time to locate and speak with Diane and Clara.

"I'm sorry to sink you into all this. These highballers sure got themselves cocked up, didn't they? I don't even know if our drug runners got down this far."

"On motorcycles?" Diane seemed tense as a drum.

"So, maybe I'm wrong?" The sheriff pulled a spiral notebook from his pocket. "From you. That's why I carry this. What do you know about motorcycles? My people seem to have lost them."

"Clara and I heard them. How far up there is the trailer?"

"You do know a lot. A few miles, why?"

"To tell the story honest, I might could make a guess why this is the spot these people picked. My deputy was talking me through the events of the past few days, and sure as taters in a bag, I think she's got a point. Drugs on the beach twice in a week, and I have a report of two people from across the Sound here just after my people pulled a bag of drugs out of the sand. I don't know what they were looking for, but I'm pretty sure you and I are thinking the same thing. Now, one of those people is dead, a woman from your county is dead at your lighthouse just down the road—"

"I don't know about that one." Sheriff Barnett frowned.

"Tonight, late. You'll read about it tomorrow in Calmont's report, I'm certain. My forensic investigator was there."

"Emily Bryant." The sheriff nodded. "Go on."

"And the man that brought these bikes over here. They were impounded in my lot, that truck, too. If they hadda stayed impounded—"

"They weren't part of a drug investigation then." Sheriff Barnett took a deep breath and let it out. He clearly knew about the impounded vehicles—and who they belonged to.

"I'm thinking there's a reason Collie Beaumarchais brought those bikes over to the shore and dropped them off. My deputy was in Kitty Hawk when the man was stopped *the first time.*"

"The first time. Tell me more."

"Clara, you want to chime in here?"

"Yes, ma'am. He was heading onto the Banks, not off like he should have been. He didn't have the bikes or the trailer with him. When I stopped him, he was being belligerent with Lavie Knight. He was very distressed, and I don't think it was just because of Lavie."

"I'm waiting," Barnett said. He had his arms crossed and was keeping an eye on his NARC officers as they concluded processing the people and their weapons.

Diane took over. "There's a reason that man drove that truck and those bikes over here and then turned around to come back before he got home. Have you heard about Amanda Sargeant?"

"I'm guessing I'm about to."

"She's from up to Knotts Island, a girlfriend to both Collie Beaumarchais and Lavie Knight—" raising the sheriff's eyebrows "—and tonight she fell from the top of the Currituck Lighthouse."

"Interesting that she fell, Diane."

"Especially as the lighthouse was closed with storm debris everywhere. And a man came running down the lighthouse after she fell."

"Tie her death in with the motorcycles."

"Collie's cousins were at the lighthouse when Amanda was found. If he was heading home from delivering the bikes and they notified him, that would have been about right for him to turn around and head back this way. Now, why would he have done that?"

"What I want to know is why the man was out in that truck at all. I believe we had a warrant out for it earlier today. If it was served, it should have been secured with police tape."

"Yes, sir," Clara chimed in. "I was there when it was secured."

"Then Collie's our man. He might have some answers. Now, ladies, my men and I are heading to the beach to see what our good neighbors left for us to find."

"We're good, then?"

"We're good."

"Then Clara," Diane said, "Let's head back south. You think that scanning machine's finished with Sean Taylor's head? I might want to stop by and see if they found a brain in there."

"Yes, ma'am." Clara chuckled. She wanted to stop by too, but her reason was a bit different. She liked the man, and she hoped beyond all hope that he was still alive. The captain hadn't seen what she had found in that hospital bed. People did die, after all, even when they were supposed to be getting better. She wanted this to be the exception, almost more than anything in the world.

WHEN THE TWO women entered the hospital, the front desk attendants noted their clothing, and one of the women set aside what she was doing and came out of the desk area.

"I saw you here earlier. Clara, isn't it?" Clara nodded, and the attendant smiled. "I'm Kitty, and I can answer any questions you might have. You came to see the sheriff's deputy, right?"

"Sergeant," Diane corrected.

"Yes, right." Kitty didn't seem bothered by the correction. "I'd forgotten. Follow me. Sean and I used to date, but that was before his promotion. It's sad what happened to him. You're Diane Turnipseed, aren't you? You were his boss when he was down in Hatteras."

"Buxton, but yes."

"I think of them as the same, although they clearly aren't. Do either of you know what happened to him?"

"Clara? Feel free." Diane was clearly done with the questions, and she passed the buck.

"He was chasing a suspect, and he was tossed down the Currituck Beach Light—"

"He just flew through the air? Like Superman?" Kitty let out a soft whistle. "I knew Sean had big dreams, but no one should dream that big. If he went off the lighthouse, no wonder he's like he is."

"That's not what I meant. I think he just tumbled down a set of steps. I wasn't there. Our forensic investigator was, and she updated me."

"That's Emily Bryant, right?"

"You know her?" Emily was a co-worker but mostly new to Clara.

"I know of her. The jokes she played on Sean are the stuff of legend."

The light banter continued as they navigated to Sean's location. Jason Romney appeared first, with his gray-streaked hair and rough-hewn good looks.

"Jason?" Diane stopped in her tracks. The tall man held a bottle of water with a drinking straw with a bendy top.

"Hey, boss," Sean called from the bed.

"Sean, you're better." Clara stepped around the captain, expecting Sean to be fully recovered, only to be surprised to find him with his head in traction, with a large gauze pad on one side. His arm was in a full cast, with his other scrapes and bruises bandaged.

"Not completely better," Jason advised them. "I'm administering the water bottle treatment. He says he's thirsty, and I offer him a drink if he's been good."

"I'm always good."

This time, Clara could hear the slurring in his words. It was better, but it wasn't gone. She asked, "What did the scan show?"

"Jason?" Sean moved just his eyes to look at him.

"Let me tell you what they did, instead. This bandage?" Jason indicated the one on Sean's head. "It covers where a tube is inserted into Sean's brain. I told them to be careful not to suck out any of the smart stuff, because he barely has enough to start with."

Jason moved the edge of the gauze pad to reveal the tube dripping into a container hooked onto the side of the bed. The fluid had a reddish look, more like pink lemonade than actual blood.

"Shouldn't it be redder?" The question burst from Clara, and she cringed as she heard herself ask it.

"It was. There's hope it's slowing down, as indicated by the slow drip."

"What does he remember of the incident?" Diane looked directly at Jason as she asked her question.

"Incident, Diane?" Jason shook his head. "You need to ask Sean."

"My mistake and my apology." She stepped closer to take in Sean's injuries more fully and to where he could see her in his limited field of vision. "Sergeant Taylor, I've got a drone assignment for you. How soon are you going to be ready to take it on?"

Sean's eyes glistened, and he tried to smile. Then he squeezed his eyes closed and fought for control of his emotions.

"Can I touch his hand?" Diane looked to Kitty for her answer.

"Of course," she said. "He's responding better, but this might take a while. Right now we're hoping we don't have to transfer him to Greenville, as that's two hours away. Be patient."

"Why Greenville?" Clara asked.

"We don't have an ICU. They do." Kitty smiled.

Diane placed her hand over Sean's, and she squeezed it gently. She leaned close and whispered, "Sean Taylor, you're doing no one any good here in this bed. I need you back on my team as soon as you can pull yourself together. Do you hear me?" She gave his hand another squeeze. Tears began to roll from under his lids, and he did his best to nod his head.

"No, don't do that." Kitty took two steps towards the head of the bed, and she placed her hands on either side of his face. "Words, please. No head movements until we know whether we can remove this brace."

A rush of activity at the hospital's emergency entrance pried everyone's attention away from the man in the bed. Flashing lights and the frantic sound of voices commanded the presence of several nurses and orderlies. Kitty said, "I need to see about this. Will you people be okay for a time?"

"I'll make sure he keeps his head still when I give him his next sip." Jason held up the cup and swirled the water inside.

"Thank you." Kitty pulled a curtain partially around the bed and the people with Sean.

Diane pulled Clara aside. "I heard a siren out yonder just before that ruckus jumped out of the bait bucket. I'm thinking you and me might need to check it out."

"Yes, ma'am. What makes you think it's special?"

"The acoustics of a motorcycle siren differ from a squad car. And I know of one man who prefers a motorcycle."

"Sheriff Barnett?" Clara had heard his comments about being a motorman, which she had taken to mean a motorcycle cop.

"Remember where we were? This is the closest hospital to bring anyone from that direction. Let's see what the net captured this time."

"Yes, ma'am."

"Jason, Clara and I will be right back. We'd be above our knees not to check this out."

"Diane!" Jason pointed at Sean.

"For all sakes, Jason. You've got his water bottle. Give him a drink, and we'll be right back. You good with that?"

Jason just shook his head as Diane and Clara swept the curtain aside and headed to see what the ruckus was all about.

WILLIAM B. BARNETT stood just inside the hospital's emergency entrance, outfitted in motorcycle leathers and holding his helmet under one arm. He watched as first one stretcher flew into the hallway, with a paramedic giving emergency heart compressions while running alongside. The man on the stretcher was a bloody lollipop, with his head wrapped in gauze and still bright red.

The second stretcher was a funeral dirge in comparison. The man didn't appear dead, as he had a breathing tube down his throat and a paramedic was rhythmically pumping a plastic bag attached to it, but no one looked like they expected him to pull through.

"William?" Diane touched him on the elbow.

"Diane. I didn't expect to see you here."

"One of my men with a brain bleed."

"From the lighthouse." The sheriff nodded. "Watch your back. That's all the advice I've got to offer. I think we all need some breathing room before we find any more dead people."

"These are from that shoot-up on the beach? Who died?"

"He hasn't been called, but that second man won't pull through. This isn't as easy as a flyover, is it? Sometimes I'd go back to being a motorman and thank God for it every day. Your man?" Barnett turned from the turbulent scene, and he gave Diane his attention. "Brain bleed, huh? That's bigger than this place can handle. Is he being transferred to Greenville?"

"Everybody's hoping not. He's drinking water and crying over every nice thing I say to him."

"He's not used to that, huh?" Barnett cracked a grin.

"For all sakes, William. Are you trying to make me feel worse than I already do?"

"Just be nice to him, Diane. If he took a brain bleed for the team, he really took it for you."

"He's not on my team anymore. He's Manteo's now."

"Not in his head. That's Sean Taylor, right? I've borrowed him several times as Drone Operator, and all he talks about is how much he admires you. Don't push him aside too easily."

Clara watched the captain as the sheriff turned and headed towards the men he'd brought in. She knew the sheriff's words must have hit home when she saw Diane's eyes glisten. Then, the boss straightened her back and announced, "Clara, I need to interview Collie Beaumarchais. I don't know if he's in custody or out on bail. You find out for me and set it up for the morning. Can you handle that?"

"Yes, ma'am!" That was what Clara wanted to hear. The boss was taking action, and Clara was certain she was on the best team that had ever been on the Outer Banks.

--- Chapter 10 ---

Disaster at The Wharf

LIEUTENANT DIANE TURNIPSEED fought to the surface from beaches erupting with explosions, massive sailboats growing from the sand, and masked drug runners spilling over the gunwales to invade the North Carolina shore she called home. Just when she felt herself beginning to drift back to sleep, the explosions picked up again, and she threw her covers back.

"For all sakes," she muttered, as she wrenched a robe off the back of a chair and tossed it over her shoulders. "Can't a woman even sleep in peace?"

Before heading to the front door, she peered out the window, surprised to see the sun fully up. She was even more surprised to see Jason Romney's massive Ford FTX truck sitting in her drive.

"I don't know what that man thinks he's doing, harassing me at my home first thing in the morning." She lived in

Elizabeth City, a good forty-minute drive from the Banks, and more than that when coming from Manteo. A glance at the clock told her it wasn't exactly first thing, and she berated herself for letting so much of the morning get away. She missed her morning "cuppa blackie" on the deck at her aunt Lucille's old beach house, but the drive to A-District had said a big no to living there, and with the Elizabeth City house sitting vacant, she would have been above her knees not to move.

Not even Elizabeth City protected her from Jason Romney.

At the front door, she pushed her hair back from her face, glanced in a mirror, and decided she would have to do. She flipped the deadbolt lever, unlocked the thumb catch on the doorknob, and pulled the door wide to the back of Jason's head. He turned at the sound of the door, and the morning sun caught his hair, slashed across half of his face, and caught at Diane's heart.

Then Jason barked, "Where have you been?" which destroyed any affection the picturesque moment might have stirred.

"What do you mean where have I been? You knew exactly where to find me, so I guess I've been right here. Do you want to come in? I haven't put the coffee on, but I'm still using your coffee machine, so if you're interested?" She kept her expression neutral, partially hoping he would consent, and also wishing he would stomp out to his truck and get on back to whatever the county had on its agenda today.

He looked in her face for a long moment, careful to keep his eyes from looking anywhere else, and relaxed slightly. "I thought it was still at the beach house. Thank you, Diane. I will. Do you have any pods for it? This needs to be quick and dirty."

"For all sakes, quick and dirty? I didn't know that applied to coffee." Diane laughed and stepped back to allow him to enter.

"Spare me, Diane. How long's my coffee machine been here?"

"I brought it up a week or so back."

"Okay, then. You do know you've missed out on the whole morning. You have no idea what's been happening. Is your phone even on?" He moved past her and headed directly to the kitchen. He called back, "Check it. Now."

Last night had run late, what with Sheriff Barnett's rowdy bunch of Bankers up in Corolla and Sean Taylor claiming everyone's attention in that hospital bed. He was always trying to be the flashiest fish in the tide pool, and he had finally gotten what he wanted, even if Diane wouldn't have wished that even on him. And Barnett's comments about Taylor's opinion of her. She didn't doubt Barnett's words, but she didn't see how Taylor wasn't glad to be in Manteo. She recognized that she had done her best to quash him at every turn, ostensibly for his own good, bur for her satisfaction, also. She let that go and rummaged through her bag. She had dumped everything on a side table after arriving, and she had no idea what level the charge on her phone was at.

She pulled it out, tapped the screen several times with no response. She walked towards the kitchen where she kept a wireless charger plugged in, frowning at how it could be dead.

"Zonked, huh?" Jason was washing out two cups. The coffee machine was already making coffee noises. He dried his hands, took the phone from her, and placed it on the charger. It remained blank for a moment before the display began to respond. "Your messages are going to light up in about two minutes."

"It won't be charged in two minutes." Diane felt her testy side crawling out. She didn't enjoy Jason gloating over being correct.

"You do remember the dead people littering two counties over the past week." He had his arms crossed and was leaning back against the countertop. His face revealed his amusement. "One catapulted off the catwalk at the top of a lighthouse. Our friend in the hospital was there for that one."

"Oh, stop it, Jason. Let Sean Taylor rest. I haven't had my morning coffee yet." Even she noticed that she called it coffee, not a cuppa blackie. What was with her this morning? Had moving to Elizabeth City stolen her beachfront vibe?

"I drove through Barco this morning." He glanced at the coffee machine and returned his attention to her. It wasn't ready yet.

"You would have to, wouldn't you, unless you took the long way round. Perhaps you should have. Taking the Albermarle Sound Bridge would have given me an extra two hours of sleep." The more alert she was becoming, the more she was glad he hadn't. Today was likely to be full of unpleasant surprises, and she needed every hour to net them in. Her phone started to ding with accumulated messages, reminding her of last night's carelessness, and she glared at it.

"I stayed on 158 up to Currituck and came down 34."

"Rather than take Shortcut Road." Shortcut Road was also 158 but just that, a more direct cutoff that was indeed a "shortcut," one that Diane preferred and usually took.

He took a long look at her phone, clearly intending to make a point. "Currituck County has a whole team up at The Wharf. I don't know but what they're all over this thing with Collie Beaumarchais. Didn't you have an interview with him on your schedule?" The coffee machine called him, and he reached for the two cups to fill them.

"If you're asking, you know I did." Diane remembered asking Clara to schedule something. What had she missed? She snatched her phone off the charger, let its facial recognition app log her in, and she began scrolling through her messages as she dropped into a chair.

Jason set one of the filled cups next to Diane's elbow. "That's why I'm here. I'm your friendly get-out-of-bed reminder. You want to get over there and see what Sheriff Barnett's got going on at The Wharf?"

"Let me see what day it is." She tapped and scrolled. She glanced at Jason. "To tell the truth, Jason, I may not have much say after today."

"Oh?" He was still standing and sipping from his cup.

"Ollie Glynne's family reunion is winding up."

"He'll want Roxie back. Have you been taking good care of her?"

"For all sakes, what point are you making, Jason? Dump it on me."

"My Roxie point is that I've seen her in action. I know she's a rescue, but when she's with Ed, and he gives her commands, that dog does everything he asks of her and more. I don't know where she was rescued from, but if she's not K9 material, no dog is."

"You can't expect me to ask Ollie to give up his dog just because she responds well to Ed's commands. His kids love her, or I suppose they do. I've not seen them together." She paused and grimaced when Jason took over the silence.

"You've hardly seen her with Ed." He paused, and when she just studied his face, he continued. "There are certification programs in place."

"She's too old for that."

"I suspect she's already certified somewhere." He took a sip and, through the steam rising from the cup, said, "Military?"

"That's out of your depth, Jason. You can't know that."

"Okay, back to your interview. If Glynne's returned today, or likely tomorrow if he's driving in today, we need to get you dressed and to that interview. It might have to happen in Barco. I hear he wasn't released after he was stopped the second time. Driving around in county evidence doesn't bode well for getting out of the county slammer."

Diane's phone dinged one last time. She glanced at it to see a message from Deputy Clara Del Ray. *Interview with Collie Beaumarchais scheduled at Barco at the Sheriff's Office. 11:00 today. Sheriff Barnett might be able to reschedule, but he suggests you do your best to be on time.*

"Eleven okay with you?" Jason fought a grin.

"For all sakes, Jason! How do you know what just showed up on my phone?"

"I told her to resend it after I got here. She sent it to me two hours ago. You probably have three other messages in there just like it."

"For all sakes!" She stood, tossed back the last of the coffee, and set the cup down hard on the table. "Thank you for the coffee. I'll be ready in twenty minutes."

"I won't go anywhere," he said.

"That's what frightens me." She muttered it, didn't think he heard, and headed to her shower for a quick freshen up to ready herself for a day on the job. It might be a long one, but then there was nothing new about that.

"I DON'T SEE why you couldn't drive your truck." They were in Diane's Explorer, and her mood hadn't improved.

"Private vehicle, not official. There's a reason the county bought me that new SUV."

"Then why didn't you drive it today?"

"I wasn't on official business. I was on Diane business."

She looked at him and caught the smile on his face. She knew what he meant, just like she'd known what he meant when he said *we need to get you dressed*. He was trying to put his spoon into the wrong pot, and she wasn't having it. However, the drive to Barco was only half that to Kitty Hawk, so she let it go and determined to remain professional.

"Are you caught up on Collie?" She thought he should be, but it was a conversation that wasn't about the two of them.

"Brother of one of our dead men and uncle to the two still in Norfolk. By the way, I hear they'll be home this afternoon."

"That's a shame. To tell the story honest, I'd as soon they stayed up there until this is resolved."

"Find something on them and that might be a thing."

"We don't finger people in Dare County without proof in hand."

"Point a finger at, I assume you mean." He grinned at her.

"Jason! Clean up your thoughts. You know exactly what I mean."

"I was in SVU for a while. My apologies, Diane." SVU was the Special Victims Unit for abuse cases.

"Accepted." She wanted to growl at him, but the hormones flooding from his every gesture and word were almost cute. "Let's focus on Collie. Clara Del Ray last night suggested something that interested me. The man had already delivered the bikes to Corolla and must have been heading home. He was clear and yet he turned around and headed back. When he saw Lavie Knight, he jumped the curb in his truck to yell at her. Everything about that is wrong. Everyone with an opinion about the man says the same thing. He's middle-aged, broken by life, and couldn't express an opinion if he had one. That's not a man who steals a truck and delivers dirt bikes to drug smugglers."

"And Lavie and his girlfriend were involved." Jason let that float untethered. What he didn't say was *with each other.*

"And his brother and nephew had just learned that Amanda Sargeant was dead."

"Not dead, Diane. This might be Wright Brothers territory, but someone who has help flying from the top of a lighthouse isn't dead. They are murdered."

"And knowing that would infuriate Collie, and he would take it out on the first person he saw who triggered him."

"Lavie Knight. I think we're on the same page."

"That beach has become a focal point. Let's see what Collie knows about the drug trade. I don't expect that he's the kingpin, but after last night, he must know something."

"He knew that Amanda served as a drug mule from Virginia. She admitted that when we met up with her on Knotts. She appeared to be still using, but if Collie claimed her as a girl-friend to protect her, he must have cared."

"And would want to vent his anger if he suspected who had wanted to harm her."

The Belcross Biscuit Company was coming up on the right, and once Diane was through the intersection where Lambs Road on the left and Belcross on the right connected at 158, she slowed for the upcoming cutoff onto 34 that would take them directly to Currituck. It was part of the reason she normally took the southern route. It was simpler to go straight on a straight road, rather than take a left that felt like going out of her way.

Even from a distance, it was clear that The Wharf had something going on. Two Currituck County vehicles were alongside an SUV labeled North Carolina State Marine Patrol, with a bulky black motorcycle wearing matching Currituck County paint in the drive. As Diane and Jason turned off the road to enter the property, around the corner of the building, Jared Johnson's gleaming black Camaro hunkered as if ready to pounce on any vehicle that dared come too close.

As they pulled up and stopped, Diane glanced at the clock on the dash: 10:30. "I wisht we had more time here."

"Good. You're remembering that you have an interview."

"It's not like I'm not paying attention this morning, Jason. Whatever's under your shell, you need to make a pearl of it, so it quits getting under your skin so much." Now irritated, she hit her seatbelt release, threw back her door, and didn't even look to see if Jason followed suit.

A small sports car honked from the direction of the road. It followed them in and pulled off onto the grass, leaving tire tracks in the damp greenery. A young man, trim, with dark hair, a fresh look, and wearing mirrored sunglasses emerged with a puzzled look on his face.

"Hello?" He said it like a question. "Why are you all here?"

"And you are?" Diane absently pulled her spiral from her shirt pocket and flipped it open.

"John Sereys. I live here with mon père and ma mère. Maman and Papa have the penthouse, and my apartment is just beneath. Is this about last night?" He leaned back in the car and lifted out two plastic bags. He held them up. "I've just been to retrieve breakfast, and none of you were here when I left."

Diane looked at Jason before answering. This was definitely about last night. She turned back to John. "Your father is Colford Sereys?" When he nodded, she continued. "When are Philippe and Creighton due back?"

"They are returning already?" John's eyes widened with surprise.

"Hold your taters. That's not my question. What I asked—"

"Diane, let me." Jason was around her car by then. "We know the hospital in Norfolk is releasing them today. As far as we know, no charges are being filed *at this time*." He emphasized the words. "We will want to talk with them as soon as they arrive."

"What have they done this time?" John seemed to slump, likely with despair. "I mean, I know they were out there with Charles-Edouard when he was, um, *found*, and they are relentless with those bikes, but I thought they were the victims in that attack."

"We just want to talk with them."

"You two are from Dare County. I've seen you. Several people from your Sheriff's Office were here yesterday. I didn't stay. I had to Uber to the lighthouse to help ma mère for most of the afternoon. She volunteers there several days a week."

"Why Uber? Is that your car?"

"Maman had it. She borrows it on days I don't use it. If you don't mind me asking, why are you people here? Some of the officers from yesterday were from your county, but that's all done with, I thought."

Diane started to answer, and Jason once more took over before she could do more than clear her throat.

"We're here on a courtesy call to check in with Sheriff Barnett—"

"The motorcycle. I know it." He turned his head in the direction of the two-wheeled conveyance as if looking at it, but behind his mirrored glasses, it was difficult to tell just where he was looking. "Hey, it's nearly eleven. I need to get this inside before it goes cold. Do you mind?" He held up the bags again.

"Almost eleven." Jason caught Diane's eyes. "Are we about finished here? We've got an appointment to keep."

Inside the car, Diane started it up, put it in reverse, and didn't say a word. They were nearly to the road when Jason broke the silence.

"Just keeping our appointment, that's all."

"My appointment, Jason." She knew she sounded terse, but she didn't like him running over her.

"I'm in the car. I'm with you. I was the one that informed you that you have this appointment." He paused and said teasingly, "You would still be in your PJs if I hadn't shown up."

"I did have a late night last night, Jason." She squirmed at admitting he was correct. "If Sheriff Barnett is here, who's running the interview?"

"Shannon, maybe." He grinned.

"That's a big no. She'd counter every question we asked and do her best to keep control of the conversation." Diane found herself smiling. Shannon Baylink worked the front desk, and while she often acted like she ran the office, her duties were rarely more than clerical. She always got the job done though, and for that, Diane liked her.

"We'll know in ten minutes. Do you want me in for backup, or are you going this one alone?"

"Hold your taters, Jason. I won't be alone, even if you're not there. But yes, I would like you to be in the interview with me. Thank you for offering."

CRIMINAL INVESTIGATIONS Division Officer Nancy Griffin greeted Diane and Jason when they arrived at the Sheriff's Office in Barco. She was neatly turned out in a skirted suit with low-heeled black pumps, and her dark hair against her pale skin gave her a crisp, businesslike air. When they headed to the interview room, two deputies at a water fountain failed to move out of their way.

"What's this, a boy's clubhouse?" When the CID officer spoke to the men, her personality changed, taking on a hard edge with a suggestive tone.

"Didn't see you there, Griffin," one of them quipped.

"What, you want me to hike my skirt for you? If that's what it takes, I don't know but what I'd rather run into you. You might pay better attention afterwards."

She had a similar tone when starting the interview. She placed her phone on the table, clicked record, and started with, "This is CID Officer Nancy Griffin with Dare County Captain Diane Turnipseed and Dare County Detention Officer Sergeant Jason Romney interviewing Collins Beaumarchais of Currituck County, North Carolina, at the request of Dare County. The date is ..."

Diane studied the man they had come to interview. He had spent the night in Barco, but he looked clean and rested. He was woefully out of shape, with a thick waistline and a balding head of hair. His jawline was coated with red growth that matched what remained up top. He barely responded while Nancy spoke into her phone.

When Diane was given the go-ahead, she asked, "You have a daughter, Mr. Beaumarchais?"

"Yes, and Collie's fine. Please." He half smiled, something that seemed to take too much effort to hold, and his face went slack again.

"Amanda had mentioned to one of my officers that your daughter stayed with her on one occasion."

"Yes." The man's impassivity cracked at the mention of Amanda's name, and he blinked rapidly several times before continuing. "DeDe—Dorothy—loved her weekend with Amanda. My brother wouldn't allow her to return."

"Which brother, Collie?" Diane spoke gently. If she could make a connection, he would bleed out everything.

"Charles-Edouard." His eyes hardened and he barely got the name out, then his forehead cracked and his eyes filled with tears.

"Was the news of Amanda why you were heading back to Corolla after delivering the bikes out there?"

His eyes jerked to Diane's face, and he chewed on his lips. A quick nod answered her question.

"Why did you take the bikes out there? We know it wasn't because of Charles. He was already gone."

"My brother …" He balled his hands into fists and his words choked out in spurts, then came like a storm surge. "I told him I still have a little money left. Not much, but we could live. He always wanted more. I didn't approve of him trafficking the drugs. I knew it would get bad. That was how I met Amanda, him using her to transport them down from Virgina. That's why I wanted her to be my girlfriend at first. I knew she was with Lavie, but I started to love Amanda. I hoped she would—" He choked off a sob. "—just hoped, you know. I thought she could love me. Then when she told me Charles asked her to hide a satchel for him, I knew what it was. And that they would come looking for it."

"What did you think was in the bag, Collie?"

"I didn't think. I knew. I'm supposed to be the head of the family, but Charles kept teasing me about being a Rothschild by fame and not by fortune. I was upset, but he was right. There's no point in trying to hide it."

"How is that, Collie?"

"If you must, I'm a failure. Those people over there—" in France, he seemed to mean "—took it all away. Now we live in that dump, and now even Amanda's dead."

Collie seemed to melt at that point, and he dropped his head onto the table, face down, and began to sob uncontrollably.

Nancy asked, "Are you finished?"

"I think we're through here." Diane was certain the man had indeed loved the young woman. He had certainly confirmed his relationship with Amanda. One thing he hadn't shared was why he had taken the bikes out to the beach.

As Nancy wrapped up the interview into her phone, Diane and Jason exited the building and headed to her car. Inside, she asked, "You want to head back to The Wharf to see what the slack tide's turned up?"

He was looking out the windshield, however, and he pointed towards the horizon. "I'm more interested in that." Eastward, over Coinjock Bay towards Monkey Island, a thin stream of black smoke stained the otherwise blue sky.

Diane's radio clicked on. "Dispatch, this is Engine 5, 10-51, structure fire at the old Knight place outside Corolla. Black smoke visible, dwelling partially engulfed."

"10-51. They are already en route," Jason said.

"The Knight place, Samuel's." Diane had just been there.

"Black smoke. That means someone's used an accelerant."

"Don't be loading me up on stuff I already know, Jason Romney."

"Let it alone, Diane. I'm just working it out."

Before she could snap back at him, the distinctive motor-cycle siren from the previous night built up, tore through the air, and disappeared south towards Point Harbor and the Wright Memorial Bridge.

"That'd be Sheriff Barnett, unless you want me to just shut up." Jason didn't try to hide a hint of a smile. "You want to follow or just you and me do traffic stops for the rest of the day?"

"For all sakes, Jason Romney. I should make you get out and walk. Yes, I'm following. If that's Samuel Knight's place, that means it's part of our investigation." She had the big truck in gear, her lights on, and she tore out of the parking lot after the sheriff.

"So, we're in hot pursuit?"

"What?"

"Well, we're headed there like a house on fire."

"Shush that, Jason, before you get so deep in you can't find your way out."

"I'll be in the hot seat, you mean?"

Diane turned to glare, quite aware the hormones were flying, and it didn't seem there was anything she could do about that.

A FIRETRUCK from Corolla Fire and Rescue flooded a rainbow of wet across the old Knight homestead. The firemen were fully suited from helmet to gloves, and the necessity of protective gear was evident in the blistered green paint that had erupted along the side of Samuel Knight's ancient Dodge pickup truck.

The smoke pouring from under the eaves and through the busted picture window billowed white by the time Diane and Jason arrived. The roof was warped and charred but seemed to be holding up, or at least as well as a roof over a burned-out house could be said to be holding up. The southern wall of the house wasn't so fortunate. A labyrinth of black charred framing now held up the roof but had turned loose of any wallboards, insulation, or siding. What had been furniture was now melted, burned, or charred into matted lumps of soaked debris.

A brick chimney rose above it all, defiant in its reach for the sky.

Diane found Samuel on an old stump. He was wearing rough jeans with the same plaid button-up she had seen him in last time. That didn't mean much. It was likely what he wore every day. When it was too soiled to wear again, then he changed to something else. She left Jason to the fire crew and Sheriff Barnett, and she raised a hand to greet the old man.

"You've redecorated since I been by. Don't know but what

I liked it better before. You aiming to redo the landscaping, too?"

His eyes soaked up the scene without acknowledging Diane for a full minute before spitting out, "I done told you people who's done this. You see? My house's been here a hundred years. My cooker was my mama's. Nothing can give that back."

"Who's done this, Samuel?" She suspected she knew who he would blame.

"Those people across the Sound. Wouldn't they whine if they got a taste of their own medicine! I ought to—"

"Shush that, Samuel." Diane didn't want that sort of talk from anyone, even if this wasn't her county. It *was* her investigation, even though she shared it with Currituck County. "You want your words coming back to you if something does happen to one of them?"

"Let me count." He held up one big, rangy hand. The tendons on the back popped out of his weathered skin. "Lavie's car. You know it was bombed, do you? Then that poor Amanda girl falling from the lighthouse. Lavie's broken up about that, you know. She thought it was a secret, but they were together, if you get my words. Then this." His arm flung out to encompass the charred remains of his home. "When I heard about Charles-Edouard, not a tear formed in my eye. Lavie rescued Amanda from that man, and Amanda … she struggled, I know she did, but let me put you right and say that she would have made it with Lavie's help."

"When did you last speak to Lavie?" Last night the woman had been accosted by Collie Beaumarchais. By all accounts, she had barely been holding it together.

"Last night. She was shaking like a leaf. She wouldn't tell me anything, but I knew it was bad. Then I heard about Amanda. I had already sent Lavie home by then."

"You think I'd be above my knees to call this an accident?" Diane was studying the firemen. The white smoke had dwindled, and it seemed the flames were snugged out. The men were inspecting the structure to see if there was anywhere left for the fire to hide.

"Lavie brought me something. It was from Amanda, and she got it from Charles." Samuel worked his hands together. His eyes studied the ground.

"Go head. Dump it on me, Samuel."

"Grown up is as grown up does, and that why I'm telling you this. Charles-Edouard still wanted Amanda to be a mule. He fed her drugs when she was having a bad time. She tried to be strong, but the drugs had a hold on her. A few weeks back, he brought her a leather satchel and told her to hide it. She did, but when he turned up dead, she looked inside and found it filled with money."

"Where do you think it was from?"

He snorted. "Where do you think? She took it to Lavie, and Lavie was having nothing to do with it. It's in that house that just burned to the ground."

"Likely not." Diane could see men going in and out, and one man was repacking equipment on the truck. "If they thought it was there, they'd retrieve it before setting fire to the house."

"Some hidey-holes are harder to find than others. I might as well show you. You think they'll let us in now?"

"I'll find out. You sit right here, and I'll be back."

She spoke to Sheriff Barnett first. It was his county and so his jurisdiction. He sent her to the fire crew, who agreed on the condition that one of them accompanied her. She motioned to Samuel, who stood, little more than an exhausted old man, and joined her.

As they entered the structure, smoke blackened the upper

portions of the walls, and while the floor was wet, anything from the waist down seemed mostly untouched. The deeper they went into the darkness, the worse the damage was, until they could see completely through the south wall. Samuel directed them to the closet. The fireman worked the floorboards up, and from underneath, tidy and dry, he retrieved a paper shopping bag. From inside, the leather satchel Samuel had placed there appeared.

Once outside, with Jason and Sheriff Barnett alongside to corroborate the contents along with Samuel's story of why it was under his floorboards, they prepared to open the leather satchel and reveal the contents. A reverberating boom from the direction of the Sound distracted them. Then a second, at which time the radio on Sheriff Barnett's bike went off; and Diane and Jason's phones began to ring.

"Diane here. Dump it on me. What did I just hear?"

"Good Lord, Diane." It was Cynthia Ellison. Her voice shook. "I got a call to come up here to help Ed with Roxie, since she's good, but we don't have a certification for her. We're letting her ride sidesaddle to Lucy, but least that I can tell, she's handling this as well as Lucy might could—" Her voice cut off.

"I'm a big girl, Cynthia. Tell me like it is." Diane caught Jason's eyes. He was equally deep in whoever he was talking to.

"I nearly lost Lucy. I can't do that again."

"Nearly lost. What does that mean?"

"I know you're over there with that fire, but if this place holds on until you can get here, I don't see how. We've got flames eating at both ends of the building."

Diane's eyes jumped to Samuel Knight. His words were already schooling around them, and although she knew he'd been here the entire time, even she found this suspicious.

"Who else is with you, Cynthia? From our side of the county line, I mean."

"Ed and Clara, your young deputy with the blonde hair. There's plenty of Currituck County people, so don't worry about that. Just no fire brigade so far."

"Was anyone inside hurt?"

"Least that I can tell, everyone's out. I don't know all their names, but I count eight, if that means anything to you. I hear the fire truck. I'm putting Lucy in the back of the Cherokee, so I'll get on to that. I'll have my phone with me if I can be of any assistance."

"You are always of assistance, Cynthia. Thank you for calling right away." She clicked off the call and was surprised to find Jason at her elbow. "Are you wanting me to have a heart attack?"

"Samuel showed us what was in that leather satchel."

"Money." Diane remembered what Samuel had told her. There was no other reason for what was happening. The drugs from the beach just a week ago; Charles-Edouard killed and his two nephews left for nearly dead; Lavie Knight's car rigged with a bomb. Then when that didn't get the money back, Amanda put out of the picture as payback. This house, then The Wharf aflame. Diane now understood why Collie Beaumarchais had risked so much to take the bikes out to the beach. Someone had twisted his arm, and now they were twisting again.

"Sheriff Barnett is headed back to Currituck. He said he trusted you to handle this, and he'd appreciate you joining him on the other side of the Sound when this is secure."

"Secure?" Diane wanted to laugh, but it would be out of frustration and not humor. "Jason, someone knows this family inside and out. They have someone's confidence and are privy to everything that's happening."

"You have any ideas?"

"Someone who doesn't care if certain people get hurt. Who's been taken out? Charles-Edouard. He's on the Currituck side. Amanda, and I also put her on the Currituck side, or at least not on the Corolla side."

"Lavie is from Corolla."

"And not injured. That's important. And before you say it, Samuel Knight is unharmed, even if his house is gone."

"Are you suggesting that Samuel—"

"To tell the story honest, no. The man's devastated that his home is gone, and he'd never hurt his niece or her car."

"Wasn't he taking potshots on the beach last night?"

Diane took a long look at Jason's face before she answered. "He weren't right in that, but he weren't wrong about it, either. He still might get served, but I'll never tell him I don't approve of someone who protects something sacred to 'em."

"So he's in the clear. Who does that leave?"

"I can account for some of 'em. The one I'm having trouble with is John Collier, Marc and Lucie's boy living in New York. By all accounts, he's successful, but no one's able to document just *how* he's so successful. In all this, his momma's not been in touch with him, and his sister, Sissy, has lost touch, too."

"That's incredibly circumstantial, Diane. That won't fly without something concrete to back it up."

"Don't be telling me stuff I already know, Jason Romney. I've just got to put together where the concrete is and get out there and dig it up."

"I don't know that I can justify an APB, as there's no concrete connection to a crime yet, but I can swing a missing person police bulletin. We might, as you say, finger his location. Do you want me to give it a try?"

"Don't get above your knees, Jason." Diane might bite his

finger off and use it for fish bait. A yellow car pulled down the drive. That would be Gippy Knight. Good. If the fire brigade were satisfied that the fire was completely out, he could watch over his brother. He might even be willing to provide Samuel a place to spend the night, meaning they could continue sorting out the fire situation tomorrow. For today, she needed to get back to her team in Currituck. She sighed. She had only thought taking this position in A-District would give her the chance to slow down. She was quickly learning better as the dying bodies piled up along the shore.

"We'd be above our knees to stand here jawing any longer. I bet tomorrow's breakfast Samuel's brother doesn't know a thing about any of this. At least he's here and can give his brother a roof over his head for the night. Let's get these fish scaled and that money in an evidence bag. We need to get back to the other side of the Sound."

If there was anything there when they arrived. She didn't say that, but it was filling her brain just the same.

BY THE TIME Diane and Jason navigated the hour-long trek down Hwy 12 and back up the Currituck Banks, the peninsula separating the Currituck Sound from the Albemarle Sound further inland, the catastrophe at The Wharf went from a one-alarm fire with visible flames to a two-alarm behemoth that threatened to consume the entire Wharf. The Incident Commander with the original contingent of firefighters from the Waterlily Fire Department south of Barco, Kyle Landon, was on the radio even as Diane and Jason were crossing the Wright Memorial Bridge from Kitty Hawk to the Currituck Banks.

"This is Incident Commander Kyle Landon with the structure fire in progress at The Wharf in Currituck. Calling for a second alarm. Again, second alarm, requesting mutual aid. This is a 10-75 emergency situation requiring a full response from any department available."

The Lower Currituck Fire Station No. 5 was already on hand when Diane turned off 158 onto Bells Island Road. They must have just arrived, as they had yet to connect their hoses, and the men were studying the structure as though assessing where they were most needed. The original structural members making up the century-old warehouse would have been waterproofed with pitch, preventing any rot or decay. Flames, however, loved to gorge on the pitch's volatile coal-tar residue. What had once protected the wood now threatened to be the very thing that consumed it. A focused effort on containment meant determining which parts of the structure were likely to burn hottest and longest.

A firefighter from the original team, his suit streaked with the residue of the past hour, separated from his men and approached the new group. Diane recognized the small sports car John Sereys had arrived in earlier. It had moved further from the building and was now clustered with several Currituck County vehicles, an older Dare County sedan, and Cynthia Ellison's rusty Jeep Cherokee. Cynthia separated from the pile when she saw Diane's Explorer and lifted an arm to catch her attention.

When Diane stopped and opened her door, the sensory input from the firestorm and the firemen's attempts to save the building was like a nor'easter of gargantuan proportions. The burning tar; men yelling instructions to one another; the hiss of the water from the hoses; the metallic clank of firefighting equipment being unattached and reattached; and the overwhelming heat from the structure fire itself. Diane recalled Samuel's green truck. The paint on one side was blistered by the flames, and it had been a small fire mostly contained to one side of the home, as compared to this massive structure divided into multiple apartments. The thick, beamed wood floors and walls of the old warehouse were likely to slow the advance of the flames, but they would also be where the fire was most difficult to locate and extinguish.

"Riding sidesaddle, Jason?" Cynthia teased him when she saw him exit the passenger's side.

"Unintended but not disappointing." He grinned.

"Shush that, Jason. He was my backup for an interview in Barco." Diane frowned at the pleased expression on his face and had to look at something else, anywhere else. "Corolla climbed out of the tidepool, and now we're back to this side of the Sound. I've been stuck with him all day."

"It don't hurt to cut the man some slack, Diane."

"I wisht …" she started and let it go. She needed to get on another topic. Having Jason in the car since the morning was about all the Jason she could stand. To have to discuss him at every turn would put her day in the collards for certain. "What about these people living here? You said eight, and I don't see none."

"Richie says I shouldn't always share what's in my head, but days like this, sometimes I don't share enough. Ed and Clara and some of the Currituck County people packed them up and are at the McDonalds up by the courthouse."

"They take Roxie?"

"The good Lord knows Roxie tried to join them. She's in the back of the Cherokee with Lucy, though least that I can tell, she's happy riding sidesaddle with my Lucy."

Jason asked, "Did Sheriff Barnett make it? He left Corolla before we did."

Cynthia seemed amused. "Those brothers in Norfolk?"

"Dump it on us, Cynthia." If this was amusing to Cynthia,

Diane wasn't sure she was going to like it.

"I heard about that truck and those bikes you had impounded. Least that I can tell, those folks up in Norfolk are about as tired of those brothers as you people."

"We heard they might be back today. I had hoped to have this resolved ahead of their arrival."

"Then get to it. The sheriff and that young deputy in that black Camaro are heading up to retrieve them."

"Jared Johnson." Jason chuckled. "Philippe and Creighton riding in that rear seat will be punishment enough. That car might have four seats but really only enough room for two."

Yet another siren caught their attention, and seeing the firetruck slow and turn towards The Wharf surprised them all, especially Diane. The Kitty Hawk Fire Station near the A-District sub-station had arrived to support the two trucks already battling the flames.

This was the best sort of collaboration: officers from two counties; firetrucks from the same two counties; and a concerted effort to provide aid whenever and wherever it was needed.

There was one thing she hoped didn't show up when the flames were quashed and they could head in to determine the cause. They had retrieved a boatload of money from Samuel Knight's place. It had survived the flames and was now secured in the back of her SUV. Money didn't choke on smoke. People did. Too many people had been piling up. When these flames were out and the smoke had cleared, she hoped John Collier wasn't one of them. If he turned out to be a bottom feeder, she wanted him in her net. The man needed to make a change and become the person his parents would want him to be, and that meant she needed to pull him in alive.

If he wasn't already dead.

"WHICH APARTMENT belonged to Charles-Edouard?" Diane and Deputy Clara Del Ray walked along a scorched hallway in The Wharf. Black fingers of residue along the ceiling revealed the in-wall heating ducts, which had allowed the flames and resulting smoke to penetrate parts of the building that hadn't burned. Most of the smoke damage was waist level or higher, with the floors being wet but unscorched. Waterproof outerwear protected their shoes while in the building.

"Just around here. I normally say that if you get your feet wet, you'll feel better, but this isn't what I normally mean." They nearly passed the door when Clara recognized a wisp of police tape and pointed.

"Then let's go in and have a look-see. Did Ed or Cynthia get in here before the fire broke out?" Diane pulled out a pair of thin nitrile gloves and slipped them on before pushing the smoke-scarred door wide.

"That's how we knew something was up. Yesterday we searched all this and didn't find anything of note, but we didn't have the dogs here, either. That's why we were back this morning. Someone must have been here in between and put in a tripwire. We didn't even get inside when the explosion happened."

"We heard two from across the water."

"The second would be the one that exploded in Marie Louise's apartment."

They were inside by then and walked into a scene of catastrophic damage. The workout equipment, once expensive, was now a collection of twisted art pieces, good for nothing except the recycle bin. The windows were blown out, whether from the blast or the intensity of the flames, and what had once been a kitchen was barely recognizable as a series of charred boxes against a wall. The refrigerator was a slumped cube that had sat too long in the rain.

"Does the other apartment look any different?"

"Worse. We can go see it also, but I don't know that I would do that. The firemen have it secured as too dangerous to enter."

"I would like to talk to Cynthia and see if the dogs can work with this." In the back of her mind, Diane heard herself and knew what she was doing. She was giving equal credit to both Roxie and Lucy. Then, if Toby were here, she knew him. Lucy was still an unknown to her, and she had seen Roxie interact with Ed. When this was up, she wanted to know her story. But that was then and this was now, and this needed to be resolved before anything happened to anyone else.

She needed to rattle the minnows in the bucket and see which one jumped out.

"Diane?" Jason's voice called her from below.

"Hold your taters, Jason. Let me get over there." She stepped through the shattered glass doors and looked over the edge of the balcony.

Just below, an actual concrete wharf fronted the water's edge. The original warehouse had boasted large doorways surrounded by massive timbers which had been closed in during the loft conversion, creating the mechanical room at the wharf level. Concrete groins extended into the Sound, forming boat slips, none of which were currently in use. From the concrete's surface to the water level was easily ten feet, high enough to prevent flooding except in the most extreme storm surges, but not too high to unload cargo from large barges or small cargo vessels. One had a metal stairway leading to a ledge about halfway down the slip, and a metal door recessed into the concrete wall stood open. The door looked like the lock had been battered open rather than using a key.

"I think we found what they were looking for." He pointed,

and about then, Ed appeared out of the dark chasm followed by Roxie, Cynthia, and Lucy. Next came NARC officers Willis Washington and Kenneth Contras, each carrying two black duffle bags, one in each hand.

"Jason, don't be spilling the tea," Washington called. "This might be laundry for all we know."

"C'mon, Willis. Don't be a buzz." Contras called to Diane, "This is the real deal. If you can get this man over here pronto, there's more where this came from." He was pointing at Jason and lifted one of the bags to the top of the wharf's edge for him to take.

"Jason, he's keeping you on your toes." Diane laughed, and she called, "I'll be right there. Don't drop it in the water."

Exiting the building, she pulled off her protective footwear and put on a fresh pair of gloves. She found Cynthia before heading over to talk to Jason.

"Did Lucy prove herself?" The brown dog was sitting at Cynthia's side looking around eagerly.

"That dog stole the show." Cynthia nodded in Roxie's direction. "Lucy fixed on the stash once the doors were open, but Roxie was the one that told us to look there. It seems that Lucy's the one riding sidesaddle today."

Across the back of the old warehouse, the different apartments were apparent. The various windows and balconies defined which rooms were living areas and which were secondary spaces, with smaller windows indicating bathrooms or kitchens. Diane located the one where she had been standing, Charles-Edouard's balcony, and far on the other end of the building, with a larger section of the superstructure blown out and blackened, what must be Marie Louise's apartment.

"That apartment. Marie Louise?"

"I believe so. The rest are—"

"Hold your taters, Cynthia. I want to talk about this particular minnow. She's the one that was interested in the man killed when that boat washed up over in Corolla. His name, Alain Valaine, I seem to recall … no, Alain Valois." Diane frowned as she pieced together the facts. "We know Charles-Edouard was in up to his boot tops. We have witnesses to say so, and that boat Alain Valois was on was spilling bags of cocaine like it was feeding the fishes. If whoever did this targeted her apartment as well as this one, that's a connection we need to put our spoon into—"

Diane intended to ask for Cynthia's take on her theory, but she was interrupted by the third explosion of the day. This came from the mechanical room in the old, converted warehouse, in the general area of the furnace Collie Beaumarchais had been working on the previous day. The heavy timber framing kept the structure mostly intact, but the walls swelled as if in slow motion, the windows directly over their heads flexed and shattered, and flames appeared in the small windows in the mechanical room, quickly crawled upward, and fingers of fire began to leap from the upper shattered window openings. Then a final rumbling built, with everyone scrambling for cover, until the roof punched skyward, belched a cloud of flame, then dropped back into the internal cavities of the top floor apartments, sending dust and soot out to shower everyone and everything within a stone's throw.

The water was littered with shredded and blackened wood and insulation. Bedding and curtains were snagged and tattered on broken stumps of balcony railings. The unburned end of the building was canted at a dizzying angle, and the entire structure groaned as though its internal ribcage had been torn from its body, and it was taking its last gasp before giving up entirely.

"Back!" Jason was one of the first to see the immediate

danger. "Willie, Kenneth, leave those bags! This place is about to go!"

He ran to Diane, who had fallen to one knee. She had been closer to the blast, and her ears rang. She shook her head, looked up at his face, and she frowned hard, unsure what had happened. She took in the litter in the water, the debris still floating in the air, and saw the two NARC officers shouldering the duffels, refusing to leave their evidence behind. They ran past her, yelling at each other with grins on their faces.

"Now, Diane." Jason stretched an arm around her and helped her stand. "We've got to move."

"What happened?" She realized her leg hurt, and when she looked down, a ragged piece of metal protruded from her pant leg.

"I've got you. Hold still." With his other hand, Jason swept her up and followed Cynthia and Lucy.

"Jason," Diane muttered. "Now's not the time—"

"Hush. Your leg has been impaled. I think that was a gas explosion. I'm surprised we're not all dead." Once at a safe distance, he gently put her down and tore open the rip in her pants to reveal the damage. The metal had pinched the wound tight on the front when it impaled her leg, sealing the entrance, but the back side was seeping blood where the ragged metal had gone completely through. "Okay, 911 for you. You need to get to the emergency room."

"Jason, this is an investigation. Sheriff Barnett is in Norfolk, and Sheriff Glynne is in West Virgina. I can't abandon my team."

"I'm not giving you a choice. Besides, I see someone who would love to take over coming down the drive."

A black Camaro in full Currituck County livery rumbled to a stop a short distance away, and the passenger door opened.

Sheriff Barnett climbed out, this time looking very polished in a dress suit. He studied the remains of the building, took a moment to take in Jason and Diane, and called, "What happened to my crime scene?"

Twin brothers, Philippe and Creighton, skinnied out on the sheriff's side. They were more patched up than whole, and the scene painted them with dismay, like little boys who'd woken up on Christmas morning to find the tree still bare of presents.

Deputy Jared Johnson didn't even bother. He did remove his sunglasses for a better look, but even that didn't make it real.

The explosion had been loud, and the cars from McDonalds pulled up alongside the Camaro. Each of The Wharf's residents had different reactions, but the look of disbelief on their faces rivaled that of Philippe and Creighton.

The final vehicle to arrive was an ambulance with the Currituck County logo and EMS on the side.

"That's a big no, Jason." Diane glared at him.

"It's a big yes, Diane, and I'm not taking no for an answer."

Diane started to growl a response when she grew light-headed, felt the world around her begin to spin, and everything around her went dark.

DIANE WOKE UP in bed with her leg wrapped in a cast. Darkness surrounded her. She tried to sit up, only to realize she was in a hospital room and her leg was immobilized with a sling. She looked around her for her phone and noticed someone in a chair at her side.

"It's on the bedside table. Let me get it for you." Jason Romney stood, handed her the phone, and returned to his chair.

"I might could have reached it if my leg wasn't all done up. Why's it like that? And thank you, Jason, for the phone."

"You're welcome. That metal shattered the bone. They had

to operate and pin it."

"Insert a rod?" Diane knew what that meant. Every airport scanner would ping her as wearing metal, metal she couldn't remove.

"Yes. You'll be able to walk, just not today. The blood results came back from Sean's hands."

"You going to tell me or let me guess?"

"The man you suspected." Jason was being unexpectedly reserved.

"Dump it on me, Jason. I don't like guessing games."

"John Collier. We located him in Maine."

"How long have I been in this bed?" She fought to sit up.

"No, don't do that." Jason was up and pressed her shoulders back to the bed.

"Dump it on me. How long, Jason?" She tried to calculate … if they had discovered John Collier in Maine, how long would it have taken them to find him on an APB …

"Nearly a week." He took a ragged breath. "That last blast at The Wharf was intended to do real damage."

"Didn't you say it was gas, a leak maybe, precipitated by the damage from the fire?"

"I did not say all that." He seemed to be relaxing. "It was gas, but it was the bomb that set it off. They had added some rather noxious chemicals to accelerate the explosion, and you got some of them. Your body didn't handle it well."

"So I was a little sick—"

"We didn't know if we would lose you. Everyone's been by but we've also been chasing down the people who did this."

"Without me?" She laughed until a cough made her stop.

"You've trained your team well. They are the best. They found John. They also implicated Marie Louise Beaumarchais. She was receiving the drug shipments from her boyfriend, Alain

Valois."

"The dead man pulled off the beach." Diane studied the ceiling for a few minutes. "So, Philippe and Creighton, innocent after all?"

"According to their parents. But no, they are in custody for receiving and transporting smuggled drugs. All those bike adventures on the beach were to retrieve drug shipments."

Diane mused, "The reason Emily was able to get pictures of Creighton with Charles-Edouard right after Ed and Clara discovered that first stash of drugs on the beach."

"You sent them up there, so thanks to you."

"Shush that, Jason. I sent them. They found them. Give them credit when it's due."

"Yes ma'am."

"So, John pushed Amanda. Payback for taking his money."

"It seems that way. They're releasing Sean Taylor today. He asked if he can come by and see you."

She started to brush off Jason's request, and she remembered Sheriff Barnett's words: "All he talks about is how much he admires you. Don't push him aside too easily."

"I'd like that. Thank you, Jason. I just need to clean up a bit."

"You look fine, Diane."

"Shush up, Jason. I've been in this bed nearly a week. No woman looks good after being in bed nearly a week."

Even so, his words made her feel good, and she wouldn't mind if he said them again.

And again.

Chapter 11

Loose Ends

"I MIGHT KNOW that a wampus cat like you would eventually find your way home." Sergeant Mary Wilson from Dare County's C-District Patrol Area had driven in from her home on Roanoke Island to Diane Turnipseed's beachfront place. It was still filled with her aunt Lucille's lifetime collection of all things beach, which Diane had never seen the need to change after her aunt died and left it to her. "If you'd cotton to, I don't suppose Tony'd mind if I stayed over for a weekend to help you out with your bum knee. I might not be the fastest cod on the coast, but I can whip up clams and red sauce any night of the week."

"Thank you, Mary." Diane stood long enough to give her old friend and long-time coworker a hug before dropping back into her chair. Her leg still hurt when she stood on it too long, but then, the doctors had said expect to give it up to six months.

"Just remember, your phone works just as well from your

end as mine does from my end. All you need to do is ask. Tony and I'll be at Danny's in Vidalia next weekend, but anything other than that and I can be here."

Mary joined the rest of Diane's coworkers and friends out on the beachfront deck where the gulls were determined to steal every tidbit of food left unattended.

"They miss you, Diane." Jason Romney placed a steaming cup of joe—a cuppa blackie, according to Diane—at her elbow and cautioned her to watch out.

"Don't be loading me up on something I already know. I can smell a cuppa as well as any person." She smiled when she said it though. Through the screen door, the early spring weather had taken the Banks by surprise, and Roxie and Lucy chased each other across the dunes.

"It was fortunate for Ed that Sheriff Glynne returned from West Virginia with a new, much smaller pup for his kids." Jason found a comfortable place next to Diane and wrapped his arm across her shoulders.

"He would. That rescue center located Roxie's paperwork and proved she was retired military. I never doubted her, and now she and Ed have trained together and she's his."

"After a manner of speaking."

"Don't you be telling me what I mean." She patted his knee, and she didn't say it hard.

"I know what you mean, but she belongs to all of A-District, too. Even me, I lay a bit of claim to her."

"It's her due." Diane paused and considered her thoughts. She was back at work, but weeks had passed before she could walk properly, and she was spending more time at her desk and less out doing what she loved. "All those people in Currituck. I don't think all of 'em were bad."

"No more than Samuel was wrong for shooting at the drug

runners on the beach. We're working to stop that. Our two sheriffs are, anyway. They're setting up an inter-county task force, the Dare-Currituck Beach Watch, to ensure that our citizens are protected now and tomorrow."

"That was niggling its way into my thoughts. I'm glad you cleared that up, Jason. I might need to get out yonder." On the far side of the screen, Sean Taylor had taken off his shirt, and he was playing a two-person volleyball game with Clara Del Ray. The scar from the tube for his brain bleed was hardly visible. "I bet tomorrow's breakfast he don't know what he's got coming with that girl. She's starry eyed if I ever saw it."

Jason laughed. "It was falling down those stairs. She saw him in the hospital all weak and helpless, and she was a goner. Just like me with you."

"Shush that! When have I ever been weak and helpless?"

"Maybe that's why I'm a goner with you, because you never are."

"Shush that, Jason. To tell the story honest, I was just waiting for you to tell me how you really felt. Enough of that. I've got a party to host outside, and this here tidepool's not nearly as interesting as that one out there."

JASON PAUSED for a minute before following Diane outside, soaking up her presence that still filled the room. He didn't know what had changed her, maybe her brush with death, or maybe that for the first time in her life, she had needed someone else around. Whatever it was, he was glad she allowed that someone to be him.

He smiled and opened the door. He called to Sean and wished him luck with Clara, only to have Sean shoot him a puzzled expression before he replied, "Thanks!" Clara waved, said, "Hey, Jason," and turned her attention back to Sean.

Sean would get what Jason meant eventually. They were no longer roommates, so what he got up to was no longer Jason's affair, and that was okay with Jason. He had other things on his mind. One of them was Diane Turnipseed, the best thing he had ever pursued with all his heart.

"Jason? I left my cuppa blackie in there."

"I'll have it right there."

Whatever she needed. He would be there every time.

A Note from the Author

Currituck Sound is a magnet for watersports and crabbing. With water depths averaging five feet and often much shallower, the mostly freshwater estuary is often awash with paddleboarders and kayakers.

Swimming is permitted, but the bottom can be mucky and dense with weeds. Snakes, especially near the lighthouse, are a consideration, also. In some areas, you might encounter otters and nutrias, which make for entertaining sightings.

The Sound extends north into Virginia and, where the line of barrier islands and the Sound crosses the state line, becomes Virginia's Back Bay. Currituck County bridges the Outer Banks between Dare County and the Virginia border and houses the iconic Currituck Beach Light.

Both the Currituck County Sheriff's Office and the one in Dare County are independent entities and eminently capable on their own. However, for the sake of my story, I have chosen for them to cooperate in the pursuit of protecting the residents and visitors of the area from those who would do them harm.